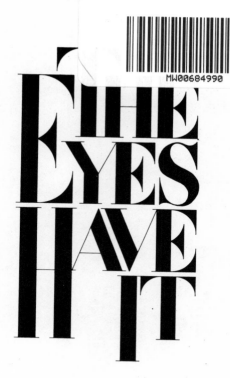

# THE EYES HAVE IT

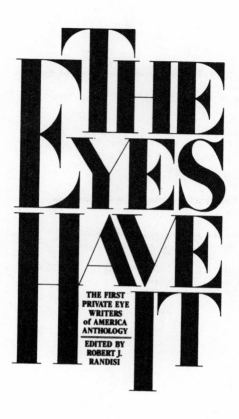

# THE EYES HAVE IT

THE FIRST
PRIVATE EYE
WRITERS
of AMERICA
ANTHOLOGY

EDITED BY
ROBERT J.
RANDISI

The Mysterious Press
New York

The Mysterious Press, 129 West 56th Street, New York, N.Y. 10019

Printed in the United States of America
First Trade Paperback Printing: June 1987
10 9 8 7 6 5 4 3 2 1

Design by John W. White

**Library of Congress Cataloging-in-Publication Data**
The Eyes have it.

1. Detective and mystery stories, American.
I. Randisi, Robert J.  II. Private Eye Writers of
America.
PS648.D4E94   1987         813'.0872'08         87-7890
ISBN 0-89296-906-7 (USA) (pbk.)
       0-89296-907-5 (Canada) (pbk.)

# Table of Contents

# Introduction

## *"With a little help from my friends . . ."*

November, 1979! That's the earliest date I've been able to find in my files for correspondence concerning this anthology.

*The Eyes Have It* started out as *my* anthology. When I first began to put it together, back in 1979, The Private Eye Writers of America was but a vaguely formed idea. I asked a few friends— Bill Pronzini, Michael Collins, Max Collins, Ed Hoch, Marcia Muller—if they would be willing to write original private eye short stories for an anthology, and they said sure . . . *if I could come up with an advance*. Those were the magic words. Advance? I couldn't even come up with a *nibble*. (Actually, that's not quite true. A brilliant and innovative editor at Charter Books—who had bought my first novel—wanted to buy it, but could not sell it to his superiors. His name will be mentioned later.)

Sometime in 1981—again, taking the date from a letter from Bill Pronzini to me—I began to put together The Private Eye Writers of America, having asked Bill if he would not only join, but be our first President. He agreed to do both. *The Eyes Have It* was still in limbo.

In January, 1982, PWA became a reality. Included among the twenty members on that first roster were most of the people who had originally promised contributions to the anthology. It was only natural, then, that *The Eyes Have It* should become the first annual PWA anthology. Stuart Kaminsky, Loren D. Estleman, Lawrence Block and Stephen Greenleaf joined the list of contributors.

The final element was added in 1983. The Mysterious Press—a small mystery publishing house founded by Otto Penzler (may his tribe increase!)—expanded. Otto asked Michael Seidman to join the new organization. (It will come as no surprise at this point to learn that Michael is the editor I was referring to earlier.) In September, some four years after the idea for the anthology was formed, *The Eyes Have It* became a reality. A long time coming, but I think you will agree that it was worth the wait.

Joining Lawrence Block, Michael Collins, Loren Estleman, Stephen Greenleaf, Edward Hoch, Richard Hoyt, Stuart Kaminsky, Michael Lewin, John Lutz, Marcia Muller, Sara Paretsky, and Bill Pronzini between these covers are five writers whose names—at least in terms of private eye fiction—are not quite as well known.

Max Collins offers a short story about private eye Nathan Heller, who was introduced in the critically acclaimed historical P.I. novel *True Detective*. This is Nathan Heller's first short story appearance.

William F. Nolan is well known for his knowledge of, and biographical work on, Dashiell Hammett, but in the nineteen sixties he published two novels about a private eye named Bart Challis. It is a pleasure to welcome both Bill Nolan and Challis back.

L. J. Washburn is one half of PWA's only husband and wife membership; Livia is married to James Reasoner, who wrote most of the Mike Shayne novelettes for *Mike Shayne Mystery Magazine* during the seventies. Livia's stories have also appeared in *MSMM*, but this publication marks the debut of Lucas Hallam.

Rob Kantner's investigator, Ben Perkins, has appeared in an impressive series of short stories in *Alfred Hitchcock's Mystery*

*Magazine.* As you read "The Rat Line," I think you will be reading one of tomorrow's stars.

Finally, Miles Jacoby, the creation of, well, me.

So there you have it: a cross-section of some of the best of today and tomorrow. Michael Z. Lewin has created a new character for this anthology. Stephen Greenleaf, Stuart Kaminsky, and Richard Hoyt have contributed their first short stories. Three women—of the eight who hold active memberships in PWA—are represented in these pages.

*The Eyes Have It* is the fulfillment of a dream. I hope all your dreams come true; in the meantime, please enjoy mine!

Robert J. Randisi
Brooklyn, N.Y.
May, 1984

# By the Dawn's Early Light

## *Lawrence Block*

*Some years ago, when Bob Randisi first proposed my
writing a story about Scudder for a collection, it seemed
safe enough to agree. The collection was as yet unsold,
the Private Eye Writers of America not yet so much as a gleam
in Randisi's eye. By the time both became realities, I had
written two more novels about my detective. In the last of
them,* Eight Million Ways to Die,
*he underwent a catharsis. It made for a book I'm
very happy with, but it also constituted a hard act to follow.
I spent much of a year trying to write a sixth Scudder
novel and concluded that, at least for the time being, it
was something I couldn't comfortably do.*

*How then could I sit down and write a short story? I told
Bob I didn't think I could. I passed the same word to
Otto Penzler. Then, relieved of my responsibilities,
I went home and saw how to manage it. I thought of the opening
line and after that everything was easy.*

*I hope you enjoy the result.*

4

ALL this happened a long time ago.

Abe Beame was living in Gracie Mansion, although even he seemed to have trouble believing he was really the Mayor of the City of New York. Ali was in his prime, and the Knicks still had a year or so left in Bradley and DeBusschere. I was still drinking in those days, of course, and at the time it seemed to be doing more for me than it was doing to me.

I had already left my wife and kids, my home in Syosset, and the NYPD. I was living in the hotel on West Fifty-seventh Street where I still live, and I was doing most of my drinking around the corner in Jimmy Armstrong's saloon. Billie was the nighttime bartender, his own best customer for the twelve-year-old Jameson. A Filipino youth named Dennis was behind the stick most days.

And Tommy Tillary was one of the regulars.

He was big, probably six-two, full in the chest, big in the belly, too. He rarely showed up in a suit but always wore a jacket and tie, usually a navy or burgundy blazer with gray flannel slacks, or white duck pants in warmer weather. He had a loud voice that boomed from his barrel chest, and a big cleanshaven face that was innocent around the pouting mouth and knowing around the eyes. He was somewhere in his late forties, and he drank a lot of top-shelf Scotch. Chivas, as I remember it, but it could have been Johnny Black. Whatever it was, his face was beginning to show it, with patches of permanent flush at the cheekbones and a tracery of broken capillaries across the bridge of the nose.

We were saloon friends. We didn't speak every time we ran into each other, but at the least we always acknowledged one another with a nod or a wave. He told a lot of dialect jokes and told them reasonably well, and I laughed at my share of them. Sometimes I was in a mood to reminisce about my days on the

5

force, and when my stories were funny his laugh was as loud as anyone's.

Sometimes he showed up alone, sometimes with male friends. About a third of the time he was in the company of a short and curvy blonde named Carolyn. "Caro-lyn from the Caro-line," was the way he occasionally introduced her, and she did have a faint southern accent that became more pronounced as the drink got to her. Generally they came in together, but sometimes he got there first and she joined him later.

Then one morning I picked up the *Daily News* and read that burglars had broken into a house on Colonial Road, in the Bay Ridge section of Brooklyn. They had stabbed to death the only occupant present, one Margaret Tillary. Her husband, Thomas J. Tillary, a salesman, was not at home at the time.

It's an uncommon name. There's a Tillary Street in Brooklyn, not far from the entrance to the Brooklyn Bridge, but I've no idea what war hero or ward heeler they named it after, or if he's a relative of Tommy's. I hadn't known Tommy was a salesman, or that he'd had a wife. He did wear a wide yellow gold band on the appropriate finger, and it was clear that he wasn't married to Carolyn from the Caroline, and it now looked as though he was a widower. I felt vaguely sorry for him, vaguely sorry for the wife I'd never even known of, but that was the extent of it. I drank enough back then to avoid feeling any emotion very strongly.

And then, two or three nights later, I walked into Armstrong's and there was Carolyn. She didn't look to be waiting for him or anyone else, nor did she look as though she'd just breezed in a few minutes ago. She had a stool by herself at the bar and she was drinking something dark from a lowball glass.

I took a seat a few stools down from her. I ordered two double shots of bourbon, drank one, and poured the other into the cup of black coffee Billie brought me. I was sipping the coffee when a voice with a Piedmont softness to it said, "I forget your name."

I looked up.

"I believe we were introduced," she said, "but I don't recall your name."

"It's Matt," I said, "and you're right, Tommy introduced us. You're Carolyn."

"Carolyn Cheatham. Have you seen him?"

"Tommy? Not since it happened."

"Neither have I. Were you-all at the funeral?"

"No. When was it?"

"This afternoon. Neither was I. There. Matt. Whyn't you buy me a drink? Or I'll buy you one, but come sit next to me so's I don't have to shout. Please?"

She was drinking Amaretto, sweet almond liqueur that she took on the rocks. It tastes like dessert but it's as strong as whiskey.

"He told me not to come," she said. "To the funeral. It was someplace in Brooklyn, that's a whole foreign nation to me, Brooklyn, but a lot of people went from the office. I could have had a ride, I could have been part of the office crowd, come to pay our respects. But he said not to, he said it wouldn't look right."

"Because—"

"He said it was a matter of respect for the dead." She picked up her glass and stared into it. I've never known what people hope to see there, although it's a gesture I've performed often enough myself.

"Respect," she said. "What's he care about respect? I would have just been part of the office crowd, we both work at Tannahill, far as anyone there knows we're just friends. And all we ever were is friends, you know."

"Whatever you say."

"Oh, *shit*," she said. "Ah don't mean Ah wasn't fucking him, for the Lord's sake. Ah mean it was just laughs and good times. He was married and he went home to Mama every night and that was jes fine, because who in her right mind'd want Tommy Tillary around by the dawn's early light? Christ in the foothills, did Ah spill this or drink it?"

We agreed that she was drinking them a little too fast. Sweet drinks, we told each other, had a way of sneaking up on a person. It was this fancy New York Amaretto shit, she maintained, not like

7

the bourbon she'd grown up on. You knew where you stood with bourbon.

I told her I was a bourbon drinker myself, and it pleased her to learn this. Alliances have been forged on thinner bonds than that, and ours served to propel us out of Armstrong's, with a stop down the block for a fifth of Maker's Mark—her choice—and a four-block walk to her apartment. There were exposed brick walls, I remember, and candles stuck in straw-wrapped bottles, and several travel posters from Sabena, the Belgian airline.

We did what grownups do when they find themselves alone together. We drank our fair share of the Maker's Mark and went to bed. She made a lot of enthusiastic noises and more than a few skillful moves, and afterward she cried some.

A little later she dropped off to sleep. I was tired myself, but I put on my clothes and sent myself home. Because who in her right mind'd want Matt Scudder around by the dawn's early light?

Over the next couple of days, I wondered every time I entered Armstrong's if I'd run into her, and each time I was more relieved than disappointed when I didn't. I didn't encounter Tommy either, and that too was a relief, and in no sense disappointing.

Then one morning I picked up the *News* and read that they'd arrested a pair of young Hispanics from Sunset Park for the Tillary burglary and homicide. The paper ran the usual photo—two skinny kids, their hair unruly, one of them trying to hide his face from the camera, the other smirking defiantly, and each of them handcuffed to a broadshouldered grimfaced Irishman in a suit. You didn't need the careful caption to tell the good guys from the bad guys.

Sometime in the middle of the afternoon I went over to Armstrong's for a hamburger and drank a beer with it, then got the day going with a round or two of laced coffee. The phone behind the bar rang and Dennis put down the glass he was wiping and answered it. "He was here a minute ago," he said. "I'll see if he stepped out." He covered the mouthpiece with his hand and looked quizzically at me. "Are you still here?" he asked. "Or did you slip away while my attention was somehow diverted?"

"Who wants to know?"

"Tommy Tillary."

You never know what a woman will decide to tell a man, or how a man will react to it. I didn't want to find out, but I was better off learning over the phone than face to face. I nodded and took the phone from Dennis.

I said, "Matt Scudder, Tommy. I was sorry to hear about your wife."

"Thanks, Matt. Jesus, it feels like it happened a year ago. It was what, a week?"

"At least they got the bastards."

There was a pause. Then he said, "Jesus. You haven't seen a paper, huh?"

"That's where I read about it. Two Spanish kids."

"You read the *News* this morning."

"I generally do. Why?"

"You didn't happen to see this afternoon's *Post*."

"No. Why, what happened? They turn out to be clean?"

Another pause. Then he said, "I figured you'd know. The cops were over early this morning, even before I saw the story in the *News*. It'd be easier if you already knew."

"I'm not following you, Tommy."

"The two Spics. Clean? Shit, they're about as clean as the men's room in the Times Square subway station. The cops hit their place and found stuff from my house everywhere they looked. Jewelry they had descriptions of, a stereo that I gave them the serial number, everything. Monogrammed shit. I mean that's how clean they were, for Christ's sake."

"So?"

"They admitted the burglary but not the murder."

"That's common, Tommy."

"Lemme finish, huh? They admitted the burglary, but according to them it was a put-up job. According to them I hired them to hit my place. They could keep whatever they got and I'd

9

have everything out and arranged for them, and in return I got to clean up on the insurance by over-reporting the loss."

"What did the loss amount to?"

"Shit, *I* don't know. There were twice as many things turned up in their apartment as I ever listed when I made out a report. There's things I missed a few days after I filed the report and others I didn't know were gone until the cops found them. You don't notice everything right away, at least I don't, and on top of it how could I think straight with Peg dead? You know?"

"It hardly sounds like an insurance set-up."

"No, of course it wasn't. How the hell could it be? All I had was a standard homeowner's policy. It covered maybe a third of what I lost. According to them, the place was empty when they hit it. Peg was out."

"And?"

"And I set them up. They hit the place, they carted everything away, and I came home with Peg and stabbed her six, eight times, whatever it was, and left her there so it'd look like it happened in a burglary."

"How could the burglars testify that you stabbed your wife?"

"They couldn't. All they said was they didn't and she wasn't home when they were there, and that I hired them to do the burglary. The cops pieced the rest of it together."

"What did they do, arrest you?"

"No. They came over to the house, it was early, I don't know what time. It was the first I knew that the Spics were arrested, let alone that they were trying to do a job on me. They just wanted to talk, the cops, and at first I talked to them, and then I started to get the drift of what they were trying to put onto me. So I said I wasn't saying anything more without my lawyer present, and I called him, and he left half his breakfast on the table and came over in a hurry, and he wouldn't let me say a word."

"And the cops didn't take you in or book you?"

"No."

"Did they buy your story?"

"No way. I didn't really tell 'em a story because Kaplan wouldn't let me say anything. They didn't drag me in because they don't have a case yet, but Kaplan says they're gonna be building one if they can. They told me not to leave town. You believe it? My wife's dead, the *Post* headline says *Quiz Husband in Burglary Murder*, and what the hell do they think I'm gonna do? Am I going fishing for fucking trout in Montana? 'Don't leave town.' You see this shit on television, you think nobody in real life talks this way. Maybe television's where they get it from."

I waited for him to tell me what he wanted from me. I didn't have long to wait.

"Why I called," he said, "is Kaplan wants to hire a detective. He figured maybe these guys talked around the neighborhood, maybe they bragged to their friends, maybe there's a way to prove they did the killing. He says the cops won't concentrate on that end if they're too busy nailing the lid shut on me."

I explained that I didn't have any official standing, that I had no license and filed no reports.

"That's okay," he insisted. "I told Kaplan what I want is somebody I can trust, and somebody who'll do the job for me. I don't think they're gonna have any kind of a case at all, Matt, but the longer this drags on the worse it is for me. I want it cleared up, I want it in the papers that these Spanish assholes did it all and I had nothing to do with anything. You name a fair fee and I'll pay it, me to you, and it can be cash in your hand if you don't like checks. What do you say?"

He wanted somebody he could trust. Had Carolyn from the Caroline told him how trustworthy I was?

What did I say? I said yes.

I met Tommy Tillary and his lawyer in Drew Kaplan's office on Court Street a few blocks from Brooklyn's Borough Hall. There was a Syrian restaurant next door, and at the corner a grocery store specializing in Middle Eastern imports stood next to an antique shop overflowing with stripped oak furniture and brass lamps and bedsteads. Kaplan's office ran to wood panelling and leather chairs and oak file cabinets. His name and the names of two partners were painted on the frosted glass door in old-fashioned gold and black lettering. Kaplan himself looked conservatively up-to-date, with a three-piece striped suit that was better cut than mine. Tommy wore his burgundy blazer and gray flannel trousers and loafers. Strain showed at the corners of his blue eyes and around his mouth. His complexion was off, too, as if anxiety had drawn the blood inward, leaving the skin sallow.

"All we want you to do," Drew Kaplan said, "is find a key in one of their pants pockets, Herrera's or Cruz's, and trace it to a locker in Penn Station, and in the locker there's a footlong knife with their prints and her blood on it."

"Is that what it's going to take?"

He smiled. "It wouldn't hurt. No, actually we're not in such bad shape. They got some shaky testimony from a pair of Latins who've been in and out of trouble since they got weaned to Tropicana. They got what looks to them like a good motive on Tommy's part."

"Which is?"

I was looking at Tommy when I talked. His eyes slipped away from mine. Kaplan said, "A marital triangle, a case of the shorts, and a strong money motive. Margaret Tillary inherited a little over a quarter of a million dollars six or eight months ago. An aunt left a million two and it got cut up four ways. What they don't bother to notice is he loved his wife, and how many husbands cheat? What is it they say? Ninety percent cheat and ten per cent lie?"

"That's good odds."

"One of the killers, Angel Herrera, did some odd jobs at the Tillary house last March or April. Spring cleaning, he hauled stuff out of the basement and attic, a little donkey work for hourly wages. According to Herrera, that's how Tommy knew him to contact him about the burglary. According to common sense, that's how Herrera and his buddy Cruz knew the house and what was in it and how to gain access."

12

"The case against Tommy sounds pretty thin."

"It is," Kaplan said. "The thing is, you go to court with something like this and you lose even if you win. For the rest of your life everybody remembers you stood trial for murdering your wife, never mind that you won an acquittal. All that means, some Jew lawyer bought a judge or tricked a jury."

"So I'll get a guinea lawyer," Tommy said. "And they'll think he threatened the judge and beat up the jury."

"Besides," the lawyer said, "you never know which way a jury's going to jump. Tommy's alibi is he was with another lady at the time of the burglary. The woman's a colleague, they could see it as completely above-board, but who says they're going to? What they sometimes do, they decide they don't believe the alibi because it's his girlfriend lying for him, and at the same time they label him a scumbag for screwing around while his wife's getting killed."

"You keep it up," Tommy said, "I'll find myself guilty, the way you make it sound."

"Plus he's hard to get a sympathetic jury for. He's a big handsome guy, a sharp dresser, and you'd love him in a gin joint but how much do you love him in a courtroom? He's a telephone securities salesman, he's beautiful on the phone, and that means every clown whoever lost a hundred dollars on a stock tip or bought magazine subcriptions over the phone is going to walk into the courtroom with a hard-on for him. I'm telling you, I want to stay the hell *out* of court. I'll *win* in court, I know that, or the worst that'll happen is I'll win on appeal, but who needs it? This is a case that shouldn't be in the first place, and I'd love to clear it up before they even go so far as presenting a bill to the Grand Jury."

"So from me you want—"

"Whatever you can find, Matt. Whatever discredits Cruz and Herrera. I don't know what's there to be found, but you were a cop and now you're a private, and you can get down in the streets and nose around."

I nodded. I could do that. "One thing," I said. "Wouldn't you be better off with a Spanish-speaking detective? I know enough to buy a beer in a bodega, but I'm a long ways from fluent."

Kaplan shook his head. "Tommy says he wants somebody he can trust," he said. "I think he's right. A personal relationship's worth more than a dime's worth of '*Me llamo Matteo y como está usted?*'."

"That's the truth," Tommy Tillary said. "Matt, I know I can count on you."

I wanted to tell him all he could count on was his fingers. I didn't really see what I could expect to uncover that wouldn't turn up in a regular police investigation. But I'd spent enough time carrying a shield to know not to push away money when somebody wants to give it to you. I felt comfortable taking a fee. The man was inheriting a quarter of a million dollars, plus whatever insurance she carried. If he was willing to spread some of it around, I was willing to take it.

So I went to Sunset Park and spent some time in the streets and some more time in the bars. Sunset Park is in Brooklyn, of course, on the borough's western edge above Bay Ridge and south and west of Greenwood Cemetery. These days there's a lot of brownstoning going on there, with young urban professionals renovating the old houses and gentrifying the neighborhood. Back then the upwardly mobile young had not yet discovered Sunset Park, and the area was a mix of Latins and Scandinavians, most of the former Puerto Ricans, most of the latter Norwegians. The balance was gradually shifting from Europe to the islands, from light to dark, but this was a process that had been going on for ages and there was nothing hurried about it.

I talked to Herrera's landlord and Cruz's former employer and one of his recent girlfriends. I drank beer in bars and the back rooms of bodegas. I went to the local stationhouse—they hadn't caught the Margaret Tillary murder case, that had been a matter for the local precinct in Bay Ridge and some detectives from Brooklyn Homicide. I read the sheets on both of the burglars and drank coffee with the cops and picked up some of the stuff that doesn't get on the yellow sheets.

I found out that Miguelito Cruz once killed a man in a tavern brawl over a woman. There were no charges pressed; a dozen witnesses reported the dead man had gone after Cruz first with a broken bottle. Cruz had most likely been carrying the knife, but several witnesses insisted it had been tossed to him by an anonymous benefactor, and there hadn't been enough evidence to make a case of weapons possession, let alone homicide.

I learned that Herrera had three children living with their mother in Puerto Rico. He was divorced, but wouldn't marry his current girlfriend because he regarded himself as still married to his ex-wife in the eyes of God. He sent money to his children, when he had any to send.

I learned other things. They didn't seem terribly consequential then and they've faded from memory altogether by now, but I wrote them down in my pocket notebook as I learned them, and every day or so I duly reported my findings to Drew Kaplan. He always seemed pleased with what I told him.

Some nights I stayed fairly late in Sunset Park. There was a dark beery tavern called The Fjord that served as a comfortable enough harbor after I tired of playing Sam Spade. But I almost invariably managed a stop at Armstrong's before I called it a night. Billie would lock the door around two, but he'd keep serving until four and he'd let you in if he knew you.

One night she was there, Carolyn Cheatham, drinking bourbon this time instead of Amaretto, her face frozen with stubborn old pain. It took her a blink or two to recognize me. Then tears started to form in the corners of her eyes, and she used the back of one hand to wipe them away.

I didn't approach her until she beckoned. She patted the stool beside hers and I eased myself onto it. I had coffee with bourbon in it, and bought a refill for her. She was pretty drunk already, but that's never been enough reason to turn down a drink.

She talked about Tommy. He was being nice to her, he said.

Calling up, sending flowers. Because he might need to testify that he'd been with her when his wife was killed, and he'd need her to back him up.

But he wouldn't see her because it wouldn't look right, not for a new widower, not for a man who'd been publicly accused of murder.

"He sends flowers with no card enclosed," she said. "He calls me from pay phones. The son of a bitch."

Billie called me aside. "I didn't want to put her out," he said, "a nice woman like that, shitfaced as she is. But I thought I was gonna have to. You'll see she gets home?"

I said I would.

First I had to let her buy us another round. She insisted. Then I got her out of there and a cab came along and saved us the walk. At her place, I took the keys from her and unlocked the door. She half sat, half sprawled on the couch. I had to use the bathroom, and when I came back her eyes were closed and she was snoring lightly.

I got her coat and shoes off, put her to bed, loosened her clothing and covered her with a blanket. I was tired from all that and sat down on the couch for a minute, and I almost dozed off myself. Then I snapped awake and let myself out. Her door had a spring lock. All I had to do was close it and it was locked.

Much of the walk back to my hotel disappeared in blackout. I was crossing Fifty-seventh Street, and then it was morning and I was stretched out in my own bed, my clothes a tangle on the straight-backed chair. That happened a lot in those days, that kind of before-bed blackout, and I used to insist it didn't bother me. What ever happened on the way home? Why waste brain cells remembering the final fifteen minutes of the day?

I went back to Sunset Park the next day. I learned that Cruz had been in trouble as a youth. With a gang of neighborhood kids, he used to go into the city and cruise Greenwich Village, looking for homosexuals to beat up. He'd had a dread of homosexuality, probably flowing as it generally does out of a fear of a part of himself, and he stifled that dread by fag-bashing.

"He still doan like them," a woman told me. She had glossy black hair and opaque eyes, and she was letting me pay for her rum and orange juice. "He's pretty, you know, and they come on to him, an' he doan like it."

I called that item in, along with a few others equally earth-shaking. I bought myself a steak dinner at the Slate over on Tenth Avenue that night, then finished up at Armstrong's, not drinking very hard, just coasting along on bourbon and coffee.

Twice, the phone rang for me. Once it was Tommy Tillary, telling me how much he appreciated what I was doing for him. It seemed to me that all I was doing was taking his money, but he had me believing that my loyalty and invaluable assistance were all he had to cling to.

The second call was from Carolyn. More praise. I was a gentleman, she assured me, and a hell of a fellow all around. And I should forget that she'd been bad-mouthing Tommy. Everything was going to be fine with them.

I told her I'd never doubted it for a minute, and that I couldn't really remember what she'd said anyway.

I took the next day off. I think I went to a movie, and it may have been *The Sting*, with Newman and Redford achieving vengeance through swindling.

The day after that I did another tour of duty over in Brooklyn. And the day after that I picked up the *News* first thing in the morning. The headline was nonspecific, something like *Kill Suspect Hangs Self in Cell*, but I knew it was my case before I turned to the story on Page Three.

Miguelito Cruz had torn his clothing into strips, knotted the strips together, stood his iron bedstead on its side, climbed onto it, looped his homemade rope around an overhead pipe, and jumped off the upended bedstead and into the next world.

That evening's six o'clock TV news had the rest of the story. Informed of his friend's death, Angel Herrera had recanted his original story and admitted that he and Cruz had conceived and

executed the Tillary burglary on their own. It had been Miguelito
who had stabbed the Tillary woman when she walked in on them.
He'd picked up a kitchen knife while Herrera watched in horror.
Miguelito always had a short temper, Herrera said, but they were
friends, even cousins, and they had hatched their story to protect
Miguelito. But now that he was dead, Herrera could admit what
had really happened.

I was in Armstrong's that night, which was not remarkable. I
had it in mind to get drunk, though I could not have told you why,
and that *was* remarkable, if not unheard of. I got drunk a lot those
days, but I rarely set out with that intention. I just wanted to feel a
little better, a little more mellow, and somewhere along the way I'd
wind up waxed.

I wasn't drinking particularly hard or fast, but I was working
at it, and then somewhere around ten or eleven the door opened
and I knew who it was before I turned around. Tommy Tillary, well
dressed and freshly barbered, making his first appearance in
Jimmy's place since his wife was killed.

"Hey, look who's here!" he called out, and grinned that big
grin. People rushed over to shake his hand. Billie was behind the
stick, and he'd no sooner set one up on the house for our hero than
Tommy insisted on buying a round for the bar. It was an expensive
gesture, there must have been thirty or forty people in there, but I
don't think he cared if there were three or four hundred.

I stayed where I was, letting the others mob him, but he
worked his way over to me and got an arm around my shoulders.
"This is the man," he announced. "Best fucking detective ever
wore out a pair of shoes. This man's money—" he told Billie "—is
no good at all tonight. He can't buy a drink, he can't buy a cup of
coffee, if you went and put in pay toilets since I was last there, he
can't use his own dime."

"The john's still free," Billie said, "but don't give the boss any
ideas."

"Oh, don't tell me he didn't already think of it," Tommy said.

"Matt, my boy, I love you. I was in a tight spot, I didn't want to walk out of my house, and you came through for me."

What the hell had I done? I hadn't hanged Miguelito Cruz or coaxed a confession out of Angel Herrera. I hadn't even set eyes on either man. But he was buying the drinks, and I had a thirst, so who was I to argue?

I don't know how long we stayed there. Curiously, my drinking slowed down even as Tommy's picked up speed. Carolyn, I noticed, was not present, nor did her name find its way into the conversation. I wondered if she would walk in—it was, after all, her neighborhood bar, and she was apt to drop in on her own. I wondered what would happen if she did.

I guess there were a lot of things I wondered about, and perhaps that's what put the brakes on my own drinking. I didn't want any gaps in my memory, any gray patches in my awareness.

After a while Tommy was hustling me out of Armstrong's. "This is celebration time," he told me. "We don't want to sit in one place till we grow roots. We want to bop a little."

He had a car, and I just went along with him without paying too much attention to exactly where we were. We went to a noisy Greek club on the East Side, I think, where the waiters looked like mob hitmen. We went to a couple of trendy singles joints. We wound up somewhere in the Village, in a dark beery cave that reminded me, I realized after a while, of the Norwegian joint in Sunset Park. The Fjord? Right.

It was quiet there, and conversation was possible, and I found myself asking him what I'd done that was so praiseworthy. One man had killed himself and another had confessed, and where was my role in either incident?

"The stuff you came up with," he said.

"What stuff? I should have brought back fingernail parings, you could have had someone work voodoo on them."

"About Cruz and the fairies."

"He was up for murder. He didn't kill himself because he was afraid they'd get him for fag-bashing when he was a juvenile offender."

Tommy took a sip of Scotch. He said, "Couple days ago, black guy comes up to Cruz in the chow line. Huge spade, built like the Seagram's Building. 'Wait'll you get up to Green Haven,' he tells him. "Every blood there's gonna have you for a girlfriend. Doctor gonna have to cut you a brand-new asshole, time you get outta there.'"

I didn't say anything.

"Kaplan," he said. "Drew talked to somebody who talked to somebody, and that did it. Cruz took a good look at the idea of playin' Drop the Soap for half the jigs in captivity, and the next thing you know the murderous little bastard was dancing on air. And good riddance to him."

I couldn't seem to catch my breath. I worked on it while Tommy went to the bar for another round. I hadn't touched the drink in front of me but I let him buy for both of us.

When he got back I said, "Herrera."

"Changed his story. Made a full confession."

"And pinned the killing on Cruz."

"Why not? Cruz wasn't around to complain. Who knows which one of 'em did it, and for that matter who cares? The thing is, you gave us the lever."

"For Cruz," I said. "To get him to kill himself."

"And for Herrera. Those kids of his in Santurce. Drew spoke to Herrera's lawyer and Herrera's lawyer spoke to Herrera, and the message was, look, you're going up for burglary whatever you do, and probably for murder, but if you tell the right story you'll draw shorter time and on top of that, that nice Mr. Tillary's gonna let bygones be bygones and every month there's a nice check for your wife and kiddies back home in Puerto Rico."

At the bar, a couple of old men were reliving the Louis-Schmeling fight, the second one, where Louis punished the German champion. One of the old fellows was throwing roundhouse punches in the air, demonstrating.

I said, "Who killed your wife?"

"One or the other of them. If I had to bet I'd say Cruz. He had those little beady eyes, you looked at him up close and you got that he was a killer."

"When did you look at him up close?"

"When they came and cleaned the house, the basement and the attic. Not when they came and cleaned me out, that was the second time."

He smiled, but I kept looking at him until the smile lost its certainty. "That was Herrera who helped around the house," I said. "You never met Cruz."

"Cruz came along, gave him a hand."

"You never mentioned that before."

"Oh, sure I did, Matt. What difference does it make, anyway?"

"Who killed her, Tommy?"

"Hey, let it alone, huh?"

"Answer the question."

"I already answered it."

"You killed her, didn't you?"

"What are you, crazy? Cruz killed her and Herrera swore to it, isn't that enough for you?"

"Tell me you didn't kill her."

"I didn't kill her."

"Tell me again."

"I didn't fucking kill her. What's the matter with you?"

"I don't believe you."

"Oh, Jesus," he said. He closed his eyes, put his head in his hands. He sighed and looked up and said, "You know, it's a funny thing with me. Over the telephone, I'm the best salesman you could ever imagine. I swear I could sell sand to the Arabs, I could sell ice in the winter, but face to face I'm no good at all. Why do you figure that is?"

"You tell me."

"I don't know. I used to think it was my face, the eyes and the mouth, I don't know. It's easy over the phone. I'm talking to a stranger, I don't know who he is or what he looks like, and he's not lookin' at me, and it's a cinch. Face to face, especially with someone I know, it's a different story." He looked at me. "If we were doin' this over the phone, you'd buy the whole thing."

"It's possible."

"It's fucking certain. Word for word, you'd buy the package. Suppose I was to tell you I did kill her, Matt. You couldn't prove anything. Look, the both of us walked in there, the place was a mess from the burglary, we got in an argument, tempers flared, something happened."

"You set up the burglary. You planned the whole thing, just the way Cruz and Herrera accused you of doing. And now you wriggled out of it."

"And you helped me, don't forget that part of it."

"I won't."

"And I wouldn't have gone away for it anyway, Matt. Not a chance. I'da beat it in court, only this way I don't have to go to court. Look, this is just the booze talkin', and we can both forget it in the morning, right? I didn't kill her, you didn't accuse me, we're still buddies, everything's fine. Right?"

Blackouts are never there when you want them. I woke up the next day and remembered all of it, and I found myself wishing I didn't. He'd killed his wife and he was getting away with it. And I'd helped him. I'd taken his money, and in return I'd shown him how to set one man up for suicide and pressure another into making a false confession.

And what was I going to do about it?

I couldn't think of a thing. Any story I carried to the police would be speedily denied by Tommy and his lawyer, and all I had was the thinnest of hearsay evidence, my own client's own words when he and I both had a skinful of booze. I went over it for a few days, looking for ways to shake something loose, and there was nothing. I could maybe interest a newspaper reporter, maybe get

Tommy some press coverage that wouldn't make him happy, but why? And to what purpose?

It rankled. But I would just have a couple of drinks, and then it wouldn't rankle so much.

Angel Herrera pleaded to burglary, and in return the Brooklyn D.A.'s office dropped all homicide charges. He went upstate to serve five-to-ten.

And then I got a call in the middle of the night. I'd been sleeping a couple of hours but the phone woke me and I groped for it. It took me a minute to recognize the voice on the other end.

It was Carolyn Cheatham.

"I had to call you," she said, "on account of you're a bourbon man and a gentleman. I owed it to you to call you."

"What's the matter?"

"He ditched me," she said, "and he got fired out of Tannahill & Co. so he won't have to look at me around the office. Once he didn't need me he let go of me, and do you know he did it over the phone?"

"Carolyn—"

"It's all in the note," she said. "I'm leaving a note."

"Look, don't do anything yet," I said. I was out of bed, fumbling for my clothes. "I'll be right over. We'll talk about it."

"You can't stop me, Matt."

"I won't try to stop you. We'll talk first, and then you can do anything you want."

The phone clicked in my ear.

I threw my clothes on, rushed over there, hoping it would be pills, something that took its time. I broke a small pane of glass in the downstairs door and let myself in, then used an old credit card to slip the bolt of her spring lock. If she had engaged the dead bolt lock I would have had to kick the door in.

The room smelled of cordite. She was on the couch she'd passed out on the last time I saw her. The gun was still in her hand, limp at her side, and there was a black-rimmed hole in her temple.

23

There was a note, too. An empty bottle of Maker's Mark stood on the coffee table, an empty glass beside it. The booze showed in her handwriting, and in the sullen phrasing of the suicide note.

I read the note. I stood there for a few minutes, not for very long, and then I got a dish towel from the pullman kitchen and wiped the bottle and the glass. I took another matching glass, rinsed it out and wiped it, and put it in the drainboard of the sink.

I stuffed the note in my pocket. I took the gun from her fingers, checked routinely for a pulse, then wrapped a sofa pillow around the gun to muffle its report. I fired one round into her chest, another into her open mouth.

I dropped the gun into a pocket and left.

They found the gun in Tommy Tillary's house, stuffed between the cushions of the living room sofa, clean of prints inside and out. Ballistics got a perfect match. I'd aimed for soft tissue with the round shot into her chest because bullets can fragment on impact with bone. That was one reason I'd fired the extra shots. The other was to rule out the possibility of suicide.

After the story made the papers, I picked up the phone and called Drew Kaplan. "I don't understand it," I said. "He was free and clear, why the hell did he kill the girl?"

"Ask him yourself," Kaplan said. He did not sound happy. "You want my opinion, he's a lunatic. I honestly didn't think he was. I figured maybe he killed his wife, maybe he didn't. Not my job to try him. But I didn't figure he was a homicidal maniac."

"It's certain he killed the girl?"

"Not much question. The gun's pretty strong evidence. Talk about finding somebody with the smoking pistol in his hand, here it was in Tommy's couch. The idiot."

"Funny he kept it."

"Maybe he had other people he wanted to shoot. Go figure a crazy man. No, the gun's evidence, and there was a phone tip, a man called in the shooting, reported a man running out of there and gave a description that fitted Tommy pretty well. Even had him wearing that red blazer he wears, tacky thing makes him look like an usher at the Paramount."

"It sounds tough to square."

"Well, somebody else'll have to try to do it," Kaplan said. "I told him I can't defend him this time. What it amounts to, I wash my hands of him."

I thought of this when I read that Angel Herrera got out just the other day. He served all ten years because he was as good at getting into trouble inside the walls as he'd been on the outside.

Somebody killed Tommy Tillary with a homemade knife after he'd served two years and three months of a manslaughter stretch. I wondered at the time if that was Herrera getting even, and I don't suppose I'll ever know. Maybe the checks stopped going to Santurce and Herrera took it the wrong way. Or maybe Tommy said the wrong thing to somebody else, and said it face to face instead of over the phone.

I don't think I'd do it that way now. I don't drink any more, and the impulse to play God seems to have evaporated with the booze.

But then a lot of things have changed. Billie left Armstrong's not long after that, left New York too; the last I heard he was off drink himself, living in Sausalito and making candles.

I ran into Dennis the other day in a bookstore on lower Fifth Avenue, full of odd volumes on yoga and spiritualism and holistic healing. And Armstrong's is scheduled to close the end of next month. The lease is up for renewal, and I suppose the next you know the old joint'll be another Korean fruit market.

I still light a candle now and then for Carolyn Cheatham and Angel Cruz. Not very often. Just every once in a while.

# The Strawberry Teardrop

## *Max Allan Collins*

*I have a great affection for the private eye story, but*
*of the dozen mystery/suspense novels that appeared under my*
*byline between 1973 and 1983, none were private eye stories*
*—exactly. They were about various latterday tough guys,*
*including a professional thief, a hired killer and a mystery*
*writer—though in many of them, the protagonist behaved much*
*as a private eye might. So why didn't I just write a novel*
*about a private eye?*

*Primarily because I couldn't make the private eye work*
*for me in modern dress; he seemed to me a walking*
*anachronism, who somehow didn't exist past about 1953.*

*Then one day it occurred to me: the private eye of*
*fiction had been around long enough now to exist in* history.
*Hammett's* Maltese Falcon *was published in 1929, making Sam*
*Spade a contemporary of Al Capone—which led to an*
*intriguing notion. Why not do a historical novel, focusing*
*on some real event shrouded in mystery/history, and use a*
*private eye as narrator?*

*True Detective (St. Martin's, 1983), the story of ex-cop*
*Nate Heller's struggle to survive in the corrupt Chicago of*

*1933, possibly the longest first-person private eye novel published to date, is—finally—my first private eye novel.*

*And what follows is my first private eye short story.*

**I**N a garbage dump on East Ninth Street near Shore Drive, in Cleveland, Ohio, on August 17, 1938, a woman's body was discovered by a cop walking his morning beat.

I got there before anything much had been moved. Not that I was a plainclothes dick—I used to be, but not in Cleveland; I was just along for the ride. I'd been sitting in the office of Cleveland's Public Safety Director, having coffee, when the call came through. The Safety Director was in charge of both the police and fire department, and one would think that a routine murder wouldn't rate a call to such a high muckey-muck.

One would be wrong.

Because this was the latest in a series of anything-but-routine, brutal murders—the unlucky thirteenth, to be exact, not that the thirteenth victim would seem any more unlucky than the preceding twelve. The so-called "Mad Butcher of Kingsbury Run" had been exercising his ghastly art sporadically since the fall of '35, in Cleveland—or so I understood. I was an out-of-towner, myself.

So was the woman.

Or she used to be, before she became so many dismembered parts flung across this rock-and-garbage strewn dump. Her nude torso was slashed and the blood, splashed here, streaked there, was turning dark, almost black, though the sun caught scarlet glints and tossed them at us. Her head was gone, but maybe it would turn up. The Butcher wasn't known for that, though. The twelve preceding victims had been found headless, and had stayed that way. Somewhere in Cleveland, perhaps, a guy had a collection in his attic. In this weather it wouldn't smell too nice.

It's not a good sign when the Medical Examiner gets sick; and the half dozen cops, and the police photographer, were looking green around the gills themselves. Only my friend, the Safety Director, seemed in no danger of losing his breakfast. He was a ruddy-cheeked six-footer in a coat and tie and vest, despite the heat; hatless, his hair brushed back and pomaded, he still seemed—years after I'd met him—boyish. And he was only in his mid-thirties, just a few years older than me.

I'd met him in Chicago, seven or eight years ago, when I wasn't yet president (and everything else) of the A-1 Detective Agency, but still a cop; and he was still a Prohibition Agent. Hell, *the* Prohibition agent. He'd considered me one of the more or less honest cops in Chicago—emphasis on the less, I guess—and I made a good contact for him, as a lot of the cops didn't like him much. Honesty doesn't go over real big in Chicago, you know.

Eliot Ness said, "Despite the slashing, there's a certain skill displayed, here."

"Yeah, right," I said. "A regular ballet dancer did this."

"No, really," he said, and bent over the headless torso, pointing. He seemed to be pointing at the gathering flies, but he wasn't. "There's an unmistakable precision about this. Maybe even indicating surgical training."

"Maybe," I said. "But I think the doctor lost this patient."

He stood and glanced at me and smiled, just a little; he understood me: he knew my wise-guy remarks were just my way of holding onto my own breakfast.

"You ought to come to Cleveland more often," he said.

"You know how to show a guy a good time, I'll give you that, Eliot."

He walked over and glanced at a forearm, which seemed to reach for an empty soap box, fingers stretched toward the Gold Dust twins. He knelt and studied it.

I wasn't here on a vacation, by any means. Cleveland didn't strike me as a vacation city, even before I heard about the Butcher of Kingsbury Run (so called because a number of the bodies, including the first several, were found on that Cleveland street). This was strictly business. I was here trying to trace the missing daughter of a guy in Evanston who owned a dozen diners around Chicago. He was one of those self-made men who started out in the greasy kitchen of his own first diner, fifteen or so years ago; and now he had a fancy brick house in Evanston and plenty of money, considering the times. But not much else. His wife had died four or five years ago, of consumption; and his daughter—who he claimed to be a good girl and by all other accounts was pretty wild—had wandered off a few months ago, with a taxi dancer from the Northside named Tony.

Well, I'd found Tony in Toledo—he was doing a floor show in a roadhouse with a dark-haired girl named FiFi; he'd grown a little pencil mustache and they did an apache routine—he was calling himself Antoine now. And Tony/Antoine said Ginger (which was the Evanston restaurateur's daughter's nickname) had taken up with somebody named Ray, who owned (get this) a diner in Cleveland.

I'd gotten here yesterday, and had talked to Ray, and without tipping I was looking for her, asked where was the pretty waitress, the one called Ginger, I think her name is. Ray, a skinny balding guy of about thirty with a silver front tooth, leered and winked and made it obvious that not only was Ginger working as a waitress here, she was also a side dish, where Ray was concerned. Further casual conversation revealed that it was Ginger's night off—she was at the movies with some girlfriends—and she'd be in tomorrow, around five.

I didn't push it further, figuring to catch up with her at the diner the next evening, after wasting a day seeing Cleveland and bothering my old friend Eliot. And now I was in a city dump with him, watching him study the severed forearm of a woman.

"Look at this," Eliot said, pointing at the outstretched fingers of the hand.

I went over to him and it. Not quickly, but I went over.

"What, Eliot? Do you want to challenge my powers of deduction, or just make me sick?"

"Just a lucky break," he said. "Most of the victims have gone unidentified; too mutilated. And a lot of 'em have been prostitutes or vagrants. But we've got a break, here. Two breaks, actually."

He pointed to the hand's little finger. To the small gold filigree band with a green stone.

"A nice specific piece of jewelry to try to trace," he said, with a dry smile. "And even better . . ."

He pointed to a strawberry birthmark, the shape of a teardrop, just below the wrist.

I took a close look; then stood. Put a hand on my stomach. Walked away and dropped to my knees and lost my breakfast.

I felt Eliot's hand patting my back.

"Nate," he said. "What's the matter? You've seen homicides before . . . even grisly ones like this . . . brace up, boy."

He eased me to my feet.

My tongue felt thick in my mouth, thick and restless.

"What is it?" he said.

"I think I just found my client's daughter," I said.

Both the strawberry birthmark and the filigree ring with the green stone had been part of my basic description of the girl; the photographs I had showed her to be a pretty but average-looking young woman—slim, brunette—who resembled every third girl you saw on the street. So I was counting on those two specifics to help me identify her. I hadn't counted on those specifics helping me in just this fashion.

I sat in Eliot's inner office in the Cleveland city hall; the mayor's office was next door. We were having coffee with some rum in it—Eliot kept a bottle in a bottom drawer of his rolltop desk. I promised him not to tell Capone.

"I think we should call the father," Eliot said. "Ask him to come and make the identification."

I thought about it. "I'd like to argue with you, but I don't see how I can. Maybe if we waited till . . . Christ. Till the head turns up . . ."

Eliot shrugged. "It isn't likely to. The ring and the birthmark are enough to warrant notifying the father."

"I can make the call."

"No. I'll let you talk to him when I'm done, but that's something I should do."

And he did. With quiet tact. After a few minutes he handed me the phone; if I'd thought him cold at the scene of the crime, I erased that thought when I saw the dampness in his gray eyes.

"Is it my little girl?" the deep voice said, sounding tinny out of the phone.

"I think so, Mr. Jensen. I'm afraid so."

I could hear him weeping.

Then he said: "Mr. Ness said her body was . . . dismembered. How can you say it's her? How . . . how can you know it's her?"

And I told him of the ring and the strawberry teardrop.

"I should come there," he said.

"Maybe that won't be necessary." I covered the phone. "Eliot, will my identification be enough?"

He nodded. "We'll stretch it."

I had to argue with Jensen, but finally he agreed for his daughter's remains to be shipped back via train; I said I'd contact a funeral home this afternoon, and accompany her home.

I handed the phone to Eliot to hang up.

We looked at each other and Eliot, not given to swearing, said, "I'd give ten years of my life to nail that butchering bastard."

"How long will your people need the body?"

"I'll speak to the coroner's office. I'm sure we can send her home with you in a day or two. Where are you staying?"

"The Stadium Hotel."

"Not anymore. I've got an extra room for you. I'm a bachelor again, you know."

We hadn't gotten into that yet; I'd always considered Eliot's marriage an ideal one, and was shocked a few months back to hear it had broken up.

"I'm sorry, Eliot."

"Me too. But I am seeing somebody. Someone you may remember; another Chicagoan."

"Who?"

"Evie MacMillan."

"The fashion illustrator? Nice looking woman."

Eliot smiled slyly. "You'll see her tonight, at the Country Club . . . but I'll arrange some female companionship for you. I don't want you cutting my time."

"How can you say such a thing? Don't you trust me?"

"I learned a long time ago," he said, turning to his desk full of paperwork, "not to trust Chicago cops—even ex-ones."

Out on the Country Club terrace, the ten-piece band was playing Cole Porter and a balmy breeze from Lake Erie was playing with the women's hair. There were plenty of good-looking women, here—low-cut dresses, bare shoulders—and lots of men in evening clothes for them to dance with. But this was no party, and since some of the golfers were still here from late afternoon rounds, there were sports clothes and a few business suits (like mine) in the mix. Even some of the women were dressed casually, like the tall, slender blonde in pink shirt and pale green pleated skirt who sat down next to me at the little white metal table and asked me if I'd have a Bacardi with her. The air smelled like a flower garden, and some of it was flowers, and some of it was her.

"I'd be glad to buy you a Bacardi," I said, clumsily.

"No," she said, touching my arm. She had eyes the color of jade. "You're a guest. I'll buy."

Eliot was dancing with his girl Evie, an attactive brunette in her mid-thirties; she'd always struck me as intelligent but sad, somehow. They smiled over at me.

The blonde in pink and pale green brought two Bacardis over, set one of them in front of me and smiled. "Yes," she said wickedly. "You've been set up. I'm the girl Eliot promised you. But if you were hoping for somebody in an evening gown, I'm not it. I just *had* to get an extra nine holes in."

"If you were looking for a guy in a tux," I said, "I'm not it. And I've never been on a golf course in my life. What else do we have in common?"

She had a nicely wry smile, which continued as she sipped the Bacardi. "Eliot, I suppose. If I have a few more of these, I may tell you a secret."

And after a few more, she did.

And it was a whopper.

*"You're* an undercover agent?" I said. A few sheets to the wind myself.

"Shhhh," she said, finger poised uncertainly before pretty lips. "It's a secret. But I haven't been doing it much lately."

"Haven't been doing what?"

"Well, undercover work. And there's a double-entendre there that I'd rather you didn't go looking for."

"I wouldn't think of looking under the covers for it."

The band began playing a tango.

I asked her how she got involved, working for Eliot. Which I didn't believe for a second, even in my cups.

But it turned out to be true (as Eliot admitted to me when he came over to see how Vivian and I were getting along, when Vivian—which was her name, incidentally—went to the powder room with Evie).

Vivian Chalmers was the daughter of a banker (a solvent one), a divorcee of thirty with no children and a lot of social pull. An expert trapshooter, golfer, tennis player and "all 'round sportswoman," with a sense of adventure. When Eliot called on her to case various of the gambling joints he planned to raid—as a socialite she could take a fling in any joint she chose, without raising any suspicion—she immediately said yes. And she'd been an active agent in the first few years of Eliot's ongoing battle against the so-called Mayfield Road Mob which controlled prostitution, gambling and the policy racket in the Cleveland environs.

"But things have slowed down," she said, nostalgically. "Eliot has pretty much cleaned up the place, and, besides, he doesn't want to use me anymore."

"An undercover agent can only be effective so long," I said. "Pretty soon the other side gets suspicious."

She shrugged, with resigned frustration, and let me buy the next round.

We took a walk in the dark, around the golf course, and ended up sitting on a green. The breeze felt nice. The flag on the pin—13—flapped.

"Thirteen," I said.

"Huh?"

"Victim thirteen."

"Oh. Eliot told me about that. Your 'luck' today, finding your client's missing daughter. Damn shame."

"Damn shame."

"A shame, too, they haven't found the son-of-a-bitch."

She was a little drunk, and so was I, but I was still shocked—well, amused—to hear a woman, particularly a "society" woman, speak that way.

"It must grate on Eliot, too," I said.

"Sure as hell does. It's the only mote in his eye. He's a hero around these parts, and he's kicked the Mayfield Mob in the seat of the pants, and done everything else from clean up a corrupt police department to throw labor racketeers in jail, to cut traffic deaths in half, to founding Boy's Town, to. . . ."

"You're not in love with the guy, are you?"

She seemed taken aback for a minute, then her face wrinkled into a got-caught-with-my-pants-down grin. "Maybe a little. But he's got a girl."

"I don't."

"You might."

She leaned forward.

We kissed for a while, and she felt good in my arms; she was firm, almost muscular. But she smelled like flowers. And the sky was blue and scattered with stars above us, as we lay back on the golf-green to look up. It seemed like a nice world, at the moment.

Hard to imagine it had a Butcher in it.

I sat up talking with Eliot that night; he lived in a little converted boathouse on the lake. The furnishings were sparse, spartan; it was obvious his wife had taken most of the furniture with her and he'd had to all but start over.

I told him I thought Vivian was a terrific girl.

Leaning back in a comfy chair, feet on an ottoman, Eliot, tie loose around his neck, smiled in a melancholy way. "I thought you'd hit it off."

"Did you have an affair with her?"

He looked at me sharply; that was about as personal as I'd ever got with him.

He shook his head no, but I didn't quite buy it.

"You knew Evie MacMillan in Chicago," I said.

"Meaning what?"

"Meaning nothing."

"Meaning I knew her when I was still married."

"Meaning nothing."

"Nate, I'm sorry I'm not the Boy Scout you think I am."

"Hey, so you've slept with girls before. I'll learn to live with it."

There was a stone fireplace, in which some logs were trying to decide whether to burn any more or not; we watched them trying.

"I love Evie, Nate. I'm going to marry her."

"Congratulations."

We could hear the lake out there; could smell it some, too.

"I'd like that bastard's neck in my hands," Eliot said.

"What?"

"That Butcher. That goddamn Butcher."

"What made you think of him?"

"I don't know."

"Eliot, it's been over three years since he first struck, and you *still* don't have anything?"

"Nothing. A few months ago, last time he hit, we found some of the . . . body parts, bones and such . . . in a cardboard box in the Central Market area. There's a Hooverville over there, or what used to be a Hooverville . . . it's a shantytown, is more like it, genuine hobos as opposed to just good folks down on their luck. Most of the victims—before today—were either prostitutes or bums . . . and the bums from that shantytown were the Butcher's meat. So to speak."

The fire crackled.

Eliot continued: "I decided to make a clean sweep. I took twenty-five cops through there at one in the morning, and rousted out all the 'bo's and took 'em down and fingerprinted and questioned all of 'em."

"And it amounted to . . . ?"

"It amounted to nothing. Except ridding Cleveland of that shantytown. I burned the place down that afternoon."

"Comes in handy, having all those firemen working for you. But what about those poor bastards whose 'city' you burned down?"

Sensing my disapproval, he glanced at me and gave me what tried to be a warm smile, but was just a weary one. "Nate, I turned them over to the Relief department, for relocation and, I hope, rehabilitation. But most of them were bums who just hopped a freight out. And I did 'em a favor by taking them off the potential victims list."

"And made room for Ginger Jensen."

Eliot looked away.

"That wasn't fair," I said. "I'm sorry I said that, Eliot."

"I know, Nate. I know."

But I could tell he'd been thinking the same thing.

I had lunch the next day with Vivian in a little outdoor restaurant in the shadow of Terminal Tower. We were served lemonade and little ham and cheese and lettuce and tomato sandwiches with the crusts trimmed off the toasted bread. The detective in me wondered what became of the crusts.

"Thanks for having lunch with me," Vivian said. She had on a pale orange dress; she sat crossing her brown pretty legs.

"My pleasure," I said.

"Speaking of which . . . about last night . . ."

"We were both a little drunk. Forget it. Just don't ask *me* to."

She smiled as she nibbled her sandwich.

"I called and told Eliot something this morning," she said, "and he just ignored me."

"What was that?"

"That I have a possible lead on the Butcher murders."

"I can't imagine Eliot ignoring that . . . and it's not like it's just *anybody* approaching him—you *did* work for him . . ."

"Not lately. And he thinks I'm just . . ."

"Looking for an excuse to be around him?"

She nibbled at a little sandwich. Nodded.

"Did you resent him asking you to be with me as a blind date last night?"

"No," she said.

"Did . . . last night have anything to do with wanting to 'show' Eliot?"

If she weren't so sophisticated—or trying to be—she would've looked hurt; but her expression managed to get something else across: disappointment in me.

"Last night had to do with showing *you*," she said. "And . . . it had a little to do with Bacardi rum . . ."

"That it did. Tell me about your lead."

"Eliot has been harping on the 'professional' way the bodies have been dismembered. He's said again and again he sees a 'surgical' look to it."

I nodded.

"So it occurred to me that a doctor—anyway, somebody who'd at least been in medical school for a time—would be a likely candidate for the Butcher."

"Yes."

"And medical school's expensive, so, it stands to reason, the Butcher just might run in the same social circles as yours truly."

"Say, you *did* work for Eliot."

She liked that.

She went on: "I checked around with my friends, and heard about a guy whose family has money, plenty of it. Name of Watterson."

"Last name or first?"

"That's the family name. Big in these parts."

"Means nothing to me."

"Well, Lloyd Watterson used to be a medical student. He's a big man, very strong—the kind of strength it might take to do some of the things the Butcher has done. And he has a history of mental disturbances."

"What kind of mental disturbances?"

"He's been going to a psychiatrist since he was a schoolboy."

"Do you know this guy?"

"Just barely. But I've heard things about him."

"Such as?"

"I hear he likes boys."

Lloyd Watterson lived in a two-story white house at the end of a dead-end street, a Victorian-looking miniature mansion among other such houses, where expansive lawns and towering hedges separated the world from the wealthy who lived within.

This wasn't the parental home, Vivian explained; Watterson lived here alone, apparently without servants. The grounds seemed well-tended, though, and there was nothing about this house that said anyone capable of mass murder might live here. No blood spattered on the white porch; no body parts scattered about the lawn.

It was mid-afternoon, and I was having second thoughts.

"I don't even have a goddamn gun," I said.

"I do," she said, and showed me a little .25 automatic from her purse.

"Great. If he has a dog, maybe we can use that to scare it."

"This'll do the trick. Besides, a gun won't even be necessary. You're just here to talk."

The game plan was for me to approach Watterson as a cop, flashing my private detective's badge quickly enough to fool him (and that almost always worked), and question him, simply get a feel for whether or not he was a legitimate suspect, worthy of lobbying Eliot for action against. My say-so, Vivian felt, would be enough to get Eliot off the dime.

And helping Eliot bring the Butcher in would be a nice wedding present for my old friend; with his unstated but obvious political ambitions, the capture of the Kingsbury Run maniac would offset the damage his divorce had done him in conservative, mostly Catholic Cleveland. He'd been the subject of near hero worship in the press here (Eliot was always good at getting press— Frank Nitti used to refer to him as "Eliot Press"); but the ongoing if sporadic slaughter of the Butcher was a major embarrassment for Cleveland's fabled Safety Director.

So, leaving Vivian behind in the roadster (Watterson might recognize her), I walked up the curved sidewalk and went up on the porch and rang the bell. In the dark hardwood door there was opaque glass through which I could barely make out movement, coming toward me.

The door opened, and a blond man about six-three with a baby-face and ice-blue eyes and shoulders that nearly filled the doorway looked out at me and grinned. A kid's grin, on one side of his face. He wore a polo shirt and short white pants; he seemed about to say, "Tennis, anyone?"

But he said nothing, as a matter of fact; he just appraised me with those ice-blue, somewhat vacant eyes. I now knew how it felt for a woman to be ogled—which is to say, not necessarily good.

I said, "I'm an officer of the court," which in Illinois wasn't exactly a lie, and I flashed him my badge, but before I could say anything else, his hand reached out and grabbed the front of my shirt, yanked me inside and slammed the door.

He tossed me like a horseshoe, and I smacked into something—the stairway to the second floor, I guess; I don't know exactly, because I blacked out. The only thing I remember is the musty smell of the place.

I woke up minutes later, and found myself tied in a chair in a dank, dark room. Support beams loomed out of a packed dirt floor. The basement.

I strained at the ropes, but they were snug; not so snug as to cut off my circulation, but snug enough. I glanced around the room. I was alone. I couldn't see much—just a shovel against one cement wall. The only light came from a window off to my right, and there were hedges in front of the window, so the light was filtered.

Feet came tromping down the open wooden stairs. I saw his legs first, white as pastry dough.

He was grinning. In his right hand was a cleaver. It shone, caught a glint of what little light there was.

"I'm no butcher," he said. His voice was soft, almost gentle. "Don't believe what you've heard. . . ."

"Do you want to die?" I said.

"Of course not."

"Well then cut me loose. There's cops all over the place, and if you kill me, they'll shoot you down. You know what happens to cop killers, don't you?"

He thought that over, nodded.

Standing just to one side of me, displaying the cold polished steel of the cleaver, in which my face's frantic reflection looked back at me, he said, "I'm no butcher. This is a surgical tool. This is used for amputation, not butchery."

"Yeah. I can see that."

"I wondered when you people would come around."

"Do you want to be caught, Lloyd?"

"Of course not. I'm no different than you. I'm a public servant."

"How . . . how do you figure that, Lloyd?" My feet weren't tied to the chair; if he'd just step around in front of me . . .

"I only dispose of the flotsam. Not to mention jetsam."

"Not to mention that."

"Tramps. Whores. Weeding out the stock. Survival of the fittest. You know."

"That makes a lot of sense, Lloyd. But I'm not flotsam *or* jetsam. I'm a cop. You don't want to kill a cop. You don't want to kill a fellow public servant."

He thought about that.

"I think I have to, this time," he said.

He moved around the chair, stood in front of me, stroking his chin, the cleaver gripped tight in his right hand, held about breastbone high.

"I *do* like you," Lloyd said, thoughtfully.

"And I like you, Lloyd," I said, and kicked him in the balls.

Harder than any man tied to a chair should be able to kick; but you'd be surprised what you can do, under extreme circumstances. And things rarely get more extreme than being tied to a chair with a guy with a cleaver coming at you.

Only he wasn't coming at me, now: now, he was doubled over, and I stood, the chair strapped to my back; managed, even so, to kick him in the face.

He tumbled back, gripping his groin, his head leaning back, stretching, tears streaming down his cheeks, cords in his neck taut; my shoe had caught him on the side of the face and broken the skin. Flecks of blood, like little red tears, spattered his cheeks, mingling with the real tears.

That's when the window shattered, and Vivian squeezed down and through, pretty legs first.

And she gave me the little gun to hold on him while she untied me.

He was still on the dirt floor, moaning, when we went up the stairs and out into the sunny day, into a world that wasn't dank,

onto earth that was grass-covered and didn't have God knows what
buried under it.

We asked Eliot to meet us at his boathouse; we told him what
had happened. He was livid; I never saw him angrier. But he held
Vivian for a moment, and looked at her and said, "If anything had
happened to you, I'd've killed you."

He poured all of us a drink; rum as usual. He handed me
mine and said, "How could you get involved in something so
harebrained?"

"I wanted to give my client something for his money," I said.

"You mean his daughter's killer."

"Why not?"

"I've been looking for the bastard three years, and you come
to town and expect to find him in three days."

"Well, I did."

He smirked, shook his head. "I believe you did. But
Watterson's family will bring in the highest-paid lawyers in the
country and we'd be thrown out of court on our cans."

"What? The son of a bitch tried to cut me up with a cleaver!"

"Did he? Did he swing on you? Or did you enter his house
under a false pretense, misrepresenting yourself as a law officer?
And as far as that goes, *you* assaulted *him*. We have very little."

Vivian said, "You have the name of the Butcher."

Eliot nodded. "Probably. I'm going to make a phone call."

Eliot went into his den and came out fifteen minutes later.

"I spoke with Franklin Watterson, the father. He's agreed to
submit his son for a lie detector test."

"To what end?"

"One step at a time," Eliot said.

Lloyd Watterson took the lie detector test twice—and on both
instances denied committing the various Butcher slayings; his
denials were, according to the machine, lies. The Watterson family
attorney reminded Eliot that lie detector tests were not admissible

as evidence. Eliot had a private discussion with Franklin Watterson.

Lloyd Watterson was committed, by his family, to an asylum for the insane. The Mad Butcher of Kingsbury Run—which to this day is marked "unsolved" in the Cleveland police records—did not strike again.

At least not directly.

Eliot married Evie MacMillan a few months after my Cleveland visit, and from the start their marriage was disrupted by crank letters, postmarked from the same town as the asylum where Watterson had been committed. "Retribution will catch up with you one day," said one postcard, on the front of which was a drawing of an effeminate man grinning from behind prison bars. Mrs. Ness was especially unnerved by these continuing letters and cards.

Eliot's political fortunes waned, in the wake of the "unsolved" Butcher slayings. Known for his tough stance on traffic violators, he got mired in a scandal when one predawn morning in March of 1942, his car skidded into an oncoming car on the West Shoreway. Eliot and his wife, and two friends, had been drinking. The police report didn't identify Eliot by name, but his license number—EN-1, well-known to Cleveland citizens—was listed. And Eliot had left the scene of the accident.

Hit-and-run, the headlines said. Eliot's version was that his wife had been injured, and he'd raced her to a hospital—but not before stopping to check on the other driver, who confirmed this. The storm blew over, but the damage was done. Eliot's image in the Cleveland press was finally tarnished.

Two months later he resigned as Safety Director.

About that time, asylum inmate Lloyd Watterson managed to hang himself with a bed sheet, and the threatening mail stopped.

How much pressure those cards and letters put on the marriage I couldn't say; but in 1945 Eliot and Evie divorced, and Eliot married a third time a few months later. At the time he was serving as federal director of the program against venereal disease

MAX ALLAN COLLINS

in the military. His attempt to run for Cleveland mayor in 1947 was a near disaster: Cleveland's one-time fairhaired boy was a has-been with a hit-run scandal and two divorces and three marriages going against him.

He would not have another public success until the publication of his autobiographical book, *The Untouchables*, but that success was posthumous; he died shortly before it was published, never knowing that television and Robert Stack would give him lasting fame.

I saw Eliot, now and then, over the years; but I never saw Vivian again.

I asked him about her, once, when I was visiting him in Pennsylvania, in the early '50s. He told me she'd been killed in a boating accident in 1943.

"She's been dead for years, then," I said, the shock of it hitting me like a blow.

"That's right. But shed a tear for her, now, if you like. Tears and prayers can never come too late, Nate."

Amen, Eliot.

*AUTHOR'S NOTE: I wish to express my indebtedness to two non-fiction works,* Four Against the Mob *by Oscar Fraley (Popular Library, 1961) and* Cleveland—The Best Kept Secret *by George E. Condon (Doubleday, 1967). Fact, speculation and fiction are freely mixed in the preceding story; with the exception of Eliot Ness, all characters—while in many cases having real-life counterparts—are fictional.*

# Eighty Million Dead

## *Michael Collins*

*Why do I write about a private detective? Well, at a point
in my writing life I discovered that the detective novel was
a form in which I could tell some stories I wanted to tell:
the best form for those stories.
As I worked I found other reasons.*

*The detective story more than any other form focuses on
human relations, on the human condition seen at naked
moments. The detective story is told by an observer, a
human "eye" that watches and tries to understand what is
happening and why. A detective seeks answers, asks
questions, and all writers are asking questions. All
writers are, after all, detectives. Detective fiction seems
to be suited to making observations about the nature of man
and society, and I want to make such observations.*

*Finally, in detective fiction the immediate story ends, but
the larger story goes on. The detective goes on. The
questions go on. The search goes on.
The attempt to understand.*

*So that is why I write detective fiction. Or maybe none of
that is true at all. Maybe there are ten others reasons. A*

*writer is probably the last person to know
why he does anything.*

WE have killed eighty million
people in eighty years. Give or take a few million or a couple of
years. Killed; not lost in hurricanes or famines or epidemics or any
of the other natural disasters we should be trying to wipe out
instead of each other. From 1900 to 1980. The Twentieth Century.

That's a hell of a way to begin a story, except in this case it
could be the whole story. The story of Paul Asher and Constantine
Zareta and me, Dan Fortune, and I want you to think about those
eighty million corpses. Most of those who killed them were fighting
for a reason, a cause. A lot of those who died had a reason, a
cause. You have to wonder what cause is worth eighty million
ended lives. You have to wonder what eighty million dead bodies
has done to the living.

I know what those eighty million deaths had done to Paul
Asher and Constantine Zareta. Those were the names they gave
me, anyway. They weren't their real names. I'm not sure they knew
their real names anymore. It was Paul Asher who walked into my
second floor office/apartment that rainy Monday.

"You are Dan Fortune? A private investigator?"

He was tall and dark. A big man who moved like a shadow. I
hadn't seen or even heard him come in. He was just there in front
of my desk—dark haired, dark eyed, soft voiced, in a dark suit.
Colorless. Nothing about him told me anything. Only his eyes,
looking at my missing arm, proved he was alive.

"I'm Fortune."

"I am Paul Asher. I wish to hire you."

"To do what, Mr. Asher?"

"You will deliver a package."

He had an accent. One I couldn't place, and not exactly even an accent. More a kind of toneless and too precise way of speaking English that told me it wasn't his native language.

"You want a messenger service," I said, "use my telephone book if you want."

"I will pay one thousand dollars," Asher said. "I wish that the package is to be delivered tonight."

No one makes a thousand dollars a day in Chelsea, not even today. Most still don't make it in a month. It was a lot of money for delivering a package. Or maybe it wasn't.

"What's in the package?" I asked.

"I will pay one thousand dollars because you will not ask what is in the package, and because Zareta is a dangerous man."

He said it direct and simple, expressionless.

"Zareta?" I said.

"Constantine Zareta. This he calls himself. It is to him you will take the package."

"Why not take it yourself?"

"He would kill me."

"Why?"

"I possess what he wants."

"Blackmail, Asher?"

"No, I ask no money. You will take the package?"

I shook my head. "Not without knowing what's in it, and why you want to send it to this Constantine Zareta."

Paul Asher thought for a time. He seemed to look again at my empty left sleeve, but his face remained expressionless. He wasn't angry or even frustrated. I had presented him with a problem, and he was thinking about it. As simple as that.

He made his decision. "The package contains documents, nothing more. I am giving them to Zareta. They are of no value except to Zareta. For him they are of great value. The papers are not a danger, simply of value to Zareta. He would kill me to get them, I am tired of danger. When he has the documents I will not be in danger. Until then, I am not safe from him. I cannot take the documents myself, so? You will take them?"

"Let's see the package."

Asher produced a flat package from an inside pocket of his dark suit. It was about as wide as a paperback book, twice as long and thick. I took it. They make bombs smaller and better every day, but the package was much too light for even a plastic bomb. It felt like a package of documents and nothing else. Even a deadly gas has to have a container. I could feel the edges, the folds, the thickness of heavy paper.

"How did you happen to pick me, Mr. Asher?"

"From the telephone book."

For the first time I didn't believe him. Too quick? Something in his voice that wasn't quite toneless this time? I'm in the phone book, but I didn't believe him. Because he wasn't the kind of man who trusted to chance? Maybe and maybe. But if it hadn't been the telephone book, how and why had he picked me out of all the detectives in New York?

"I take the package to Zareta," I said. "What do I bring back?"

"Nothing."

"Who pays me? When?"

"I will pay you," Asher said. "Now."

He took a thin billfold from his inside pocket, counted out ten hundred dollar bills. He wasn't telling me the truth, not the whole truth, but I knew that. Warned, what could happen that I couldn't handle? If anything looked a hair out of line I'd toss the package and walk away. I took the ten bills. Crisp and new, straight from the bank. Maybe I wanted to know why he had picked me for the job. I wanted to know something.

"What's the address?"

"It is on the package."

"How do I contact you later?"

"You do not. You are paid, I will know if you do not do what you have been paid to do."

"Anything else?"

"Yes," Paul Asher said. "You will deliver the package at midnight. Precisely midnight."

He walked out. I tilted back in my chair. I was a thousand dollars richer. Why didn't I feel good?

# 2

The address was on the East Side up in Yorkville far over near the river. Asher's instructions had been definite—midnight—and the slum street was dark and silent in the rain when the taxi dropped me. There was no one on the street. No one in sight anywhere, but I felt the eyes. When you grow up near the docks, start stealing early because you have to eat even if your father ran out long before and your mother drinks too much, you learn to feel when eyes are watching.

I walked slowly along the dark street in the rain and knew that I wasn't alone. I sensed them all around. The address was an old unrenovated brownstone with the high front steps. Two men appeared at the far end of the street. They leaned against a dark building. Two more appeared behind me where the taxi had dropped me. Two stood in the shadows on another stoop across the street. Shadows of shadows all around in the dark and rain. The glint of a gun.

I went up the steps to the front door and into the vestibule. There was only one mailbox and doorbell. I had my finger on the bell when I saw the man outside on the steps. He stood two steps below the vestibule with an automatic rifle. A short, powerful man behind a bandit mustache. There were two more behind him at the foot of the steps. They had guns too. They stood there doing nothing. Too late I knew why, felt the inner vestibule door open behind me.

An arm went around my throat, a hand went over my mouth, another hand held my arm, and I was dragged back into the dark of the entrance hall. I didn't resist. The short one with the bandit mustache and automatic rifle followed us in. They dragged me into a small room, sat me in a chair, came and went in rapid groups. They barely glanced at me. They were busy. Except two I felt close behind me keeping watch.

"What's going on?" I tried.

"Do not talk!" He was the short, powerful man with the automatic rifle. He seemed to be the leader, sent the other men in and out with the precision of a drill sergeant. They spoke some language I didn't even recognize. I didn't have to know the language to know what they were doing. They were all armed, and they were searching the street outside and the neighborhood for anyone who might have come with me. It was half an hour before the mustachioed leader sat down astride a chair in front of me. He still carried his automatic rifle, and the package Paul Asher had sent me to deliver.

"Your name is Fortune. What do you want here?"

"I came to deliver that package."

"Who are you?"

"You've searched my papers."

"You came to deliver this package to who?"

"Constantine Zareta. Is that you?"

"What is in the package?"

"Papers. Documents."

He studied the package a moment, turned it over in his heavy hands. Then he gave it to one of the other men.

"From who does the package come?"

"Paul Asher."

"We know no Paul Asher."

"It's the name he gave me."

"Your papers say you are a private investigator. We know what that means. A man who will sell his weapon to anyone. A hired murderer. An assassin. You came to kill Constantine Zareta!"

"I came to deliver a package," I said. "I don't have a gun. I don't even know who Zareta is or what he looks like."

"Of course not. They would not tell you who you kill or why. They have hired you only to kill. Do not lie!"

"If someone is trying to kill Zareta, go to the police. That's their work."

I had been watching all their faces as I talked. They were grim, unsmiling, and they didn't look like hoodlums. They looked like soldiers, *guerillas*. They were nervous and armed, but they didn't act like gunmen. And as I watched them I saw their faces come alert, respectful. Someone else had come into the room somewhere behind me. A low voice with good English.

"The police could not help me, Mr. Fortune."

I felt him standing close behind me. His voice had that power of command, of absolute confidence in himself and what he did. Constantine Zareta. I started to turn.

"Do not turn, Mr. Fortune."

I looked straight ahead at the mustachioed man. "Maybe the police can't help you because you want to kill Paul Asher."

The mustache reached out and hit me.

"Emil!"

Emil glared down at me. "He's another one, Minister! I can smell them!"

"Perhaps," Zareta's slow voice said. "Let us be sure."

"We cannot take the chance, Minister! Kill him now. If they did not send him, what does it matter?"

There was a silence behind me. A chair scraped. I felt hot breath on the back of my neck. Slow breathing. Zareta had sat down close behind me. That was fine. As long as I could feel his breath I was ahead of the game. As long as I could feel anything.

"A man sent you to me at this address."

"Yes."

"Why did he pick you?"

"Out of the telephone book."

"Do you believe that?"

"No."

I could almost hear him nod.

"What was his reason for not coming himself?"

"He said you'd kill him."

"Why would I kill him?"

"Because he had what you wanted. Documents, not dangerous to you, but so important you'd kill to get them."

"And these documents are in the package?"

"Yes. He said he was tired of danger, wanted to give them to you, but was afraid to come himself."

It was strangely unreal to be talking straight ahead into the empty air of the dark room, the silent face of Emil.

"This man's name was Paul Asher."

"Yes."

"I know no Asher, but that does not surprise me. You will decribe him."

I described Paul Asher down to the flinty calm of his dark eyes, his silent movement despite his size.

"I do not recognize him, but that does not surprise me either, Mr. Fortune. I do recognize the type of man you have described. It sounds true. You have saved your life, Mr. Fortune. For now."

Emil did not like my reprieve. "The risk, Minister!"

"I think we can take some risk, Emil," Zareta said, his breath still brushing the back of my neck. "Mr. Fortune could be lying, but I think not. This Asher sounds like all the men we have known, yes? Mr. Fortune has acted exactly as he would have if his story is true, and you found no one else who could have been with him. Then, he clearly does not know what was in the package he brought to us, or he would have told a better tale, yes? And he has no weapon of any kind."

That seemed to stop Emil. I've said it before, most of the time a gun does nothing but get you in trouble. Sooner or later you'll use it if you have to or not, and someone else will use theirs. If I'd had a gun this time, I'd probably be dead. I wasn't dead, and I wondered what had been in the package that would have made me tell a different story if I'd known?

"Why?" Zareta said slowly. "I cannot understand what reason this Asher had to send you to me. That makes me uneasy. Tell me everything once more. Leave nothing out."

I told him all of it again. I was uneasy too. Why had Paul Asher sent me if the package wasn't the reason? Or was it Zareta who was conning me now? Lulling me to get me to lead him back to Asher? If that was his scheme he wouldn't get far. I couldn't lead anyone to Paul Asher.

"I do not understand," Zareta said when I finished the story again, "but you have done me an important service. I know now what this Paul Asher looks like." The chair scraped behind me. "Take your money, Mr. Fortune, and go home. Forget that you ever heard of Paul Asher or me."

There was a silence, and then a door closed somewhere in the dark brownstone. The troops began to disperse. The boss had spoken. Emil's heart wasn't in it, but Zareta was boss.

"Tonight you are a very lucky man," Emil said.

I looked around. I saw no one that looked like a boss, but I saw the package I'd carried lying on a table. It was torn open to show—a stack of folded papers. Just what Asher had said it was. Only there *was* something wrong, something odd about the package. Not quite right. What? They didn't give me the time to look longer or closer.

They hustled me back out into the dark hall. Then I was out on the street where I'd started. I walked to the nearest corner without looking back. I didn't run, that would have been cowardly. I waited until I was around the corner. Then I ran.

By the time I got down to Chelsea and my one room office apartment I felt pretty good. I had no more interest in Asher and Zareta and their private feud, whatever it was. I was a thousand dollars richer and still alive. I figured I was home free. I should have known better.

## 3

I awoke in the pitch dark to a violent pounding on my door. My arm was aching. The missing arm. That's always a sign. It's what's missing that hurts when the days become bad.

The pounding went on. Cop pounding. As I got up and pulled on my pants, a gray light began to barely tinge the darkness. Captain Pearce himself led his Homicide men into my office area. The men fanned out and began to look behind the doors and under the beds. Pearce sat down behind my desk.

"What's it about, Captain?" I asked.

"Paul Asher," Pearce said.

"Nice name. Is there more?"

"Asher is enough," Pearce said. "He was a client of yours? Or was there some other connection?"

"Was?" I said.

"Asher's dead," Pearce said. "You should give him his money back."

Pearce doesn't like any private detective much, but especially me. I was too close to old Captain Gazzo. Pearce took Gazzo's place after the Captain was gunned down on a dark city roof. One of the new breed, a college man, and he doesn't like me bringing Gazzo's ghost with me. But he's a good cop, he does his job first.

"We found Asher an hour ago," Pearce said. "Dumped under the George Washington Bridge. Shot up like Swiss cheese. Any ideas?"

The George Washington Bridge is a long way from Yorkville, but that I would expect.

"Constantine Zareta," I said.

I told Pearce about Zareta and Asher, about Emil and all those silent gunmen. Pearce got up, signalled for his forces.

"Let's pick them up."

We went in the Captain's car. He sat silent and edgy as we headed uptown at the head of his platoon of squad cars, drumming his fingers on his knee. He had no more questions. I had questions.

"You said you found Asher an hour ago, Captain. How did you dig up my connection so fast?"

"Your business cards in his pocket."

"Cards?"

Pearce nodded as he watched the dawn city, gray and empty of people but teeming with trucks. "He must have had ten, and your name was in his little black book with a thousand dollars and yesterday's date noted next to it."

Business cards cost money, I don't hand them out without necessity. Asher had found me, there had been no reason to give him a card, not even one. I leave some with uptown contacts in case anyone up there wants a kidnapped poodle rescued, so Asher may have picked up the cards from whoever sent him to me before he came down to my office. Or he could have palmed them off my desk when he walked out. But why? And why ten?

In the dawn the Yorkville street was as deserted as it had been last night. We parked all along the gray morning street. Windows popped open all along the block, but nothing moved in Constantine Zareta's brownstone. The building was as dark and silent as some medieval fortress.

It turned out to be as hard to get into as a medieval fortress. Rings, knocks, shouts and threats failed to open the vestibule door, the building remained dark.

"Break it down," Pearce said.

His men broke the door open, and Pearce strode into the dim entrance hall. The mustachioed Emil faced him. Emil had his automatic rifle aimed at the Captain's heart. Other gunmen stood in the doorways of the rooms and on the stairs. We were all covered. It took Captain Pearce almost a minute to find his voice.

"Police, damn it! Put those guns down! We're the police!"

Constantine Zareta spoke from somewhere behind Emil, out of sight in the dim hallway. I knew that slow voice by now.

"You will tell me your name, your rank, and your badge number. I will verify that you are police. You will make no moves, my men watch your people in the street also."

The color began to suffuse Pearce's face. The Captain isn't a patient man, and I wondered how long it had been since anyone had asked him to prove who he was. He opened his mouth, looked slowly around the dark hallway at the silent *guerillas* and their guns, and closed his mouth. If Constantine Zareta was as tough as he sounded, we could have a blood bath in the dark hallway and out on the morning street.

"Captain Martin Pearce," the Captain said through thin lips, and explained that a captain's shield does not have a number.

In the silent hallway we all waited.

I imagined the scene down at Police Headquarters when they got the call asking about a Captain Pearce, and would they please describe the Captain! It took some time, but whatever they thought down there they must have gone along with it and given an accurate description. Constantine Zareta appeared in the dim light, and I saw him for the first time—a short, thick man as wide as he was tall, with a shaved bullet head attached to his massive shoulders as if he had no neck. He said something in his unknown language. The guns vanished and the gunmen disappeared.

"Very well, Captain," Zareta said to Pearce. "We will talk in the living room."

Pearce and Zareta faced each other in the same room where I had been interrogated earlier. The Captain stood. Zareta sat on a straight chair, Emil close behind him. Neither Zareta nor Emil had seen me yet.

"Just who and what are you, Zareta?" Pearce said. "Why do you need armed men?" His voice was controlled, but I heard the edge in it. No policeman can tolerate a private army.

"A poor exile, Captain," Zareta said. "My men have permits for their weapons."

"Exile from where?"

"Albania."

That was the language I hadn't recognized—Albanian.

"Was Paul Asher an Albanian too?" Pearce said. "Is that why he was afraid of you? Is that why you killed him?"

For a moment there was a heavy silence in the small living room lit only by a single lamp behind its drawn curtains. Then Emil grunted. Others made other noises. Constantine Zareta leaned forward in his chair.

"This Asher, he is dead? You are sure?"

"We're sure," Pearce said.

Zareta laughed aloud. "Good! He is one *we* will not have to kill! You bring me good news, Captain, I am grateful. But how did you know that this Asher's death would be something I would want to know? How did you know of Asher and myself? How . . . Ah, of course! Mr. Fortune. You have talked with Mr. Fortune. It is the only way." He looked around the small room. "Are you here again, Mr. Fortune?"

I stepped out into the dim light where Zareta could see me, flashed my best smile at the glowering Emil, and missed it. I missed the whole impossible, monstrous plan.

# 4

Sometimes I wonder if there is anyone left who hasn't killed. I know there are millions, but sometimes it seems there can't be a man alive who hasn't killed. I've killed. In my work you kill sooner or later, but I never get used to it. It always shakes me up, killing and death, and maybe that was why I missed what I should have heard in what Constantine Zareta said when I stepped out where he could see me and only smiled at him.

Pearce wasn't smiling. "You're saying you didn't kill Paul Asher?"

"We did not."

"But you would have?"

"If he came here, yes."

"Why?"

"Because he would have killed me."

"Why didn't you ask for protection?"

"The police?" Zareta shook his head. "No, Captain. I am not precisely a friend of your government. I am a Communist. I have no love for your capitalist regime, they have no love for me. In my country the present leaders and I have no love for each other either. They want me dead, *must* have me dead, or someday I will destroy them. Six times they have tried. In four countries. Twice we had police protection. Once the police could not stop the assassin, once they did not want to stop the assassins. Each time I was close to death. I have survived, I have killed four of them, but they will not give up. If I were them I would not give up. One of us must kill the other."

That was when I first thought about the eighty million dead in eighty years. Zareta said the word *kill* the way other men say the word *work*—a fact of life, a necessity. Neither good nor bad, just a tool of life. I remember when we used to say that a man who killed for the fun of it was an animal, inhuman, a monster. Today we kill without even having any fun from it. We just kill. A job, a duty, our assigned role. And it has nothing to do with being a Communist. It isn't only the Communists who have swallowed those eighty million corpses like so many jelly beans.

Pearce said, "So you have your own army, trust no one to come near you, not even the police."

"That is why I still live, Captain," Zareta said. "But we do not kill unless we are sure a man is our enemy."

"You knew Paul Asher was your enemy. Fortune told you."

"Yes, but Asher did not come here."

"Someone else just killed him for you. A lucky accident."

"I ask no questions, Captain," Zareta said.

Pearce seemed to think. He glanced toward me. If Zareta or his men hadn't killed Paul Asher, it didn't leave many known candidates except me. I didn't like that much, but I couldn't think of anyone else to hand the Captain. While I was thinking about it, and Zareta and the glowering Emil had relaxed a hair now that they knew Paul Asher was dead, Pearce nodded sharply to his men. They grabbed Zareta, had their guns out before Zareta's men knew what had happened.

"Maybe you didn't kill Paul Asher," Pearce said. "But I need to know more. We'll go down to headquarters and sort it out there."

"No!" Emil cried. "The Minister does not go with you!"

The police had the edge now, but if Emil and the rest went for their guns it could be nasty. It was a tense moment in the small, dim room. Zareta broke it.

"Very well, Captain," he said. He had little choice. He was an alien, they were the police, and his own chances of surviving a shootout would be slim. "But not alone. I will take Emil and two other men, yes? A precaution of safety in numbers we who do not come from free countries need."

"Okay, but they leave all their guns. My men will stay around here to help protect the rest of your people."

"Agreed," Zareta said.

"Minister!" Emil was uneasy.

"Come, Emil, they are the police," Zareta said.

They laid their weapons on a table, followed Captain Pearce out of the room.

I was uneasy too. Constantine Zareta would kill any enemy, without anger or remorse. He seemed to draw the line at killing without *some* reason, and that had probably saved me the first time around, but it wasn't exactly high morality. Yet, as I watched them go out with Pearce I was suddenly sure that they had *not* killed Paul Asher.

Zareta wouldn't have waited to be caught if he or any of his men had killed Asher. He would have known that the moment Asher turned up dead I would tell the police all about him and his connection to Asher. No, Zareta would have been long gone before the police could connect Asher to me, and I could connect Zareta to Asher and lead the police to him, and the police . . .

And I knew the answer. The whole thing.

I felt colder than I had ever felt in my life.

And I knew what had been wrong about the package I had delivered. It was still there, open on the table next to the guns of Zareta and Emil and the other two men. The sheets of folded paper, the *documents*, were blank. I had been paid a thousand dollars to deliver a package of blank paper to Constantine Zareta.

And all the time I was thinking all this I was out of that room and running along the dark hallway to the gray dawn light of the front door. I thought it all, and grabbed Zareta's own automatic from the table, and was running out the front door into the morning like a racer coming around the last turn.

They had reached the sidewalk at the foot of the brownstone steps. The door of Pearce's black car was open. The man stood in the dawn not ten feet from the Captain's car. A stocky patrolman with an automatic in his hands. In both hands. A long-barreled automatic that was no part of the equipment of a New York city patrolman. An automatic aimed straight at Constantine Zareta.

I had no time to shout or even aim.

Zareta had seen the man now. And Captain Pearce. Emil had seen him. None of them could have moved in time.

I fired on the run. Three shots.

I never did know where the first went.

The second shot smashed a window of Pearce's black car.

The third hit the fake cop in the arm. Not much, a graze that barely needed a Band-Aid later, but enough. The assassin's arm jerked and he missed Constantine Zareta by inches.

Pearce, Emil and five real patrolmen swarmed the gunman under like an avalanche on the Yorkville street.

# 5

I never learned Paul Asher's real name, or who he really was, or where he came from. No one did. No one ever will.

No one will visit his grave in Potter's Field out on Hart Island in the East River. He's buried out there under a marker with only his false name on it. Nameless, even to his partner in the assassination plot, the phony patrolman.

The fake policeman never told us his real name either. No one came forward to identify him or even visit him. No one ever has or ever will where he serves his time up in Auburn. He never told us who sent them to kill Zareta, or what their cause was, their reason, but he didn't mind telling us the unimportant parts, and that it had been Paul Asher's plan all the way. A plan that had very nearly worked.

"Himself," Captain Pearce said as we sat in his office.

It was late evening. Somehow it was hard to think that it was still the same day the police had pounded on my door at dawn. A century ago. The Captain looked out toward the distant East River as if waiting for it to rise up and drown us all.

"Himself," I said. "He had himself killed just to smoke Zareta out into the open where his partner could get a clear shot, to lull Zareta into dropping his guard for an instant. He died so Zareta would die."

"To do his job," Pearce said. "And he almost made it."

"Because I missed it," I said. "Missed that package of blank paper, and missed what Zareta really told me. When he asked how you knew about him and Asher, and realized that it had to be through me, I should have seen it all. I was the only one in New York, probably in the world, who could have connected Asher and Zareta, brought the police to Zareta. He said it, and I missed it."

"We all missed it then," Pearce said. "Even Zareta."

Six killers had tried for Constantine Zareta and failed. So Paul Asher made his own plan. The fake patrolman told us all about it. He was proud of the plan, proud of Paul Asher.

"He picked you," Pearce went on in the silent office, "because he heard you were especially close to the police through Gazzo. He sent you to Zareta so you'd know where Zareta was, and so Zareta wouldn't be alarmed when you brought the police. He put your cards in his pocket, wrote your name and the date in his book, and had his partner kill him and dump his body under the bridge. So we would go to you, and you would take us to Zareta, and we'd bring Zareta out into the open."

Paul Asher, dead, had sent the police to me, and I had taken them to Zareta. Asher's plan to kill Constantine Zareta. Even a rat fights to survive, but Paul Asher died just to do his job. His life and death no more than a tool in nis own plan.

I said, "Every assassin expects to die if he succeeds, maybe even if he fails, but Asher died without knowing if he would succeed or fail. Anything could go wrong. He died on the *chance* that his plan would work."

"He wasn't human," Pearce said.

There are people all over this world who will say that Paul Asher was a hero. The same people who can live with those eighty million dead, and maybe eight hundred million tomorrow or the next day, and go right on drinking beer and grabbing for a dollar. The Paul Ashers and Constantine Zaretas kill the way other men swat flies, and we let them. We're used to it.

"He was human," I said. "That's the horror."

Paul Asher was human. And it's not the eighty million dead that really worry me, it's what those piled corpses have done to the rest of us in those eighty years.

It's not the dead that scare me, it's the living.

# The Prettiest Dead Girl in Detroit

## Loren D. Estleman

*This story was written specifically for* The Eyes Have It. *As has happened with many of the Amos Walker novels and short stories, it began with a title. I then envisioned the dead body of a beautiful naked girl lying on the floor of a room in an elegant old hotel going to seed. At that point I commenced writing with no clear idea of where the story was headed or how it would end. I'm told this is a very bad method of plotting fiction, but as it's seen me through fifteen books and a score of short stories I imagine it's too late to change.*

NO one sat in the lobby of the Hotel Woodward any more. The ceiling was too high, the brass balls on the banister posts were too big, the oak paneling on the walls was carved too deep. The dark red crushed-leather chairs and sofa ached to wrap themselves around someone's thighs and when I stepped through the front door and closed it against an icy

LOREN D. ESTLEMAN

gust the potted fern that occupied the spot on the Persian rug where
Theodore Roosevelt had stood to register stirred its dusty fronds
like an old man raising his face to the sun. In six months it was all
coming down to make room for a ladies' gym.

A geezer with a white moustache growing straight out of his
nostrils moved his lips over my ID on the front desk and directed
me to Room 212. I climbed a staircase broad enough to roll a
rajah's dead elephant down and paused outside an open door with
cigarette smoke curling through it. The girl lying on the floor was
looking straight at me, but she didn't invite me in. She had learned
her lesson the last time. She was a redhead, which I don't guess
means much of anything these days, but the red was natural and
would look blond in some lights. She had a tan the shade of good
brandy covering her evenly from hairline to pink-polished toenails
without a bikini line anywhere. It was the only thing covering her.
Her body was slim and sleekly muscled, a runner's body. Her eyes
were open and very blue. The dark bruises on her throat where the
killer's thumbs had gone were the only blemishes I could see.

The investigation business was the same as ever. All the
beautiful women I meet are either married or guilty or dead.

There were three men in the room with her, not dead. One was
tall and fifty with crisp gray hair to match his suit and very black
features carved along the coarse lines of a Masai warrior chief.
Standing next to him, almost touching him, was a smaller man
fifteen years younger with dark hair fluffed out on the sides to draw
your eyes down from his thinning top to a handlebar moustache
someone else trimmed for him and one of those outfits you grin at in
magazine ads, plaid jacket over red vest over diamond-patterned
sweater over shirt over pink silk scarf with red cherries on it. He
looked very white next to the other man. The third man, also white,
was very broad across the shoulders, bought his suit in Sears, and
combed his hair with a rake. His age had leveled off somewhere
between the others'. Guess which one of these men is the hotel
dick.

He spotted me first and walked around the body, transferring

64

his cigarette to his lips to take my hand. He had a grip like a rusted bolt. "Amos Walker? Trillen, security officer. I'm the one who called you."

"What seems to be the problem?"

He started a little and looked at me closely. He had gray eyes with all the depth of cigarette foil. "Yeah, I heard you were a comic. The night man, Applegate, gave me your name. You helped him clear up an employee matter a few months back before it got to the papers."

I remembered the case. One of the hops had been letting himself into rooms with a passkey and taking pictures of people who would rather not have had their pictures taken together in hotel rooms. One night he went into 618 looking to Allen-Funt a city councilman with his male aide and got me.

"This is Charles Lemler," Trillen said. "He's with the mayor's press corps. I'll let him tell it."

"Everyone calls me Chuck. Amos, right?" The moustached man in the noisy outfit grasped the hand Trillen had finished with. Afterward I left it out to dry. "The woman was here when we checked in, just as you see her. The clerk offered to move Mr. De Wolfe to another room before the police got here, but it's going to get out anyway that he registered the day a dead body turned up in the hotel. Trillen suggested you by way of putting some kind of face on this before we call in the authorities."

"Mr. De Wolfe?"

"I'm sorry. Clinton De Wolfe, Amos Walker."

The tall black man standing with his back to the body inclined his head a tenth of an inch in my direction. Well, I'd had my hand wrung enough for one morning.

"Mr. De Wolfe is a former Chicago bank officer," Chuck Lemler explained. "He's the mayor's choice for city controller here."

"Ah."

"'Ah' means what?" snapped De Wolfe.

"That my mouth is too big for my brain. Sorry. Can I look at the body?"

They made room for me. I checked the face and forehead for bruises and the hair for clotting, found nothing like that, spread my fingers to measure the marks on her neck. The spread was normal and while the dark spots were bigger than my thumbtips they weren't the work of an escaped orangutan or Bigfoot. It takes less strength to strangle a healthy woman than you might think. There was some darkening along her left thigh and under her fingernails. I did a couple of ungallant things with the body and then stood up. My hands felt colder for the contact with her skin. "Cover her."

"You don't like 'em boned?" asked Trillen.

"Trillen, for God's sake!" Lemler's moustache twisted.

"Yeah, yeah." The dick strolled into another room and came back carrying a hotel bedspread under one arm. I took an end and we covered the body. I asked if anyone knew her.

Trillen shook his shaggy head and squashed out his butt in a glass ashtray atop the television set. Well, he'd hear about that from someone. "Just another night rental. I hustle 'em out the back door and they come in again through the side and prowl the bar for fresh meat. This one's new."

"This isn't just another fifty-a-pop career girl," I said. "It takes income to maintain an all-over tan in Michigan in November and the body stinks exclusive health club. Also she didn't die here, or if she did someone moved her. She was lying on that thigh until not too long ago."

"I'd heard politics were rotten in this town," said De Wolfe.

"That's just the sort of knee-jerk assumption we've been fighting for years," Lemler told him harshly. To me: "There's some opposition to Mr. De Wolfe's choice as controller. But they wouldn't go this far."

"You mean trash a hooker and stash the body in his suite to stir up bad press. It's been done." I shook a Winston out of my pack but stopped short of lighting it. Why later. "My consulting fee's two-fifty, same as my day rate." Lemler nodded. I said,

66

"There's a lieutenant in Homicide named Alderdyce. If you ask him to sit on it he'll do it till it sprouts feathers. But only if you ask him."

De Wolfe glared. "That's your professional advice? Call the police?"

"Not the police. John Alderdyce."

"It's the same thing."

"I just got through telling you it isn't."

Lemler said, "We'll think about it."

I said, "You'll do it. Or I will. Maybe this is common practice at the City-County Building, but on Woodward Avenue it's failure to report a homicide. I have a license to stand in front of."

Trillen said, "Tell him to keep the name of the hotel out of it too."

"That's for the newspapers to decide when it breaks. And whether you advertise with them heavily enough to make it worth deciding."

"Will you stay on the case regardless?" Lemler asked. "The sooner this gets squared away the better for us, but we can't throw the city's weight behind an ordinary homicide investigation without drawing flies."

"I'll stay as long as the two-fifty holds out. Or until Alderdyce orders me off it," I added.

Lemler produced a checkbook from an inside pocket and began writing. "Will a thousand buy a week of your services?"

"Four days. Not counting expenses."

"The mayor will howl."

"Tell him to make his new raise retroactive to August instead of July."

Trillen called the number I gave him for Alderdyce from downstairs. I was smoking my cigarette in the hall outside when they came, the lieutenant towing a black photographer with a beard like a shotgun pattern and a pale lab man with a shrinking hairline and a young oriental carrying a black metal case. Alderdyce stopped in front of me. He's black, my age, big through the chest and shoulders, with facial features hacked out of a charred tree stump blindfolded.

"You didn't burn any tobacco in there?" he demanded. I shook my head. "Thank Christ for small miracles." The group swept in past me. I killed my stub in a steel wall caddy and brought up the rear.

Chuck Lemler broke off a conversation with Clinton De Wolfe to greet the newcomers. But Trillen intercepted Alderdyce and their clasped hands quivered grip for grip until the hotel dick surrendered. Alderdyce wasn't even looking at him. "The body was covered like that when it was found?" Trillen said no. The lieutenant barked at the lab man to take some fiber samples from the blanket and subtract them from whatever else was found on the corpse. He lifted one corner of the blanket.

Damn."

"Jesus," said the photographer, and took a picture.

I said, "Yeah."

Alderdyce flipped aside the blanket. "Bag her hands," he told the lab man. "There's matter under her fingernails."

"Blood and skin," I said. "Somebody's wearing her brand."

He looked at me. "I guess you better feed me all of it."

"Strangulation maybe," said the young oriental, before I could speak. He was down on one knee beside the body with his case open on the floor, prying open one of the dead eyelids with a thumb in a surgical glove. "Maybe O.D. I'll say what when I get her open."

"No tracks," said Alderdyce, glancing at her wrists and legs.

I said, "There's scar tissue between her toes. I checked."

"Damn nice of you to think to call us in, Walker."

I let that one drift.

"Get some Polaroids," Alderdyce told the photographer. "Last time the shots were three days coming back from the lab." He stopped looking at the body and pointed at the used ashtray. "Careful with that butt. The girl's wearing lipstick. It isn't."

"Uh, that's mine," said Trillen.

The lieutenant swore.

The rest was routine. Under questioning Trillen revealed that the suite had been cleaned the afternoon before and that no one had been inside between then and when the body was found. There were enough passkeys floating around and keys that had gone off with former guests to spoil that angle, and while Lemler maintained that De Wolfe's arrival and the number of his suite had been kept confidential, Trillen admitted that there was no standing on the staff grapevine. Meanwhile the lab men quartered the carpet for stray paperclips and the photographer, having traded the camera he'd been using for another strung around his neck, took more pictures of the body and laid them on the telephone stand to finish developing. I palmed a good one and let myself out while Alderdyce was politely grilling De Wolfe.

Barry Stackpole came out of the YMCA showers scrubbing his sandy hair with a towel, hesitated when he saw me by the lockers, then grinned and lowered the towel to cover his lower body modestly. Only it wasn't his nakedness that embarrassed him, just his Dutch leg. I said, "Doesn't that warp or something?"

He shook his head, reaching for his pants. "Fiberglass. I could've used you out on that handball court a few minutes ago."

"No, you couldn't. I was watching you."

I've known Barry since we shared a shell crater in Cambodia, years before he started his column on organized crime for the Detroit *News* and got his leg and two fingers blown off for his syntax. Someone at the paper had told me I'd find him creaming a Mob attorney on the courts. I held the Polaroid I'd swiped in front of his face while he was tying his shoes. He whistled. "Actress?"

"Prostitute," I said. "Maybe. Know her?"

"Not on my salary. Who squiffed her?"

"Why I'm here. Can you float it among your friends on the well-known street, put a name to the face? It wouldn't have stayed so pretty very long if she wasn't connected."

He finished drawing on his shirt and put the picture in the breast pocket. "User?"

"Yeah. Either someone throttled her unconscious and then shot too much stuff to her or shot too much stuff to her and couldn't wait. While you're at it, feed Clinton De Wolfe to your personal computer and see what it belches out."

"I know that name."

"If you do you heard it from your guy on city government. He'll be fine-tuning the books if the mayor gets his way."

"That isn't it. When I remember what it was I'll get back to you." He took down a bottle of mouthwash from the shelf in his locker and unscrewed the cap. "How rich does this little errand stand to make me?"

"A century, if I like what I hear. Otherwise seventy-five."

"Century either way. Plus a fifth of Jack Daniel's."

"I thought you were on the wagon."

"It's a cold dry ride." He hoisted the mouthwash. "Cold steel."

"Hot lead," I returned. The joke toast was as old as the last Tet offensive and the stuff in the bottle smelled like rye. I left him.

My office waiting room was full of no customers. I unlocked the door to the brain trust, forward-passed a sheaf of advertising circulars I found under the mail slot to the wastebasket, pegged my hat and coat, and set the swivel behind the desk to squeaking while I broke the Scotch out of the deep drawer. There was frost on the window, frost on my soul. I guessed Barry had found my breath sweet enough not to need help. As the warmth crawled through my veins I dialed my service. John Alderdyce had tried to reach me twice. I knew why. I asked the girl to hold any further calls from him and thumbed down the plunger and tried another number from memory. A West Indies accent answered on the third ring, cool and female.

"Iris, this is Amos."

"Amos who?"

"It's a funny hooker," I said dryly. "I'm trying to identify a lady who might have been in your line. Five-six and a hundred and ten, red and blue, Miami tan, about thirty. She showed up dead in a suite in the Woodward this morning. Drugs and strangulation. She wasn't a stranger to the drugs."

"Sound a little rich for the street."

"You get around."

"In blacktown. You're talking Grosse Pointe chic. Try the escort services."

"The real ones or the fronts?"

"There's a difference?"

"That's all you can tell me, huh."

"Every one of us don't know everyone else," she retorted, her class slipping. "Amos?"

I'd started to peg the receiver. I raised it again and said yeah. After a pause she said, "I'm going home."

"Home where?"

"Home where. Home the island. I'm going back to live with my mother."

"I'm glad," I said after a moment. "It's what you've been wanting."

"That's all? I thought maybe you'd try to talk me out of it."

"I don't have any hold on you, Iris."

"No. I guess you don't."

"Have a good flight." I was speaking into a dead line.

I looked at the calendar on the wall across from my framed investigator's license. Then I looked at a pigeon shivering alone on the ledge of the apartment house facing my building. Then I looked at the calendar again to see what the date was. I winched the Yellow Pages out of the top drawer and looked up Escorts.

I tried the display advertisements first and got three possibles. Then I tried the cheaper listings and lucked out on the first call.

"I need an escort for a business party Friday night," I told the woman who answered, by rote. "What I'm interested in is a specific redhead I saw with a friend of mine in the restaurant of the Hotel

LOREN D. ESTLEMAN

Woodward recently. I didn't get her name but I think she's with your service." I described her.

"That sounds like Myra Langan," said the woman. "But she doesn't work here any more."

"Did she resign?"

"I'm not at liberty to say."

"That means she was fired."

"I'm not—"

"Can I talk to you about her in person? It's important."

"We have another redhead," she started to say. I told her I'd pay for her time. She hesitated, then said, "Our regular escort fee is a hundred dollars." I said that sounded fair and agreed to meet her in the office at three. "Ask for Linda."

It was just past noon. I thought about the woman's voice. She sounded pleasant and young. You can't always get the accent you want. I skipped lunch and drove to a downtown theater where an old Robert Mitchum detective film was playing in revival. I took notes. In the lobby afterwards I used the pay telephone to call Barry Stackpole's private number at the *News*.

"Nobody I showed the picture to knows her from Jane Fonda," he told me. "Could be I'm working the wrong level. All the *capos* are browning their bellies at Cannes this time of year."

"Try Myra Langan. I've got an appointment today with a woman she worked with at a legit floss rental firm." I named the place.

"Our guy on cophouse might turn something. It means bringing him in."

"Cut the best deal you can." I took the instrument away from my ear.

"Don't you want to hear what I found out about Clinton De Wolfe?"

I paused. "I'm on pins and noodles."

"I get an exclusive when this breaks, right?"

"Feed it to me."

"I finally remembered where I'd heard the name and hooked a

72

snitch," he said. "De Wolfe is on the books as having resigned his vice-presidency at a Chicago bank in September. The dope is he was forced out for making unsecured loans to a Mob subsidiary in Evanston and accepting repayment in cash skimmed from the tables in Vegas."

I looked at a stiff face reflected in the telephone's shiny steel cradle. "Laundering?"

"Yeah. They let him quit to duck bad press. Good?"

"Listen, I'm on my way to your office with a C-note and a fifth of JD. Have that picture ready, okay?"

"Bring a glass for yourself." He broke the connection.

It was a quick stop and a quicker drink. From there I drove downriver to a low yellow brick building between a beauty salon and a hairpiece emporium with the escort firm's name etched in elegant script across the front. Inside was an office decorated like a living room with a white shag rug and ivory curtains and a lot of blond furniture, including a tall occasional table with turned legs and a glass top, but it didn't fool me, I know a desk when I see one. A brunette with her hair piled atop her head in blue waves and the kind of cheeks girls used to have their back teeth hauled out to get sat behind it wearing a black dress with a scoop neck and pearl buttons in her ears. I took off my hat and asked for Linda.

"You're Mr. Walker?" I said I was. "I'm Linda."

I glanced around. The room took up the entire ground floor and we were the only ones in it. "Who was I supposed to ask?"

"I wanted to get a look at you. In this business we have to go out with whoever has the price and no bloodstains on his necktie. When I get the chance to choose I leap on it. Are you a daylighter or a sundowner?" I must have looked as stupid as I felt, because she said, "A sundowner waits for darkness before he'll take a drink. It's dark in England."

"My father's family was English."

She smiled and rose. "I'll get my coat and purse."

We went to a place down the street with a blue neon cocktail glass on the roof and took a booth upholstered in red vinyl around a table the size of a hubcap. She ordered something green. I took Scotch and when the waitress left I slid the Polaroid shot I had gotten back from Barry across the table. Linda's nostrils whitened when she glanced down at it. Then she looked at me.

"You're not a policeman. Your eyes are too gentle."

"I'm a private investigator." I tapped the picture. "Myra Langan?"

"It's her. Are you looking for her murderer?"

"Who said murder?"

"She was the kind of a girl who would wind up murdered or suicided. Did she kill herself?"

"Not unless she found a way to strangle herself barehanded. What kind of a girl is the kind that would wind up murdered or suicided?"

She sipped her drink and set it down. After a beat I passed her two fifties. With what I'd given Barry, that left me just fifty from the first day of my retainer. I was on the wrong end of the information business.

"Myra got fired for her action on the side," said Linda, snapping shut her purse. "The police keep a tight eye on the escort business for just that. It was can her or risk a raid."

"Who snitched on her?"

"Another girl, Susan. They were at the same party and Susan overheard Myra discussing terms with her escort. Myra tried to cut her in but she wasn't having any."

"Myra got canned on just her word?"

"The boss lady ran a check. Her brother's a retired cop. He interviewed some of Myra's regular customers. The same pimp put six of them on her scent."

"What'd he interview them with, a Louisville Slugger?"

"He's retired like I said." She licked a drop off the end of her swizzle stick, eyeing me. "Married?"

"Not recently. Was she using when she worked for the firm?"

"You mean drugs. She couldn't have been. A complete physical is part of the screening process for new employees."

"Could've happened after she was hired. She worked there how long?"

"She was there when I came. A year, maybe. You think the pimp turned her on to get a handle on her?"

"It's not new. Looks like hers run high in executive circles. He have a name?"

"Probably. Talk to Max Montemarano. That's the boss lady's brother. He's a day guard at the Detroit Bank & Trust. The main branch."

I got up and left money on the table for the drinks. "Thanks. I have to see a man."

"Me too." She swung a mile of silk-paved leg out from under the table. "What do you do when you're not detecting?"

I watched her stand up. Some women know how to get out of a booth. I asked her if she'd ever lived on an island.

"What? No."

"Okay, thanks again."

On my way out a man in a blue suit seated near the door looked from me to the woman in the black dress standing by the booth and then back to me. I agreed with him.

I called the bank from an open-air booth outside a service station. A receptionist got me Montemarano, who explained in a hard fat man's voice that his shift didn't change for another hour but agreed to stop by my office on his way home for a quick fifty. The expenses on this one had just caught up with my fee.

Letting myself in the door of my building I smelled cop. A kid in a plaid overcoat stood in the foyer reading the sign on the building super's door. The sign read MANAGER. He was still studying when I reached the second-floor landing.

I found Lieutenant John Alderdyce sitting on the bench in my waiting room learning about the Man of some other Year from a copy of *Time* he'd unstuck from the coffee table. He had on a tan jacket and a red knit tie over a champagne-colored shirt. Since I knew him he'd dressed from nowhere closer to the street than J.L. Hudson's second floor. "This year it's a computer," he said, flicking his fingers at the photograph on the cover. "What do you think about a machine making the cover of *Time*?"

"Electricity's cheap. You and I run on tobacco and alcohol." I unlocked the inner office door. "Someone should enroll your boy in the lobby in a remedial reading course."

"He's on loan from the commissioner's office. His Police Positive has an ivory handle." He got up and followed me inside, where I shed my outerwear and sat down and got an old bill from under the desk blotter and pretended to check the arithmetic. He thumped his hand down on the desk, palm up. "The photog used up a twelve-pack of Polaroid film at the Woodward. He wound up with eleven pictures."

I started to reach for my inside breast pocket, then remembered I'd left the picture of Myra Langan on the table where I'd had drinks with Linda. "I'll stand the department to a new pack tomorrow."

"You wouldn't be prowling around in an open homicide investigation," he said. "Not you."

"It happens we're both working for the city this one time. Check with Lemler."

"No thanks. Every time I look at that guy's clothes and shut my eyes I see spots. What'd you turn?"

I watched him. He had sad eyes. Cops do, and it doesn't mean anything more than a croc's smile. Finally I said, "Her name was Myra Langan. She worked for an escort service downtown till they booted her for soliciting." I told him which service and gave him Linda's name. I didn't mention Max Montemarano or the pimp. It weighed light without them and Alderdyce saw it. He said, "I guess you stopped here on your way to Headquarters."

"More or less."

"More less than more. You passed Headquarters on your way here."

"I wanted to see if I had customers."

"No good. Go again."

"I'm a small guy in a small business, John. I don't have your resources."

"Resources. The redhead—Myra?—rode the springs with some guy not long before she was killed, the M.E. said. He took a smear and the type matches the blood we found under her fingernails. She was alive until four this morning. I've got men knocking on doors in the hotel looking for busted lamps and shaving cuts that don't fit a razor and scouting up the night staff, which by now is scattered between here and Ann Arbor. It's a big hotel, Walker. It has a big staff and lots of rooms. If I could put the squad on it I'd have the answers I need in an hour. But police reporters notice when the squad's missing and start asking questions. I've got Junior downstairs and one other detective and two uniforms borrowed from Traffic. I can't even get priority at the lab because someone who knows the number of one of this town's three TV stations might be looking."

He stuck his brutal face inches from mine. "Those are my resources, Walker. Four men, and the mayor's dresser asking me every five minutes when I'm going to arrest someone. You're a detective. Does it look to a detective like I need a keyholer playing Go Fish with me too?"

"Is this where you threaten to yank my ticket, or does that come after intermission?"

Alderdyce lifted weights when he wasn't sifting leads. He gave the desk a shove and it struck me in the solar plexus and I rolled backward on squealing casters and came to a rest pinned against the window. He leaned on the desk.

"We've never mixed it up, you and me," he said. "You'd lose."

We stayed like that for a long moment, he resting his weight on the desk, I trying to breathe with the edge pressing my sternum and cold from the window glass soaking clammily through my jacket and shirt to my back. Then he pushed off and turned around and left. The door drifted shut against the pressure of the pneumatic closer.

John and I had played together as kids, a million years ago. Max Montemarano found me straightening the furniture in the office a few minutes later. He wasn't fat at all, just large and slope-shouldered with a civilian overcoat over his gray guard's uniform and a visored cap on the back of his white head. His face was broad and ruddy, and burst blood vessels etched purple tributaries on his cheeks. "Colder'n a witch's tit," he said by way of greeting.

I blew dust out of a pair of pony glasses and filled them with Scotch from the bottle I kept in the deep drawer of the desk. He managed to snatch one up without spilling anything, lifted it in a sort of toast, and knocked it back the way they used to do in westerns. When the glass came down empty I poked a fifty-dollar bill into it. "Myra Langan," I said.

He looked down at the bill without touching it. "What about her?"

"You followed up another girl's complaint about her for your sister. She had a pimp. He had a name."

He set the glass down on the desk and drew himself up, squaring his visor. "I'm not a cop any more. She ain't working for my sister now. I never dipped a finger in twenty-three years on the force and I ain't about to start now."

I said, "She's dead. There's a better than even chance her pimp killed her or knows who did."

He hesitated. I uncapped the bottle again and moved it toward his glass. He scooped out the bill and straightened it between his fingers and folded it and put it in his breast pocket and snapped the flap shut. I poured. He put down half.

"He was a regular customer of Myra's until he stopped coming in," he said. "That was about the time the first John was approached." A brow got knitted. "Wilson. Jim Wilson."

"Fat, short, tall, skinny, black, white, what?"

"White. Not fat. Thick like me. He had the widest shoulders

for his height of any man I ever seen. Wider than yours. Wore cheap suits."

I was lighting a Winston. I avoided burning any fingers putting out the flame. "Shaggy head? A smoker?"

"Like a stack at the River Rouge plant. And if the guy combed his hair at all—"

I came around the desk and armed him toward the door. "Thanks for coming in."

"My drink."

I handed him the glass and the bottle and held the door. "Happy Thanksgiving."

After the outer door closed on Montemarano I made a call and then unlocked the top drawer of the desk and checked my Smith & Wesson for cartridges and clipped the holster to my belt under the tail of my jacket. It was heavier than a rabbit's foot but felt just as good.

The same geezer was sorting mail into the pigeonholes behind the desk at the Woodward when I strode past heading for the stairs. The letters might have come Pony Express. I knocked at 212 and Trillen opened the door. The hotel dick was alone in the suite with a chalk outline on the carpet where the dead girl had been lying. I asked him where Chuck Lemler and Clinton De Wolfe were.

"Coming. De Wolfe changed hotels. What's it about?"

I walked around, poking my head into the other rooms. The air smelled of cigarettes and there were three butts in the ashtray on the television set, all Trillen's brand. He'd been waiting there since taking my call. "Applegate offered me a job nightside," I said. "The pay stunk. Head of security pay any better?"

"Not much. Why?"

I lifted a shoulder.

De Wolfe and Lemler arrived fifteen minutes later. The black controller-to-be looked tall and gaunt in a dark overcoat and gray scarf. Lemler had on a horse blanket and one black glove and the other in his fist posing as a riding crop. "I hope you have

79

something," Lemler demanded. "The mayor wants to avoid identifying Mr. De Wolfe with this hotel any more than is absolutely necessary."

"I agree. It's bad enough he's identified with his old bank."

De Wolfe measured me out some of his icy glare.

I said, "You took early retirement. The board of directors was all for it. If the stockholders found out you'd been using bank funds to launder Mob money they'd clear the executive offices."

"You're drunk!" Lemler was paler than usual.

"It was a frame," said De Wolfe. "A good vice-president makes enemies. It was the only way they could get rid of me."

"It's probably true or you would've let it go to court," I said. "But it rules out the theory that your opponents here dumped a body in your suite to embarrass you. They have access to my information; the publicity from that Mob tie-in alone would have been enough to take you out of the running for city office. They didn't have to commit murder too." I turned to Lemler. "Chuck, I owe you five hundred from the retainer you gave me. I spent two-fifty. I'll eat the price of the whiskey."

"I didn't pay you to fork up dirt on my employer's choice for controller." He was twisting his glove.

"No, you paid me to find out who killed Myra Langan. That was the name of the murdered girl.

"Someone thought she was too pretty to throw away on old men at dinner parties in Birmingham and Grosse Pointe," I went on. "This someone started seeing her as a customer of the escort service she worked for and when he had confidence he hooked her on drugs to make her easier to steer. He was in a line of work that put him in contact with useful people on every level. When it came time to collect for the stuff he was supplying her, he put her to work. Some men would pay two hundred dollars for twenty minutes with a girl like Myra. For a time it was sweet. But one night something tilted, as things will in business relationships of that nature, and she became a liability. As her pimp he was used to favors other than money; he picked an intimate moment to strangle her senseless and then load her with enough dope to send her over. It would look like accidental death or suicide. Only he hadn't counted on her throat showing the bruises his fingers made after death. He'd forgotten how strong his hands were."

It was warm in the room, but none of us who were wearing overcoats had moved to take his off. Trillen, wearing the same baggy gray suit I had met him in, hadn't stirred at all. I put my hands in the pockets of my coat and said, "But pimps are nothing if not resourceful. It happened that a political big gun was stopping at the hotel later that morning. If her body were found in his suite it would change the whole complexion of the investigation. This particular pimp had access to the service elevator and the authority to see to it that all the employees that might be prowling the halls at four in the morning were in another part of the hotel when he moved the corpse. The bare chance that a stray guest might spot him was worth taking. Bringing in a PI later to muck things up worse didn't hurt.

"How's the back, Wilson?" I asked Trillen. "You ought to get iodine on those scratches before they infect."

The hotel dick's mouth smiled. "You're just stirring ashes. No proof."

"Applegate, the night man, will remember you were in the hotel this morning, hours before your shift started. Whatever excuse you made won't stand. You're wearing Myra's marks and I spoke to a man today who will identify you as her pimp. Take a fellow sleuth's advice and plead guilty to second-degree. The city will want to get this one under glass in a hurry. Am I right, Chuck?"

"I'll advise the mayor," said Lemler. He and De Wolfe were staring at Trillen, who was moving his huge shoulders around under his jacket. The dick said:

"I didn't hook her. She was shooting between her toes when I met her. Whatever croaker gave her the nod at the escort place wasn't thorough. It was business all the way with us; I got her the stuff, she wiggled her tail at conventions and sometimes for me."

"What was she doing, moonlighting on you?" I asked.

"That wouldn't have been so bad, but she started doing it here where I work. I like this job and I busted my butt to get it. I left something here last night and when I came in for it I found her working the bar. She tried to sugar me out of my mad in 110. I went crazy in the middle of it. I thought she was dead. I O.D.'d her to make it look like an accident, but then the bruises started to show. Well . . ." He put a hand behind his back as if to stretch and brought it around with a gun in it.

"Let it go."

Trillen swung toward the new voice, bringing the gun with him. John Alderdyce, standing in the open door to the hallway, crouched with his .38 stretched out in front of him in both hands. The hotel man dropped his weapon and threw his palms into the air.

"Okay," called the lieutenant.

The kid in the plaid overcoat entered from the bedroom with his gun drawn. He holstered it, frisked Trillen against a wall, cuffed him, and started droning from a printed card he carried in his shirt pocket.

"Fire escape," explained Alderdyce, tucking away his own gun. "Junior was still in your building when Montemarano came out. We questioned him. I figured you'd come straight here. You should have called me."

"I had to earn my fee first," I said.

"You cut it fine."

"Not so fine." I pulled my right hand out of my coat pocket wrapped around the butt of the Smith & Wesson and returned it to its holster.

We shook hands.

De Wolfe said, "Lieutenant, may I go now? I just have time to book the evening flight back to Chicago."

Lemler was standing by the window with his face on the floor. I went over there. "We didn't know about De Wolfe," he said.

"I believe you. Look on it as a break. The opposition would

have run it up the nearest flagpole. Everybody crapped out on this one. The mayor lost an appointee, De Wolfe lost a good job, Trillen's out the next ten to twenty, and Myra Langan's behind one life. She was too pretty to live."

"You're the only one better off than he was this morning," Lemler said.

I looked out the window. My lone pigeon or one like it had followed me there and was perched on the ledge between gimcracks, looking cold and dirty and miserable and like the only pigeon in the whole world.

"Yeah, I'm way ahead."

# Iris

## *Stephen Greenleaf*

*This is John Marshall Tanner's first appearance in
a short story. I find the form difficult, because of the premium
placed on plot, because of its suggestion if not its demand that
the conclusion offer an epiphany of sorts. I don't often see
life in terms of epiphanies, but I agreed to do the story because
it offered a chance to experiment—a chance to present Mr. Tanner
in the third person rather than the first.*

*After Hammett, first person narration became common
to the hardboiled detective novel. The question is whether
the first person is essential to the form, or is merely conventional. My conclusion is that third person narration works
fairly well in* Iris, *distancing the detective from his audience
enough to allow the plot to advance steadily and economically,
as of course it must in a short story. But I also conclude
that the third person works in* Iris *in large measure because I
was able, at the risk of some confusion to the reader, to
make all narrative references to Tanner pronominal, a feat
impossible in a longer work. This device seems to complement
the atmosphere of solitude and alienation I sought to achieve.
A few 'Tanner said's' would, I'm afraid, have added an aristocratic
note that would be incongruous, and a suggestion of companionship*

*and confederacy that would undermine the mood of the piece.*
*So the experiment was, in a peculiar way, successful. But*
*it may not be worth repeating.*

T HE Buick trudged toward the
summit, each step slower than the last, the automatic gearing
slipping ever-lower as the air thinned and the grade steepened and
the trucks were rendered snails. At the top the road leveled, and
the Buick spent a brief sigh of relief before coasting thankfully
down the other side, atop the stiff gray strap that was Interstate 5.
As it passed from Oregon to California the car seemed cheered. Its
driver shared the mood, though only momentarily.

He blinked his eyes and shrugged his shoulders and twisted
his head. He straightened his leg and shook it. He turned up the
volume of the radio, causing a song to be sung more loudly than it
merited. But the acid fog lay still behind his eyes, eating at them.
As he approached a roadside rest area he decided to give both the
Buick and himself a break.

During the previous week he had chased a wild goose in the
shape of a rumor all the way to Seattle, with tantalizing stops in
Eugene and Portland along the way. Eight hours earlier, when he
had finally recognized the goose for what it was, he had headed
home, hoping to make it in one day but realizing as he slowed for
the rest area that he couldn't reach San Francisco that evening
without risking more than was sensible in the way of vehicular
manslaughter.

He took the exit, dropped swiftly to the bank of the Klamath
River and pulled into a parking slot in the Randolph Collier safety
rest area. After making use of the facilities, he pulled out his map
and considered where to spend the night. Redding looked like the
logical place, out of the mountains, at the head of the soporific
valley that separated him from home. He was reviewing what he
knew about Redding when a voice, aggressively gay and musical,

STEPHEN GREENLEAF

greeted him from somewhere near the car. He glanced to his side, sat up straight and rolled down the window. "Hi," the thin voice said again.

"Hi."

She was blond, her long straight tresses misbehaving in the wind that tumbled through the river canyon. Her narrow face was white and seamless, as though it lacked flesh, was only skull. Her eyes were blue and tardy. She wore a loose green blouse gathered at the neck and wrists and a long skirt of faded calico, fringed in white ruffles. Her boots were leather and well-worn, their tops disappearing under her skirt the way the tops of the mountains at her back disappeared into a disc of cloud.

He pegged her for a hitchhiker, one who perpetually roams the roads and provokes either pity or disapproval in those who pass her by. He glanced around to see if she was fronting for a partner, but the only thing he saw besides the picnic and toilet facilities and travelers like himself was a large bundle resting atop a picnic table at the far end of the parking lot. Her worldly possessions, he guessed; her only aids to life. He looked at her again and considered whether he wanted to share some driving time and possibly a motel room with a girl who looked a little spacy and a little sexy and a lot heedless of the world that delivered him his living.

"My name's Iris," she said, wrapping her arms across her chest, shifting her weight from foot to foot, shivering in the autumn chill.

"Mine's Marsh."

"You look tired." Her concern seemed genuine, his common symptoms for some reason alarming to her.

"I am," he admitted.

"Been on the road long?"

"From Seattle."

"How far is that about?" The question came immediately, as though she habitually erased her ignorance.

"Four hundred miles. Maybe a little more."

She nodded as though the numbers made him wise. "I've been to Seattle."

"Good."

"I've been lots of places."

"Good."

She unwrapped her arms and placed them on the car door and leaned toward him. Her musk was unadulterated. Her blouse dropped open to reveal breasts sharpened to twin points by the mountain air. "Where you headed, Marsh?"

"South."

"L.A.?"

He shook his head. "San Francisco."

"Good. Perfect."

He expected it right then, the flirting pitch for a lift, but her request was slightly different. "Could you take something down there for me?"

He frowned and thought of the package on the picnic table. Drugs? "What?" he asked.

"I'll show you in a sec. Do you think you could, though?"

He shook his head. "I don't think so. I mean, I'm kind of on a tight schedule, and . . ."

She wasn't listening. "It goes to . . ." She pulled a scrap of paper from the pocket of her skirt and uncrumpled it. "It goes to 95 Albosa Drive, in Hurley City. That's near Frisco, isn't it? Marvin said it was."

He nodded. "But I don't . . ."

She put up a hand. "Hold still. I'll be right back."

She skipped twice, her long skirt hopping high above her boots to show a shaft of gypsum thigh, then trotted to the picnic table and picked up the bundle. Halfway back to the car she proffered it like a prize soufflé.

"Is this what you want me to take?" he asked as she approached.

She nodded, then looked down at the package and frowned. "I

don't like this one," she said, her voice dropping to a dismissive rasp.

"Why not?"

"Because it isn't happy. It's from the B Box, so it can't help it, I guess, but all the same it should go back, I don't care *what* Marvin says."

"What is it? A puppy?"

She thrust the package through the window. He grasped it reflexively, to keep it from dropping to his lap. As he secured his grip the girl ran off. "Hey! Wait a minute," he called after her. "I can't take this thing. You'll have to . . ."

He thought the package moved. He slid one hand beneath it and with the other peeled back the cotton strips that swaddled it. A baby—not canine but human—glared at him and screamed. He looked frantically for the girl and saw her climbing into a gray Volkswagen bug that was soon scooting out of the rest area and climbing toward the freeway.

He swore, then rocked the baby awkwardly for an instant, trying to quiet the screams it formed with every muscle. When that didn't work, he placed the child on the seat beside him, started the car and backed out. As he started forward he had to stop to avoid another car, and then to reach out wildly to keep the child from rolling off the seat.

He moved the gear to park and gathered the seat belt on the passenger side and tried to wrap it around the baby in a way that would be more safe than throttling. The result was not reassuring. He unhooked the belt and put the baby on the floor beneath his legs, put the car in gear and set out after the little gray VW that had disappeared with the child's presumptive mother. He caught it only after several frantic miles, when he reached the final slope that descended to the grassy plain that separated the Siskiyou range from the lordly aspect of Mt. Shasta.

The VW buzzed toward the mammoth mountain like a mad mouse assaulting an elephant. He considered overtaking the car, forcing Iris to stop, returning the baby, then getting the hell away from her as fast as the Buick would take him. But something in his memory of her look and words made him keep his distance, made him keep Iris in sight while he waited for her to make a turn toward home.

The highway flattened, then crossed the high meadow that nurtured sheep and cattle and horses below the lumps of the southern Cascades and the Trinity Alps. Traffic was light, the sun low above the western peaks, the air a steady splash of autumn. He checked his gas gauge. If Iris didn't turn off in the next fifty miles he would either have to force her to stop or let her go. The piercing baby sounds that rose from beneath his knees made the latter choice impossible.

They reached Yreka, and he closed to within a hundred yards of the bug, but Iris ignored his plea that the little city be her goal. Thirty minutes later, after he had decided she was nowhere near her destination, Iris abruptly left the interstate, at the first exit to a village that was hand-maiden to the mountain, a town reputed to house an odd collection of spiritual seekers and religious zealots.

The mountain itself, volcanic, abrupt, spectacular, had been held by the Indians to be holy, and the area surrounding it was replete with hot springs and mud baths and other prehistoric marvels. Modern mystics had accepted the mantle of the mountain, and the crazy girl and her silly bug fit with what he knew about the place and those who gathered there. What didn't fit was the baby she had foisted on him.

He slowed and glanced at his charge once again and failed to receive anything resembling contentment in return. Fat little arms escaped the blanket and pulled the air like taffy. Spittle dribbled down its chin. A translucent bubble appeared at a tiny nostril, then broke silently and vanished.

The bug darted through the north end of town, left, then right, then left again, quickly, as though it sensed pursuit. He lagged behind, hoping Iris was confident she had ditched him. He looked at the baby again, marvelling that it could cry so loud, could for so long expend the major portion of its strength in unrequited pleas. When he looked at the road again the bug had disappeared.

He swore and slowed and looked at driveways, then began to plan what to do if he had lost her. Houses dwindled, the street became dirt, then flanked the log decks and lumber stacks and wigwam burners of a sawmill. A road sign declared it unlawful to sleigh, toboggan or ski on a county road. He had gasped the first breaths of panic when he saw the VW nestled next to a ramshackle cabin on the back edge of town, empty, as though it had been there always.

A pair of firs sheltered the cabin and the car, made the dwindling day seem night. The driveway was mud, the yard bordered by a falling wormwood fence. He drove to the next block and stopped his car, the cabin now invisible.

He knew he couldn't keep the baby much longer. He had no idea what to do, for it or with it, had no idea what it wanted, no idea what awaited it in Hurley City, had only a sense that the girl, Iris, was goofy, perhaps pathologically so, and that he should not abet her plan.

Impossibly, the child cried louder. He had some snacks in the car—crackers, cookies, some cheese—but he was afraid the baby was too young for solids. He considered buying milk, and a bottle, and playing parent. The baby cried again, gasped and sputtered, then repeated its protest.

He reached down and picked it up. The little red face inflated, contorted, mimicked a steam machine that continuously whistled. The puffy cheeks, the tiny blue eyes, the round pug nose, all were engorged in scarlet fury. He cradled the baby in his arms as best he could and rocked it. The crying dimmed momentarily, then began again.

His mind ran the gauntlet of childhood scares—diphtheria, smallpox, measles, mumps, croup, even a pressing need to burp. God knew what ailed it. He patted its forehead and felt the sticky heat of fever.

Shifting position, he felt something hard within the blanket, felt for it, finally drew it out. A nippled baby bottle, half-filled, body-warm. He shook it and presented the nipple to the baby, who sucked it as its due. Giddy at his feat, he unwrapped his package further, enough to tell him he was holding a little girl and that she seemed whole and healthy except for her rage and fever. When she was feeding steadily he put her back on the floor and got out of the car.

The stream of smoke it emitted into the evening dusk made the cabin seem dangled from a string. Beneath the firs the ground was moist, a spongy mat of rotting twigs and needles. The air was cold and damp and smelled of burning wood. He walked slowly up the drive, courting silence, alert for the menace implied by the hand-lettered sign, nailed to the nearest tree, that ordered him to KEEP OUT.

The cabin was dark but for the variable light at a single window. The porch was piled high with firewood, both logs and kindling. A maul and wedge leaned against a stack of fruitwood piled next to the door. He walked to the far side of the cabin and looked beyond it for signs of Marvin.

A tool shed and a broken-down school bus filled the rear yard. Between the two a tethered nanny goat grazed beneath a line of drying clothes, silent but for her neck bell, the swollen udder oscillating easily beneath her, the teats extended like accusing fingers. Beyond the yard a thicket of berry bushes served as fence, and beyond the bushes a stand of pines blocked further vision. He felt alien, isolated, exposed, threatened, as Marvin doubtlessly hoped all strangers would.

He thought about the baby, wondered if it was all right, wondered if babies could drink so much they got sick or even choked. A twinge of fear sent him trotting back to the car. The baby was fine, the bottle empty on the floor beside it, its noises not wails but only muffled whimpers. He returned to the cabin and went onto the porch and knocked at the door and waited.

Iris wore the same blouse and skirt and boots, the same eyes too shallow to hold her soul. She didn't recognize him; her face pinched only with uncertainty.

He stepped toward her and she backed away and asked him what he wanted. The room behind her was a warren of vague shapes, the only source of light far in the back by a curtain that spanned the room.

"I want to give you your baby back," he said.

She looked at him more closely, then opened her mouth in silent exclamation, then slowly smiled. "How'd you know where I lived?"

"I followed you."

"Why? Did something happen to it already?"

"No, but I don't want to take it with me."

She seemed truly puzzled. "Why not? It's on your way, isn't it? Almost?"

He ignored the question. "I want to know some more about the baby."

"Like what?"

"Like whose is it? Yours?"

Iris frowned and nibbled her lower lip. "Sort of."

"What do you mean, 'sort of?' Did you give birth to it?"

"Not exactly." Iris combed her hair with her fingers, then shook it off her face with an irritated twitch. "What are you asking all these questions for?"

"Because you asked me to do you a favor and I think I have the right to know what I'm getting into. That's only fair, isn't it?"

She paused. Her pout was dubious. "I guess."

"So where did you get the baby?" he asked again.

"Marvin got it."

"From whom?"

"Those people in Hurley City. So I don't know why you won't take it back, seeing as how it's theirs and all."

"But why . . ."

His question was obliterated by a high glissando, brief and

92

piercing. He looked at Iris, then at the shadowy interior of the cabin.

There was no sign of life, no sign of anything but the leavings of neglect and a spartan bent. A fat gray cat hopped off a shelf and sauntered toward the back of the cabin and disappeared behind the blanket that was draped on the rope that spanned the rear of the room. The cry echoed once again. "What's that?" he asked her.

Iris giggled. "What does it sound like?"

"Another baby?"

Iris nodded.

"Can I see it?"

"Why?"

"Because I like babies."

"If you like them, why won't you take the one I gave you down to Hurley City?"

"Maybe I'm changing my mind. Can I see this one?"

"I'm not supposed to let anyone in here."

"It'll be okay. Really. Marvin isn't here, is he?"

She shook her head. "But he'll be back any time. He just went to town."

He summoned reasonableness and geniality. "Just let me see your baby for a second, Iris. Please? Then I'll go. And take the other baby with me. I promise."

She pursed her lips, then nodded and stepped back. "I got more than one," she suddenly bragged. "Let me show you." She turned and walked quickly toward the rear of the cabin and disappeared behind the blanket.

When he followed he found himself in a space that was half-kitchen and half-nursery. Opposite the electric stove and Frigidaire, along the wall between the wood stove and the rear door, was a row of wooden boxes, seven of them, old orange crates, dividers removed, painted different colors and labelled A to G. Faint names of orchards and renderings of fruits rose through the paint on the stub ends of the crates. Inside boxes C through G were babies, buried deep in nests of rags and scraps of blanket. One of them was crying. The others slept soundly, warm and toasty, healthy and happy from all the evidence he had.

"My God," he said.

"Aren't they beautiful? They're just the best little things in the whole world. Yes they are. Just the best little babies in the whole wide world. And Iris loves them all a bunch. Yes, she does. Doesn't she?"

Beaming, Iris cooed to the babies for another moment, then her face darkened. "The one I gave you, she wasn't happy here. That's because she was a B Box baby. My B babies are always sad, I don't know why. I treat them all the same, but the B babies are just contrary. That's why the one I gave you should go back. Where is it, anyway?"

"In the car."

"By itself?"

He nodded.

"You shouldn't leave her there like that," Iris chided. "She's pouty enough already."

"What about these others?" he asked, looking at the boxes. "Do they stay here forever?"

Her whole aspect solidified. "They stay till Marvin needs them. Till he does, I give them everything they want. Everything they need. No one could be nicer to my babies than me. *No* one."

The fire in the stove lit her eyes like ice in sunlight. She gazed raptly at the boxes, one by one, and received something he sensed was sexual in return. Her breaths were rapid and shallow, her fists clenched at her sides. "Where'd you get these babies?" he asked softly.

"Marvin gets them." She was only half-listening.

"Where?"

"All over. We had one from Nevada one time, and two from Idaho I think. Most are from California, though. And Oregon. I think that C Box baby's from Spokane. That's Oregon, isn't it?"

He didn't correct her. "Have there been more besides these?"

"Some."

94

"How many?"

"Oh, maybe ten. No, more than that. I've had three of all the babies except G babies."

"And Marvin got them all for you?"

She nodded and went to the stove and turned on a burner. "You want some tea? It's herbal. Peppermint."

He shook his head. "What happened to the other babies? The ones that aren't here any more?"

"Marvin took them." Iris sipped her tea.

"Where?"

"To someone that wanted to love them." The declaration was as close as she would come to gospel.

The air in the cabin seemed suddenly befouled, not breathable. "Is that what this is all about, Iris? Giving babies to people that want them?"

"That want them and will *love* them. See, Marvin gets these babies from people that *don't* want them, and gives them to people that *do*. It's his business."

"Does he get paid for it?"

She shrugged absently. "A little, I think."

"Do you go with Marvin when he picks them up?"

"Sometimes. When it's far."

"And where does he take them? To Idaho and Nevada, or just around here?"

She shrugged again. "He doesn't tell me where they go. He says he doesn't want me to try and get them back." She smiled peacefully. "He knows how I am about my babies."

"How long have you and Marvin been doing this?"

"I been with Marvin about three years."

"And you've been trading in babies all that time?"

"Just about."

She poured some more tea into a ceramic cup and sipped it. She gave no sign of guile or guilt, no sign that what he suspected could possibly be true.

"Do you have any children of your own, Iris?"

Her hand shook enough to spill her tea. "I *almost* had one once."

"What do you mean?"

She made a face. "I got pregnant, but nobody wanted me to keep it so I didn't."

"Did you put it up for adoption?"

She shook her head.

"Abortion?"

Iris nodded, apparently in pain, and mumbled something. He asked her what she'd said. "I did it myself," she repeated. "That's what I can't live with. I scraped it out of there myself. I passed out. I . . ."

She fell silent. He looked back at the row of boxes that held her penance. When she saw him look she began to sing a song. "Aren't they just perfect?" she said when she was through. "Aren't they all just perfect?"

"How do you know where the baby you gave me belongs?" he asked quietly.

"Marvin's got a book that keeps track. I sneaked a look at it one time when he was stoned."

"Where's he keep it?"

"In the van. At least that's where I found it." Iris put her hands on his chest and pushed. "You better go before Marvin gets back. You'll take the baby, won't you? It just don't belong here with the others. It fusses all the time and I can't love it like I should."

He looked at Iris' face, at the firelight washing across it, making it alive. "Where are you from, Iris?"

"Me? Minnesota."

"Did you come to California with Marvin?"

She shook her head. "I come with another guy. I was tricking for him when I got knocked up. After the abortion I told him I wouldn't trick no more so he ditched me. Then I did a lot of drugs for a while, till I met Marvin at a commune down by Mendocino."

"What's Marvin's last name?"

"Hessel. Now you got to go. Really. Marvin's liable to do

something crazy if he finds you here." She walked toward him and he retreated.

"Okay, Iris. Just one thing. Could you give me something for the baby to eat? She's real hungry."

Iris frowned. "She only likes goat's milk, is the problem, and I haven't milked today." She walked to the Frigidaire and returned with a bottle. "This is all I got. Now, git."

He nodded, took the bottle from her, then retreated to his car.

He opened the door on the stinging smell of ammonia. The baby greeted him with screams. He picked it up, rocked it, talked to it, hummed a tune, finally gave it the second bottle, which was the only thing it wanted.

As it sucked its sustenance he started the car and let the engine warm, and a minute later flipped the heater switch. When it seemed prudent, he unwrapped the child and unpinned her soggy diaper and patted her dumplinged bottom dry with a tissue from the glove compartment. After covering her with her blanket he got out of the car, pulled his suitcase from the trunk and took out his last clean T-shirt, then returned to the car and fashioned a bulky diaper out of the cotton shirt and affixed it to the child, pricking his finger in the process, spotting both the garment and the baby with his blood. Then he sat for a time, considering his obligations to the children that had suddenly littered his life.

He should go to the police, but Marvin might return before they responded and might learn of Iris' deed and harm the children or flee with them. He could call the police and wait in place for them to come, but he doubted his ability to convey his precise suspicions over the phone. As he searched for other options, headlights ricocheted off his mirror and into his eyes, then veered off. When his vision was re-established he reached into the glove compartment for his revolver. Shoving it into his pocket, he got out of the car and walked back to the driveway and disobeyed the sign again.

A new shape had joined the scene, rectangular and dark. Marvin's van, creaking as it cooled. He waited, listened, and when he sensed no other presence he approached it. A converted bread truck, painted Navy blue, with sliding doors into the driver's cabin and hinged doors at the back. The right fender was dented, the rear bumper wired in place. A knobby-tired motorcycle was strapped to a rack on the top. The door on the driver's side was open, so he climbed in.

The high seat was rotted through, its stuffing erupting like white weeds through the dirty vinyl. The floorboards were littered with food wrappers and beer cans and cigarette butts. He activated his pencil flash and pawed through the refuse, pausing at the only pristine object in the van—a business card, white with black engraving, taped to a corner of the dash: 'J. Arnold Rasker, Attorney at Law. Practice in all Courts. Initial Consultation Free. Phone day or night.'

He looked through the cab for another minute, found nothing resembling Marvin's notebook and nothing else of interest. After listening for Marvin's return and hearing nothing he went through the narrow doorway behind the driver's seat into the cargo area in the rear, the yellow ball that dangled from his flash bouncing playfully before him.

The entire area had been carpeted, ceiling included, in a matted pink plush that was stained in unlikely places and coming unglued in others. A roundish window had been cut into one wall by hand, then covered with plasticine kept in place with tape. Two upholstered chairs were bolted to the floor on one side of the van, and an Army cot stretched out along the other. Two orange crates similar to those in the cabin, though empty, lay between the chairs. Above the cot a picture of John Lennon was tacked to the carpeted wall with a rusty nail. A small propane bottle was strapped into one corner, an Igloo cooler in another. Next to the Lennon poster a lever-action rifle rested in two leather slings. The smells were of gasoline and marijuana and unwashed flesh. Again he found no notebook.

He switched off his light and backed out of the van and walked to the cabin, pausing on the porch. Music pulsed from the interior, heavy metal, obliterating all noises including his own. He walked to the window and peered inside.

Iris, carrying and feeding a baby, paced the room, eyes closed, mumbling, seemingly deranged. Alone momentarily, she was soon joined by a wide and woolly man, wearing cowboy boots and Levi's, a plaid shirt, full beard, hair to his shoulders. A light film of grease coated flesh and clothes alike, as though he had just been dipped. Marvin strode through the room without speaking, his black eyes angry, his shoulders tipping to the frenetic music as he sucked the final puffs of a joint held in an oddly dainty clip.

Both Marvin and Iris were lost in their tasks. When their paths crossed they backed away as though they feared each other. He watched them for five long minutes. When they disappeared behind the curtain in the back he hurried to the door and went inside the cabin.

The music paused, then began again, the new piece indistinguishable from the old. The heavy fog of dope washed into his lungs and lightened his head and braked his brain. Murmurs from behind the curtain erupted into a swift male curse. A pan clattered on the stove; wood scraped against wood. He drew his gun and moved to the edge of the room and sidled toward the curtain and peered around its edge.

Marvin sat in a chair at a small table, gripping a bottle of beer. Iris was at the stove, her back to Marvin, opening a can of soup. Marvin guzzled half the bottle, banged it on the table, and swore again. "How could you be so fucking stupid?"

"Don't, Marvin. Please?"

"Just tell me who you gave it to. That's all I want to know. It was your buddy Gretel, wasn't it? Had to be, she's the only one around here as looney as you."

"It wasn't anyone you know. Really. It was just a guy."

"What guy?"

"Just *a guy*. I went out to a rest area way up by Oregon, and I talked to him and he said he was going to Frisco so I gave it to him and told him where to take it. You *know* it didn't belong here, Marvin. You know how puny it was."

Marvin stood up, knocking his chair to the floor. "You stupid bitch." His hand raised high, Marvin advanced on Iris with beer dribbling from his chin. "I'll break your jaw, woman. I swear I will."

"Don't hit me, Marvin. Please don't hit me again."

"Who was it? I want a name."

"I don't *know*, I told you. Just some guy going to Frisco. His name was Mark, I think."

"And he took the kid?"

Iris nodded. "He was real nice."

"You bring him here? Huh? Did you bring the son-of-a-bitch to the cabin? Did you tell him about the others?"

"No, Marvin. No. I swear. You know I'd never do that."

"Lying bitch."

Marvin grabbed Iris by the hair and dragged her away from the stove and slapped her across the face. She screamed and cowered. Marvin raised his hand to strike again.

Sucking a breath, he raised his gun and stepped from behind the curtain. "Hold it," he told Marvin. "Don't move."

Marvin froze, twisted his head, took in the gun and released his grip on Iris and backed away from her, his black eyes glistening. A slow smile exposed dark and crooked teeth. "Well, now," Marvin drawled. "Just who might you be besides a fucking trespasser? Don't tell me; let me guess. You're the nice man Iris gave a baby to. The one she swore she didn't bring out here. Right?"

"She didn't bring me. I followed her."

Both men glanced at Iris. Her hand was at her mouth and she was nibbling a knuckle. "I thought you went to Frisco," was all she said.

"Not yet."

"What do you want?" Her question assumed a fearsome answer.

Marvin laughed. "You stupid bitch. He wants the *rest* of them. Then he wants to throw us in jail. He wants to be a hero, Iris. And to be a hero he has to put you and me behind bars for the rest of our fucking lives." Marvin took a step forward.

"Don't be dumb." He raised the gun to Marvin's eyes.

Marvin stopped, frowned, then grinned again. "You look like you used that piece before."

"One or twice."

"What's your gig?"

"Detective. Private."

Marvin's lips parted around his crusted teeth. "You must be kidding. Iris flags down some bastard on the freeway and he turns out to be a private cop?"

"That's about it."

Marvin shook his head. "Judas H. Priest. And here you are. A professional hero, just like I said."

He captured Marvin's eyes. "I want the book."

"What book?" Marvin burlesqued ignorance.

"The book with the list of babies and where you got them and where you took them."

Marvin looked at Iris, stuck her with his stare. "You're dead meat, you know that? You bring the bastard here and tell him all about it and expect him to just take off and not try to *stop* us? You're too fucking dumb to breathe, Iris. I got to put you out of your misery."

"I'm sorry, Marvin."

"He's going to take them *back*, Iris. Get it? He's going to take those sweet babies away from you and give them back to the assholes that don't want them. And then he's going to the cops and they're going to say you *kidnapped* those babies, Iris, and that you were bad to them and should go to jail because of what you did. Don't you see that, you brain-fried bitch? *Don't you see what he's going to do?*"

"I . . . ." Iris stopped, overwhelmed by Marvin's incantation. "Are you?" she asked, finally looking away from Marvin.

STEPHEN GREENLEAF

"I'm going to do what's best for the babies, Iris. That's all."

"What's best for them is with me and Marvin."

"Not any more," he told her. "Marvin's been shucking you, Iris. He steals those babies. Takes them from their parents, parents who love them. He roams up and down the coast stealing children and then he sells them, Iris. Either back to the people he took them from or to people desperate to adopt. I think he's hooked up with a lawyer named Rasker, who arranges private adoptions for big money and splits the take with Marvin. He's not interested in who loves those kids, Iris. He's only interested in how much he can sell them for."

Something had finally activated Iris' eyes. "Marvin? Is that true?"

"No, baby. The guy's blowing smoke. He's trying to take the babies away from you and then get people to believe you did something bad, just like that time with the abortion. He's trying to say you did bad things to babies again, Iris. We can't let him do that."

He spoke quickly, to erase Marvin's words. "People don't give away babies, Iris. Not to guys like Marvin. There are agencies that arrange that kind of thing, that check to make sure the new home is in the best interests of the child. Marvin just swipes them and sells them to the highest bidder, Iris. That's all he's in it for."

"I don't believe you."

"It doesn't matter. Just give me Marvin's notebook and we can check it out, contact the parents and see what they say about their kids. Ask if they wanted to be rid of them. That's fair, isn't it?"

"I don't know. I guess."

"Iris?"

"What, Marvin?"

"I want you to pick up that pan and knock this guy on the head. Hard. Go on, Iris. He won't shoot you, you know that. Hit him on the head so he can't put us in jail."

He glanced at Iris, then as quickly to Marvin and to Iris once again. "Don't do it, Iris. Marvin's trouble. I think you know that now." He looked away from Iris and gestured at her partner. "Where's the book?"

"Iris?"

Iris began to cry. "I can't, Marvin. I can't do that."

"The book," he said to Marvin again. "Where is it?"

Marvin laughed. "You'll never know, detective."

"Okay. We'll do it your way. On the floor. Hands behind your head. Legs spread. Now."

Marvin didn't move. When he spoke the words were languid. "You don't look much like a killer, detective, and I've known a few, believe me. So I figure if you're not gonna shoot me I don't got to do what you say. I figure I'll just take that piece away from you and feed it to you inch by inch. Huh? Why don't I do just that?"

He took two quick steps to Marvin's side and sliced open Marvin's cheek with a quick swipe of the gun barrel. "Want some more?"

Marvin pawed at his cheek with a grimy hand, then examined his bloody fingers. "You bastard. Okay. I'll get the book. It's under here."

Marvin bent toward the floor, twisting away from him, sliding his hands toward the darkness below the stove. He couldn't tell what Marvin was doing, so he squinted, then moved closer. When Marvin began to stand he jumped back, but Marvin wasn't attacking, Marvin was holding a baby, not a book, holding a baby by the throat.

"Okay, pal," Marvin said through his grin. "Now, you want to see this kid die before your eyes, you just keep hold of that gun. You want to see it breathe some more, you drop it."

He froze, his eyes on Marvin's fingers, which inched further around the baby's neck and began to squeeze.

The baby gurgled, gasped, twitched, was silent. Its face reddened; its eyes bulged. The tendons in Marvin's hand stretched taut. Between grimy gritted teeth, Marvin wheezed in rapid streams of glee.

He dropped his gun. Marvin told Iris to pick it up. She did, and exchanged the gun for the child. Her eyes lapped Marvin's face, as though to renew its acquaintance. Abruptly, she turned and ran around the curtain and disappeared.

"Well, now." Marvin's words slid easily. "Looks like the worm has turned, detective. What's your name, anyhow?"

"Tanner."

"Well, Tanner, your ass is mine. No more John Wayne stunts for you. You can kiss this world good-bye."

Marvin fished in the pocket of his jeans, then drew out a small spiral notebook and flashed it. "It's all in here, Tanner. Where they came from; where they went. Now watch."

Gun in one hand, notebook in the other, Marvin went to the wood stove and flipped open the heavy door. The fire made shadows dance.

"Don't."

"Watch, bastard."

Marvin tossed the notebook into the glowing coals, fished in the box beside the stove for a stick of kindling, then tossed it in after the notebook and closed the iron door. "Bye-bye babies." Marvin's laugh was quick and cruel. "Now turn around. We're going out back."

He did as he was told, walking toward the door, hearing only a silent shuffle at his back. As he passed her he glanced at Iris. She hugged the baby Marvin had threatened, crying, not looking at him. "Remember the one in my car," he said to her. She nodded silently, then turned away.

Marvin prodded him in the back and he moved to the door. Hand on the knob, he paused, hoping for a magical deliverance, but none came. Marvin prodded him again and he moved outside, onto the porch then into the yard. "Around back," Marvin ordered. "Get in the bus."

He staggered, tripping over weeds, stumbling over rocks, until he reached the rusting bus. The moon and stars had disappeared; the night was black and still but for the whistling wind, clearly Marvin's ally. The nanny goat laughed at them, then trotted out of reach. He glanced back at Marvin. In one hand was a pistol, in the other a blanket. "Go on in. Just pry the door open."

He fit his finger between the rubber edges of the bus door and opened it. The first step was higher than he thought, and he tripped and almost fell. "Watch it. I almost blasted you right then."

He couldn't suppress a giggle. For reasons of his own, Marvin matched his laugh. "Head on back, Tanner. Pretend you're on a field trip to the zoo."

He walked down the aisle between the broken seats, smelling rot and rust and the lingering scent of skunk. "Why here?" he asked as he reached the rear.

"Because you'll keep in here just fine till I get time to dig a hole out back and open that emergency door and dump you in. Plus it's quiet. I figure with the bus and the blanket no one will hear a thing. Sit.

He sat. Marvin draped the blanket across the arm that held the gun, then extended the shrouded weapon toward his chest. He had no doubt that Marvin would shoot without a thought or fear. "Any last words, Tanner? Any parting thoughts?"

"Just that you forgot something."

"What?"

"You left the door open."

Marvin glanced quickly toward the door in the front of the bus. He dove for Marvin's legs, sweeping at the gun with his left hand as he did so, hoping to dislodge it into the folds of the blanket where it would lie useless and unattainable.

"Cocksucker."

Marvin wrested the gun from his grasp and raised it high, tossing off the blanket in the process. He twisted frantically to protect against the blow he knew was coming, but Marvin was too heavy and strong, retained the upper hand by kneeling on his chest. The revolver glinted in the darkness, a missile poised to descend.

Sound split the air, a piercing scream of agony from the cabin or somewhere near it. "What the hell?" Marvin swore, started to retreat, then almost thoughtlessly clubbed him with the gun, once, then again. After a flash of pain a broad black creature held him down for a length of time he couldn't calculate.

When he was aware again he was alone in the bus, lying in the aisle. His head felt crushed to pulp. He put a hand to his temple and felt blood. Midst throbbing pain he struggled to his feet and made his way outside and stood leaning against the bus while the night air struggled to clear his head.

He took a step, staggered, took another and gained an equilibrium, then lost it and sat down. Back on his feet, he trudged toward the porch and opened the door. Behind him, the nanny laughed again.

The cabin was dark, the only light the faint flicker from the stove behind the curtain. He walked carefully, trying to avoid the litter on the floor, the shapes in the room. Halfway to the back his foot struck something soft. As he bent to shove it out of his way it made a human sound. He knelt, saw that it was Iris, then found a lamp and turned it on.

She was crumpled, face down, in the center of the room, arms and legs folded under her, her body curled to avoid asssault. He knelt again, heard her groan once more, and saw that what he'd thought was a piece of skirt was in fact a pool of blood and what he'd thought was shadow was a broad wet trail of the selfsame substance leading toward the rear of the cabin.

He ran his hands down her body, feeling for wounds. Finding none, he rolled Iris to her side, then to her back. Blood bubbled from a point beneath her sternum. Her eyelids fluttered, open, closed, then open again. "He shot me," she said. "It hurt so bad I couldn't stop crying so he shot me."

"I know. Don't try to talk."

"Did he shoot the babies, too? I thought I heard . . ."

"I don't know."

"Would you look? Please?"

He nodded, stood up, fought a siege of vertigo, then went behind the curtain, then returned to Iris. "They're all right."

*106*

She tried to smile her thanks. "Something scared him off. I think some people were walking by outside and heard the shot and went for help. I heard them yelling."

"Where would he go, Iris?"

"Up in the woods. On his dirt bike. He knows lots of people up there. They grow dope, live off the land. The cops'll never find him." Iris moaned again. "I'm dying, aren't I?"

"I don't know. Is there a phone here?"

She shook her head. "Down at the end of the street. By the market."

"I'm going down and call an ambulance. And the cops. How long ago did Marvin leave?"

She closed her eyes. "I blacked out. Oh, God. It's real bad now, Mr. Tanner. Real bad."

"I know, Iris. You hang on. I'll be back in a second. Try to hold this in place." He took out his handkerchief and folded it into a square and placed in on her wound. "Press as hard as you can." He took her left hand and placed it on the compress, then stood up.

"Wait. I have to . . ."

He spoke above her words. "You have to get to a hospital. I'll be back in a minute and we can talk some more."

"But . . ."

"Hang on."

He ran from the cabin and down the drive, spotted the lights of the convenience market down the street and ran to the phone booth and placed his calls. The police said they'd already been notified and a car was on the way. The ambulance said it would be six minutes. As fast as he could he ran back to the cabin, hoping it would be fast enough.

Iris had moved. Her body was straightened, her right arm outstretched toward the door, the gesture of a supplicant. The sleeve of her blouse was tattered, burned to a ragged edge above her elbow. Below the sleeve her arm was red in spots, blistered in others, dappled like burned food. The hand at its end was charred and curled into a crusty fist that was dusted with gray ash. Within the fingers was an object, blackened, burned, and treasured.

He pried it from her grasp. The cover was burned away, and the edges of the pages were curled and singed, but they remained decipherable, the written scrawl preserved. The list of names and places was organized to match the gaily painted boxes in the back. Carson City. Boise. Grant's Pass. San Bernardino. Modesto. On and on, a gazetteer of crime.

"I saved it," Iris mumbled. "I saved it for my babies."

He raised her head to his lap and held it till she died. Then he went to his car and retrieved his B Box baby and placed her in her appointed crib. For the first time since he'd known her the baby made only happy sounds, an irony that was lost on the five dead children at her flank and on the just dead woman who had feared it all.

# The Rented Scar

## *Edward D. Hoch*

*Although this is the thirteenth story I've published about private eye Al Darlan, he remains one of the least familiar of my series characters. One reason for this is probably that the series has never found a regular home. Beginning in 1957, the stories have appeared in such assorted magazines as* Crime & Justice, Killers, Fast-Action Detective, Off Beat Detective, Manhunt, Alfred Hitchcock's Mystery Magazine, Mike Shayne Mystery Magazine, *the literary quarterly* Antaeus, *and the newly revived* Saint Magazine.

*Then too, Al Darlan was named Al Diamond in his first two adventures. Editor Robert A.W. Lowndes changed the name with the third story, to avoid confusion with radio and TV detective Richard Diamond, and I stuck with the change. One Darlan story, published in* Manhunt *and narrated uncharacteristically in the third person, seems to have been an attempt to kill off my character. But like better writers before and since, I relented and Darlan lived.*

*Maybe I kept him alive for all these years because I knew someday there'd be a PWA.*

THE sun seemed especially bright on that September afternoon, possibly because we'd finally convinced the landlord he had to wash the windows of *Darlan & Trapper Investigations* so the place would look a bit more inviting. I'd paid for a couple buckets of paint myself, and my young partner Mike Trapper had promised to paint the office over the weekend.

"By Monday morning you won't know it," he promised. "A nice cool green on the walls to make everyone relax. And then if we get that secretary you've been promising us, she won't be ashamed to be seen here."

"We need clients worse than we need a secretary," I reminded him. Since I'd taken him on as a partner in an attempt to save the business, we'd had only a handful of decent cases. Even the money he'd invested in the partnership was just about gone.

"Don't worry so much, Al. We can have both."

I'd promised to spend the weekend with an old war buddy who was passing through town, so I left Mike with his paint cans and his optimism. "I'll see you Monday. But don't hire a secretary without me."

"The first thing that has to go is that old iron safe of yours."

I grinned at him. "Where would I keep my gun?"

"Think of a new place. That safe's gotta go."

"We'll talk about it Monday."

It was something of a shock meeting Griff Cary after nearly forty years. We'd fought together as teen-agers in the final months of the war in Europe, and been together at Bastogne when a German artillery shell ripped away part of his face one sunny December afternoon. They said I saved his life that day, dragging him a hundred yards to a field hospital while shells kept landing all around us, but I never thought of myself as much of a hero even after they gave me a medal for it.

At first, seeing what Griff's face looked like in the army hospital where I visited him, I wondered if I'd done him any favors by rescuing him. The left side of his cheek seemed almost gone, and I couldn't imagine the number of operations necessary to restore it—if any sort of restoration was possible. I visited him a few times before the tide of battle shifted and we were on the offensive once more. Then I moved on, and I hadn't seen Griff Cary since.

Oh, we kept up a correspondence of sorts for the first few years, and even tried to arrange a meeting in New York after the war, but we never quite got together. A few Christmas cards over the years, and a note one time telling me he was happily married— that was about all. Then, a week ago, he'd phoned to say he'd be passing through town by bus. He planned to get off and spend the weekend with me. His wife was gone—dead or divorced—and he was alone. I'd expected him to phone me Thursday night, but the call hadn't come till Friday. I met him at the bus station.

He was the same age as me, pushing sixty, and despite the scar on his left cheek he still looked rugged and handsome. His hair was white, and the skin grafts on his face were noticeable, but outside of that he was holding up better than I was. "Hey, fella— those army docs did a pretty fair job on you!"

He shook my hand. "I've been living with it nearly forty years. I don't think about it any more. I had twelve operations before I called it quits. They said they could help this scar, but I was sick of hospitals by that time."

"Don't blame you. I guess we got a lot to talk about."

He nodded. "You married, Al?"

I shook my head. "Never found a wife who'd put up with my line of work. I've still got the agency, you know."

"Sure, that's how I found your number. I never figured you for Sam Spade. You make money at it?"

"Just barely. I almost folded a couple of years back. Finally took in a young fellow as a partner. God, he's young enough to be my son!"

"I've got a son," Griff Cary said glumly. "Never see him, though. He's out on the west coast."

"You said you were married."

"Yeah. It worked for about ten years, and I guess that's pretty good these days. But I've been alone a long time now. I had a pretty fair job in St. Louis till the company went bankrupt. I'm just sort of drifting now, seeing the country, living off my savings. Guess I'm too old for anyone to hire."

"You'll find something."

He put a gentle hand on my arm. "I figured I needed to see you, Al, to show you what sort of a life you saved."

"What sort of life has it been?"

"Average, I guess, but I'm not kicking. I wouldn't have wanted to miss it."

We had dinner together and I took him back to my apartment where there was a spare bed. He glanced around at my few possessions and asked, "What'd you ever do with the medal you got for rescuing me?"

"Hell, it's around here somewhere. I didn't pawn it or anything."

The following morning after breakfast I said I'd show him the office. I'd forgotten that Mike was in there repainting the place, and we had to move gingerly around the ladders and drop cloths.

"This is my old buddy Griff Cary," I told him. "Griff, meet Mike Trapper, my partner."

Mike wiped off the paint and shook hands. "The place doesn't always look this bad. Pleased to meet you."

"Nice location here," Griff observed. "Right near the center of things."

"We get some business from the local lawyers," I told him. "Nothing very exciting."

We drifted out after a bit and Mike returned to his painting. I had to admit it was looking good. "Nice young fellow," Griff said as we took the elevator down. "He must be a big help to you."

"We keep each other company when business is slow."

"Look," he said suddenly, "if you can put me up for one more night I'll be leaving in the morning."

"You're welcome as long as you want to stay, Griff. You know that."

"No, just one more night."

I showed him around the town for a bit, and it was mid-afternoon by the time we returned to the apartment. The telephone was ringing as I walked through the door. I wasn't used to getting calls at home and I figured it might be Mike Trapper. It was.

"Al," he said, speaking softly, "I've got a client here at the office."

"On a Saturday afternoon?"

"Two guys. They just walked in off the street."

"Tell them to come back Monday. Tell them you're the painter."

"It's too late for that now. They're talking about hiring us on a five hundred dollar retainer. They're in the outer office with cash in hand."

"Take it, then. Don't fight it."

"I'm not, Al. Here's the point. They need an older man with a scarred face. My first thought was that we could put makeup on you—"

"Mike—"

"—but then I thought of that friend of yours. What's his name? Cary? Griff Cary. It would only be a day's work and we could pay him a hundred or two. He sounded like he was at loose ends."

I glanced across the room at Griff. "Yeah. But I don't know. What's the deal?"

"Could you come down here and see these guys?"

I glanced at Griff again. "Not very well. Look, bring them over to my apartment in about a half-hour. OK?"

"Sure, Al."

I hung up and thought about it. I'd never liked coincidences. "Anyone else know you're in town?" I asked Griff.

He looked puzzled. "No. You're the only one I know around here."

I opened the cupboard and took down a bottle. "How about a drink, or is it too early for you?"

"Sure, I'll join you, Al. A little water in mine."

"That was Mike on the phone, from the office. We've got a couple of clients on the way over with special needs. There might be a day's pay in it for you if you could stay over."

"How much?"

"A hundred and a half. Maybe more."

"Doing what?"

"That's what I don't know yet."

"Then how do you know I can do it?"

"They want someone with a scar on his face. Don't ask me why. That's why I asked if you knew anyone else in town."

Griff Cary touched his left cheek. "Never thought this thing would bring me any money."

"It hasn't yet. Look, Mike's on his way over with the clients. Why don't you wait in the bedroom while I talk to them, see what the deal is. If it sounds OK, I'll call you out."

"Fine by me."

We finished our drinks just as Mike arrived. The two men with him were an odd pair. The one who did most of the talking, Daniel McCarthy, wore a conservative suit and looked like a banker or lawyer. The other one, Phil Rush, was a huskier man with a mustache that didn't fit his face. He wore a dark jacket and gray pants, and his shirt was open at the neck. For a moment I entertained the notion that he might be McCarthy's bodyguard.

They seated themselves on my worn leather couch and McCarthy opened the conversation. "Good of you to have us up to your apartment, Mr. Darlan."

"The office is a bit of a mess. We're not usually open on Saturdays. What can we do for you?"

"I need something picked up tomorrow. That's why I couldn't wait till Monday."

"What business are you in, Mr. McCarthy? You must realize we're licensed private investigators. Any illegal activity, especially concerning narcotics—"

"There are no drugs involved. I'll be frank, Darlan. My daughter ran off with a most undesirable chap. One or both of them took some valuable papers from the house when they left."

"How long ago was this?"

"Last month. While my wife and I were vacationing in Europe."

"What business are you in?" I asked again.

"Real estate."

"Are the missing papers concerned with your business?"

"They are. My business of real estate development is such that I'm often involved in confidential negotiations for parcels of land—putting together property for a new suburban shopping mall or a downtown office complex. We have to keep our secrets or the price of the necessary land could be driven up considerably."

"Your daughter and her friend stole documents concerning this?"

"I'm afraid so, and I need them back. My relations with Karen aren't the best these days. Phil here has been acting as intermediary."

Phil Rush took over the conversation for the first time, and I realized he wasn't a bodyguard after all. His voice had a soft cultured quality that surprised me. "I'm Karen's godfather," he explained with a wry smile, "trying to keep peace in the family. This fellow Serces is bad news and I can't blame Dan and Jane for disliking him. He stole their daughter and took this briefcase full of papers besides. But I'm doing what I can for Karen. I met her and told her they had to give back the briefcase. She's agreed, and we're to send someone for it tomorrow afternoon."

"Why can't you go?" I wondered.

"Serces has the briefcase, and I'm no friend of his. He wears long hair and earrings—you know the type. He told Karen we should send Dan's chauffeur, Wentworth, for the briefcase. Trouble is, Wentworth isn't with him any more."

"I hate to disrupt the arrangements when we're this close to recovering the papers," Daniel McCarthy said. "Wentworth had a scar on the left side of his face from an old auto accident, and when he drove for me he wore a peaked cap. Serces couldn't have seen him more than once and I figure any older man with a scar would pass muster. If I sent anyone else Serces might think it was a cop and be frightened off."

It sounded logical but not quite right. I was bothered by the whole business. "If these papers are all that valuable, Serces probably has a hundred copies by now."

"He doesn't know they're valuable," McCarthy explained. "They don't *look* valuable. And there are lots of other papers mixed in with them. I think Karen took the briefcase just so I wouldn't send the police after them immediately. It was a bargaining chip. Let them alone and they'd give it back."

"But you said it's been a month now."

"It took me a while to contact Karen," Rush explained. "I had dinner with her a few days ago, and then she had to get Serces to agree to surrender the briefcase."

They had an answer for everything, but I still didn't like it. "What's the schedule for tomorrow?"

"Serces says he'll be at the South Street Park with the briefcase at four in the afternoon. Near the fountain. He should be easy to spot."

"That fountain attracts a lot of his type on a Sunday afternoon," Mike Trapper said.

"But not carrying a briefcase."

"One other thing," I said. "Why'd you come to a private detective agency with this?"

"I need those papers back," McCarthy explained. "In that park on a Sunday afternoon someone could get mugged and robbed even after Serces delivered them. I figured you private eyes could handle yourselves."

Mike and I exchanged glances. "It won't be one of us, Mr. McCarthy, though we'll provide backup." I walked to the bedroom door and opened it. "Come out, Griff."

He stepped smiling into the room, like a job applicant trying to make a good impression. "He'll do," McCarthy said at once. "He's about the same build as Wentworth."

I pulled Mike aside. "What price did you quote them?"

"A thousand. Five hundred down. They never blinked an eye."

I nodded. "If it goes well I might give Griff three. He could use it."

I stopped worrying about coincidences.

Sunday was a breezy, sunny day with seasonable temperatures. Mike Trapper had gone out to the McCarthy home and returned with a chauffeur's cap that the departed Wentworth had worn. It was a bit large for Griff's head, but we fooled around with some tissue paper stuffing until it was a reasonable fit. He had a dark blue suit jacket that looked like something a chauffeur might wear.

"Never thought I'd be renting out my body like this," he remarked with a smirk. "And the pay is good too."

"We're only renting your scar," I reminded him. "You just happened to be in the right place at the right time."

"Like in Bastogne. Only I guess that was the wrong place at the wrong time."

"We'd better get going," Mike said. "What's the plan?"

"There are some wooded areas overlooking the fountain. You and I will cover him from there. Got your gun?"

Mike nodded. "I suppose yours is still in the safe."

"One should be enough. I don't expect trouble." I turned to Griff. "You know what you're to do?"

"Look for a young guy with a briefcase and take it when he gives it to me. You're sure he doesn't expect money in return?"

"No money. He'll have long hair and earrings and his name is Serces." I glanced at my watch. "Come on. It's time we were going."

There was a fair crowd of young people in the area of the

117

fountain, but not as many as there might have been earlier in the summer. I headed toward an unoccupied bench near a clump of trees and sent Mike Trapper in the opposite direction. Griff adjusted his cap, smiled his slightly off-center smile, and started down toward the fountain. It was five minutes to four.

I tried to pick out some likely long-haired types, but there was no one carrying a briefcase or any large package. As four o'clock came and went I began to wonder if he'd show up at all.

Then a dark-haired girl wearing a long gypsy skirt and scoop-necked blouse suddenly appeared, walking quickly across the paved area around the fountain. She headed directly for the spot where Griff Cary lounged against the fountain's base. I watched her speak to him, and Griff glanced around uncertainly. Then the two of them started walking.

I looked across at the opposite clump of trees, trying to spot Mike Trapper. Whatever was happening, it wasn't according to plan.

Finally I moved off my bench, following the two of them at a distance, hoping that Mike was doing the same. They went up the path and turned out of sight while I hurried through the afternoon crowd behind them. There was still no sign of the man with the briefcase, but perhaps the girl was leading Griff to the real meeting place.

Then I heard the shot.

It was muffled but unmistakable to experienced ears. I broke into a run, rounding the bend in the path to find Griff Cary sprawled on the ground. There was no sign of the girl.

"Griff!" I shouted, dropping to my knees beside him.

But this time I was too late to save his life. Griff Cary was dead.

The single bullet had penetrated his chest at the level of the heart. I'd established that by the time Mike Trapper arrived, slightly out of breath, his revolver in hand. "What happened?" he asked. "I saw him following the girl."

"I heard a shot and found him. Either she did it or Serces was waiting here."

"But why?"

"I don't know. We'd better get the police."

He studied my face. "Are you all right, Al?"

"It's not the first body I've seen."

"I know, but—"

"Get the police. Then you'd better phone Daniel McCarthy and tell him what's happened."

I stayed with the body until the first officers arrived, remembering that sunny December day at Bastogne when I'd dragged Griff Cary to safety as the shells burst around us. He'd had nearly forty years of life because of what I did, but now he was dead because of what I did in getting him involved in this. How does anyone figure life when it plays tricks like that on you?

When the police arrived I left them with the body and started searching the general area. I didn't have to look far. About ten yards away I found the gun, stuck into the middle of a lilac bush. It was a .38 caliber revolver, wrapped in a white handkerchief to partly muffle the sound and guard against fingerprints, and the spot of white had caught my eye. The handkerchief seemed unused except for the powder-burnt bullet hole and a few green spots on one corner.

I left the gun where it was and pointed it out to the cops. Some detectives and technicians were arriving, along with a photographer and the assistant medical examiner. I talked to Sergeant Gold, a homicide detective who knew me, and told him what little I could. Mike Trapper was back from making his phone calls, and he filled in his part of it.

"What's the full name of this Serces?" Gold asked.

"I don't know. Maybe McCarthy can tell us." I turned to Mike. "Is he coming down?"

"Not a chance, Al. He claims he's got a bad ankle. As soon as I told him Griff was dead he washed his hands of it."

119

"I'll change his mind about that," Gold assured us. "If his daughter was this woman you saw, she's a prime suspect."

"That handkerchief around the gun—any initials on it?"

"No such luck. Killers don't leave their initials at the scene of the crime."

"But it was a man's handkerchief, not a woman's."

"Doesn't mean a thing," Gold assured us. "Come on—we'll go see this Daniel McCarthy."

McCarthy lived in a big suburban house befitting a successful dealer in real estate. There was a limo in the driveway, but no sign of Wentworth the chauffeur's replacement, if there was one. A handsome woman with graying hair opened the door as we started up the front walk. I guessed it was McCarthy's wife, and it was a good guess.

"I'm Jane McCarthy," she announced in a cultured voice. "Come in, please. I'm sorry my husband was so abrupt on the telephone."

"I understand," Mike told her, and introduced us. She looked pained at the presence of Sergeant Gold, as if this was hardly a matter that called for the police.

Daniel McCarthy appeared from the spacious living room, walking with a bit of a limp. "This is a bad day all around," he explained as he shook hands with Gold. "I fell in the yard and twisted my ankle."

"It was a bit worse for Griff Cary," I said. "He's dead."

"I'm sorry about that. But I suppose those things happen all the time in your line of business."

"Mr. McCarthy," Gold interrupted, "is it correct that you hired the murdered man to make contact with the boyfriend of your runaway daughter, to secure the return of some papers?"

"That's right. Or I should say I employed Darlan and Trapper for that task. We needed a man with a scar to impersonate a former chauffeur of mine, and they suggested this man Cary."

"You'd never met him before?"

"No."

"How about your daughter?"

"Griff Cary was just passing through town," I explained. "He didn't know anyone here but me."

Sergeant Gold turned to me. "You said a young woman approached him, possibly the missing Karen McCarthy."

"Possibly. You must have a picture of your daughter in the house."

Jane McCarthy disappeared into the living room and returned with a framed photograph showing the family standing by their limo. I could see the scarred face of an older man in chauffeur's uniform, standing behind the car, and I noticed the whip antenna that told me the car was equipped with a telephone. I studied the smiling girl in the middle of the group. "That's her," I decided.

"Why would she shoot this man Cary?" Gold asked.

"She wouldn't shoot anyone!" Jane McCarthy insisted.

"But when she met him she knew at once that he wasn't Wentworth," I said. "Back among the trees, she probably told Serces. He panicked and shot Griff."

"Maybe," Gold said, thinking about it.

"That's what must have happened," Jane McCarthy insisted. "My daughter never killed anyone."

Mike Trapper asked, "Do you know where Karen and Serces are living?"

"No," McCarthy said. "If I knew, I'd go down there myself and drag her back home."

Gold took out his notebook. "Give me a description of this Serces."

"He's a hippy type," Jane McCarthy said. "Long hair that he wears in a band, and earrings too!"

While Gold questioned her and Mike stood by, McCarthy motioned me aside. "Darlan, I still want that briefcase back. Get it for me and I'll double your fee."

"That might be difficult now," I said. "I'll try." What I really wanted to find was Griff's killer. If the briefcase turned up along the way, so much the better.

\* \* \*

I left Mike with Sergeant Gold and decided to try an idea of my own. I checked the phone book for Phil Rush's address and drove out to the swank apartment where he lived alone. When he answered the door it was obvious he knew what had happened. "Dan just phoned," he told me. "The police were at his house."

"I know. The thing went wrong and my man Cary is dead. Look, you've got to stop covering up for your goddaughter, Mr. Rush."

"I don't—"

"Cut it! I don't have time for lies. You told us you met her to arrange this deal today, and that means you know how to contact her. You know where she and this guy Serces are holed up."

"She didn't kill anyone."

"Maybe not, but I think Serces did. You can't protect them any longer. We're talking about murder now."

He flopped onto the couch as if I'd cut the wires that supported him. "All right, Darlan. What do you want?"

"Where are they?"

"Last I knew Karen was with him at a boat repair yard near the Bay Marina. You go past the marina down a single-lane road, close to the water. Serces worked there during the summer, and the owner let him live in an extra room."

"Thanks," I said. "Don't tip them off I'm coming."

"You think I'm crazy? I'm staying out of this!"

I left him and went back to my car, stopping at a sidewalk pay phone to call the office. I was hoping Mike had decided to return to his painting, but there was no answer. I drove over to the office myself and took my .38 caliber revolver out of the old iron safe. Then I left a note on Mike's desk telling him where I was.

The sun was low in the sky by the time I passed the Bay Marina and headed down the dirt road to the boat repair yard. There were yachts and cabin cruisers beached on both sides of the road, some on trailers, waiting to be carted away or put in storage for the winter. It was a depressing place at this time of the year, devoid of most activity.

I pulled up and parked before I reached the repair yard. There was a little foreign sports car parked there, and it looked like the sort of vehicle Karen McCarthy might be driving. Her father hadn't mentioned bringing her back, just the briefcase.

Keeping in the shelter of the big boats as best I could, I made my way forward, heading for a tin-roofed structure that seemed to house the only likely living quarters. I was about fifty yards from it when Karen herself suddenly appeared in the doorway. She saw me, and said something over her shoulder. I broke into a run, trying to cover the remaining ground between us.

"Karen!" I shouted as she stepped back inside. "I'm a friend!"

I hit the door before she could quite close it, hoping I wouldn't get a bullet for my trouble. She tried to slip away but I grabbed her arm. "Where is he?" I demanded.

"Who the hell are you?"

I heard a clatter from the rear of the building and drew the revolver with my free hand. "Your father hired me to get the briefcase."

Then he was in the back doorway, framed against the fading evening light on the bay. I released her and made a dive for him, leading with my .38. He tripped on the back step and went down with me on top of him. "Cool it, Serces," I said into his ear, trying to forget that he was half my age. I yanked at his long hair and turned him so I could see his face.

It had a scar on the left cheek like Griff's and the chauffeur Wentworth's, and I knew there was more to this case than I'd ever dreamed.

"Suppose you tell me what's been going on," I told Karen McCarthy when I'd brought Serces back inside.

"Are you some thug my father hired?" she demanded.

"Al Darlan. Private investigator. He hired me to get back his briefcase and a friend of mine died this afternoon trying to do just that. Want to tell me about it, or should I call the cops?"

Serces twisted in my grip and I finally released him, keeping the gun where he could see it. "You've got nothing on me!" he said.

"How about a murder charge?"

"I didn't kill him."

"Who did?" I asked, glancing at Karen.

"We don't know," she said. "I led him back to Russ and we'd just left him when we heard the shot. I was scared and we ran."

"Russ?"

"I'm Russ Serces."

"Were you also one of the McCarthy chauffeurs?" I asked, taking a wild guess.

He snorted. "I had to wear my hair under that fool cap so no one could see how long it was. I only lasted a month."

"So you two fell in love and ran off."

"Why not?" Karen asked defensively. "Now he's got a job at this boatyard, earning an honest living."

"What about the briefcase?"

"We thought it contained money," she answered. "Sometimes it did. I figured they owed me that much for saving them the cost of an expensive wedding."

"Was there money in it?"

"No, just some papers. My father wanted them back so we agreed to meet with someone he sent."

"You didn't ask for Wentworth?"

"He was the chauffeur before me," Serces said. "I figured the guy who came was my replacement."

"Where's the briefcase now?"

"We threw it away after the shooting," Karen said. "He told us he just wanted the papers. He folded them and put them in his pocket."

My mind was spinning. Nothing seemed to make sense. "Why do your parents dislike Russ so much?" I asked her. "It couldn't be his long hair, or they wouldn't have hired him in the first place."

Russ Serces snorted. "It was her mother disliked me. She wanted a roll in the hay and I liked her daughter better."

That told it all, and I should have seen it coming. The scar, especially. "How'd you get it?" I asked him, pointing to his cheek.

"Fell on a milk bottle when I was small, when milk still came in bottles. My mother thought it was sexy and never had it fixed. She told me some women like scars."

"Mrs. McCarthy does," I said.

I saw a car coming down the road as I left. It was Mike Trapper, riding to rescue me. "I thought you'd be dead," he said with relief.

"What, and leave the business to you? Come on, we've got a call to make."

We found Jane McCarthy alone on the main floor of her big house. "My husband has gone out," she said. "Is there anything I can do for you?"

I stepped across the threshold. "We need some truth, Mrs. McCarthy. From you."

"About what?"

"Neither you nor your husband told us that Karen had run off with your chauffeur."

"What difference does that make?"

I walked to the side table with the framed picture of the family by their car. "The man in this photo with the scarred face—it's not Russ Serces. It's an older man. Your chauffeur ahead of Serces, this guy Wentworth, also had a scarred cheek. You like men with scars, don't you, Mrs. McCarthy?"

Her eyes blazed at me. "Get out of this house—both of you!"

I replaced the picture and nodded to Mike. "Let's go."

As we walked back to the car, he asked, "What about our fee?"

"We'll collect it, with a bit of luck."

"You think McCarthy saw Griff Cary's scar, thought he was another one of his wife's lovers, and shot him?"

"That's one possibility," I admitted.

"And he twisted his ankle escaping from the murder scene!"

I laughed at that. "You're missing the most obvious clue of all, Mike. It's as big as the wall of our office, and you're missing it."

"Huh?"

"Come on. We're going to earn our fee."

Phil Rush was wearing a dressing gown when he answered the door of his apartment. He eyed us bleakly and asked, "It's a bit late to be visiting, isn't it?"

"We didn't think you'd mind," I said. "We're wrapping up the case and I thought you'd want a report."

"Dan McCarthy is really your employer. The report should go to him."

I sat down and took out my notebook. "Let me tell you what I think happened, from the beginning. Dan McCarthy's wife Jane has a liking for men with scars on their face. Especially chauffeurs. I'm sure a head doctor could find roots for it in her childhood, but that's not my line. Her husband handles a great many confidential real estate transactions. A spy in his household, acting as his driver, could deliver some valuable information. He has a phone in his car. The driver could overhear phone calls, listen in on back seat conversations, and keep a record of real estate sites that McCarthy was inspecting."

"Why are you telling me all this?"

"You noticed Jane McCarthy's liking for scar-faced chauffeurs, and decided to take advantage of it. You went out and found a scar-faced man."

"We came to you for one. That's no secret."

"I think you found Griff Cary first and recruited him for your own purpose. You were looking for drifters, and naturally you checked out the bus station. I was expecting him to arrive Thursday night, but he didn't phone till Friday morning. You picked him up Thursday, but you still had to bring him to the McCarthys' attention in a way that didn't directly involve you. Griff told you he was in town to visit an old friend who was a private detective, so you concocted this idea of Karen insisting the chauffeur pick up the briefcase. You told McCarthy they needed a scar-faced man, because Karen and Russ would be expecting one. You persuaded McCarthy to hire us, and naturally we had a perfect scar-faced man. You figured Jane McCarthy would offer Griff the chauffeur's job when he returned the briefcase, and your spy would be planted. He was still a good-looking guy, after all, and she liked them all ages."

"You think you're pretty smart," Rush said, his right hand in the dressing gown pocket.

"But my friend Griff got greedy. He stuffed those papers in his pocket and told Karen to keep the briefcase. Maybe he decided he wouldn't like being a chauffeur. You were watching from the bushes, and when he saw you maybe he said you'd have to pay for the papers. You shot him in an instant, took the papers out of his pocket, and hid behind a tree as I came running up."

"You think you can prove that?"

"I think so. I don't know why you had the gun with you in the first place, but you took it out, wrapped in a handkerchief to muffle the sound and guard against fingerprints. The handkerchief had spots of green paint on it—from our office, Mr. Rush. You must have wiped wet paint off your fingers on Saturday without remembering it. Only you and McCarthy and Griff and I were in that office while Mike's paint was wet. Griff didn't shoot himself and drop the gun in a bush ten yards away. And McCarthy was at his suburban home to answer Mike's call five minutes after the killing. That leaves you, Rush. It's your handkerchief, and you shot Griff."

He moved faster than I'd expected. The tiny pistol in his dressing gown wouldn't have done much damage, but I was still relieved to see Mike's big fist connect with his jaw before the gun was free of the pocket.

"Call Sergeant Gold," I told Mike, kicking the weapon away from Rush's limp right hand. "Then let's search this place for those papers. They're the evidence Gold'll need, and they'll earn our fee from McCarthy."

"Think he knew about his wife and those chauffeurs, Al?"

"He'd have to be blind not to."

He nodded and moved toward the phone. "You know, your friend Griff brought it on himself. You weren't responsible for his death after all."

"I'd like to think that," I admitted. "It would help me sleep better at night."

# Private Investigations

## *Richard Hoyt*

*I first got hooked on private detective novels in 1957 when
I was a sixteen-year-old truck driver in the wheat fields of
eastern Oregon and had a twenty-minute wait between combines.
The hired man had a cardboard box filled with Richard S. Prather
and Mickey Spillane. I was able to read two or three Shell Scott
or Mike Hammer adventures in a twelve hour shift. I turned the
corners of the pages back to help me find the places where the
detective got the lady's clothes off.*

*Twenty years later, I sat down at a 1929 Royal to try my
hand at the genre and came up with John Denson, who works out of
Seattle. I gave Denson my background: former newspaper reporter,
former intelligence agent. No Ph.D. in American studies for him,
however. He drinks screw-top red, throws darts in working men's
taverns and cons his way out of violence.*

Ihad a hunch which is why I
watched his house in the first place. The brunette arrived in a little
Honda. I thought I recognized her when he opened his front door,
but I couldn't be sure. Ada was a brunette and drove a Honda. I
watched the lights go on as the two of them made their way inside.
It was an expensive Bellevue house overlooking Lake Washington.
The streets were wet from an earlier rain but there was a white
moon now.

I drank some coffee out of my thermos and waited. They had a
drink or two or maybe smoked a joint in a room up front—his den if
I remembered the layout right. I had only been there once. He had
shown me the whole house. He was proud of it. He had a room of
his own and so had his wife. He would show the brunette mementos
of his past. He was a successful man.

Later, the light was doused and they made their way to the
rear of the house, to the bedroom.

I wondered why he did it. He had so much to lose. His wife
was a handsome, articulate woman. Why? A couple of hours later
the lights were turned on in the front of the house again and the
brunette left. I followed the Honda across the floating bridge over
Lake Washington into Seattle. I was sure I had seen her before.
Was it Ada? Was my hunch right?

She parked her Honda in front of a warm little cafe and went
inside. She joined a well-dressed blonde in a booth; the blonde was
Madeliene, my client's wife. The brunette sat with her back to me.
She was soft spoken so I couldn't hear her. I could only hear
Madeliene. I ordered a cup of coffee and deep fried onion rings and
listened in.

"No, no," Madeliene said. "I want to hear it all. The whole
thing." She looked right at me without seeing me. I ate my onion
rings impassively, my mind apparently on other things.

The brunette said something I couldn't hear.

"Believe me, I won't get embarrassed. I want the details," Madeliene said. She paused. "Sure, sure. Go ahead."

The brunette got up to go to the women's room. On the way back she saw me at my booth. Ada. She acknowledged me with her eyes. She sat down and continued her story.

Madeliene smiled ruefully. "Really? I didn't think he had the imagination. That sounds like fun." She waited, listening. "Why that devil! You know, they put you on a pedestal and won't give you a chance, then complain that you're frigid or something."

Ada continued.

"Did he say anything about me? What did he say?" Madeliene waited. She was suddenly angry. "He did, did he? It was the other way around, I swear. How could he say that? How could he? He was the one who would never do anything adventurous or unusual. I thought he was repressed or something. What else? Tell me."

Ada told her.

"Did he? Did he?" Madeliene said. "I would have done that for free? No problem! How was I supposed to know if he never did anything? Never said anything. Why didn't he give me a chance?"

Ada finished her story.

Madeliene said, "Men are so damned timid. So stupid. He's so boring. I wonder if he really thinks I spend all my time in department stores on my shopping trips. Not all men are gay in San Francisco, you know." She opened her handbag and wrote a check which she gave to Ada.

Ada said something, then rose and shook Madeliene's hand. She headed my way toward the front door. Madeliene was left behind, staring at her cup of coffee.

"Have a good time, Ada?" I said.

"Had a heck of a time, John Denson. I think he paid me for what he could have gotten for free, though. You on the job?"

"We should work together, maybe make some real bucks."

Ada grinned. She knew I'd tell my client everything. "Give me a call tomorrow, we'll compare notes." She walked on out and got into her Honda. The exhaust puffed into the cold night when she turned the ignition.

I found a phone booth and called the man in the impressive Bellevue house. He said I should come on over.

He stood in the open doorway, looking worried. He had been thinking about my call. "Well?" he said.

"You said to let you know immediately if I found anything out."

"And?"

"You're right. She's onto you."

"Let's go have a brandy and you can tell me about it." I followed him into his den and waited while he poured our drinks, saying nothing. The den was lined with mementos and with books. He was a reader. His wife was a reader too, only her room was filled with women's magazines. "When did you find out?" he asked.

"Tonight."

He turned and saw me reading the titles on the spines of the books. "Freud could probably tell me what went wrong."

"Probably," I said. I accepted the brandy. He was a brandy drinker and so read Freud and argued in the abstract.

"I really do love Madeliene, you know. Only she's so damned conventional, so straight. After a while a man's mind wanders. He wants to do something different, maybe a little forbidden. He thinks of what he might be doing, could be doing if he wanted."

"Your wife's a beautiful woman," I said.

"A beautiful woman can be intimidating. It's like they're different, special, like you shouldn't soil them. I got bored after a while. It's the hormones that do it."

I didn't say anything. Misunderstandings like he had with his wife helped keep shrinks and lawyers in business, not to mention private detectives.

"She knows it for a fact? She can prove it in court? She's supposed to be shopping in San Francisco; that's why I thought it was okay to use the house. How can you know all this?"

"She's not in San Francisco," I said. "She got her proof tonight."

He looked stunned. "Oh, no."

"I had a hunch so I watched you."

"My, uh . . ." He was uncertain of what term to use.

"She wasn't a call girl. She was a private investigator."

He looked at me in disbelief.

"Her name's Ada. There was an article about her in *Ms.* magazine a couple of months ago. I saw the issue in your wife's study when you showed me the house that day."

"A private detective?"

"It's a new world. Times change. Ada specializes in these kinds of cases. Finds things out for women clients."

His shoulder slumped. He shook his head. "And here I thought I was being so damned careful. Madeliene never comes back early from San Francisco. Never. She's charming, good company. I love her."

"Maybe you should talk to your wife," I said. "Open up a little. She might surprise you."

"You think so?"

"She knows why you're restless now. That was Ada's job."

He wrote me a check. His signature was neatly rendered, the letters well formed. I left wondering if he had it in him to be honest with his wife. If he did, Ada and I might turn out to be a better deal than counselors and divorce courts.

# The Man Who Shot
# Lewis Vance

## *Stuart M. Kaminsky*

*After nine novels, this is Toby Peters' first
appearance in a short story. It was inevitable that since
Duke Wayne and the Pevsner brothers were all brought up in
Glendale in the 1920s that they met and might well run
into each other again.*

*This tale introduces a new character to the Toby Peters world,
Straight-Ahead Beeson who, I have a feeling, will turn up in a
novel or two.*
*In fact, the whole tale will probably form the basis
for a future novel-length adventure.*

WHEN I opened my eyes, I saw
John Wayne pointing a .38 at my chest. It was my .38. I closed my
eyes.

The inside of my head seemed to be filled with strawberry
cotton candy with little unnamed things crawling through its sickly
melting strands. Nausea forced my eyes open again. John Wayne

was still there. He was wearing trousers, a white shirt and a lightweight tan windbreaker. He was lean, dark and puzzled.

"Don't close your eyes again, Pilgrim," he said.

I didn't close them. He was standing over me and I slumped in a badly sprung cheap understuffed hotel chair. I tried to sit up and speak but my tongue was an inflated, dry, pebbly football. There was a flat, half full glass of brown Pepsi on the stained yellow table in front of me but I didn't reach for it. That glass, and what had been in it, had put me out.

I wasn't sure of the day and the time. When I took that last few gulps of Pepsi, it had been a Sunday night in the winter of 1942. I had been sitting in a cheap Los Angeles hotel room with a guy who had identified himself as Lewis Vance.

Lewis Vance had left a message for me at my office, but I had been out of town filling in for a gate guard at an old people's home in Goleta. It had netted me $20 minus gas. The message on my desk, left in the uncertain hand of Sheldon Minck, the dentist I rent space from, had said I should call Lewis Vance in Room 303 of the Alhambra Arms over on Broadway. I'd called and Vance had told me to come right over. I didn't even have to drive. My office was on Hoover a few blocks away and I ambled over knowing I needed a shave and worrying about which island the Japanese had taken while I was in Goleta.

My grey seersucker was crumpled but reasonably clean if you ignored the remnants of mustard stain on the sleeve. It was the best suit I had. The sky threatened rain but no one on the street seemed concerned. Soldiers, sailors, overly painted women laughing too hard to make a buck and sour-faced visitors flowed with me. Before the war, the crowds had been thick on Broadway on a Sunday, but tourists didn't make their way to Los Angeles after the first threats of an invasion by the Japanese.

Now Broadway was kids in uniform, waiting women and girls and people who couldn't afford to or were too stubborn to leave. I was one of the latter.

Vance had said he had a job for me. Since I am a private investigator, I assumed it had something to do with my profession. At 46 with a bad back, pushed-in nose and black greying hair, I was a reasonably formidable sight as a bodyguard. If I were over five foot-nine, I'd probably be busy nine or ten months a year with celebrities who wanted to show they could afford protection they usually didn't need. But there were plenty of muscle builders from the beaches—Santa Monica, Venice—who could be bought cheap and looked bigger and meaner than I did. They weren't meaner, but they were fine for show as almost everything was and is in Los Angeles.

The people who hire me usually get my name from someone who has used me in the past. They really want protection or a grandmother found or a stern word or two to a former friend who owes them a few hundred bucks. Vance hadn't said what he wanted me for.

The lobby of the Alhambra Arms was wilting badly, had been since long before the war. There were four big wooden pots in the lobby which had once held small palm trees. The palms had sagged to the floor years before and now the chipped green pots were used as ash trays and garbage bins. It didn't look too bad because you couldn't see much of anything in the Alhambra lobby. There was a strict policy of not replacing light bulbs as they died. The ceiling was a cemetery of darkened bulbs with a few dusty die-hards still glowing away. Considering the way I looked, I didn't mind the shadows of the Alhambra. I had filled in as hotel detective here twice in the last two years, both times on weekends. There had been no detecting involved, no thefts. The job was to keep the uniformed kids and ununiformed prostitutes from destroying the place and each other. It had kept me busy. The last time I had held down the duty I had done almost as much damage to the Allies as the Japanese fleet. Two sailors in diapers had taken umbrage at my telling them to refrain from destroying the lobby. Had they been sober I might have had a problem. They walked away from our discussion with a concussion, broken thumb, badly lacerated thigh, and a black eye. The damage was divided rather evenly between them.

The guy behind the desk when I walked into the Alhambra lobby on Sunday was named Theodore Longretti, better known on the streets as Teddy Spaghetti. Teddy is about 50, long, lean and faintly yellow from whatever it is cheap hotel clerks put into themselves to make the world think they are awake and relatively sane. Teddy's once white hair was even turning yellow again, not the yellow it might have been when and if he was a kid, but the yellow of white yarn dipped in cheap bourbon.

"Teddy," I said walking across the empty morning lobby and listening to my shoes clap the worn linoleum made to look like Spanish tiles.

"Toby?" he said, squinting through the darkness in my direction.

A desk lamp stood on the counter next to Teddy. Lights bounced off of the center making the welcoming clerk look like the skeleton of Woodrow Wilson.

"You've got a Lewis Vance, 303?" I said coming near the desk but not too close. A little of Teddy Spaghetti can go a long way. Besides he thought we were buddies.

"I've got a Lewis Vance," he admitted looking down at his open book, "and a half dozen Browns, a sprinkling of Andersons, a Kelly or two, but no Smiths. It's a fallacy that people use the name Smith when they go to a hotel. You know what I mean?"

"I know," I said.

"Even people named Smith avoid saying they're Smith. It looks too suspicious," Teddy said seriously, finally looking up from his book. "So what can I do for you?"

"Vance look kosher?"

Teddy shrugged, his yellow face moving into a thoughtful pout. "Never saw him before, but looks like a straight arrow," he said. "But I ask you, if he's so straight, what's he checking in here for?" Teddy looked around, into the dark corners, past the chipped green former palm holders. I had to admit he had a point.

"Thanks," I said and headed for the stairway.

"No trouble, Toby," he stage whispered. "I see you're packing heat. I'm in for two shifts and I don't want to identify the remains of former guests. You know what I mean?"

"I know, Teddy," I said whispering back. "The gun's just for show, to impress the client. You know what I mean?"

I patted the holster under my seersucker jacket and winked at Teddy though I doubted if he could see me.

"I know what you mean," he said and I jogged up the stairs.

The holster thumped against my chest as I went up and my back told me not to be so athletic. I slowed down and followed the trail of dimly lit landings to the third floor. Room 303 was next to Room 301 where what sounded like a child soprano was singing "Praise the Lord and Pass the Ammunition" with frequent stops for giggling. I knocked on the door of 303, adjusted my jacket, ran a hand through my hair and tried to look as if I wasn't afraid of anything less than a Panzer attack.

The guy who opened the door looked familiar, at least his outline did against the back light. He was tall, good shoulders, a full size nose and a good head of dark hair.

"Peters?" he said.

"Right," I answered. He opened the door and I walked in.

When I turned to face him, he didn't look quite so much like John Wayne as I had thought, but the resemblance was there.

Vance had a glass of amber liquid in his hand. He was wearing a weary smile and a lightweight brown suit with a white shirt and no tie. It wasn't Beverly Hills but it beat what I was wearing and he was the client.

"How about a drink?" he said holding up the glass.

"Nothing hard," I said looking around the small room, seeing nothing but shabby furniture, an open unmade Murphy bed and a dirty window.

"Coke?" he asked.

"Pepsi if you've got it," I answered sinking into the worn chair next to the splintery yellow coffee table.

"I've got it," he said moving to the dresser where a group of bottles huddled together. One, indeed, was a Pepsi. "Even got some ice."

His back was to me as he poured and started to talk. He kept talking as he turned and handed me the glass.

"Job is simple," he said. "I'm John Wayne's stand-in. Maybe you can see the resemblance."

"I can see it," I said.

"I'm doing Duke a little favor here." He went on swirling his glass and sitting across from me on a wooden chair pulled away from the spindly-legged desk in the corner. "He owes some people and they want to collect. Word's out that the Duke is registered at a downtown hotel as Lewis Vance. Meanwhile, the Duke is out calling in some loans to pay these guys off. My job, our job, is to keep them busy and away from Duke till he collects and pays them off. Don't worry about your money. We're talking big bills here. He can pay you with pocket money. No offense."

"None taken," I said, picking up the Pepsi. I wasn't offended by the money insult. It was true. It was the story that offended me. It had more holes than the U.S. Navy ships in Pearl Harbor. There were lots of possibilities here, I thought as I took a sip of the Pepsi. First, the story is true and John Wayne is dong one of the most stupid things imaginable. Second, Lewis Vance, who sat across from me watching for a reaction through dancing brown eyes, was a first-class nut who had thought this up for ends I couldn't imagine. Three, I was being set up for something though I couldn't begin to figure what that something might be. I took a deep drink of the slightly bitter Pepsi and pretended to weigh the offer. What I really wanted to do was get the hell out of this room before I found out what was going on.

I finished the Pepsi, put the glass down and stood up. Vance was bigger than me, younger too, but I was used to getting past people or keeping them from getting past me. He didn't look as if he had too much experience with either. I didn't see anything on him that looked like a gun bulge.

"I think I'll pass on this one, Mr. Vance," I said.

He stood up quickly not loosening his grip on his glass.

"Wait," he said with real panic. "I can pay whatever your fee is. Duke authorized me to pay. Cash. Just one day's work. He'll really be grateful."

"Sorry," I said. "Truth is, Mr. Vance, you don't smell right to me."

Something went dull inside my head and should have been a warning, but I've taken so many blows over the years that I tend to regard occasional aches, pains and ringing bells as natural.

"I'll prove it," Vance said holding out his free hand to get me to wait. "We'll call Duke. He'll tell you."

Maybe John Wayne had gone mush-headed. My head certainly wasn't feeling too good. Maybe the 48 hours straight in Goleta and the drive back was getting to me.

"Make the call," I said. Hell, I needed the money.

"Fine," he said with a smile, his hand still out. "Just sit down again and I'll get him."

I sat down again. Actually, I fell backwards.

"Fine," I repeated.

Vance walked slowly to the phone on the desk, his eyes on me all the time as if to keep me from moving. My upper lip felt numb and my eyes didn't want to stay open, but I forced them to as Vance slowly, very slowly made his call or pretended to. I was rapidly losing my grip on the room and the situation.

"Right," Vance said. He kept looking at me and nodding his head. "Right. Mr. Peters is right here and he wants to talk to you."

Vance was looking at me now with a triumphant and mean little grin. He held out the phone.

"It's the Duke," he said. "He wants to talk to you. All you have to do is walk over here and take the phone."

I tried to get up, but it couldn't be done. It was at that point, long after a lobotomized chimp would have figured it out, that I knew I had been slipped something in my Pepsi. I could but hope that it wasn't lethal as I gave up, sank back and closed my eyes.

It rained while I was asleep. I don't know how I knew it while clowns danced before me, but I knew it and it was confirmed when I woke up with John Wayne, the real John Wayne, holding my gun on me. I looked at the single window and watched the downpour splatter and ask to come in.

"Water," I said.

"That it is, Pilgrim," he agreed, the gun steady and level.

"No, need water," I said pointing to my tongue.

He nodded, understanding and pointed to the sink in the corner. I made three tries at getting up and succeeded on the fourth. I staggered to the sink, turned on the tap and looked down at the brown stain near the drain. The stain looked a little like the state of Nevada. I put my head under the warm water, cupped my hand and sloshed liquid into my mouth and over my inflated tongue. The tongue deflated slightly and, using the sink for support, I turned around.

Beyond Wayne, who looked at me with his forehead furrowed in curiosity, the Murphy bed stood open and on it lay the former Lewis Vance. He was definitely not asleep, not with that hole through his forehead.

I must have looked sick, surprised or bewildered.

"You did that?" Wayne said pointing his gun at the corpse.

"No," I said as emphatically as I could. I even shook my head which was one hell of a mistake. The red cotton candy inside my skull turned to liquid and threatened to come out of every available opening.

Slowly, painfully, I told my tale. The call, the offer from Vance, the drugged Pepsi. Wayne listened, nodding once in a while.

"And," I concluded, "I've got a feeling that hole in Vance's face came from a bullet in my gun, the one in your hand, the one with your fingerprints on it."

Wayne looked at the gun, shrugged and said, "Supposing I believe you. Where do we go now?"

First I asked him why he was in the room, holding my gun.

"Got a call," he said, gun still on me though he looked over at the corpse from time to time. "Man said I should get over here fast, a friend of mine named Dick Lang had taken an overdose of something. I came fast and walked in to find you out with the gun in your hand and your friend Vance. He's never been my stand-in. I don't owe anyone any money and no one is looking for me. I was planning on going to a party at C.B. DeMille's to celebrate the finish of *Reap the Wild Wind* when the call came. I don't think old C.B. is going to be too happy that I didn't come. Won't surprise me if I've worked for him for the last time."

The rain got louder and the day darker.

"Why should I believe you Peters?"

"When you were a kid you used to go in the driveway of Pevsner's grocery store in Glendale," I said making my way back to the chair and dropping into it. "About two blocks from your dad's drug store. You used to go to that driveway and throw a ball against the wooden wall. You did that for about two weeks till Pevsner's son came out and hit you in the head."

Wayne's mouth opened slightly and his hand went up to his head, a spot right behind the ear.

"That was you?" he said.

"My brother Phil," I said. "He's a Los Angeles cop now."

I figured Wayne was about 35 or 36 now, but there was still a little of that kid in him.

"I thought you said your name was Peters?" Wayne said suspiciously.

"Professional change," I said. "I thought your name was Marion Morrison?"

"You made your point," he agreed. "But knowing your brother

beat me up when I was a kid doesn't exactly prove you didn't shoot that fella over there."

I got out of the chair again and started to stagger around the room in the hope of clearing my head and returning my agonized body to its former, familiar level of constant ache.

"Let's go over it," I said, looking at Vance. "Someone wanted me here. Vance or someone else. Let's figure the idea was to set me up for Vance's murder. Vance thought it was for something else. Who knows what? He put me out with the drink and our killer steps in, takes my gun and punctuates Vance."

"And then," Wayne interrupted, "the killer calls me and I come over and step into it. Publicity could ruin the DeMille picture and maybe my career. Could be we're dealing with an old enemy of mine."

"Could be we're dealing with an old enemy of both of us," I said. "The only one I can think of is my brother Phil and I doubt if he'd go this far to get either one of us. Maybe it's a blackmail deal. The phone will ring and we'll get . . . No. It would have happened by now. It's a frame-up, simple and dirty."

"Let's try it another way," Wayne said furrowing his brow. "Fella over there puts something in your drink. You feel you're going out, get out the gun, put some holes in him and pass out. I come in, find the gun in your hand and. . . "

"Who called you?" I said. My mind was starting to work again, not as well as I would have liked, but that's what I feel even if I haven't had a boiled Pepsi.

"Beats me, Pilgrim," Wayne shrugged.

The knock at the door cut off our further exploration of possibilities. We looked at each other and he delegated me with a wave of the .38 to be the door opener. I opened the door. The woman standing there was more than 30 and less than 50 but that was about the best I could do with her age. She had a body that could pass for 25. Her hair was red and frilly. So was her tight dress.

She looked at me, at Wayne—who she didn't seem to recognize—and over at Vance on the bed who had his head turned away.

"You didn't say anything about three," she said. "Three is more."

She stepped in, looked at Wayne and added appreciatively, "Maybe not much more." He had pocketed the gun in his windbreaker and was looking at me for an explanation.

"What did I say?" I said. "On the phone."

She stepped in, put her small red handbag on the yellow table next to my lethal Pepsi and looked at me as if I had a few beans loose, which I did.

"You said ten in the night," she said looking now at the body of Vance with the first hint of awareness. "It's ten and here I am." Then she turned to Wayne, looked at him enough to get him to look away and added, "You really are Randolph Scott."

"John Wayne," I said.

"Right," she said with a snap of the fingers. "That's what you said, John Wayne." Her eyes stayed on Wayne who gave me a sigh of exasperation and said,

"Thanks for clearing it up for the lady, Peters. I wouldn't want her to forget who she met here."

She took a few steps of curiosity toward the Murphy bed and Vance and I eased over as fast as my retread legs would let me to cut her off.

"Are you sure it was me on the phone?" I said, putting my face in front of hers.

"You don't know if you called me?" she said trying to look over my shoulder at Vance. "Voice on a phone is all I know. You trying to back out of this? And what's with the guy on the bed?"

Wayne was leaning against the wall now, his arms folded, watching. He wasn't going to give me any help.

"We're not backing out," I said. "You'll get paid, Miss. . ."

"Olivia Fontaine," she said.

"Classy," I said.

"Thanks," she answered with a smile that faded fast. "That guy on the bed. Is he hurt or something?"

"Or something," I said.

"He's dead, lady," Wayne said pushing away from the wall. "And we're going to call the police."

"Dead?" she repeated and backed away from me. "I don't want no part of 'dead,'" she said, looking for something, spotted her red bag and clacked her red high heels toward it.

"You're going to have to stay awhile, ma'm," Wayne said, stepping in front of the door. "I don't like this much, but you walk out of here and that's one more complication that has to be unwound."

"You didn't talk like that to Claire Trevor in *Stagecoach*," Olivia Fontaine said with her hands on her hips. "She was a hooker and you was . . . were nice to her, for Chrissake."

"That was a movie, lady," Wayne said.

"Me, other girls I know, love that movie," she said forgetting for a second the corpse on the bed. "I saw it five times. Hooker goes riding off with you at the end to a new life, ranch or something. Only thing is I thought you were Randolph Scott."

This knock at the door was louder than Olivia's. It was the one-two knock of someone who is used to knocking at hotel room doors . . .

Olivia, Wayne and I looked at each other. Then Wayne nodded at me.

"Who is it?" I asked.

"Hotel detective," came a familiar voice. "Got a call to come up here."

Wayne shrugged, Olivia looked for someplace to hide, found nothing and sat in the chair I had recently passed out in. I opened the door and he came in. He was Merit Beeson, 60, a massive white-haired man who had once been shot by a Singapore sailor. The shot had hit him in the neck and when it was clear he would survive, it also became clear that he would never be able to turn his neck again. Hence Merit Beeson became known as Straight-Ahead

Beeson. The stiff neck lost him his job as a Los Angeles cop but it gave him a strange dignity which got him steady if not high-paying work in hotels. Straight-Ahead looked like a no-nonsense guy, a stand-up almost British butler in appearance with strong ham arms and a craggy face. His suit was always pressed and he always wore a tie. Straight-Ahead avoided a lot of trouble just by looking impressive, but he wasn't going to be able to avoid this one.

He took it all in fast, Olivia, me, Wayne and the body.

"You know the guy on the bed, Merit?" I said.

He stepped into the room, closed the door behind him and looked at me carefully.

"Before we talk," he said without turning his body to John Wayne which would have been the only way to acknowledge the actor, "I want the cowboy to ease the radiator out of his pocket and put it nice and gentle on the dresser. You think we can arrange it?"

Wayne took the gun out and did just what Straight-Ahead wanted.

"Good start," Beeson said, though he hadn't turned to watch. In the thirty years he had looked straight ahead, he had developed great peripheral vision. "I've seen the gent staining the Murphy around the lobby now and then. Gave him a light rousting. Mean customer. Threatened to cut up Merit Beeson. Can you imagine that, Toby?"

"Can't imagine it, Merit," I said shaking my head for both of us. Something he said hit me gently and whispered back that I should remember it.

"You or the cowboy or the lady shoot him?" Merit said.

"None of us," I answered.

"Speak for yourself," Olivia said jumping up. "I didn't shoot him is all I know."

"Sal," Beeson said, his body moving toward the corpse, "I thought you agreed to stay out of the Alhambra after the unfortunate incident of the trollop and the ensign. You recall that tale?"

"I recall," she said. "I'm not Sal anymore. I'm Olivia, Olivia Fontaine."

Straight-Ahead was leaning forward over the bed in that awkward stiff-back way he had. When Merit moved, people watched.

"And I am now General Douglas MacArthur," he sighed touching the body carefully. "The former Mr. Vance has been with his maker for maybe five hours. That how you peg it Toby?"

"'Bout that, Merit," I agreed.

He stood up, pushing his bulk from the bed with dignity. The springs squealed and the body of Lewis Vance bounced slightly.

"And what do we do now?" he said.

"We call the police," said Wayne.

"That the way you want it?" Beeson said.

"No," Wayne admitted, stepping forward. "It's not the way I want it, but it's the way it has to be, isn't it?" He pointed at the bed and said, "We've got a murdered man here."

"Not the first in the Alhambra," Straight-Ahead said. He now had his hands folded over his belly like a satisfied Sunday School teacher. "You even had one the last time you filled in for me if my memory serves me, right Toby?"

"You've got it, Merit," I agreed. "Salesman in 512, but it was suicide, not murder."

"Not that time," he agreed. "not that time." Then to Wayne, "No, you see Mr. Wayne, hotels usually don't like to promote the number of people who get killed within them. It's not like they keep charts and compete with each other because it will bring in new trade. No, we usually do our best to keep such things from the attention of the populace."

I explained, "It is not unheard of for a corpse to be carted off to some alley by a house dick."

Wayne shook his head and looked at us as if he had been trapped in a room with the incurably insane.

"You mean you're suggesting that we just take . . ."

"Vance," I supplied, "Lewis Vance."

"Right, Vance," Wayne said. "that we take Vance and dump him in some alley and walk away?"

"No," I said emphatically.

"Of course not," Straight-Ahead concurred. "Too many people involved now and you're too big a name. Sal . . ."

"Olivia," she corrected from her chair as she reached for my unfinished Pepsi.

"Olivia," Merit said, "would be happy to walk away and forget it. Toby knows the routine. He'd walk in a twinkling."

I nodded agreement and reached Olivia just as she was bringing the glass to her mouth. I took it from her. She gave me a dirty look but I weathered it and put the flat, warm drink on the dresser near the gun.

"So," Wayne said. "What now?"

"We get the killer in here and try to work something out," I said.

"That's the way of it," Straight-Ahead agreed.

"But we don't know who killed him," Wayne said, running his hand through his hair.

"Sure we do," said Straight-Ahead looking straight ahead at Wayne.

"We do now," I agreed. Olivia didn't give a damn.

I moved to the telephone, picked it up and dialed a number.

"The who of it is easy," said Merit, unfolding his hands and scratching his white mane. It didn't do his image much good but his head clearly itched. "It's the why we have to figure. Then we'll know what to do."

The killer answered the phone on the third ring and I said, "Get up to 303 fast." I hung up.

The rain took this pause in the conversation to get really mad and start rocking the window in its loose fitting. It rocked and rattled and said bad things while we waited.

"Can I go?" Sally Olivia asked Merit.

"Let's all just stay cosy till we wind it up," Merit said. "That's how you put it in the movies, right?"

"Wrap it up," Wayne volunteered with a sigh. "Call it a wrap."

Straight-Ahead nodded and filed that information for future use.

"You think he might skip?" I asked.

"Human nature is a fickle thing, Toby," Straight-Ahead said now facing the door, "a fickle thing. He might skip, it's true, but where's he to go? And going will be a confession. No, he'll bluff it out or try. Besides, he doesn't yet know that we know."

"That's the way I see it," I agreed.

Wayne and Olivia looked at each other for an answer, got none and joined Straight-Ahead in looking at the door and listening to the rain and the rattling window. I glanced at Lewis Vance's body trying not to be angry about what he had done to my head and gotten me into. Then the knock came, almost unheard under the noise of the rain.

"Come right in," Merit shouted.

A key turned in the lock and the door opened to reveal Theodore Longretti. He stepped in, eyes darting around and closed the door behind him.

"What is this all about?" he said, his eyes finding John Wayne and fixing on him.

"Murder," I said. "Over on the bed."

Teddy Spaghetti turned his long, yellow face to the bed and registered fake surprise.

"He's dead?" he said.

"You ought to know," I said. "You put the bullet in him with my gun." I nodded toward the dresser and Teddy's eyes followed me.

"Me?" he said, pointing to his thin chest and looking around at each of us for a touch of support, a sign of realization that it was too absurd to consider the possibility of his having killed anyone.

"You," I said.

"I'm calling the police," Teddy said stepping toward the phone. I stepped in front of him.

"Let's just work it through," Straight-Ahead said, turning

slowly to look at us. "Then we'll decide what to do about it. Give it
to him, Toby."

I stepped away from Teddy knowing I had his attention and
that of everyone else in the room. I eased back to the metal railing
of the Murphy bed.

"Number one, Vance has been seen hanging around the
lobby," I began. "Which means you knew him. But you told me
you'd never seen him before."

"I knew him, but . . ." Teddy began looking around the
group for support. All he got was distant curiosity.

"I get a call on a Sunday to come to a room in this hotel, your
hotel, while you are on the desk. You know me. You know Vance.
Nothing tight here yet, but it's adding up. You following me?"

"Toby . . ." Teddy started but he was stopped by Straight-
Ahead who put his finger to his ample lips and said, "Shhhhhh."

"Then Sal . . . Pardon me, Olivia shows up. Someone
called her. Someone who knows she is for rent. You know Olivia,
don't you Teddy?"

He looked at her and she looked back at him.

"I've seen her," he said. "I've seen lots of whores."

"Seen is right," she said disdainfully. "Just seen."

"I've done plenty," Teddy said standing straight and thin.

"We're not questioning your manhood," Merit said. "We're
trying to clean a dirty room. Hush it now."

"Then John Wayne gets a call," I said.

Teddy looked at John Wayne, who nodded.

"And finally, Merit gets a call to come up here," I went on.
"Seems to me whoever did the dialing knew a lot about who was
coming and going not just to the Alhambra but Room 303. You
follow my reasoning?"

"No," Teddy said stubbornly.

"We could be wrong," Straight-Ahead said.

"We could be," I agreed.

"But we're not," Straight-Ahead added.

"We're not," I agreed again.

"Hold it just a minute here," John Wayne said, shaking his head. "You mean this fella here set this all up, killed that fella on the bed, fixed it so it would look like you did it and fixed it so I'd be found here with the corpse, you and . . . the lady."

"Looks that way to me," I said.

"What in the name of God for?" Wayne asked reasonably.

"You want to answer that one, Teddy?" I asked as if I knew the answer but was willing to give up the stage to let the supporting cast take over. I had tried to set it up this way with Merit's help and the moment of truth or lies had come. All Teddy had to do was keep his mouth shut and we'd be stuck with having to make a decision. There was about enough evidence to nail him on a murder charge as there was to get Tojo to give up by midnight. A little digging might put him in the bag but a little digging would mean enough time for the newspapers to make John Wayne and the Alhambra big news. That gave me an idea.

"Publicity," I prompted. "You want to talk about publicity, Teddy?"

Teddy didn't want to talk about anything. He looked as if he were in a voodoo trance, his face almost orange as the thunder cracked outside.

"Teddy," Merit prompted. "I've got work to do and no one is on the desk downstairs."

Teddy shook himself or rather a wave or chill went through him.

"It got all crazy," he said. "I'll tell you it got all crazy."

Olivia sighed loudly to let us know she had no interest in hearing Teddy tell it, but she had no choice.

"I didn't plan on killing him, you see," Teddy said, playing with his shirt front and looking down. "Idea of it was to get you here, Toby, put you out or something, get Wayne in and then Sally and have Merit walk in on it. Idea was to give the *Times* a tip about a love nest thing at the Alhambra, have a photographer and reporter maybe right behind. You'd confirm the whole thing and. . . ."

"That was one hell of a stupid idea," Olivia said angrily from the chair.

Teddy shrugged. It hadn't worked out the way he planned.

"Idea was publicity," he whispered to his shirt.

"That John Wayne was making it with a prostitute in your hotel?"

"You think the Alhambra is such a hot-shot address?" Teddy came back defensively with a little animation. "Kind of people we got coming it could be a real attraction, you know what I mean? Idea was to set something up like this with a whole bunch of movie people, you know, real he-man types, Wild Bill Elliott, Alan Ladd, you know."

"And then the girls would be kicking back a few bucks to you just to work the rooms," Straight-Ahead said.

"Never thought of that," said Teddy, who had evidently considered just that. "But it was the publicity. Rooms aren't going as good as they should. Management needs it at seventy-eight percent or they'll sell and I'll lose my job."

"Hold it," John Wayne pitched in. He walked over to Teddy who shrank back, almost flopping like a dry noodle over the coffee table. "This is one hell of a harebrained scheme, Pilgrim, and I've got a mind to snap a few pieces off of you, but I want to know why you shot that man."

Teddy was still backing away from Wayne toward the wall. He almost stumbled over Olivia's stretched-out legs but she pulled them in just in time.

"An accident," Teddy said. "An accident. Vance called me, said Toby had passed out. I had already made the calls to Sally and Wayne, got his phone number from a friend at Republic. Vance called me up, said he wanted more than the ten bucks I promised him, wanted in on whatever I was doing. I told him I didn't have more than ten bucks to give him, that there might be more money later, but he wouldn't listen. It was not a good situation."

"Not a good situation at all," Straight-Ahead agreed, turning toward him. "So you took Toby's gun and shot Lewis Vance between the eyes."

"He threatened to beat me up, kill me," Teddy whined. "It was self-defense."

"That's the story I'd tell," I agreed.

"It's the truth," Teddy squealed, bumping into the wall with Wayne advancing. I realized what was coming but I couldn't stop it. It should have been plain to a room in which half the living people were detectives, but it wasn't. Teddy reached up in the dresser at his elbow and came down with my .38 in his right hand. It reached out at the end of his spindly arm and pointed at the stomach of John Wayne who stopped abruptly and put up his hands.

"You are making me mad, mister," Wayne said through his teeth but he took a step backward.

"Teddy, Teddy, Teddy," I said shaking my head. "You are not going to shoot all four of us. Put the gun down and let's talk."

I could see no good reason why he wouldn't shoot all four of us but I hoped that the prospect of mowing down citizens would not appeal to the shaking desk clerk whose experience in mayhem, as far as I knew, had been limited to one unfortunate scrape a few hours earlier with an apparently unpleasant third-rate bully. "Think of the publicity."

He thought of the publicity and his mouth went dry. He reached over and took a sip of the flat Pepsi to moisten it. I didn't stop him. No one moved. We just watched him and hoped he would down the whole thing.

"Five bodies in one room, one a famous actor," Straight-Ahead chimed in. "The Alhambra might have a hell of a time surviving that."

"I can shoot you and get away," Teddy reasoned. He took another drink.

"Never get away with it," I said. People always said that in situations like this. My experience was that they very often did get away with it, but you don't tell things like that to killers holding guns. You just hoped they saw the same movies and listened to the same radio shows you did. The room suddenly went quiet. The rain had stopped.

Teddy blinked his eyes and looked at us. I couldn't tell whether he was considering who to shoot first or was realizing that he couldn't pull the trigger. I never got the chance to ask him.

"I've had just about enough," Wayne said and took a step, the final step, forward. Teddy, already a little drowsy from the drink, moved his gun-holding hand and fired. It missed Wayne, breezed past me and shattered the window, letting in a rush of rain-smelling air. Wayne's punch slammed Teddy against the wall. The gun fell, hit the floor, bounced a few times and rested.

Olivia screamed and Straight-Ahead walked slowly straight ahead toward the slumped figure. Wayne, fists still clenched, stepped back to let the house detective take over. It was a show and a half to see Merit get to his knee, lift the now silent desk clerk up and deposit him on the chair near the desk.

"Let's go," I said exchanging a look of understanding with Merit when he turned around.

"Go?" asked Wayne, his dark hair over his forehead. "What are you talking about? This man killed that man and we . . ."

"Can go," I said.

Olivia didn't need persuading. She grabbed her red bag and headed for the door.

"You've never been in this room," Straight-Ahead said to her.

"I've never been in this hotel," she answered. "Nice to meet you, John." And out she went.

"Merit will work a deal with Teddy," I explained to the bewildered Wayne. "Teddy says he shot Vance in self-defense and no one else was around. Merit backs him up. Story's over. Teddy doesn't want it that way. Merit calls him a liar trying to save his skin but that won't happen. Teddy will back it up and you're out of it."

"With some embellishments, that's the way it really was," Merit said looking at Teddy.

"It's. . . ." John Wayne began.

"Not like the movies," I finished. "Not this time, anyway. The rain's stopped. You want to stop for a cup of coffee?"

"I guess," said Wayne, shaking his head. "It's too late for DeMille's party." He took a last look at the corpse on the bed and the scrawny killer in the chair. The Ringo Kid wouldn't have handled it like this, but what the hell. He looked at Straight-Ahead who said, "Go on. It's my job."

Wayne nodded and went into the hall after I said, "I'll be right there."

Teddy was showing no signs of waking up.

"The gun," I said.

"The gun," Merit repeated giving up on a revival of Teddy Spaghetti in the near future. "We say you left it here for Teddy. Protection. He was threatened by all kinds. That sort of thing. It'll hold up."

"It'll shake a lot," I said, "but it'll hold. Take care."

A breeze from the broken window swirled around the room as Straight-Ahead waved his arm at me and sat slowly in the overstuffed chair to wait for Teddy to wake up. I closed the door quietly and joined John Wayne in the hall.

"This happen to you a lot?" he said as we got onto the elevator.

"When things are going well," I said. "Only when things are going well."

My head began to ache again and I longed for a plate of tacos from Manny's a few blocks away. I wondered if I could talk Wayne into a trip to Manny's.

# The Rat Line

## Rob Kantner

*Every mystery buff knows that the work done by real-life
private detectives bears little (if any) resemblance to that
done by their fictional counterparts.*

*Despite this—and, possibly, because of it—I try to
place Ben Perkins firmly in a world of work, bills, family,
obligations; just like the rest of us.*

*But if all fictional detectives (including Perkins)
operated the same way as real ones, the genre would not remain
the enduring one it is. The Rat Line is an example of how a
mundane, real-life type case turns into something very
different—and, in addition, shows how a crime,
even a very old one, never dies.*

IT sounded like a regular old adultery investigation, except for one thing.

"He's *how* old?" I asked, startled.

"D. P. Charlie? Oh, lots younger than me," my Uncle Dan replied, shifting his thin, withered frame under the sheets. "Late seventies."

"And his wife thinks he's having an affair," I prodded skeptically.

"That's what Peggy told me." Uncle Dan clasped his white skeletal hands together behind his bald head, making his hospital gown tighten around his thin shoulders. "I told her my nephew was in the investigating business. I said you'd check it out for her."

Normally I don't like being volunteered for things, but this was Uncle Dan asking. I scratched my head and sat down clumsily in a cheap plastic chair next to his bed. I wanted a cigar, but the nice folks at Wayne County General Hospital would get unnice in a hurry if I lighted up. I asked, "You known these people long?"

Uncle Dan's crystal clear blue eyes glinted with humor. "At my age, I've known *everyone* long. D. P. Charlie and I worked together on the Rouge line. We were neighbors in Detroit, lived a block apart. They moved to east Dearborn back in nineteen sixty something." His offhand attitude toward the passing of years was understandable; Uncle Dan was my age in 1937.

"Charlie Steel," I muttered. "What's the 'D. P.' mean?"

"Oh, just a nickname. Stands for Displaced Person. He was a refugee from Poland or somewhere, emigrated here after the war."

I sighed. Not that I'm particularly picky about the jobs I take on, but this one sounded like a dead snore. I said to my uncle, "So she thinks he's sleeping out on her. Doesn't this strike you as a little, uh, eccentric?"

"No," Uncle Dan said from his hospital bed.

"I personally don't buy it."

"You personally are forever telling me how slow the investigating business is. You personally are forever telling me how broke you are. Peggy Steel has money and this problem, and I promised her you'd look into it."

I'd do anything for Uncle Dan, and he knew it. Plus he was bang-on right about my financial situation. I don't earn money, I rent it.

"Well," I snorted, "it'll be like shooting fish in a barrel, but sure, I'll check into it. What's their address?"

\* \* \*

They built lots and lots of these boxy little cookie-cutter homes in east Dearborn right after the war. The Steels' tiny two-bedroom had the looks of a place that had been inhabited by the same people for many years. Trim little patch of lawn, little shrubs carved into various geometric shapes, blankets of gaily colored flowers, a birdbath, a plastic ostrich, dwarf fruit trees. Every square inch of landscape had been attended to by people who obviously had plenty of time to do it.

Mrs. Steel answered the door, let me in, and wobbled away toward the bathroom after inviting me to sit. When she returned, her dentures were back in her mouth. Peggy Steel was a short, round woman who'd fought the fat fight for fifty years and then said to hell with it, I'm pushing eighty and I like to eat. Her smooth skin hadn't seen sun in a quarter century. She wore a tight reddish wig, lots of rings on her plump little hands, a pink-flowered house dress and pink 29-cent thongs. Despite her age, she looked alert and moved well and probably still clogged up traffic on Michigan Avenue from behind the wheel of the sky-blue '65 Ford Fairlane which sat in the driveway outside.

She snapped off the game show on the gigantic color TV set, sat with a sigh in a big overstuffed swivel chair in the corner beneath a framed needlepoint hanging on the wall which declared that the occupants of this home wanted to live by the side of the road and be a friend to man, and smiled nervously. "So you're Benjy. Dan's told us so much about you."

I don't hear my childhood nickname that much anymore. I said courteously, "Ben Perkins, ma'am. Nice meeting you too."

She nodded, smile fixed, not knowing where to start.

The small house tocked with the sound of a dozen clocks. It had the old-house smell of old folks and old furniture and recently cooked food, and each piece of furniture, each picture, each knick-knack was put precisely into place.

I said, "Listen, I know this isn't easy. Let me start. You told Uncle Dan that Mr. Steel has been acting strangely. You think he might be seeing another woman." I delivered the line straight and was quite proud of myself. "What is he doing that makes you believe that's the case?"

She sniffed, eyes fluttering, cleared her throat, and said, "It's—a lot of it is instinct, I suppose. When you've known a man for many many years, you develop an instinct."

"Uh-huh. Let's get to that in a minute. What specifically is he doing?"

She breathed deeply. "Charles is retired, as you probably know. He's not as active as he once was. He spends his days on the lawn and the garden or here, watching the TV. We don't get out much. Charles tires easily, his leg is bad, he's got the sciatica and has to walk with a cane, but he can still drive. But he doesn't leave home much except to go to the market with me. Until late last week."

In the pause, I studied her. She was staring down at her white knees half-covered by the pink house dress. I asked quietly, "What happened?"

She looked up suddenly. "He began going out. Walking. He's spent several afternoons away from home. He was late for supper last night. He's out right now, God knows where."

"You ask him where he's going?"

"I haven't asked," she answered with some pride. "He's told me he's going to the main library over on Michigan. That's ten blocks from here. He goes to read, he says." She leaned forward, staring intently at me through unaged eyes. "Benjy, my husband has never been a reader. His eyes are bad anyhow, it's all he can do to get through the sports pages."

"Mm-hm," I nodded judiciously. Suspicious as hell, all right. "What makes you think it's a woman?"

"Well, I'll tell you. He's gotten very quiet these past few days. But inside he's very excited. He moves around in his sleep at night and mutters nonsense words in a jolly voice. He stares off into space while we eat, God knows what he's thinking.

"*I* think it's a woman. After all these years, *that's* what I think.

Why else walk? Why not take the car? He doesn't want the car spotted by somebody, that's why. Maybe she's married too. He just walks out of the house and up the street and vanishes for hours." She leaned back, burst of energy dissipated, facial skin sagging. "I just want to know," she said plaintively.

A long, long silence. I rubbed my forehead with my fingertips and said, finally, "Well, I look into these things on a pretty regular basis. I'll say to you what I say to everyone who wants to hire me to do this. That is: before you turn me loose, make sure you really want to know. Decide right now what you'll do if the answer I get for you is the worst one. Because I can get the answer, but then you're the one who's going to have to deal with it."

Her stare was on her lap again. "I'll just talk to him, that's all," she whispered. "But I have to know."

My feeling is, you get enough bad news on a regular basis, why go pay somebody to bring you more? But people pay me to do, not to think. I asked her a few more questions and didn't learn anything new. We settled the money part—I violated normal custom and didn't get an advance—and I left after promising her a report in a couple of days.

D. P. Charlie didn't go for a stroll the next day, causing me to spend an incredibly boring afternoon sitting in my '71 Mustang half a block down from his house, watching, wasting time. The next day, though, he set off alone on foot.

It wasn't exactly the chase scene out of *The French Connection*, though.

D. P. Charlie hobbled out of the house and headed up the sidewalk. He was a short stocky man, obviously powerfully built once, big-knuckled hand tight on the cane he used to help his right leg. He wore a white shirt, dark pants, heavy black work shoes. He still had a lot of hair and it was bristly, snow white, trimmed in a military cut. He didn't go fast. He couldn't have herded turtles. I felt silly in my Mustang with the hot 302 motor, three-quarter cam, four-barrel carb and Hurst shifter, getting ready to trail a man who'd have lost a one-on-one race with a tree.

I thought about dumping the car and following on foot, but I'm a Detroit boy, I like wheels under me. I let him get a full block's lead, then fired up the motor and rolled up the street after him and past him and took up watch in the following block. We played leapfrog like that for about half an hour till he got to Michigan Avenue. There he stood at the corner, cane gripped in both hands propping him up, till a SEMTA bus came, which he boarded.

Forget the library then. It was only three blocks away now, he could have walked it and maybe gotten there by the end of the month. I blew the stop sign at the corner, cut off the onrush of westbound traffic with a cheerful wave of the middle digit, and followed the bus up Michigan, glad to be out of first gear. We passed the main part of downtown and went a couple of blocks with me snuggled up to the back end of the bus, inhaling diesel.

The bus stopped and D. P. Charlie got out. He hobbled north away from Michigan past a row of old dirty brick buildings, then went into the Q Room. I parked at the curb a half block up and followed him inside.

Despite the name, the Q Room isn't a gay joint, not in Dearborn, Michigan, no sir. It's a pool hall and gin joint and a neighborhood hangout that was old when the first Model T parked there. It was jammed, even that early in the day. I cruised up to the bar and ordered a beer when I had a chance, eyes casually on old D. P. Charlie, who headed back to the tables.

There were four of them, all in use. Cues thwacked, balls clattered, men called their shots, talked and laughed and occasionally shouted. The noise from the patrons and the juke was deafening. D. P. watched the play, standing quietly against the wall. Then a table cleared and he got a cue. A thin, intense young man, wearing a dress shirt and slacks and no tie, got a cue also and the two of them began playing and talking.

They played several games, badly, and talked all the while. I couldn't hear what they were talking about and didn't see any need to. D. P. didn't drink, didn't ogle the barmaids, didn't do anything but shoot pool badly and talk to the young fella and smile a lot and have a wonderful time. I was disgusted, not with him at all, but with the whole thing. I was wasting a tired old woman's money. I paid my bill and left.

"He doesn't play pool," Mrs. Steel said tersely on the phone.

"Not too well, anyhow," I allowed.

"I've known Charles better than thirty years," she insisted. "He's never played pool." She spaced the words out as if I was hard of hearing.

"Mrs. Steel," I said, "maybe not, but that's what he's doing. I followed him yesterday and today. He's getting out and having a little harmless fun. Nothing wrong with that. Fact, there's a lot right with it."

"What's *not* right," she said, voice rasping, "is that he's not being truthful with me about where he's going."

I said respectfully, "Well, ma'am, now you know. There's no more to it than that."

A pause, then a sigh. "Very well. I'll mail you a check, Mister Perkins."

At least she'd quit calling me Benjy.

I was more than mildly surprised when Dick Dennehy, an inspector with the Office of Special Investigations of the Michigan State Police, appeared on the barstool next to mine that night at Under New Management, my favorite dark dingy little drinking hangout.

He was a tall, half-out-of-shape, square-faced blond. His aviator glasses glinted as he grinned at me and ordered a beer from Bill. I said, "Long way from Lansing just to have a beer."

He grinned and lighted a Lucky straight-end, pulling the smoke knee-deep. "Came looking for you, buddy."

"Oh yeah?" Dick's okay but not exactly a pal, and he's usually only where trouble is. "Got a knotty investigative problem you need a hand on?"

"Yeah, right." He grinned sarcastically, picked up his beer, and swigged. "No actually, I'm a message boy this time."

"Ooh." My mind automatically flashed through my recent activities. No guilty conscience. No little nags and tugs and worries. Unless, of course, he was doing free-lance collecting for Master Card. "So what is it?"

Dennehy's beer was half gone. He inhaled on his cigarette and let the smoke wander out of his mouth as he talked. "I got this because I know you and I'm here to give you a friendly word."

This was starting to smell real bad. "Yeah?"

He looked at me square-on. "Charles Steel," he said.

"Huh? Who?" I asked, startled.

"Lay off him," Dick said.

"Never met the man in my life," I said truthfully. Why in the hell would the Michigan State Police be interested in an old wheeze like D. P. Charlie?

Dick Dennehy squinted. "Don't argue with me, 'cause there's no point, I don't know what the story is, I really don't. This word comes from real top-siders, folks who get their way, period. Lay off Charles Steel. Roger?"

I answered evenly, "You can tell them, 'Message received.'"

The policeman loosened a little bit. "Take my word, Ben. Get the arch out of your back and I mean right now. Whatever's going on, back offa it."

"Message received," I answered, softer.

Dick Dennehy tossed some coins on the bar, slid off the stool and pushed his way out.

I'd received Peggy Steel's check that morning, and it was cashed and gone. But she was still my client, and so in a more fundamental way was my Uncle Dan, and besides, once you let someone strongarm you and get away with it, they get in the habit of doing it over and over and over again.

The next day I got on D. P. Charlie's trail again.
Same deal. Walked up to Michigan Avenue, took the bus

through town and went into the Q Room. Played pool and chatted with the same thin young man he'd talked to the other days. I found this interesting. The man looked like a professional, neatly dressed and groomed and apparently friendly. I wondered who he was, and what he was doing in a place like the Q Room, and, most important, why he spent so much time talking to D. P. Charlie. I didn't get any answers, though, and couldn't without getting too close. And I didn't feel like doing that yet.

The next day was Friday. Hot and miserable, ninety-five plus temp, ninety-plus humidity, naked uncaring sun staring down baking everything. Some folks don't think we ever swelter in Michigan, but we do, we do. I followed D. P. Charlie's bus up Michigan again, parked, and strolled after him into the Q Room.

It was jammed. Friday: payday for the assembly line workers out of the Rouge, the Clark Street Cadillac plant, Wayne Assembly, Michigan Truck and Detroit Diesel Allison. Afternoon shift guys were loading up prior to going on shift; graveyard guys were hanging around soaking up brew and fun prior to going to their complaining wives and sweltering homes.

D. P. hobbled back to the pool area, as usual. I took up position at the bar, as usual. D. P. began shooting pool with his friend. I noticed several other youngish men entertaining themselves at the tables—men dressed like D. P.'s friend, but paying no attention to anyone else.

This time, by God, I was going to eavesdrop a bit. I drifted over toward the pool tables and spotted a row of video arcade games against the wall. Wonderful. I don't like the dumb things—I prefer more athletic pursuits, like poker—but no one was dealing cards in the Q Room. I fished a handful of quarters out of my pocket and cruised up to a game called Mister Do and began "playing."

It took me a buck and a half to figure out the point of the game. From that point on I'd have been bored if I hadn't been doing something else—mainly listening to D. P. Charlie talk in his gravelly voice.

I could only get snatches of his words what with the noise of my game, the jukebox and the general commotion, but I gathered that they were reminiscing about the war. I heard reference to Germany and France, Belgium and the Russians. I could make no sense out of it.

After about an hour I heard D. P.'s friend say casually, "Hey, Charlie, how about it, I gotta go, okay?"

They stepped away from the table and other players swooped in to take over. I pretended to rattle the coin return on Mister Do and listened intently. D. P. said, sounding disappointed, "Okay, Paul, guess I'll head on home too."

"Listen, D. P.," the young man named Paul said, "How about I drop you off? You don't wanna walk all the way back there. My car's just outside. Okay?"

D. P. slapped his friend on the back with a hamlike hand. "That's kind of you. Very kind of you." He thumped his cane on the floor as they started toward the front door.

I pushed off from the game, walked as quickly as I could through the mob, and beat the pair to the door, mainly because D. P. Charlie was so slow. My car was about three spaces down at the curb and hotter than hell inside. I fired up the engine and waited for the men to emerge.

Before that happened, a black Buick Regal sedan pulled up to the entrance of the Q Room and stopped, engine running.

Then D. P. Charlie and Paul came out the door and down the steps, clumsily.

And three of the other young well-dressed men came out after them, fanning out to herd D. P. Charlie in toward the car.

As the back door of the Regal was opened from the inside, I threw the Mustang into gear and screeched out onto the street. D. P. looked angrily at the men and tried to push his way past them, but they wore frozen smiles and kept trying to nudge him into the car. I flung the Mustang in front of the Regal, punched the emergency brake, popped my .45 automatic out from the clip under my front seat, hurled the car door open, and stood, reaching the pistol over the roof of the car toward the men.

Everything freeze-framed, mouths and eyes wide.

Then I said, "Turn him loose."

Paul's mouth was ugly. "We had you warned. Buzz off."

D. P. took care of that problem by punching Paul in the face with the crook of his cane. The straight end he used at the throat of one of the other men, who went down gagging. D. P. hobbled around the front of the Regal toward me as I asked the other men, "Bullet holes, anybody?"

No one tested me. D. P., gasping, made it to the Mustang, opened the door, and tumbled in. I waited till he'd shut his door, then lowered the automatic and with two very satisfying shots blew out the driver's-side tires of the Regal. Dropping back into the car, I mashed her into gear, popped the clutch, and roared out of there, making a sliding rubber-burning turn onto westbound Michigan Avenue.

D. P. Charlie was pasty faced, sweating, and breathing hard. I concentrated on the traffic and building speed and distance between us and the trouble. It was a good thing I let D. P. speak first.

Because he said, "So you've been watching me after all." Voice tinny, gravelly, jagged.

Weird question. I grunted. "Yeah."

"I didn't think you men would forget about me. Thank God you didn't."

We blasted out of east Dearborn and were on the open stretch of Michigan Avenue in Ford country. I laid my automatic down on my lap and glanced at the old man. "Who were those guys?"

D. P. made an ugly, triumphant chuckle. "Well, they *said* they were one of you people. U. S. intelligence. Wanted to debrief me about my work for you after the war. But they weren't. I think they were . . . they were . . . some kind of hunters."

"Yeah," I said, bewildered.

D. P. Charlie's breathing was back under control. He said coldly, "After all these years, they're still after us. Thank God you men are around. You understand these matters. You remember what I did for you." I felt his flinty eyes on me. "You weren't in action in the war," he said.

"Came along after that."

We hit the fringe of west Dearborn and Michigan Avenue clogged up with traffic, slowing us down. D. P. Charlie was silent for a minute, then said flatly, "You should have put those bullets into the men, not the tires."

"We have to be cautious these days," I said noncommittally.

The traffic started moving and we crossed west Dearborn slowly. "Ah," Charlie snorted, "not like the old days. By God, it was interesting talking about that again, when that *Paul*—" he spat the name—"asked me about the old days in Bruges. We knew how to handle terrorists then. For every one of our men killed in terrorist attacks, we'd shoot ten civilian hostages. *That* was the way to handle those things. And the Communists, they're nothing but terrorist scum. But I helped you with the Communists after the war, didn't I? You men haven't forgotten how much I helped."

I became conscious of the .45 sitting on my lap, within the old man's reach. I casually slid it under the seat. We were advancing on the Telegraph Road interchange now, and I figured out how to handle it. I pulled into a side street and into the parking lot of Miller's Bar. "Listen," I said to Charlie as I shut down the engine, "I got to make some arrangements. You need a new place. We'll go in here where it's quiet and I'll make some phone calls."

"Very well," he answered crisply, an officer accepting the suggestion of a subordinate.

We walked into the bar slowly. It was quiet, air-conditioned, peopled with a few regulars. I parked D. P. at the bar. "Get yourself a drink. This'll take a few minutes." Then I went to the pay phone, dropped a quarter, and called Dick Dennehy.

Fifteen minutes later, as D. P. Charlie happily swilled beer and chatted with the friendly bartender, the place was overrun by feds.

\* \* \*

167

ROB KANTNER

"Karl Stahlen," I said to Uncle Dan.

He sighed deeply and took a sip of his hospital Coke. "A German?"

"Yes. Second in command of the Gestapo office in Bruges, Belgium, from 1942 to 1944."

Uncle Dan's piercing blue eyes fixed on me. His expression was totally vacant. "A war criminal," he said flatly.

I nodded. "Not a big shot, but on the list. Convicted of murder in absentia in 1946. The Belgians never found him. Till last week, that is."

"How did he get here?" my uncle asked unwillingly.

I sat in the dumb uncomfortable plastic chair again, wanting a cigar badly. Thank God, in a few days my uncle would be back in his retirement community apartment where I could smoke when I visited him. "After the war he was recruited by U. S. intelligence. They used him to get information on communist sympathizers and activities in western Europe. They paid him in cigarettes, liquor, women, and lodging. He delivered the goods for them for several years, I guess. He was quite useful."

"And the intelligence people were grateful," Dan said bitterly.

"Yeah. Grateful as hell. Kept him out of sight of the Belgians. When his usefulness ran out, they smuggled him to Genoa, where he boarded ship under an assumed name—Steel—and sailed to Bolivia. From there he made his way to the States. It was an escape route that our intelligence people used with several of the war criminals they became friendly with. The Rat Line, it was called."

"The Rat Line," Uncle Dan repeated softly.

"Came to Detroit," I said, feeling the need to finish the story, "married Peggy, went to work for Ford's, made friends with you, and all that.

"God," Uncle Dan said wearily. "Poor Peggy."

I had no answer for that.

Uncle Dan asked, "So what happened then?"

"You mean his little walks? I guess the Belgians got a tip as to his whereabouts somehow. Maybe tumbled to the Rat Line, after all these years. I don't know. Anyway, they approached the CIA and told them they knew about American complicity in hiding war criminals. Steel, in particular, by now number one on their list; the rest are dead or in jail. The CIA, in its wisdom, made a deal with the Belgians. They could put a snatch on Steel and smuggle him out and the Americans would look the other way. As long as the identification was absolutely positive, and as long as word about the Rat Line wasn't made public."

"Very accommodating."

"Sure." God, I wanted a smoke; I could smell a fresh cigar calling from my shirt pocket. "I don't know how the Belgians first made contact with Steel. But they did—this guy Paul—and he began meeting with Steel at the Q Room, a nice public place where you can talk about anything. Paul pretended to be an intelligence guy wanting to debrief Steel on his wartime intelligence activities. Actually, Paul is a Belgian intelligence operative and he was questioning Steel to make sure he was actually Karl Stahlen, Gestapo, Bruges. Once he was sure, he tried to put the snatch on him, as agreed with CIA."

"But you were there," Uncle Dan commented.

"Yeah."

Dan finished his coke and set it on the tray table next to his bed. "Why did the feds confide all this to you?"

"Hell, they had to. I was there, I knew too much. They're scared to death the story of the Rat Line will get out. It would be embarrassing as hell, American intelligence agents recruiting Nazi war criminals and then helping them escape justice. I agreed to keep my mouth shut in return for the whole miserable story. I'm sure there's juicy parts they left out, but it's all essentially there."

"And D. P. Charlie? Where is he now?"

I shrugged. "Probably in Canada by now. Our people kept their deal with the Belgians. He'll surface again in a Brussels jail on war-crimes charges in a few days, no doubt. And our people will never have heard of him."

We didn't say anything for a while. Footsteps went by in the corridor outside. My nicotine hunger grew. My uncle was staring blankly out the window at the dismal skyline of Inkster. I asked, "What are you thinking about, Uncle?"

"War crimes," he answered, not looking at me.

"Yeah. Well, you couldn't have guessed. He had everybody fooled, including his wife."

"I was thinking about myself." He looked at me and he was pale. "I had thirty-one confirmed victories in World War I. Thirty-one men dead. That doesn't count at least that many victories unconfirmed. And the strafing missions." He groped for words. "There's blood on my hands too. But they haven't come to judge me, only D. P. Charlie."

I stood and said angrily, "Don't ever make that comparison again. The men you killed were combatants. Volunteers. Equally armed. You were better than them, that's all, and just doing your job. Stahlen's victims were innocent civilians." I calmed down. "Jesus, Uncle. What got you thinking like that?"

He sighed. "D. P. Charlie was my friend. I have to adjust, that's all." He looked up at me and I was glad to see that sardonic twinkle come back to his ancient eyes. "I was one of the good guys, huh?"

"One of the good guys," I grinned.

His grin faded and I knew he was thinking about D. P. Charlie again. "It's hard to tell who the good guys are anymore."

# The Reluctant Detective

## *Michael Z. Lewin*

*I was pleased when I heard about the plans for this book and
even more pleased when asked to contribute a story to it.
The only problem for me was that there are no* stories *about my
Indianapolis-resident private detective, Albert Samson.
Samson was born in a novel and he has never appeared in
anything else. I wouldn't say that he is too big a character for
the smaller vehicle—maybe he just needs all the novel's body
and trim to get anywhere at all. So what have we here? Although
my books are set in Indiana, I live in England. There are
advantages to that arrangement as well as the obvious dis-
advantages. But from time to time it occurs to me that thirteen
years in Somerset might be about enough to begin to provide
some settings, some background, some flavo(u)r for a tale
or two. So here we have Freddie Herring. An American—as I
inevitably remain—who rather casually opens up shop in
Frome (the town I live in) and gets swept along by circumstance.
Not the makings of classic stuff, perhaps, but as Samson
himself proves often enough, P.I.s can't be smart all the time.*

IT was a Tuesday. I remember because when the doorbell rang I was reading the weekly basketball column in *The Guardian* newspaper—I try to keep up with some of my old interests from the U.S.A., see. It was about ten o'clock and I thought it might be the man to read the gas meter. Dawn was out, visiting her cousin—she's got as many relatives in this little town as I have none, so to speak. A lot is what I am saying.

At the door was a sallow faced little man—well, I suppose he was about average height for England, but I am awkwardly tall at 6'8" so I have a distorted perspective on people. He wore a jacket and tie and, even though it wasn't raining just then, he looked unhappy.

I thought, not the gas man but maybe a local government official.

'Are you Mr. Herring?' he asked.

'Yes.'

'May I talk to you?'

'What about?' I asked.

He glanced at the sign on the house wall by the door. It's so small you can hardly see it even if you know it's there. The minimum size to fulfill legal requirements, Dawn's half-nephew George said. George and his wife run a sign business here in town.

The man said, 'Are you the Mr. Herring who is a private inquiry agent?'

And I suddenly realized he had come on business. I was stunned. I was shocked. Things had been going so well.

I began to shake though I don't know if he noticed but I said, 'Yes, yes, of course. Fredrick Herring. Do come in.'

For lack of anywhere better, I led him to our living room.

'I like to keep things informal,' I said as I cleared the cat off the couch to make some sitting space for the man. 'I think people often find it hard to speak freely in a formal office atmosphere,' I said. Which I thought was pretty good off the cuff.

We sat down.

I didn't know what to say next.

But the man made the running. 'My name is Goodrich,' he said.

'Hi.'

'I don't know whether I should even be here.'

'It's not a step to take lightly,' I said.

'I'm not,' he said. 'I'm not.'

'Oh.'

'I don't know whether you know me?'

'No.'

'I am a solicitor with Malley, Holmes and Asquith, but I need someone to conduct an investigation for me on a private matter.'

'I see.'

'Well, you do that kind of thing, don't you?'

He looked at me. There was something devious in his eyes. And I had another sudden shock—suspicion.

You see, Dawn and I had agreed that if ever anybody tried to hire us, we would say we were too busy to take the case on. But there was something about this guy. The same thing that made me think he might be a council official. I suddenly got this idea that he was from one of the tax offices, that he might be checking up on us.

My initial hot flush of embarrassment that somebody might actually want to hire *me* as a detective was replaced by the cold draught of imminent accusation, prosecution.

'Of course,' I said. 'Fredrick Herring, private detective, at your service.'

# 2

It all began as a tax fiddle, see. Just about the time I had convinced myself for the tenth and final time that I did not want to spend the rest of my life being a bad lawyer, I inherited this house in England

and this bit of an income from my Uncle Ted. So, what more natural than to skip over the ocean for a while, see my house, have a think?

Oh, have I said where I am? It's in this little town called Frome, which they pronounce like it was spelled Froom. It's out in the country and is pretty enough that even some English people come as tourists.

Well, you know how life goes. I was here a while and I damaged my knee and met this girl who was just deciding she didn't want to spend the rest of her life being a bad physiotherapist. And after I had a bit of treatment she moved in with me. What with my having this money coming in regularly, we were having a most sympatico time. Not dropouts. Just taking our time deciding about futures and careers.

The tax fidd . . . tax avoidance structurization didn't come up till I had been here a year or so. In fact, it was Dawn's idea, like so many of the crafty things are. In that sense everything that's happened is down to her. In another sense it's down to the root of all evil.

It's just we began to realize there were things we would like to do but didn't have the money for.

Get a car for instance. Nothing flash, but some wheels to see some more of the country with. And to take some strain off my knee. Yes, it was wanting a car that set us thinking in the first place.

Or set Dawn thinking, actually. She's like that. Don't know whether it comes from fighting for survival in a big family, but she's got this kind of mind that finds ways to do things. There's something tricky about it, and I sometimes think that maybe *she* would have made the good lawyer. She says I have physiotherapeutic potential too, but that's something else.

Well, her idea was this. If I set up in business, as a self-employed person, I could save money in taxes by claiming a lot of our expenses were for the business. The details were all British tax law stuff but Dawn worked it out, and there was no question, it would pay for the car. And maybe a little bit more as we went along.

The question was what kind of business to supposedly set up in. That was Dawn's idea too. See, in Britain you don't need a licence of any kind. And, I have to admit, we yielded to a certain pleasant absurdity attached to the notion. I mean, a private detective, in Frome!

As well, the chances of anybody coming to us for business were, of course, nil.

We didn't want the business to succeed, or, indeed, for there to be any work at all. What we wanted were the deductions. It was all a tax fiddle. As I've mentioned.

And everything was going great until I found myself in my living room listening to a guy in a jacket and tie unburdening his problems to me.

## 3

Dawn was not pleased when she returned to the house and found that I had taken a case. She's not a big girl, Dawn, not in the sense of tall, but when she's upset she kind of grows. And shakes. And goes all red in the face.

'We agreed!' she said when I told her. 'We agreed!' She was vermillion and wobbling and I feared for the tray of eggs that she had brought back from her cousin who had got it half price from a guy who works part-time at the egg farm on the Marston side of town.

But I explained what had happened and about this devious look in the guy's eyes and then she accepted the situation as a fact.

We put the eggs away and had a hug and when she was back to her normal color I told her what this Mr. Goodrich wanted us to do.

'It's about his brother-in-law, a guy named Chipperworth, who is a crook,' I said.

'Chipperworth . . .' Dawn said. She was thinking. She's lived in Frome all her life and knows a lot of people.

'He has a company that manufactures beds, up on the industrial development. The brand name is Rest Easy.'

175

'Ah.'

'You know it?'

'Rest Easy, yes. My Auntie Vi worked up there a few years ago until she had the twins.'

'And this man Goodrich says that Chipperworth set fire to a warehouse next to his factory and collected the insurance for it.'

'I read about the fire,' Dawn said. 'But not that it was on purpose. How does Goodrich know?'

'He says Chipperworth was bragging yesterday that he had just collected a cheque for over three hundred thousand pounds and it was for beds he wasn't going to be able to sell.'

Dawn seemed to hear this information with at least a little touch of envy, but she said, 'But why doesn't Goodrich go to the police?'

'Because that's not what he's trying to sort out.'

'Oh.'

'What he's worried about is his sister. That Chipperworth is a crook, and that he's dangerous. He wants his sister to divorce Chipperworth.'

Dawn cocked her head.

'But his sister refuses to believe the stuff about the insurance fraud.'

'What are *we* supposed to do about that?'

'Nothing. What Goodrich wants us to prove is that Chipperworth has a woman on the side. If we can do that then the sister will divorce him and will be safe. Goodrich is sure that his sister will get a divorce in the end anyway, but if he precipitates it at least she'll be well off financially. It he waits till Chipperworth's activities catch up with him then it might ruin the sister too.'

'Oh,' Dawn said.

'I agreed to try. I felt in the circumstances I had to.'

She nodded resignedly. Then she looked at me.

And I looked at her.

We were thinking the same thing.

I said, 'What the hell do we do now?'

# 4

All we knew about private detecting was what we'd seen in the movies. But we talked about it over a cup of tea and decided that we would try to go through the motions, as best we could think of them. The first motion was to find Chipperworth and identify him.

It wasn't hard. Mr. Goodrich had given me a photograph and we took the car and hung around outside Rest Easy Beds toward the end of the work day. We realized that we might be sitting around in the car for quite a while with nothing to do, so we brought the cat and when we got tired of trying to teach it tricks Dawn spent some time telling me about her wild youth.

About five thirty we heard a horn from inside the factory and people began to leave. Rest Easy was not a big company. We counted fifteen before Chipperworth came out. He left about six and got into a new red Mercedes.

'OK,' Dawn said. 'There he is. What do we do now?'

'Drive along after him, I guess,' I said.

Chipperworth went directly to a house on the Prowtings Development. He pulled the car into the driveway. Got out. Went to front door. Was met by a woman, 6:06 pm.

Then Chipperworth went into the house and closed the door.

That would have wrapped the case up if the house hadn't been his home address and the woman his wife.

Dawn and I sat.

'At least we know the licence number of his car now,' I said after ten minutes.

But we were both sinking fast.

After another twenty minutes the cat showed distinct signs of feline restlessness. So did Dawn. She said, 'This is no good. What are we going to do, sit out here all night without any food or anything? The cat's hungry. I'm hungry.'

After some consideration, we decided to get fish and chips from Pangs, satisfying all palates.

When we got back, Chipperworth's car was gone.

# 5

Solicitor Goodrich rang up at 9 the next morning. He seemed annoyed that I didn't have anything to report.

I explained that in the detective business progress is not always rapid, that we'd had less than a day on the job, that patience was a virtue.

But Goodrich knew that Chipperworth had been out the previous night. He'd called his sister and she told him.

'If you want to do the surveillance yourself,' I said, 'please say so. Otherwise, leave it to us.'

He took a breath, then apologized—rather unconvincingly I thought—and we hung up.

I told Dawn about the call. Neither of us was happy.

'I'm going to see a couple of my cousins,' she said.

I looked puzzled.

'Nigel is a telephone engineer. He's a nut case and would probably enjoy finding a way to tap the Chipperworths' telephone. And Paul works in the photographic section at B & T.' Butler and Tanner is the big local printing firm. 'He is a camera buff. He'll lend us a camera with a telephoto lens.'

I sat silently for a moment. 'Look, babe,' I said. 'We're on the verge of taking this seriously in spite of ourselves.'

'I know,' she said quietly. She took my hand. 'But what can we do? If we don't get it sorted out quickly it's going to mess up our lives for weeks. We can hardly go to London next Friday if we've got a client calling up every day asking for a list of the things we've done on his case.'

We take a lot of little trips now we have the car, me and Dawn. This one to London was for a basketball tournament. Sometimes it's concerts. She's crazy for The Police, Dawn. Some perverse appeal about the name, I always think. We also go to plays and look at museums and keep track of what's happening in the world. We may live like wastrels now, but we always planned to amount to something. One day.

'If it goes on for long,' she said, 'we'll have to do shifts to cover Chipperworth for the whole day. We may have to borrow another car. I ought to be able to use Adele's Mini. You remember Adele?'

'No.'

'She's the small one with the big—'

'I remember now,' I said

Biggest feet I'd ever seen.

'I just wish I knew someone who could lend us a two-way radio.'

'There's your step-brother Mike,' I said remembering his reputation as a CB hobbyist.

'So there is,' she said. Then made a face. 'But he already pinches and pokes whenever I get close enough. What he'd want for doing me a favor. . . .'

'We'll get along without,' I said firmly.

# 6

In the end it only took a day.

It was the afternoon of my first shift. I was fitted out with a thermos, sandwiches and a radio. Even a specimen bottle—from Dawn's friend Elaine, the nurse—in case time was short and need was great.

As you can tell, when Dawn and I get down to it, we're impressive.

The camera from Paul was one of those instant print jobs. No time waiting for the film to come back from the developers. And, Paul said, 'Considering what kind of pictures you may get, a commercial firm might not print them.' Does a great leer, does Paul.

He also gave us a foot-long lens for the thing. 'It'll put you in their pockets. If they're wearing pockets.'

And Cousin Nigel jumped at the chance to plant a tape recorder up a telephone pole outside the Chipperworths' home. He volunteered to tap the company phone too. Well, you don't turn down offers like that.

It's struck me that *all* of Dawn's family are just that little bit shady. I offer it as an observation, not a complaint. It's part of what makes her an unusual girl. She can juggle too. I'm terrifically fond of her.

Anyway, after an hour's lunch at home, Chipperworth did not go back to his office. He drove instead out Bath Road and pulled into the driveway of a detached brick house just beyond the town limits. I parked in front of the cottage next door. I left the car and got the camera aimed and focused just in time to see Chipperworth open the door to the house with a key.

The picture came out a treat.

I stood there in the road looking at it. And wondering what to do next.

But Dawn and I had talked it through. First I made a note of the time, date and location on the back of the photograph. Then I set about trying to find out who lived in the house.

I went to the cottage and rang the bell. And had a little luck.

A tiny old woman with big brown eyes came to the door. I said, 'Excuse me. I have a registered letter for the people next door but nobody answers when I knock on the door.'

'That's because Wednesday afternoons Mrs. Elmitt has her fancy man in,' the old woman said. 'And she wouldn't want to be answering the door then, would she? Some of the things I've seen! And they don't even bother to draw the curtains.'

Old women can do pretty good leers too, when they try.

'Come in,' she said. 'Have a look for yourself.'

# 7

Dawn was chuffed, which means pleased as punch. I was pretty pleased too. The wretched case would soon be over and we could get back to life as usual. I resolved to try to arrange for my income to arrive from America so that it looked more like proceeds of the business. Then we wouldn't have to worry about being inspected by the tax people. Worry is a terrible thing.

But just about the time that Dawn and I were getting ready to be chuffed with each other, Cousin Nigel showed up at the front door.

He punched me on the shoulder as he came in, and gave Dawn a big kiss. A hearty type is Nigel.

'I've got your first tape,' he said jovially. 'Thought you would want to hear it sooner rather than later, so I put another cassette in the machine and brought this one right over. Got any beer?' He dropped into our most comfortable chair. 'Hey Dawnie, how about something to eat? Egg and chips? Hungry work, bugging telephones.'

The tape was a revelation.

Right off, the very first phone call, and the man was saying, 'Darling, I can't wait until I see you again.'

And the woman: 'I don't know whether I'll be able to bear not being with you full time for very much longer.'

'It will be soon. We'll be together, forever. Someplace nice. Away from your wretched husband.'

'I don't know what will become of me if our plan doesn't work.'

'It will work. We'll make it work.'

'Oh darling, I hope so.'

And on and on. There were a lot of slobbering sounds too. I would have been embarrassed if I hadn't been so upset.

'Wow!' Nigel said. 'All that kissy-kissy, and before lunch too. They must have it bad.'

Dawn said, 'Isn't that great! We've got all we need now, Freddie, don't you think?'

But I was not happy, not even close.

Because, unlike my two colleagues, I had recognized one of the voices. The man's. The conversation was not between Mr. Chipperworth and Mrs. Elmitt. The man on the telephone was our client, Mr. Goodrich, and the object of his affection was, presumably, Mrs. Chipperworth. His 'sister.'

# 8

We got rid of Nigel without even offering seconds of chips.

There was no law that a client had to tell us the truth. But neither of us liked it. Yet what can you do?

What we did first was go the next morning to Dawn's Great Uncle Steve, who is a police sergeant. We asked him about the fire in the Rest Easy Beds warehouse.

'Always knew it was arson,' Great Uncle Steve said. 'But we couldn't prove who did it. The owner was the only possible beneficiary, but he had an airtight alibi. He was at a civic function with the mayor and he was in full sight, the whole evening.'

'I see,' Dawn said.

'I interviewed Chipperworth myself,' Great Uncle Steve said, 'and he was quite open about being delighted about the fire. Business wasn't very good and he was having trouble moving the stock that was destroyed. Personally, I don't think he *did* have anything to do with it. I've been at this job long enough to get a good sense of people and that's the way he came across.'

'I see,' Dawn said.

'But we never got so much as a whiff of any other suspect. Checked current and past employees for someone with a grievance. Sounded out all our informants in town for a word about anybody who had heard anything about it. But we didn't get so much as a whisper. It's very unusual for us not to get some kind of lead if we try that hard. In the end, it was written off to kids. There are so many of them unemployed these days that we are getting all sorts of vandalism.'

'Thanks, Uncle Steve,' Dawn said.

'Helps you, does that?' he asked.

'I think so.'

Great Uncle Steve gave Dawn a hard squint. 'If you know anything about the case, you must tell me. You know that, don't you, Dawn?'

'Yes, Uncle Steve.'

He studied her and shook his head. Then he said to me, 'Young man, there is a look in her eyes that I don't like. You watch yourself.'

He was right, of course. Dawn was cooking something up, and it wasn't chips.

When we got home we sat down over a nice cup of tea. She hadn't said a word for the whole drive.

I couldn't bear it any longer. I said, 'All right. What *is* the significance of that funny look?'

'I've decided we're going to get Mrs. Chipperworth that divorce after all.'

'We are?'

'It's what we were hired to do, isn't it?'

# 9

I called Solicitor Goodrich to tell him that we had had success in our investigation and to ask if he wanted our report.

He did. He was with us within twenty minutes.

I explained what I had seen the previous afternoon. I gave him the photographs I had taken of Chipperworth entering Mrs. Elmitt's house with a key and, later, adjusting his tie as he came out. Also

one or two pocketless ones in between. I explained that the old
woman would be willing to testify to the lurid details of what she
had seen through Mrs. Elmitt's undrawn curtains. 'But I think she
would like a little expense money if she does testify,' I said.

'I'm sure that can be arranged,' Goodrich said through his
smiles.

A little ready cash might help the old woman get some
curtains for her own windows.

After Goodrich left I rang Rest Easy Beds.

I explained to Mr. Chipperworth that Dawn and I wanted to
speak to him immediately.

'What is it that is so urgent, Mr. Herring?' he asked.

'We want to tell you about your wife's plans to sue you for
divorce,' I said.

As soon as we arrived we were ushered into Chipperworth's
office.

'But Felicity's known about Madeleine for years,' he said
when I explained what we'd been hired to do. 'It's an arrangement
we have. Felicity doesn't like *it*, you see. So Madeleine keeps me
from making . . . demands.'

'Felicity doesn't seem to mind *it* with her lover,' Dawn said.

'Her what?' Chipperworth asked, suddenly bug-eyed.

'Why don't you ask about her recent telephone calls,' Dawn
suggested. 'We have to be going now. Ta ta.'

After stopping at Nigel's we went on home.

We didn't have long to wait.

A few minutes after noon the bell rang. Before I could get to
it, pounding started on the door. When I opened it I faced a furious
Solicitor Goodrich. He swung fists at me.

For the most part being as tall as I am is an inconvenience.
But at least I have long arms and could keep him out of reach.
When he finished flailing, he started swearing. The language

seemed particularly unseemly for a member of the legal profession. I would have been embarrassed for Dawn if I hadn't heard worse from her own family. But they are foul mouthed in a friendly way. Goodrich was vicious.

Also defamatory. He claimed that we had sold information to Mr. Chipperworth.

I was about to deny it when Dawn said, 'What if we did?'

'I'll have you jailed for this,' Goodrich said. 'It's illegal.'

'That's fine talk from somebody who set fire to a warehouse,' Dawn said.

Suddenly Goodrich was still and attentive. 'What?'

'You are the arsonist responsible for the fire at Rest Easy Beds.'

'That's ridiculous,' Goodrich said. But he wasn't laughing.

'The plan,' Dawn said, 'was that when Mr. Chipperworth collected his insurance money Mrs. Chipperworth would divorce him, which would entitle her to half of it. Between the insurance cash and her share of the rest of the joint property, you and Mrs. Chipperworth would have a nice little nest egg to run away on.'

'Prove it,' Goodrich said furiously.

'I suppose you have an alibi for the night of the fire?' Dawn said charmingly.

'Why should I need one?'

'Well, I'm sure when we go to the police . . .'

'Don't do that!' Goodrich burst out.

'Ah,' Dawn said. 'Now we're getting down to serious business.' She batted her eyelashes. 'We never actually gave our evidence to Mr. Chipperworth, you know, and as long as Mrs. Chipperworth has denied everything . . .'

'You want money, I suppose,' Goodrich said.

'Well, poor Freddie is terribly tall, and a bigger car would be so much easier for him to get in and out of.'

'All right,' Goodrich said. 'A car.'

'And there are so many improvements that ought to be made on this house.'

'How about just getting to a bottom line figure.'

'I think thirty thousand would come in very handy, don't you, Freddie?'

'Oh, very handy.'

'Thirty thousand!' Goodrich said.

'Yes,' Dawn said. 'See how reasonable we are!'

# 10

When the trial came along it was plastered all over the local papers. Frome is not so big a town that it gets serious court cases involving local people very often.

Especially cases involving solicitors and arson and windowless curtains. Goodrich pleaded guilty, but the local reporter, Scoop Newton, tracked down Mrs. Elmitt's neighbor and she was photographed pointing to the windows she had been forced to witness indescribable acts through. Well, the descriptions didn't make the papers anyway.

However Great Uncle Steve was not pleased at first when he heard what we had done.

Heard is the operative word because we had tape recorded the entire conversation with Goodrich on equipment borrowed from Cousin Nigel.

But Dawn explained. After all this time the only way Goodrich's arson could be proved was if he confessed to it. The police couldn't have used the threat of exposing his relationship to Mrs. Chipperworth the way we did because that would have transgressed legal niceties. 'So it was up to Freddie and me,' Dawn said.

Eventually Great Uncle Steve laughed.

'I warned you about her,' he said to me.

But it worked out all right in the end.

Except . . . Scoop Newton tracked down Dawn and me too.

We begged her not to put anything about us in the paper, for business reasons.

But she refused. We were key figures in bringing a dangerous solicitor to justice. It was news. And besides, Dawn has good legs and photographs well.

It's not that we weren't proud of what we—or let's be fair— what Dawn had done.

But it meant that the Fredrick Herring Private Inquiry Agency burst from its quiet and total obscurity into the glare of public attention.

We started getting calls. We started getting visitors. We started getting letters. Find this, look for that, unravel the other.

And in the end it wasn't actually the attention which was the problem.

What upset us at first was that we found we quite liked it. We hadn't expected to be inclined to *work*.

Yet, some of the cases we were offered were pretty interesting. And after giving it our very best vertical and horizontal thought we finally decided to compromise on principle and take maybe one more. Or two.

# Typographical Error

## *John Lutz*

*"Typographical Error" is the seventh short story to
be published featuring private detective Nudger,
who also has been featured in the novels* Buyer Beware
*and* Nightlines. *Though he is in the classic mold
of fictional detectives, I hope there is something more to Nudger.
The streets he walks down are not only mean, but
also dark, steep, and unevenly paved. He negotiates
them tentatively, fearfully, yet with a well-worn,
undying optimism, while Murphy's Law courses in his blood.
Things tend to go wrong for Nudger. He carries on.
He has no choice.
Sound familiar?*

NUDGER walked into the Kit-Kat lounge and looked around, waiting for his eyes to adjust to the dimness. It was ten A.M. and the lounge was barren of customers. That was okay. The person he wanted to talk with stood behind the long, vinyl-padded bar, idly leafing through a newspaper. Lani Katlo was her name, proprietor and manager of the Kit-Kat. She was a woman sneaking up on menopause, attractive in a still-youthful if shopworn fashion. When she saw Nudger approaching the bar, she smiled and nodded, waiting for him to order.

"Coffee if you have it," Nudger told her.

"We don't. There's a restaurant across the street." Her smile remained, taking any edge off her words.

"Never mind," Nudger said, "What I really want is to talk, Lani." He handed her one of his cards with his Saint Louis address.

She appeared vaguely surprised that he knew her name as she accepted the card and folded the newspaper closed. "You're in what line of work," she asked, studying the card, "that brings you to Florida?"

"I'm a private detective," Nudger told her.

"This says defective, with an 'f.' "

"That's a printer's error."

"Why don't you return the cards?"

"I had a thousand of them made up, then the printer went out of business. What can I do but use the cards anyway?"

"I see your point," Lani Katlo said. "These cards aren't cheap. But what would a private detective from Saint Louie want to talk to me about?"

"Harmon Medlark. And nobody from Saint Louis says 'Saint Louie.' "

"You mean Meadowlark?"

"Medlark." Nudger spelled the name for her.

Lani Katlo shrugged. "I thought maybe he was somebody who'd used your printer."

"Medlark was in business over in Clearwater six months ago, selling time shares in vacation condominium units. The deal where the customers purchase part ownership in a unit and have the right to use it one or two weeks out of each year before turning it over to the next part owner."

"I'm familiar with the system," Lani said. "I own one fifty-second of a unit in Hawaii myself." ·

Nudger settled himself onto a soft barstool. "Harmon Medlark ran into problems when he used his own peculiar calendar that divided the year into hundreds of weeks. After collecting big down payments he managed to finagle by offering ridiculously low interest rates on loans, he disappeared with the money. Some of the Saint Louis fleeced have hired me to find him and recover the wool."

"Did he build any of the condominiums?"

Nudger shook his head sadly. "There is a tract of graded ground in Clearwater supporting only weeds and a sign reading 'Sun Joy Vacation Limited.' That is all. Medlark bought the ground with a small deposit and a large smile then defaulted on the loan when he disappeared."

"With all that wool."

Nudger nodded. He watched Lani Katlo pour herself two fingers of Scotch in a monogrammed glass and winced at the thought of hundred proof booze cascading down a throat at ten in the morning.

Lani downed half the Scotch without visible effect and asked, "Why are you telling me all this?"

"Because your name and address were found among the few items Medlark left behind in his hasty departure."

Lani Katlo appeared mystified. "Honest, Nudger, I never heard of the man."

Nudger reached into an inside pocket of his sports coat and withdrew a fuzzy snapshot of a graying man with regular features and kindly blue eyes. He showed the photograph to Lani Katlo.

"Him I think I know," she said. "I thought his name was Herman Manners. He's a friend of Eddie Regal, who owns a florist shop over on Citrus Drive. They used to come in here together now and then, a few times they came in with Eddie's wife and a tall oversexed-acting redhead that looked like a watermelon festival queen." Lani used cupped hands before her own gaunt torso to illustrate her meaning.

"Do you know the redhead's name?" Nudger asked. That

could be useful information even if there was no longer a connection with the evasive Medlark.

"No," Lani said, "I only saw her maybe twice. Eddie Regal could probably tell you."

Nudger reached into his pocket again, unfolded a slip of beige notepaper and laid it on the bar. "Does this note we found along with your name tell you anything?" he asked Lani Katlo. The neatly typed note read:

Dear Mrs Cupcake,
   I still can't believe you love an old greybeard like me, but I'll keep living in a dream. See you in Shangri-la.
                                          Mr Moneybags

"It doesn't mean a thing to me," Lani Katlo said, handing back the note. "Where's Shangri-la, anyway. Isn't that a place up the coast?"

"It's a place in a book," Nudger told her. "Not real."

"Maybe it's the name of a night spot or resort or something. Ever think of that?"

"Thought of it and checked," Nudger said. "It's possible that was what Medlark meant when and if he typed the note."

"Maybe Eddie Regal can tell you something about it," Lani Katlo suggested. She unfolded her newspaper again, as a signal that she was losing interest in the conversation.

Nudger thanked her for her cooperation and left.

On the sidewalk he stood in the heat and glare of the Florida sun and felt his stomach contract. Talking with people like Lani Katlo did that to him. Nerves. She was hiding something and Nudger knew it but couldn't pinpoint how he knew. He couldn't draw her out of concealment. Frustration. He wished, as he had so many times, that he knew another trade, was in some other line of work. But he didn't. He wasn't. He regretted the Spanish omelet he'd eaten for breakfast, popped an antacid tablet into his mouth and walked toward his dented Volkswagen Beetle.

\* \* \*

"This card says defective," Eddie Regal said from behind a display of chrysanthemums. He was a swarthy, hairy man with oversized knuckles. He did not look like a florist.

"A typographical error," Nudger said. "I use them anyway. Have you ever heard of a man named Harmon Medlark?"

"You mean Meadowlark?"

Nudger explained that he didn't. "Possibly you knew him as Herman Manners." Nudger flashed the obscure photograph of Medlark.

"Sure," Regal said. "that's Herman. I met him a few months ago at a place called the Kit-Kat. We talked a while over drinks and found we were both interested in the dog races. So we went a few times."

"Alone?"

"Sometimes. A couple of times we took my wife Madge and a girl Herman went out with, a redhead name of Delores."

"Do you know where I can find Delores?"

Regal snipped a bud and shook his head no. "I only met her a few times, when she was with Herman. I think she lives around Orlando, near Disney World."

"Did Manners ever mention where he lived?"

"Nope. It wasn't that kind of friendship. And Herman is a kind of tight-lipped guy anyway."

"What's Delores's last name?"

"That I remember because it's unusual. Bookbinder. It stuck in my mind because she isn't a bookish kind of girl at all."

"So I hear," Nudger said. "Did Manners ever mention a time-sharing deal in a condominium project in Clearwater?"

"Nope. We talked dogs and women and that's about all."

"Okay, Mr. Regal. You have my card with my motel phone number penned on it. Will you call me if you think of anything else about Manners?"

"Oh, be glad to, Mr. Nudger. It interests me, how a detective works. Where you going now? Back to Saint Louie?"

"To Orlando, to try to find Delores Bookbinder."

"We specialize in funeral wreaths," Regal said, "but we got a special today on long-stemmed roses if you're interested."

"Thanks," Nudger said, "but I don't think I'll need either." He walked from the aromatic shop and heard the little bell above the door tinkle cheerily behind him.

Bookbinder, he thought. That *is* an unusual name.

She was easy to find, was Delores Bookbinder. She lived in Orlando proper and was listed in the phone directory. When Nudger called her she readily agreed to see him after learning only his name and hearing Regal's name mentioned. She gave directions to her apartment in a sultry telephone voice that kicked his imagination around like a bent tin can.

Delores's directions led Nudger to a long, two-story stucco apartment building on Soltice Avenue, just off the Bee-line expressway. She lived on the top floor, and when he knocked she answered the door wearing a simple green dress that hugged her curves the way he found himself yearning to hug. Delores was a tall, lushly proportioned woman in her early thirties, with that flawless milky complexion possessed by only a minority of natural redheads.

"Nudger?" she asked.

He nodded, and she stepped back to usher him into a small but neatly furnished apartment that featured thick blue carpet, cool white walls and a large oil painting of a leopard luxuriously sunning itself on some far away African plain. A window air-conditioner was humming a gurgly, suggestive melody. Nudger handed Delores one of his cards.

"This says defective," she told him.

"Don't let it fool you."

Delores smiled and motioned for Nudger to sit on a low cream-colored sofa. She sat across from him in a dainty chair and crossed her long legs with a calculated exaggerated modesty that brought a

JOHN LUTZ

familiar tightness to his groin. He decided he was an idiot for what
he was thinking. He reached for the foil-wrapped cylinder in his
shirt pocket, thumbnailed off an antacid tablet and popped it into
his mouth.

Delores was staring at him curiously.

"Sensitive stomach," Nudger explained. "Nerves."

"Isn't that something of a drawback in your profession?"

"Yes and no," he answered. "It causes me discomfort, but it
sometimes acts as a warning signal." As it was doing now. Nudger
decided not to lay a hand or anything else on Delores Bookbinder,
if that was her name.

"Do you know a man named Herman Manners?" he asked.

She threw him the kind of curve he wasn't thinking about.
"You mean Harmon Medlark?"

"The same." Nudger was becoming uncomfortable on the
underslung soft sofa; it was for lying down, not sitting. "Eddie
Regal and a number of other people seem to know him as Herman
Manners."

Delores waved an elegant, ring-adorned hand. "Oh, that's a
name Harmon sometimes uses."

Nudger showed her the photograph. "Is this the man we're
talking about?"

She crossed the room, leaned over Nudger with a heavy scent
of perfume and squinted at the photo. "That's so fuzzy it could be
anyone," she said, "but I can say with some certainty it's Harmon."
Her hand rested very lightly on Nudger's shoulder. He wondered if
she could feel his heartbeat. He chomped down hard on the antacid
tablet to create a diversionary vibration.

"Where can I get in touch with Medlark?" he asked as
casually as possible.

"I don't know exactly," Delores said. "We had an argument. I
haven't seen Harmon for over a week."

"What did you argue about?"

Delores didn't seem offended by Nudger's nosiness. Her hand

194

remained steady on his shoulder and he could feel the warmth of her breath on the back of his neck, as if she still needed to study the photograph that he'd now replaced in his pocket. "His drinking," she said. "Harmon drinks too much. Between the two of us, he's a sick man." She gave a mindless little laugh. "I do pick the losers. You look like a winner."

Now that was fairly direct. Nudger turned to say something to her and they were kissing. After what seemed an enjoyable full minute, he pulled away. He stood up.

"I don't see this as a wise move in the game," he said.

Delores appeared mystified, her green eyes wide. "What game?"

"I'm not sure. That's why it's not a wise move." He smiled at her. "I'm going to leave while I still can, Delores."

She frowned and ran a long-fingered hand over her svelte curves, as if to reassure herself that they were still there. "You're nuts," she said, "or something else."

"Nuts," Nudger assured her.

"If you're really leaving," Delores said in a resigned and disappointed voice, "I guess I ought to tell you about a rumor I heard that Harmon is in a 'rest home' that's actually a place for alcoholics to dry out and take the cure."

"Rest home where?" Nudger asked.

"Over near Vero Beach. Shady Retreat, it's called, like it's a religious place for meditation or something. Well it's not; it's for problem drinkers."

Nudger moved toward the door.

"After I told you that," Delores said in an injured tone, "you're not still leaving, are you?"

Nudger got out of there. The tropical Florida sun seemed cool.

Vero Beach was a resort town on the Atlantic coast, a few hours' drive from Orlando. Nudger gassed up the Beetle and drove there.

Shady Retreat was south of the town, one of several buildings erected on relatively undeveloped beachfront property secluded from the highway by thick brush and palm trees. It was a converted large beach-house, behind a mobile home office that rested with an air of permanence on a stone foundation that hid any sign of wheels or axles. The sunlight glinted brightly off the mobile home's white aluminum siding, causing Nudger's eyes to ache as he approached along a brick walkway flanked by azaleas. The sea slapped at the beach beyond the cast concrete structure behind the mobile home. Nudger pressed a button beside the glass storm door and heard a faint buzzing that reminded him of a fly trapped in a jar.

A dark-eyed man with black hair and wire-rimmed glasses opened the door. He was wearing a neat blue business suit with a maroon tie. He introduced himself as Dr. Mortimer and invited Nudger inside.

Nudger stepped into the coolness of the sparsely furnished office and handed Dr. Mortimer his card. The doctor glanced at it and slipped it into his pocket, then sat behind a tan metal desk, and in the manner of doctors asked Nudger how he could help him.

"Do you have a patient here named Harmon Medlark?" Nudger asked.

The doctor's face didn't change expression. "We don't ordinarily give out information on our patients."

"How many patients do you have at one time?" Nudger asked.

"Sometimes ten, at maximum. Right now we have five."

"And Harmon Medlark is one of them?"

The doctor seemed to struggle with his sense of ethics.

"The information is very important to a lot of people, Doctor," Nudger said.

Doctor Mortimer nodded and finally said, "Yes, Mr. Medlark is here."

"For treatment of chronic alcoholism?"

Dr. Mortimer nodded. "As are all our patients."

Nudger's stomach was kicking up violently.

"Could you describe Harmon Medlark?"

"Average height, middle-aged, a rather handsome man." The

doctor reached into a desk drawer and handed Nudger a slip of yellow paper. "Here's his admission form, filled out and signed by Medlark himself. His description and vital statistics are on it."

Nudger read: "Mr Harmon Medlark/age 46/hgt. 5' 10"/wgt. 160/hair: gray/eyes: blue/occupation: real estate." He handed Doctor Mortimer the photograph. "Is this Medlark?" he asked.

Dr. Mortimer nodded.

"Would you mind doing me a favor, Doctor?" Nudger asked. "Just jot down Medlark's description on the back of the photo. It's kind of fuzzy and the color of hair and eyes and complexion couldn't be right. Here, just copy off this if you want." Nudger laid the yellow admission form on the desk before the doctor.

"Certainly," Dr. Mortimer agreed with a smile, withdrew a gold pen from his pocket and took a few minutes to comply with Nudger's request.

Nudger took the photograph the doctor handed back and read: "Mr. Harmon Medlark/age 46/hgt. 5' 10"/wgt. 160/hair: grey/eyes: blue/occupation: real estate."

"Now, do you mind if I see Mr. Medlark?" Nudger said.

"How important is it, Mr. Nudger?"

"Very. And if I don't see him now, someone with authority certainly will later."

Dr. Mortimer sighed and laced his manicured fingers together tightly. "All right, if it's necessary, though I don't like the patients disturbed during withdrawal. Mr. Medlark is in Unit C."

Nudger thanked the doctor and left the office. He walked back along an extension of the brick path to the main building. A white-uniformed attendant seated in a webbed chair near the front doors smiled and nodded to him. Nudger returned the smile but said nothing as he walked past and inside.

Unit C was one of the four ground floor units. Nudger knocked on the door, heard a muffled voice invite him to enter, and went in.

Before him in a white wicker rocking chair, reading a *Time* magazine, sat his quarry.

"Harmon Medlark?" Nudger asked.

The handsome gray-haired man nodded. "I am. Are you Doctor Mortimer's assistant?"

"I am not. My name is Nudger. I'm a private detective hired by the so called owners of Sun Joy Vacation Limited."

The wicker rocker stopped its gentle movement. "I know nothing about such a development."

"Who said it was a development? I might have been talking about a travel club."

"I'm not a travel agent, Mr. Nudger, I'm in real estate."

"Delores Bookbinder told me where to find you," Nudger said.

For an instant surprise showed in the blue eyes that surveyed Nudger. "Never heard of her. She sounds like a librarian."

"How about Eddie Regal?"

"I knew an Eddie Rogers once. Sold billiard accessories."

"Not the same fella, Herman."

"It's Harmon." The chair resumed its gentle back-and-forth motion. Its occupant ignored Nudger and cracklingly turned a page of *Time*.

Nudger stood listening to the creak of the wicker runners for a while, then turned and left the room. He asked the attendant if it was okay to use the telephone he'd noticed on the way in. The attendant said sure.

After using the phone, Nudger returned to the office in the white aluminum trailer. Dr. Mortimer was still at his desk, ostensibly studying an open file. He smiled at Nudger.

"Did you see Mr. Medlark?" he asked.

"I'm impressed," Nudger told him.

"We try to keep our facilities modern and—"

"I mean I'm impressed by the way I was led by the nose," Nudger said. "From Lani Katlo to Eddie Regal to Delores Bookbinder to here. Of course, I wouldn't have come here at all if Delores had been able to entice and derail me with her own special diversion. And then there was the deliberate absence of periods in Medlark's note to 'Mrs Cupcake'—Delores no doubt—and signed

'Mr Moneybags,' and the same absence of a period in the admission form you showed me. And let's not forget the fuzzy photograph."

"This is somewhat confusing," Dr. Mortimer said, raising an eyebrow at Nudger.

"It's simple once you have the key," Nudger said. "A network was set up in case anyone came looking for Medlark. That network guided me to Delores, where I would have wound up anyway in time, and if Delores couldn't deal with me she was to send me here and phone to warn you I was on my way. I was supposed to collar the wrong man here, and give the right man plenty of time to make other hideaway arrangements."

"Wrong man?" Dr. Mortimer asked.

"That isn't Harmon Medlark in Unit C," Nudger said. "That's someone hired to play a role as long as possible for the police while the heat is off the real Medlark. You're Harmon Medlark, behind that dyed hair and dark contact lenses. And that sound you hear is the law from Vero Beach turning into your driveway."

Dr. Mortimer seemed to absorb a powerful kick in the solar plexus. He slumped back in his chair, and his head lolled forward over his maroon tie that suddenly resembled a long tongue.

"It was a good idea, attempting to deflect rather than simply stonewall an investigator," Nudger said. "It might have worked. It was the note that put me onto you."

"The note?" Medlark-Mortimer croaked.

Nudger nodded. "The British spelling of gray, with an 'e,' was in the note to 'Mrs Cupcake.' The form filled out by the man in Unit C contained 'gray' with an 'a,' the common American spelling. But your description jotted on the back of the photograph contains 'grey' with an 'e,' like on the Medlark note. That was a genuine unconscious similarity you hadn't intended."

Car doors slammed outside.

"But it was our introduction that really tipped me," Nudger said.

Medlark glared at him from behind the desk, counting his remaining seconds of freedom. "I don't understand."

"You're the only one I gave a business card to who didn't comment on the misspelling of detective. You were expecting me today, Mr. Medlark, and knew who and what I was, so you barely glanced at my card."

The police were pounding on the door.

"I'll let them in," Nudger said.

Harmon Medlark was studying the card Nudger had handed him earlier.

"Defective," he muttered. "That isn't true at all."

# Wild Mustard

## *Marcia Muller*

*"Wild Mustard" takes place in the spring, shortly after
Sharon McCone's investigation in* The Cheshire Cat's Eye *and
before her break-up with Lieutenant Gregory Marcus, prior to*
Games to Keep the Dark Away. *In this early story, I've tried
to portray the private side of a private eye—the Sunday brunches
at a favorite restaurant and hand-in-hand walks by the seaside
with a close friend. What the story really shows, however, is
that there is no completely private side to Sharon's life. The
inquiring qualities that made her choose her profession cause
her to observe her surroundings with greater-than-average
curiosity— thus noticing evidence of a crime
that many others fail to see.*

T HE first time I saw the old Jap-
anese woman, I was having brunch at the restaurant above the
ruins of San Francisco's Sutro Baths. The woman squatted on the
slope, halfway between its cypress-covered top and the flooded
ruins of the old bathhouse. She was uprooting vegetation and
stuffing it into a green plastic sack.

"I wonder what she's picking," I said to my friend Greg.

He glanced out the window, raising one dark-blond eyebrow, his homicide cop's eye assessing the scene. "Probably something edible that grows wild. She looks poor; it's a good way to save grocery money."

Indeed the woman did look like the indigent old ladies one sometimes saw in Japantown; she wore a shapeless jacket and trousers, and her feet were clad in sneakers. A gray scarf wound around her head.

"Have you ever been down there?" I asked Greg, motioning at the ruins. The once-elegant baths had been destroyed by fire. All that remained now were crumbling foundations, half submerged in water. Seagulls swam on its glossy surface and, beyond, the surf tossed against the rocks.

"No. You?"

"No. I've always meant to, but the path is steep and I never have the right shoes when I come here."

Greg smiled teasingly. "Sharon, you'd let your private eye's instinct be suppressed for lack of hiking boots?"

I shrugged. "Maybe I'm not really that interested."

"Maybe not."

Greg often teased me about my sleuthing instinct, but in reality I suspected he was proud of my profession. An investigator for All Souls Cooperative, the legal services plan, I had dealt with a full range of cases—from murder to the mystery of a redwood hot tub that didn't hold water. A couple of the murders I'd solved had been in Greg's bailiwick, and this had given rise to both rivalry and romance.

In the months that passed my interest in the old Japanese woman was piqued. Every Sunday that we came there—and we came often because the restaurant was a favorite—the woman was scouring the slope, foraging for . . . what?

One Sunday in early spring Greg and I sat in our window booth, watching the woman climb slowly down the dirt path. To complement the season, she had changed her gray headscarf for bright yellow. The slope swarmed with people, enjoying the release from the winter rains. On the far barren side where no vegetation had taken hold, an abandoned truck leaned at a precarious angle at the bottom of the cliff near the baths. People scrambled down, inspected the old truck, then went to walk on the concrete foundations or disappeared into a nearby cave.

When the waitress brought our check, I said, "I've watched long enough; let's go down there and explore."

Greg grinned, reaching in his pocket for change. "But you don't have the right shoes."

"Face it, I'll never have the right shoes. Let's go. We can ask the old woman what she's picking."

He stood up. "I'm glad you finally decided to investigate her. She might be up to something sinister."

"Don't be silly."

He ignored me. "Yeah, the private eye side of you has finally won out. Or is it your Indian blood? Tracking instinct, papoose?"

I glared at him, deciding that for that comment he deserved to pay the check. My one-eighth Shoshone ancestry—which for some reason had emerged to make me a black-haired throwback in a family of Scotch-Irish towheads—had prompted Greg's dubbing me "papoose." It was a nickname I did not favor.

We left the restaurant and passed through the chain link fence to the path. A strong wind whipped my long hair about my head, and I stopped to tie it back. The path wound in switchbacks past huge gnarled geranium plants and through a thicket. On the other side of it, the woman squatted, pulling up what looked like weeds. When I approached she smiled at me, a gold tooth flashing.

"Hello," I said. "We've been watching you and wondered what you were picking."

"Many good things grow here. This month it is the wild mustard." She held up a sprig. I took it, sniffing its pungency.

"You should try it," she added. "It is good for you."

"Maybe I will." I slipped the yellow flower through my buttonhole and turned to Greg.

"Fat chance," he said. "When do you ever eat anything healthy?"

"Only when you force me."

"I have to. Otherwise it would be Hershey bars day in and day out."

"So what? I'm not in bad shape." It was true; even on this steep slope I wasn't winded.

Greg smiled, his eyes moving appreciatively over me. "No, you're not."

We continued down toward the ruins, past a sign that advised us:

CAUTION!
CLIFF AND SURF AREA
EXTREMELY DANGEROUS
PEOPLE HAVE BEEN SWEPT
FROM THE ROCKS AND DROWNED

I stopped, balancing with my hand on Greg's arm, and removed my shoes. "Better footsore than swept away."

We approached the abandoned truck, following the same impulse that had drawn other climbers. Its blue paint was rusted and there had been a fire in the engine compartment. Everything, including the seats and steering wheel, had been stripped.

"Somebody even tried to take the front axle," a voice beside me said, "but the fire had fused the bolts."

I turned to face a friendly-looking sunbrowned youth of about fifteen. He wore dirty jeans and a torn t-shirt.

"Yeah," another voice added. This boy was about the same age; a wispy attempt at a mustache sprouted on his upper lip. "There's hardly anything left, and it's only been here a few weeks."

"Vandalism," Greg said.

"That's it." The first boy nodded. "People hang around here and drink. Late at night they get bored." He motioned at a group of unsavory-looking men who were sitting on the edge of the baths with a couple of six-packs.

"Destruction's a very popular sport these days." Greg watched the men for a moment with a professional eye, then touched my elbow. We skirted the ruins and went toward the cave. I stopped at its entrance and listened to the roar of the surf.

"Come on," Greg said.

I followed him inside, feet sinking into coarse sand which quickly became packed mud. The cave was really a tunnel, about eight feet high. Through crevices in the wall on the ocean side I saw spray flung high from the roiling waves at the foot of the cliff. It would be fatal to be swept down through those jagged rocks.

Greg reached the other end. I hurried as fast as my bare feet would permit and stood next to him. The precipitous drop to the sea made me clutch at his arm. Above us, rocks towered.

"I guess if you were a good climber you could go up, and then back to the road," I said.

"Maybe, but I wouldn't chance it. Like the sign says . . ."

"Right." I turned, suddenly apprehensive. At the mouth of the tunnel, two of the disreputable men stood, beer cans in hand. "Let's go, Greg."

If he noticed the edge to my voice, he didn't comment. We walked in silence through the tunnel. The men vanished. When we emerged into the sunlight, they were back with the others, opening fresh beers. The boys we had spoken with earlier were perched on the abandoned truck, and they waved at us as we started up the path.

And so, through the spring, we continued to come to our favorite restaurant on Sundays, always waiting for a window booth. The old Japanese woman exchanged her yellow headscarf for a red one. The abandoned truck remained nose down toward the baths, provoking much criticism of the Park Service. People walked their dogs on the slope. Children balanced precariously on the ruins, in spite of the warning sign. The men lolled about and drank beer.

The teenaged boys came every week and often were joined by friends at the truck.

Then, one Sunday, the old woman failed to show.

"Where is she?" I asked Greg, glancing at my watch for the third time.

"Maybe she's picked everything there is to pick down there."

"Nonsense. There's always something to pick. We've watched her for almost a year. That old couple are down there walking their German Shepherd. The teenagers are here. That young couple we talked to last week are over by the tunnel. Where's the old Japanese woman?"

"She could be sick. There's a lot of flu going around. Hell, she might have died. She wasn't all that young."

The words made me lose my appetite for my chocolate cream pie. "Maybe we should check on her."

Greg sighed. "Sharon, save your sleuthing for paying clients. Don't make everything into a mystery."

Greg had often accused me of allowing what he referred to as my "woman's intuition" to rule my logic—something I hated even more than references to my "tracking instinct." I knew it was no such thing; I merely gave free rein to the hunches that every good investigator follows. It was not a subject I cared to argue at the moment, however, so I let it drop.

But the next morning—Monday—I sat in the converted closet that served as my office at All Souls, still puzzling over the woman's absence. A file on a particularly boring tenants' dispute lay open on the desk in front of me. Finally I shut it and clattered down the hall of the big brown Victorian toward the front door.

"I'll be back in a couple of hours," I told Ted, the secretary.

He nodded, his fingers never pausing as he plied his new Selectric. I gave the typewriter a resentful glance. It, to my mind, was an extravagance, and the money it was costing could have been better spent on salaries. All Souls, which charged clients on a sliding fee scale according to their incomes, paid so low that several of the attorneys were compensated by living in free rooms on the second floor. I lived in a studio apartment in the Mission District. It seemed to get smaller every day.

Grumbling to myself, I went out to my car and headed for the restaurant above Sutro Baths.

"The old woman who gathers wild mustard on the cliff," I said to the cashier, "was she here yesterday?"

He paused. "I think so. Yesterday was Sunday. She's always here on Sunday. I noticed her about eight, when we opened up. She always comes early and stays until about two."

But she had been gone at eleven. "Do you know her? Do you know where she lives?"

He looked curiously at me. "No, I don't."

I thanked him and went out. Feeling foolish, I stood beside the Great Highway for a moment, then started down the dirt path, toward where the wild mustard grew. Halfway there I met the two teenagers. Why weren't they in school? Dropouts, I guessed.

They started by, avoiding my eyes like kids will do. I stopped them. "Hey, you were here yesterday, right?"

The mustached one nodded.

"Did you see the old Japanese woman who picks the weeds?"

He frowned. "Don't remember her."

"When did you get here?"

"Oh, late. Really late. There was this party Saturday night."

"I don't remember seeing her either," the other one said, "but maybe she'd already gone by the time we got here."

I thanked them and headed down toward the ruins.

A little further on, in the dense thicket through which the path wound, something caught my eye and I came to an abrupt stop. A neat pile of green plastic bags lay there, and on top of them was a pair of scuffed black shoes. Obviously she had come here on the bus, wearing her street shoes, and had only switched to sneakers for her work. Why would she leave without changing her shoes?

I hurried through the thicket toward the patch of wild mustard.

There, deep in the weeds, its color blending with their

foliage, was another bag. I opened it. It was a quarter full of wilting mustard greens. She hadn't had much time to forage, not much time at all.

Seriously worried now, I rushed up to the Great Highway. From the phone booth inside the restaurant, I dialed Greg's direct line at the SFPD. Busy. I retrieved my dime and called All Souls.

"Any calls?"

Ted's typewriter rattled in the background. "No, but Hank wants to talk to you."

Hank Zahn, my boss. With a sinking heart, I remembered the conference we had had scheduled for half an hour ago. He came on the line.

"Where the hell are you?"

"Uh, in a phone booth."

"What I mean is, why aren't you here?"

"I can explain—"

"I should have known."

"What?"

"Greg warned me you'd be off investigating something."

"Greg? When did you talk to him?"

"Fifteen minutes ago. He wants you to call. It's important."

"Thanks!"

"Wait a minute—"

I hung up and dialed Greg again. He answered, sounding rushed. Without preamble, I explained what I'd found in the wild mustard patch.

"That's why I called you." His voice was unusually gentle. "We got word this morning."

"What word?" My stomach knotted.

"An identification on a body that washed up near Devil's Slide yesterday evening. Apparently she went in at low tide, or she would have been swept much further to sea."

I was silent.

"Sharon?"

"Yes, I'm here."

"You know how it is out there. The signs warn against climbing. The current is bad."

But I'd never, in almost a year, seen the old Japanese woman near the sea. She was always up on the slope, where her weeds grew. "When was low tide, Greg?"

"Yesterday? Around eight in the morning."

Around the time the restaurant cashier had noticed her, and several hours before the teenagers had arrived. And in between? What had happened out there?

I hung up and stood at the top of the slope, pondering. What should I look for? What could I possibly find?

I didn't know, but I felt certain the old woman had not gone into the sea by accident. She had scaled those cliffs with the best of them.

I started down, noting the shoes and the bags in the thicket, marching resolutely past the wild mustard toward the abandoned truck. I walked all around it, examining its exterior and interior, but it gave me no clues. Then I started toward the tunnel in the cliff.

The area, so crowded on Sundays, was sparsely populated now. San Franciscans were going about their usual business, and visitors from the tour buses parked at nearby Cliff House were leery of climbing down here. The teenagers were the only other people in sight. They stood by the mouth of the tunnel, watching me. Something in their postures told me they were afraid. I quickened my steps.

The boys inclined their heads toward one another. Then they whirled and ran into the mouth of the tunnel.

I went after them. Again, I had the wrong shoes. I kicked them off and ran through the coarse sand. The boys were halfway down the tunnel.

One of them paused, frantically surveying a rift in the wall. I prayed he wouldn't go that way, into the boiling waves below.

He turned and ran after his companion. They disappeared at the end of the tunnel.

I hit the hard-packed dirt and increased my pace. Near the end, I slowed and approached more cautiously. At first I thought the boys had vanished, but then I looked down. They crouched on a ledge below. Their faces were scared and young, so young.

I stopped where they could see me and made a calming motion. "Come on back up," I said. "I won't hurt you."

The mustached one shook his head.

"Look, there's no place you can go. You can't swim in that surf."

Simultaneously they glanced down. They looked back at me and both shook their heads.

I took a step forward. "Whatever happened, it couldn't have—" Suddenly I felt the ground crumble. My foot slipped and I pitched forward. I fell to one knee, my arms frantically searching for a support.

"Oh, God!" the mustached boy cried. "Not you too!" He stood up, swaying, his arms outstretched.

I kept sliding. The boy reached up and caught me by the arm. He staggered back toward the edge and we both fell to the hard rocky ground. For a moment, we both lay there panting. When I finally sat up, I saw we were inches from the sheer drop to the surf.

The boy sat up too, his scared eyes on me. His companion was flattened against the cliff wall.

"It's okay," I said shakily.

"I thought you'd fall just like the old woman," the boy beside me said.

"It was an accident, wasn't it?"

He nodded. "We didn't mean for her to fall."

"Were you teasing her?"

"Yeah. We always did, for fun. But this time we went too far. We took her purse. She chased us."

"Through the tunnel, to here."

"Yes."

"And then she slipped."

The other boy moved away from the wall. "Honest, we didn't mean for it to happen. It was just that she was so old. She slipped."

"We watched her fall," his companion said. "We couldn't do anything."

"What did you do with the purse?"

"Threw it in after her. There were only two dollars in it. Two lousy dollars." His voice held a note of wonder. "Can you imagine, chasing us all the way down here for two bucks?"

I stood up carefully, grasping the rock for support. "Okay," I said. "Let's get out of here."

They looked at each other and then down at the surf.

"Come on. We'll talk some more. I know you didn't mean for her to die. And you saved my life."

They scrambled up, keeping their distance from me. Their faces were pale under their tans, their eyes afraid. They were so young. To them, products of the credit-card age, fighting to the death for two dollars was inconceivable. And the Japanese woman had been so old. For her, eking out a living with the wild mustard, two dollars had probably meant the difference between life and death.

I wondered if they'd ever understand.

# A Long Time Dying

## *William F. Nolan*

*My hard-fisted private op, Bart Challis, was born
in the gaudy pages of* Chase *in May of 1964. In that issue,
I had him slug his way through a story I called "Strippers Have To
Die"—which later formed the basis for my first Challis novel,*
Death Is For Losers *(published in 1968). Bart's second case,
"The Pop Op Caper," was printed in* Playboy
*in October of 1967, and formed the
basis for my sequel novel,* The White Cad Cross-Up *(published in
1969.) I was proud to find that these two novels were enough
to place Bart among the top 30 private eyes in the 1920-1970 survey
listing for* The Armchair Detective *(Summer 1983).*

*The present story marks his return to action for the first
time in 15 years and, alas, it may be his final bow. My present
intention is to kill him off in the first chapter of a new novel
I'm planning—which will feature his younger brother, Nick
Challis. The truth is, Bart is
just too damn old to sustain a savage beating in a Beverly
Hills alley or bed a man-hungry blonde who demands multiple
orgasms. But, happily, Nick will be around to carry on
this lurid tradition. God, how I love tough private eyes!*

I'VE had me a hell of a ten days. Insane. Incredible. In the course of my doubtful career a lot of freak things have happened, but this was fruitcake with all the nuts. Let me run it down for you . . .

It's July in the armpit. That's where my office is, on Spring, in downtown Los Angeles. Geek Street. Where the smog is thick enough to choke a hippo. Once, about a thousand years ago, this was a nice place to be. Now even the winos complain. But with business the way it is I can't afford a suite in Century City.

Anyhow, it's July, with the heat so bad my .38 is melting. I'm busy drinking at my desk when this pop-eyed kid comes in carrying a big leather suitcase. Asks me if my name is Bart Challis. I tell him yes.

"And you are a licensed private detective?"

"If I'm not, I've sure been kidding myself for thirty years."

"Splendid! My name is Ronald Strongheart." He reaches across the desk to pump my hand. "I'm delighted to meet you."

"I don't believe that," I said.

"You don't believe that I'm delighted to meet you?"

"No—I don't believe your name is Ronald Strongheart. *Nobody* is named Ronald Strongheart."

"My great-grandfather was a Blackfoot. I'm part Indian."

I shrugged. "Okay, Strongheart, what can I do for you?"

"I've been fascinated with private detectives since childhood," he said. "I tend to think of your kind as the last of the urban cowboys—members of a vanishing breed."

"I'm still able to get around without a cane."

"I was speaking metaphorically, not personally. No offense intended."

"Look," I said, "you've interrupted my drinking. If you came in here to hire me, then let's skip the metaphors and get down to it."

"Well, I do in fact wish to hire you. How much do you charge?"

"Hundred a day, plus expenses."

"There won't be any expenses. You will not be required to leave your office—but the hundred a day is quite satisfactory. My father is extremely well-fixed, and he's financing this. You're my thesis."

"I'm your *what*?"

"I'm working for my Master's degree at UCLA," the kid explained. "I'm doing my thesis on hard-boiled private detectives, tracing their development through the pulp magazines of the '20s and '30s, and relating these rough-hewn pulpwood operatives to today's real life independent investigators. I have chosen you as my focal subject."

I put away the office bottle and leaned back in my swivel chair. "Are you on the level, kid, or is someone after you with a net?"

"Splendid hard-boiled repartee," the kid said, popping his eyes. "I'm really very pleased. I feel that I've made an excellent choice."

"Show me some of Daddy's money and maybe I'll agree with you."

He smiled, reached into his wallet and laid ten crisp new hundred-dollar bills on my shabby desk blotter. I picked up the bills one at a time, held them toward the window. They looked genuine. "Well, well, well," I said.

"May we begin our relationship?" the kid asked.

"We may indeed," I told him.

He opened the big leather suitcase and began stacking magazines on my desk. Magazines with gaudy covers featuring chesty chicks in off-the-shoulder blouses, and tough mugs with smoking automatics. Each time he laid one of these on the desk he named it, verbally caressing each title:

"*Candid Detective . . . Crack Detective . . . Amazing Detective . . . Snappy Detective . . . Smashing Detective . . .*

*Super Detective . . . Famous Detective . . . Double Detective . . . Triple Detective . . . Giant Detective . . . Mammoth Detective . . ."*

"So what am I supposed to do with these?"

"Read them, Mr. Challis. Study them. Then tell me how the fictional detectives in these issues differ from the reality of your chosen profession. When you have read all of them, I shall question you regarding your notes and observations."

"And *this* is what your rich daddy is paying for?"

"Of course," he said. "You are to be my primary source of research."

I sighed, picked up one of the magazines, flipped it open to the lead story. In the illustration, a big, square-jawed detective had just kicked his way through a door, a .45 in each fist, and was blazing away at a roomful of unshaven knife-wielding goons who had a full-breasted blonde tied to a wooden chair. She was half-naked, and her eyes were popping, like the kid's. She looked as if she could use a drink. The story's title was "Gangster Guns for the Grinning Ghouls of Gothamtown."

"Been at least two weeks since I've shot my way into a room to save a kidnapped blonde," I said.

The kid chuckled. "Splendid!" he said, jotting down my comment in a notebook. He handed me an engraved card. "My unlisted number's at the bottom. Phone me when you wish to discuss the material." He hesitated, and his grape eyes rolled. "And I beg of you, Mr. Challis, handle these issues with extreme care. They are all collectors' items. Quite impossible to replace."

"That's what I told my second wife *I'd* be. But she dumped me anyhow."

He chuckled again, snapping the suitcase shut. "Love your repartee!"

And he was through the door and gone.

For the next ten days at the office, between belts of Old Turkey, I read pulp-paper detective stories. About smashing, crashing, dashing detectives and classy, sassy, sexy dames, in cases filled with bullets, blood and bootleg gin. There was a killing in every pulp paragraph, with master criminals evil enough to make Attila the Hun look like Little Red Riding Hood.

I kept reading. Eight hours a day. Until I used up the kid's thousand.

Then I picked up his engraved card and gave him a jingle.

"Strongheart here."

"Challis here," I said.

"Ah, and how are you progressing, Mr. Challis?"

"Well, I've progressed right through your grand," I told him. "Ten days, ten hundred bucks."

"Then you need more money?"

"That's the general idea," I said. "I've still got a stack of kidnapped blondes to get through."

"How many more days will it take you to finish the material?"

"Ten days more ought to do it."

"Fine. I'll send you a check for another thousand."

"Cash," I said. "No checks."

"But I've *never* had a check bounce," he said in an injured tone. "Why do you insist on cash?"

"*I* don't, but my bookie does," I told him. "I played a long shot on a three-legged wonder horse and lost. If the money's not paid before midnight I'll be looking for a new set of teeth."

"Wait just a second," he said. "I want to get all that down in my notebook. Superb hard-boiled vernacular!"

"What about the grand? I need it today. In cash."

"I don't have that much with me at the moment," he said.

"Then how about I meet you at your bank, okay?"

"Yes, that would be fine. It's the Agoura Hills First National. The one with the splendid nostalgic decor. It just opened this week."

"How do I get there?"

"Take the Ventura Freeway west—all the way out through the

Valley. Then take the Reyes Adobe turnoff. The bank is just over the rise, in the Plaza area. Can't miss it."

"Oke," I said. "What time?"

"Twoish. How does twoish sound?"

"Does that mean two o'clock?"

"Yes," said Ronald Strongheart.

"See you there," I said.

I hung up, got out the office bottle and poured myself a stiff jolt. "*Twoish* . . . Jesus!" I said.

Entering the Agoura Hills First National was like stepping out of a time machine. The joint was designed to look exactly like a bank of the 30s—with brass railings, varnished wood counters, old-fashioned tellers' cages and antique lighting. All part of the Greater Los Angeles Nostalgia Craze. Even the tall black door on the main safe looked like it had been built back in those days, with its fat hinges and big round combination knobs.

Ronald was waiting for me. He shook my hand, popped his eyes, and asked me what I thought of the place. "It's simply fascinating, isn't it?"

"Yeah, fascinating," I growled sourly. For the past week and a half I'd been up to my kazoo in the 1930s so I didn't really appreciate more of the same. I just wanted my grand.

Ronald was in line in front of a teller's cage when this incredible old guy walks in the door. That's the word for him— incredible. He's maybe seventy-five or eighty. Tough, wrinkled mug. Seedy moustache. Wearing a straw hat, the kind they used to call a boater. Black and white perforated wing-tip shoes. Dark blue pin-striped suit with a silver watch chain draped across his vest.

And, swear to God, he's packing a Tommy. Thompson submachine gun, with a circular snap-in ammo drum.

"This is a stickup," he yells in a cracked voice. "Everybody—get yer mitts in the air!"

People start to grin. One of the cashiers begins to giggle. Even the bank guard looks amused. They all figure it's a gag, part of the bank's opening week celebration.

But it's for real. The old gink in the straw boater cuts loose with a burst from the Thompson—and a dozen antique lamps jump into glass splinters along the side counter. Then he slugs the guard, knocking him flat with the barrel of the gun.

"Hit the deck," the old guy shouts. "Everybody! *Do* it!"

Nobody's laughing now. Faces are pasty white; jaws are hanging slack. Everybody flops belly-down, including Ronald and yours truly.

"Are you armed, Mr. Challis?" Ronald whispers.

"I've got my .38," I whisper back, "but I'm not dumb enough to pull it against a Tommy."

He raised his head. "Maybe I can divert him, and then you can—"

I pushed his face into the rug. "Cut the crap," I whispered fiercely. "This weirdo means business!"

The old guy didn't bother with petty cash. He proceeded to leap over the front counter toward the main safe. I mean, he *vaulted* over that counter. I was impressed.

Then he jammed his Tommy into the bank president's gut. "Get me seventy-five thousand three hundred and forty-six dollars—and be quick about it!"

I raised an eyebrow. Bank robbers take what they can get; they don't name specific sums. But this guy waited until that exact amount had been counted out to him before he vaulted back over the counter and split.

Everybody jumps up. Alarm bells are ringing. People are yelling at each other. The bank president looks like he's just survived World War III.

"Do something!" Ronald says to me.

"Do what?"

"You're a detective. Go after him!"

"I'm also a 56-year-old man," I said. "I don't chase bank robbers."

"Not even ones in their late seventies?"

I blinked at him. He *meant* it. He wanted me to go after the old gink in the straw hat.

So I did. Don't ask me why, because I couldn't tell you. I just suddenly took off with Ronald at my heels, out the door and into my Honda Civic.

He was easy to follow. I mean, who *else* in Los Angeles uses a 1933 Hudson Terraplane as a getaway car?

The weird part of this whole thing was *I* seemed to be the only one to realize this. The folks in the Agoura First National were so stunned by the whole nutso scene that nobody had managed to get a fix on the old guy's car.

Otherwise, by now, as we roared east along the Ventura Freeway, through the San Fernando Valley toward downtown L.A., there would have been cops' cars and copters all over the landscape.

But it was just me and Ronald in my Honda, hotdogging it after the old guy's antique Hudson.

"I think he's spotted us," says Ronald. "He's speeding up."

Sure enough, he's trying to lose us. And that old fart could *drive*, I tell you. Had that teakettle doing 85, weaving in and out of traffic, skinning past slower cars, really putting on a show. But I stuck with him.

"Maybe you could shoot out one of his tires," Ronald suggests.

"Are you nuts?" I yell, "It's all I can do just to keep *up* with him!"

We zip on down onto the Hollywood Freeway, with him switching lanes like Mario Andretti in the Indy 500, but with me hanging on his tailpipe all the way.

To the old Union Station. The downtown train depot. That was his destination. He dry-skids into the parking lot, judders his antique to a smoking stop, jumps out and runs inside. Leaves his straw hat in the car. By now he's wearing a long kind of furry raccoon coat with the Tommy and the bag of money hidden under it.

I followed him inside, with Ronald right behind me.

The depot was practically deserted, like a convention hall without the convention. Huge, and full of echoes.

The old guy seemed confused. Guess he'd expected to find the place jammed with people and trains. Maybe figured to lose himself in the crowd, then hop a train out of town. That's how they did it in the '30s. Only this was the '80s—the Jet Age—with damn few train passengers and fewer trains. The depot was more like a marble mausoleum than an active center of travel.

The old guy didn't know what to do about it. So he did the only thing possible; he swung around in the middle of the big depot's main waiting room, opened his raccoon coat, and let fly with the Tommy.

I took a fast nosedive behind one of the long wooden benches, pulling Ronald down with me. A line of hot slugs ripped across the top of the bench, showering us with wood dust.

By then I had my .38 in hand.

"Shoot *back* at him!" Strongheart urged. He was popping his eyes at me again. "Don't let him get the best of you!"

"Shut up, Ronald," I said. "This isn't 'High Noon' and I'm not Gary Cooper. That wizened old shitface is *dangerous!*"

"Well, you can't just let him shoot up the entire depot like this. He *could* kill innocent people!"

"Yeah, like for instance, *us*," I said. "Besides, there's nobody left in here. They all ran out when he cut loose."

"Will someone call the police?"

"Maybe."

"I truly feel that you should take affirmative action," said Ronald. "This fellow is a public menace."

It was quiet now. The old geezer had quit firing. Probably he was reloading, slipping in a new ammo drum. I peered cautiously over the top of the splintered bench—in time to see him disappearing through the waiting room doors at the far end of the station.

He was headed for the outside platform.

We took off after him.

The platform was very silent. No trains this time of day. Nothing but a long expanse of dusty concrete with the late afternoon sun painting everything pale yellow. The corner shadows were deep.

"He's out here *somewhere*," whispered Ronald. "Maybe I can act as a decoy . . . flush him out."

"Fine," I said. "You *do* that," Ronald. Then your bullet-riddled body will show me where he's hiding."

"Uh . . ." Ronald hesitated. "Maybe we need another plan."

Suddenly the pillar we've been crouching behind begins to disintegrate under a hail of bullets. He's cut loose again with the Thompson and we do a fast duck behind a high wooden baggage cart.

"There he is!" yells Ronald, pointing.

I spot him, about fifty feet in front of us, on his belly, firing from the shadows. I squeeze off three shots of my own.

Silence again.

"Hey, Pop! Give it up," I yell. "Cops are coming. They'll blow your ass off."

No reply. I expected another burst, but what I got back was more silence.

"You stay here," I told Ronald. "I'm going to check him out."

"All right, but be *careful*, Mr. Challis."

I gave him a sour look; never had a piece of advice been more superfluous.

Dodging between concrete pillars, I closed on the old guy, my gun up and ready. But he didn't fire at me, and he didn't move. Had I nailed him with one of my shots? Jesus, maybe I'd *killed* him!

Somehow the thought depressed me. This whole business,

from the moment I'd walked into the bank, had been like an act out of Barnum and Bailey. Strictly circus. And you don't end up killing the head clown.

He was still belly down on the platform, with most of his body in shadow, the Thompson angled out in front of him. Sunlight played along the barrel.

I edged closer. No movement.

Then I heard a groan. Low, muffled. He was in pain.

I reached him, my .38 aimed at his head. "Are you hit, Pop?" I asked him.

"No . . . no . . ." he said in a low, strained voice, letting go of the Tommy and rolling over on his back. Both hands clutched at his chest, but I couldn't see any blood.

"Heart . . ." he said softly. "Heart attack."

His face was all splotchy, eyes tensed with pain. But, by damn, he was *smiling*. That I couldn't figure. Later, I knew why.

I holstered the .38 and knelt beside him. "I'll call a doctor."

"Too late." He shook his head. "This time it's curtains."

"I'm going for help," I said, standing up. He reached out to grab my sleeve with a clawed hand.

"Do you know who I am?" he asked me.

"How could I?"

"Important . . . important for you to know." His voice was full of pain; each word took effort.

He pulled me toward him and began whispering in my ear. By now, Ronald was standing off to one side of the platform, watching us. He started forward, but I waved him back.

When the old guy told me who he was I let out a yelp of disbelief. "Hey, that's crazy!" I said. "You *can't* be . . . he's dead. Has been for fifty years."

He chuckled, a wet, broken sound deep in his throat. "Ah, yes . . . I was a long time dying . . . but I lasted long enough to do it. They all said I couldn't, but I *did*!"

Then, with fading strength, he began to whisper things into

222

my ear that convinced me. Little things. Details. Convincing as
hell.

"People should *know*," I said finally.

He shook his head again. "Wrong . . . Don't want to . . .
spoil the legend. Don't want them to know I died . . . *this* way
. . . sick . . . old . . . alone . . ."

His eyes, in that ancient bulldog face, were moist now. The
last of his strength was slipping away. His eyelids fluttered down.

And then he was gone.

A long time dying.

After the cops had arrived and the body had been removed
and the money was on its way back to the bank I told Ronald I
needed to do some research. Alone. At the downtown Central
Library.

"But I've got *questions* to ask," he declared.

"Look, go back to Agoura and get my grand. From Daddy.
And bring it to my office at five. Then I'll answer your questions.
Right now, I've still got a lot of my *own* to deal with."

"Okay, Mr. Challis. See you at five."

At the library I found the book I was looking for, checked it
out, and took it back to the office.

It satisfied me.

Promptly at five, Ronald showed. With the grand. I told him
my bookie would be very grateful.

"Now," said Ronald. "What was all that whispering about
between you and the deceased? Who *was* that guy?"

"The name in the wallet was Frank Sullivan," I said. "And
that's who the cops think he is."

"But Sullivan wasn't his real name?"

"No," I said. "He used a lot of others—John Hall . . . Joe
Harris . . . Carl Hellman . . . John Donovan . . . but they
were all phony."

I lit a cigarette, took a long drag, let smoke seep from the
corners of my mouth. "In late October of 1933," I said, "the

223

Dillinger gang robbed the Central National Bank in Greencastle, Indiana, and got away with $75,346. It was the biggest haul of Dillinger's career and the papers said he'd never be able to match it. So, half a century later, he comes back to prove 'em wrong."

A long moment of pop-eyed silence. Ronald's tone is slow and measured. "Are you telling me that John Dillinger robbed the Agoura Hills First National this afternoon? . . . *the* John Dillinger?"

"That's exactly what I'm telling you."

"But that's flatly impossible. Everybody knows that Dillinger was killed by the FBI in Chicago in an alley next to some theater, back in . . . in . . ."

"In 1934," I said. "On the night of July 22nd."

"But *this* is July 22nd!"

"Uh huh," I said. "That's why he chose today. For his rebirth. Exactly fifty years after he'd retired. He wanted to see if he could still do it at the age of eighty. And I guess he damn well proved he *could.*"

"Retired?"

"Sure. The poor gink who died in that alley, full of FBI slugs, wasn't John Dillinger. The shooting was a setup, and the public bought it. So did Hoover and his boys at first—until they performed an autopsy on the dead man and found out the truth. Then, to save their own reputation, they faked the prints and buried the autopsy report. Claimed that the reason the guy didn't *look* like Dillinger was because of extensive plastic surgery."

"Well, that would have explained it," said Ronald. "How do you know it *wasn't* really Dillinger?"

"Before he croaked, the old guy told me that a book had been published that would back up his story. Well, he wasn't lying. I found it at the library."

"What book are you talking about?"

"This one." I took *Bloodletters and Badmen* out of a drawer and shoved it across the desk. The author was Jay Robert Nash.

Ronald opened it to the entry on Dillinger, read it, then

looked at me numbly. "Shows his year of birth as late 1903, but the year of his death is a question mark."

"Right," I said. "They can fill it in with the next edition—July 22, 1984."

"And the guy they killed next to the Biograph movie house back in '34 was named James Lawrence?"

"Right again." I took another drag on my cigarette. "He was a small-time Chicago hood. Had a moustache and dark hair. Looked enough like Dillinger to make the whole setup work."

"The autopsy report—"

"—was 'lost.' For thirty years nobody could find it. The FBI made sure of that. But this writer guy, Nash, he got hold of a copy and put all the facts together." I ticked them off, one by one: "Lawrence was shorter and heavier than Dillinger. And you can't alter a man's height. He had a rheumatic heart. Dillinger didn't. His eyes were brown. Dillinger's were blue. The dead man lacked *all* of Dillinger's known body scars and birthmarks. And, to top it, Lawrence had *not* had plastic surgery. It was a total fakeout, pure and simple. Dillinger was able to retire, probably to South America, and Hoover's boys were able to tell the world they'd killed America's Public Enemy Number One."

"And—despite this book—people still believe that?"

"Sure. People believe what they *want* to believe. It's like director John Ford used to say about his westerns: 'Given the truth, and given the legend, film the legend.' And the legend of John Dillinger, the notorious bank robber, remains secure. The old geezer who died of a heart attack today at Union Station was Frank Sullivan. He wanted it that way. He wanted to be remembered as going out in a blaze of FBI gunfire at the height of his fame. That job today in Agoura was a *personal* thing, just to prove he still had the stuff in him, that he could still vault over a bank counter and drive like hell in a getaway car. He told me what a great day it had been. His heart failed from all the excitement—but he died happy."

Ronald nodded. "And that's why he demanded exactly $75,346. To match his best job."

"Yeah," I said.

"But why the Agoura First National?"

"Nostalgia . . . with the 1930s decor old Johnny felt right at home."

Ronald Strongheart closed the book with a sigh. "It's like a story out of the pulps," he said. "Only better. A whole *lot* better."

Then he began gathering the pulp magazines together and putting them back into his leather suitcase.

"Hey," I protested. "You've paid me for another ten days' reading."

"No, Mr. Challis, please consider the extra thousand as a bonus. I've got what I need now for my thesis. I've decided on a new theme—a comparative analysis regarding truth versus legend. With John Herbert Dillinger as my new focal subject. I've even got the title."

"And what's that?"

"I'll call it . . . 'A Long Time Dying.'"

*AUTHOR'S NOTE: For factual confirmation of the "fictional" elements in this story, I refer the reader to* Bloodletters and Badmen: A Narrative Encyclopedia of American Criminals From the Pilgrims to the Present *by Jay Robert Nash. New York: Evans and Company, 1973, pp. 159–178.*

# Three-Dot Po

## *Sara Paretsky*

*"Three-Dot Po" is a tribute to the golden retriever in general and to Capo, my family's retriever, specifically. On Christmas Day, 1983, I sat discussing a possible V.I. story with my brother Jonathan, my son Tim, and my husband. They demanded a story that would have a golden retriever as the heroine, and one featuring Jonathan, who does have long golden hair but is a German scholar, not a pianist.*
*"Three-Dot Po" is in fact ". . . po."*

CINDA Goodrich and I were jogging acquaintances. A professional photographer, she kept the same erratic hours as a private investigator; we often met along Belmont Harbor in the late mornings. By then we had the lakefront to ourselves; the hip young professionals run early so they can make their important eight o'clock meetings.

Cinda occasionally ran with her boyfriend, Jonathan Michaels, and always with her golden retriever, Three-Dot Po, or Po. The dog's name meant something private to her and Jonathan; they only laughed and shook their heads when I asked about it.

Jonathan played the piano, often at late-night private parties. He was seldom up before noon and usually left exercise to Cinda and Po. Cinda was a diligent runner, even on the hottest days of summer and the coldest of winter. I do five miles a day as a grudging way to fight age and calories, but Cinda made a ten mile circuit every morning with religious enthusiasm.

One December I didn't see her out for a week and wondered vaguely if she might be sick. The following Saturday, however, we met on the small promontory abutting Belmont Harbor—she returning from her jaunt three miles further north, and I just getting ready to turn around for home. As we jogged together, she explained that Eli Burton, the fancy North Michigan Avenue department store, had hired her to photograph children talking to Santa. She made a face. "Not the way Eric Lieberman got his start, but it'll finance January in the Bahamas for Jonathan and me." She called to Po, who was inspecting a dead bird on the rocks by the water, and moved on ahead of me.

The week before Christmas the temperature dropped suddenly and left us with the bitterest December on record. My living room was so cold I couldn't bear to use it; I handled all my business bundled in bed, even moving the television into the bedroom. I didn't go out at all on Christmas Eve.

Christmas Day I was supposed to visit friends in one of the northern suburbs. I wrapped myself in a blanket and went to the living room to scrape a patch of ice on a window. I wanted to see how badly snowed over Halsted Street was, assuming my poor little Omega would even start.

I hadn't run for five days, since the temperature first fell. I was feeling flabby, knew I should force myself outside, but felt too lazy to face the weather. I was about to go back to the bedroom and wrap some presents when I caught sight of a golden retriever moving smartly down the street. It was Po; behind her came Cinda, warm in an orange down vest, face covered with a ski mask.

"Ah, nuts," I muttered. If she could do it, I could do it. Layering on thermal underwear, two pairs of wool socks, sweatshirts, and a down vest, I told myself encouragingly, "Quitters never win and winners never quit," and "It's not the size of the dog in the fight that counts but the size of the fight in the dog."

The slogans got me out the door, but they didn't prepare me for the shock of cold. The wind sucked the air out of my lungs and left me gasping. I staggered back into the entryway and tied a scarf around my face, adjusted earmuffs and a wool cap, and put on sunglasses to protect my eyes.

Even so, it was bitter going. After the first mile the blood was flowing well and my arms and legs were warm, but my feet were cold, and even heavy muffling couldn't keep the wind from scraping the skin on my cheeks. Few cars were on the streets, and no other people. It was like running through a wasteland. This is what it would be like after a nuclear war: no people, freezing cold, snow blowing across in fine pelting particles like a desert sand-storm.

The lake made an even eerier landscape. Steam rose from it as from a giant cauldron. The water was invisible beneath the heavy veils of mist. I paused for a moment in awe, but the wind quickly cut through the layers of clothes.

The lake path curved around as it led to the promontory so that you could only see a few yards ahead of you. I kept expecting to meet Cinda and Po on their way back, but the only person who passed me was a solitary male jogger, anonymous in a blue ski mask and khaki down jacket.

At the far point of the promontory the wind blew unblocked across the lake. It swept snow and frozen mist pellets with it, blowing in a high persistent whine. I was about to turn and go home when I heard a dog barking above the keening wind. I hesitated to go down to the water, but what if it were Po, separated from her mistress?

The rocks leading down to the lake were covered with ice. I slipped and slid down, trying desperately for hand and toeholds—even if someone were around to rescue me I wouldn't survive a bath in sub-zero water.

I found Po on a flat slab of rock. She was standing where its edge hung over the mist-covered water, barking furiously. I called to her. She turned her head briefly but wouldn't come.

By now I had a premonition of what would meet me when I'd picked my way across the slab. I lay flat on the icy rock, gripping my feet around one end, and leaned over it through the mist to peer in the water. As soon as I showed up, Po stopped barking and began an uneasy pacing and whining.

Cinda's body was just visible beneath the surface. It was a four-foot drop to the water from where I lay. I couldn't reach her and I didn't dare get down in the water. I thought furiously and finally unwound a long muffler from around my neck. Tying it to a jagged spur near me I wrapped the other end around my waist and prayed. Leaning over from the waist gave me the length I needed to reach into the water. I took a deep breath and plunged my arms in. The shock of the water was almost more than I could bear; I concentrated on Cinda, on the dog, thought of Christmas in the northern suburbs, of everything possible but the cold which made my arms almost useless. "You only have one chance, Vic. Don't blow it."

The weight of her body nearly dragged me in on top of Cinda. I slithered across the icy rock, scissoring my feet wildly until they caught on the spur where my muffler was tied. Po was no help, either. She planted herself next to me, whimpering with anxiety as I pulled her mistress from the water. With water soaked in every garment, Cinda must have weighed two hundred pounds. I almost lost her several times, almost lost myself, but I got her up. I tried desperately to revive her, Po anxiously licking her face, but there was no hope. I finally realized I was going to die of exposure myself if I didn't get away from there. I tried calling Po to come with me, but she wouldn't leave Cinda. I ran as hard as I could back to the harbor, where I flagged down a car. My teeth were chattering so hard I almost couldn't speak, but I got the strangers to realize there was a dead woman back on the promontory point. They drove me to the Town Hall police station.

I spent most of Christmas Day in bed, layered in blankets, drinking hot soup prepared by my friend Dr. Lotty Herschel. I had some frostbite in two of my fingers, but she thought they would recover. Lotty left at seven to eat dinner with her nurse, Carol Alvarado, and her family.

The police had taken Cinda away, and Jonathan had persuaded Po to go home with him. I guess it had been a fairly tragic scene—Jonathan crying, the dog unwilling to let Cinda's body out of her sight. I hadn't been there myself, but one of my newspaper friends told me about it.

It was only eight o'clock when the phone next to my bed began ringing, but I was deep in sleep, buried in blankets. It must have rung eight or nine times before I even woke up, and another several before I could bring myself to stick one of my sore arms out to answer it.

"Hello?" I said groggily.

"Vic. Vic, I hate to bother you, but I need help."

"Who is this?" I started coming to.

"Jonathan Michaels. They've arrested me for killing Cinda. I only get the one phone call." He was trying to speak jauntily, but his voice cracked.

"Killing Cinda?" I echoed. "I thought she slipped and fell."

"Apparently someone strangled her and pushed her in after she was dead. Don't ask me how they know. Don't ask me why they thought I did it. The problem is—the problem is—Po. I don't have anyone to leave her with."

"Where are you now?" I swung my legs over the bed and began pulling on longjohns. He was at their apartment, four buildings up the street from me, on his way downtown for booking and then to Cook County jail. The arresting officer, not inhuman on Christmas Day, would let him wait for me if I could get their fast.

I was half dressed by the time I hung up and quickly finished pulling on jeans, boots, and a heavy sweater. Jonathan and two policemen were standing in the entryway of his building when I ran up. He handed me his apartment keys. In the distance I could hear Po's muffled barking.

"Do you have a lawyer?" I demanded.

Ordinarily a cheerful, bearded young man with long golden hair, Jonathan now looked rather bedraggled. He shook his head dismally.

"You need one. I can find someone for you, or I can represent you myself until we come up with someone better. I don't practice any more, so you need someone who's active, but I can get you through the formalities."

He accepted gratefully, and I followed him into the waiting police car. The arresting officers wouldn't answer any of my questions. When we got down to the Eleventh Street police headquarters, I insisted on seeing the officer in charge, and was taken in to Detective Sergeant John McGonnigal.

McGonnigal and I had met frequently. He was a stocky young man, very able, and I had a lot of respect for him. I'm not sure he reciprocated it. "Merry Christmas, Sergeant. It's a terrible day to be working, isn't it?"

"Merry Christmas, Miss Warshawski. What are you doing here?"

"I represent Jonathan Michaels. Seems someone got a little confused and thinks he pushed Miss Goodrich into Lake Michigan this morning."

"We're not confused. She was strangled and pushed into the lake. She was dead before she went into the water. He has no alibi for the relevant time."

"No alibi! Who in this city does have an alibi?"

There was more to it than that, he explained stiffly. Michaels and Cinda had been heard quarreling late at night by their neighbors across the hall and underneath. They had resumed their fight in the morning. Cinda had finally slammed out of the house with the dog around nine-thirty.

"He didn't follow her, Sergeant."

"How do you know?"

I explained that I had watched Cinda from my living room. "And I didn't run into Mr. Michaels out on the point. I only met one person.

He pounced on that. How could I be sure it wasn't Jonathan? Finally agreeing to get a description of his clothes to see if he owned a navy ski mask or a khaki jacket, McGonnigal also pointed out that there were two ways to leave the point—Jonathan could have gone north instead of south.

"Maybe. But you're spinning a very thin thread, Sergeant. It's not going to hold up. Now I need some time alone with my client."

He was most unhappy to let me represent Michael, but there wasn't much he could do about it. He left us alone in a small interrogation room.

"I'm taking it on faith that you didn't kill Cinda," I said briskly. "But for the record, did you?"

He shook his head. "No way. Even if I had stopped loving her, which I hadn't, I don't solve my problems that way." He ran a hand through his long hair. "I can't believe this. I can't even really believe Cinda is dead. It all happened too fast. And now they're arresting me." His hands were beautiful, with long, strong fingers. Strong enough to strangle someone, certainly.

"What were you fighting about this morning?"

"Fighting?"

"Don't play dumb with me, Jonathan; I'm the only help you've got. Your neighbors heard you—that's why the police arrested you."

He smiled a little foolishly. "It all seems so stupid now. I keep thinking, if I hadn't gotten her mad, she wouldn't have gone out there. She'd be alive now."

"Maybe. Maybe not. What were you fighting about?"

He hesitated. "Those damned Santa Claus pictures she took. I never wanted her to do it, anyway. She's too good—she was too good a photographer to be wasting her time on that kind of stuff. Then she got mad and started accusing me of being Lawrence Welk, and who was I to talk. It all started because someone phoned her at one this morning. I'd just gotten back from a gig—" he grinned suddenly, painfully "—a Lawrence Welk gig, and this call came in. Someone who had been in one of her Santa shots. Said he was very shy, and wanted to make sure he wasn't in the picture with his kid, so would she bring him the negatives?"

"She had the negatives? Not Burton's?"

"Yeah. Stupid idiot. She was developing the film herself. Apparently this guy called Burton's first. Anyway, to make a long story short, she agreed to meet him today and give him the negatives, and I was furious. First of all, why should she go out on Christmas to satisfy some moron's whim? And why was she taking those dumb-assed pictures anyway?"

Suddenly his face cracked and he started sobbing. "She was so beautiful and I loved her so much. Why did I have to fight with her?"

I patted his shoulder and held his hand until the tears stopped. "You know, if that was her caller she was going to meet, that's probably the person who killed her."

"I thought of that. And that's what I told the police. But they say it's the kind of thing I'd be bound to make up under the circumstances."

I pushed him through another half hour of questions. What had she said about her caller? Had he given his name? She didn't know his name. Then how had she known which negatives were his? She didn't—just the day and the time he'd been there, so she was taking over the negatives for that morning. That's all he knew; she'd been too angry to tell him what she was taking with her. Yes, she had taken negatives with her.

He gave me detailed instructions on how to look after Po. Just dry dog food. No table scraps. As many walks as I felt like giving her—she was an outdoor dog and loved snow and water. She was very well-trained; they never walked her with a leash. Before I left, I talked to McGonnigal. He told me he was going to follow up on the story about the man in the photograph at Burton's the next day but he wasn't taking it too seriously. He told me they hadn't found any film on Cinda's body, but that was because she hadn't taken any with her—Jonathan was making up that, too. He did agree, though, to hold Jonathan at Eleventh Street overnight. He could get a bail hearing in the morning and maybe not have to put his life at risk among the gang members who run Cook County jail disguised as prisoners.

I took a taxi back to the north side. The streets were clear and we moved quickly. Every mile or so we passed a car abandoned on the roadside, making the Arctic landscape appear more desolate than ever.

Once at Jonathan's apartment it took a major effort of will to get back outside with the dog. Po went with me eagerly enough, but kept turning around, looking at me searchingly as though hoping I might be transformed into Cinda.

Back in the apartment, I had no strength left to go home. I found the bedroom, let my clothes drop where they would on the floor and tumbled into bed.

Holy Innocents' Day, lavishly celebrated by my Polish Catholic relatives, was well advanced before I woke up again. I found Po staring at me with reproachful brown eyes, panting slightly. "All right, all right," I grumbled, pulling the covers back and staggering to my feet.

I'd been too tired the night before even to locate the bathroom. Now I found it, part of a large dark room. Cinda apparently had knocked down a wall connecting it to the dining room; she had a sink and built-in shelves all in one handy location. Prints were strung around the room and chemicals and lingerie jostled one another incongruously. I borrowed a toothbrush, cautiously smelling the toothpaste tube to make sure it really held Crest, not developing chemicals.

I put my clothes back on and took Po around the block. The weather had moderated considerably; a bank thermometer on the corner stood at 9 degrees. Po wanted to run to the lake, but I didn't feel up to going that far this morning, and called her back with difficulty. After lunch, if I could get my car started, we might see whether any clues lay hidden in the snow.

I called Lotty from Cinda's apartment, explaining where I was and why. She told me I was an idiot to have gotten out of bed the night before, but if I wasn't dead of exposure by now I would probably survive until someone shot me. Somehow that didn't cheer me up.

While I helped myself to coffee and toast in Cinda's kitchen I started calling various attorneys to see if I could find someone to represent Jonathan. Tim Oldham, who'd gone to law school with me, handled a good-sized criminal practice. He wasn't too enthusiastic about taking a client without much money, but I put on some not very subtle pressure about a lady I'd seen him with on the Gold Coast a few weeks ago who bore little resemblance to his wife. He promised me Jonathan would be home by supper time, called me some unflattering names and hung up.

Besides the kitchen, bedroom and darkroom, the apartment had one other room, mostly filled by a grand piano. Stacks of music stood on the floor—Jonathan either couldn't afford shelves or didn't think he needed them. The walls were hung with poster-sized photographs of Jonathan playing, taken by Cinda. They were very good.

I went back into the darkroom and poked around at the pictures. Cinda had put all her Santa Claus photographs in neatly marked envelopes. She'd carefully written the name of each child next to the number of the exposure on that role of film. I switched on a light table and started looking at them. She'd taken pictures every day for three weeks, which amounted to thousands of shots. It looked like a needle-in-the-haystack type task. But most of the pictures were of children. The only others were ones Cinda had taken for her own amusement, panning the crowd, or artsy shots through glass at reflecting lights. Presumably her caller was one of the adults in the crowd.

After lunch I took Po down to my car. She had no hesitation about going with me and leaped eagerly into the back seat. "You have too trusting a nature," I told her. She grinned at me and panted heavily. The Omega started, after a few grumbling moments, and I drove north to Bryn Mawr and back to get the battery well charged before turning into the lot at Belmont Harbor. Po was almost beside herself with excitement, banging her tail against the rear window until I got the door open and let her out. She raced ahead of me on the lake path. I didn't try to call her back; I figured I'd find her at Cinda's rock.

I moved slowly, carefully scanning the ground for traces of— what? Film? A business card? The wind was so much calmer today and the air enough warmer that visibility was good, but I didn't see anything.

At the lake the mist had cleared away, leaving the water steely grey, moving uneasily under its iron bands of cold. Po stood as I expected on the rock where I'd found her yesterday. She was the picture of dejection. She clearly had expected to find her mistress there.

I combed the area carefully and at last found one of those grey plastic tubes that film comes in. It was empty, however. I pocketed it, deciding I could at least show it to McGonnigal and hope he would think it important. Po left the rocks with utmost reluctance. Back on the lake path, she kept turning around to look for Cinda. I had to lift her into the car. During the drive to police headquarters, she kept turning restlessly in the back seat, a trying maneuver since she was bigger than the seat.

McGonnigal didn't seem too impressed with the tube I'd found, but he took it and sent it to the forensics department. I asked him what he'd learned from Burton's; they didn't have copies of the photographs. Cinda had all those. If someone ordered one, they sent the name to Cinda and she supplied the picture. They gave McGonnigal a copy of the list of the seven hundred people requesting pictures and he had someone going through to see if any of them were known criminals, but he obviously believed it was a waste of time. If it weren't for the fact that his boss, Lieutenant

Robert Mallory, had been a friend of my father's, he probably wouldn't even have made this much of an effort.

I stopped to see Jonathan, who seemed to be in fairly good spirits. He told me Tim Oldham had been by. "He thinks I'm a hippy and not very interesting compared to some of the mob figures he represents, but I can tell he's doing his best." He was working out the fingering to a Schubert score, using the side of the bed as a keyboard. I told him Po was well, but waiting for me in the car outside, so I'd best be on my way.

I spent the rest of the afternoon going through Cinda's Santa photographs. I'd finished about a third of them at five when Tim Oldham phoned to say that Jonathan would have to spend another night in jail: because of the Christmas holidays he hadn't been able to arrange for bail.

"You owe me, Vic; this has been one of the more thankless ways I've spent a holiday."

"You're serving justice, Tim," I said brightly. "What more could you ask for? Think of the oath you swore when you became a member of the bar."

"I'm thinking of the oaths I'd like to swear at you," he grumbled.

I laughed and hung up. I took Po for one last walk, gave her her evening food and drink and prepared to leave for my own place. As soon as the dog saw me putting my coat back on, she abandoned her dinner and started dancing around my feet, wagging her tail, to show that she was always ready to play. I kept yelling "No" to her with no effect. She grinned happily at me as if to say this was a game she often played—she knew humans liked to pretend they didn't want her along, but they always took her in the end.

She was very upset when I shoved her back into the apartment behind me. As I locked the door, she began barking. Retrievers are quiet dogs; they seldom bark and never whine. But their voices are deep and full-bodied, coming straight from their huge chests. Good diaphragm support, the kind singers seldom achieve.

Cinda's apartment was on the second floor. When I got to the ground floor, I could still hear Po from the entryway. She was clearly audible outside the front door. "Ah, nuts!" I muttered. How long could she keep this up? Were dogs like babies? Did you just ignore them for awhile and discipline them into going to sleep? Did that really work with babies? After standing five minutes in the icy wind I could still hear Po. I swore under my breath and let myself back into the building.

She was totally ecstatic at seeing me, jumping up on my chest and licking my face to show there were no hard feelings. "You're shameless and a fraud," I told her severely. She wagged her tail with delight. "Still, you're an orphan; I can't treat you too harshly."

She agreed and followed me down the stairs and back to my apartment with unabated eagerness. I took a bath and changed my clothes, made dinner and took care of my mail, then walked Po around the block to a little park, and back up the street to her own quarters. I brought my own toothbrush with me this time; there didn't seem much point in trying to leave the dog until Jonathan got out of jail.

Cinda and Jonathan had few furnishings, but they owned a magnificent stereo system and a large record collection. I put some Britten quartets on, found a novel buried in the stack of technical books next to Cinda's side of the bed, and purloined a bottle of burgundy. I curled up on a bean-bag chair with the book and the wine. Po lay at my feet, panting happily. Altogether a delightful domestic scene. Maybe I should get a dog.

I finished the book and the bottle of wine a little after midnight and went to bed. Po padded into the bedroom after me and curled up on a rug next to the bed. I went to sleep quickly.

A single sharp bark from the dog woke me about two hours later. "What is it, girl? Nightmares?" I started to turn over to go back to sleep when she barked again. "Quiet, now!" I commanded.

I heard her get to her feet and start toward the door. And then I heard the sound that her sharper ears had caught first. Someone was trying to get into the apartment. It couldn't be Jonathan; I had his keys, and this was someone fumbling, trying different keys, trying to pick the lock. In about thirty seconds I pulled on jeans, boots and a sweatshirt, ignoring underwear. My intruder had managed the lower lock and was starting on the upper.

Po was standing in front of the door, hackles raised on her back. Obedient to my whispered command she wasn't barking. She followed me reluctantly into the darkroom-bathroom. I took her into the shower stall and pulled the curtain across as quietly as I could.

We waited there in the dark while our intruder finished with locks. It was an unnerving business listening to the rattling, knowing someone would be on us momentarily. I wondered if I'd made the right choice; maybe I should have dashed down the back stairs with the dog and gotten the police. It was too late now, however; we could hear a pair of boots moving heavily across the living room. Po gave a deep, mean growl in the back of her throat.

"Doggy? Doggy? Are you in here, Doggy?" The man knew about Po, but not whether she was here. He must not have heard her two short barks earlier. He had a high tenor voice with a trace of a Spanish accent.

Po continued to growl, very softly. At last the far door to the darkroom opened and the intruder came in. He had a flashlight which he shone around the room; through the curtain I could see its point of light bobbing.

Satisfied that no one was there, he turned on the overhead switch. This was connected to a ventilating fan, whose noise was loud enough to mask Po's continued soft growling.

I couldn't see him, but apparently he was looking through Cinda's photograph collection. He flipped on the switch at the light table and then spent a long time going through the negatives. I was pleased with Po; I wouldn't have expected such patience from a dog. The intruder must have sat for an hour while my muscles cramped and water dripped on my head, and she stayed next to me quietly the whole time.

At last he apparently found what he needed. He got up and I heard more paper rustling, then the light went out.

"Now!" I shouted at Po. She raced out of the room and found the intruder as he was on his way out the far door. Blue light flashed; a gun barked. Po yelped and stopped momentarily. By that time I was across the room, too. The intruder was on his way out the apartment door.

I pulled my parka from the chair where I'd left it and took off after him. Po was bleeding slightly from her left shoulder, but the bullet must only have grazed her because she ran strongly. We tumbled down the stairs together and out the front door into the icy December night. As we went outside, I grabbed the dog and rolled over with her. I heard the gun go off a few times but we were moving quickly, too quickly to make a good target.

Streetlamps showed our man running away from us down Halsted to Belmont. He wore the navy ski mask and khaki parka of the solitary runner I'd seen at the harbor yesterday morning.

Hearing Po and me behind him he put on a burst of speed and made it to a car waiting at the corner. We were near the Omega now; I bundled the dog into the backseat, sent up a prayer to the patron saint of Delco batteries, and turned on the engine.

The streets were deserted. I caught up with the car, a dark Lincoln, where Sheridan Road crossed Lake Shore Drive at Belmont. Instead of turning onto the Drive, the Lincoln cut straight across to the harbor.

"This is it, girl," I told Po. "You catch this boy, then we take you in and get that shoulder stitched up. And then you get your favorite dinner—even if it's a whole cow."

The dog was leaning over the front seat, panting, her eyes gleaming. She was a retriever, after all. The Lincoln stopped at the end of the harbor parking lot. I halted the Omega some fifty yards away and got out with the dog. Using a row of parked cars as cover, we ran across the lot, stopping near the Lincoln in the shelter of a van. At that point, Po began her deep, insistent barking.

This was a sound which would attract attention, possibly even the police, so I made no effort to stop her. The man in the Lincoln reached the same conclusion; a window opened and he began firing

241

at us. This was just a waste of ammunition, since we were sheltered behind the van.

The shooting only increased Po's vocal efforts. It also attracted attention from Lake Shore Drive; out of the corner of my eye I saw the flashing blue lights which herald the arrival of Chicago's finest.

Our attacker saw them, too. A door opened and the man in the ski mask slid out. He took off along the lake path, away from the harbor entrance, out toward the promontory. I clapped my hands at Po and started running after him. She was much faster then I; I lost sight of her in the dark as I picked my way more cautiously along the icy path, shivering in the bitter wind, shivering at the thought of the dark freezing water to my right. I could hear it slapping ominously against the ice-covered rocks, could hear the man pounding ahead of me. No noise from Po, her tough pads picking their way sure and silent across the frozen gravel.

As I rounded the curve toward the promontory I could hear the man yelling in Spanish at Po, heard a gun go off, heard a loud splash in the water. Rage at him for shooting the dog gave me a last burst of speed. I rounded the end of the point. Saw his dark shape outlined against the rocks and jumped on top of him.

He was completely unprepared for me. We fell heavily, rolling down the rocks. The gun slipped from his hand, banged loudly as it bounced against the ice and fell into the water. We were a foot away from the water, fighting recklessly—the first person to lose a grip would be shoved in to die.

Our parkas weighted our arms and hampered our swings. He lunged clumsily at my throat. I pulled away, grabbed hold of his ski mask and hit his head against the rocks. He grunted and drew back, trying to kick me. As I moved away from his foot I lost my hold on him and slid backwards across the ice. He followed through quickly, giving a mighty shove which pushed me over the edge of the rock. My feel landed in the water. I swung them up with an effort, two icy lumps, and tried to back away.

As I scrabbled for a purchase, a dark shape came out of the water and climbed onto the rock next to me. Po. Not killed after all. She shook herself, spraying water over me and over my assailant. The sudden bath took him by surprise. He stopped long enough for me to get well away and regain my breath and a better position.

The dog, shivering violently, stayed close to me. I ran a hand through his wet fur. "Soon, kid. We'll get you home and dry soon."

Just as the attacker launched himself at us, a searchlight went on overhead. "This is the police," a loudspeaker boomed. "Drop your guns and come up."

The dark shape hit me, knocked me over. Po let out a yelp and sunk her teeth into his leg. His yelling brought the police to our sides.

They carried strong flashlights. I could see a sodden mass of paper, a small manila envelope with teethmarks in it. Po wagged her tail and picked it up again.

"Give me that!" our attacker yelled in his high voice. He fought with the police to try to reach the envelope. "I threw that in the water. How can this be? How did she get it?"

"She's a retriever," I said.

Later, at the police station, we looked at the negatives in the envelope Po had retrieved from the water. They showed a picture of the man in the ski mask looking on with intense, brooding eyes while Santa Claus talked to his little boy. No wonder Cinda found him worth photographing.

"He's a cocaine dealer," Sergeant McGonnigal explained to me. "He jumped a ten million-dollar bail. No wonder he didn't want any photographs of him circulating around. We're holding him for murder this time."

A uniformed man brought Jonathan into McGonnigal's office. The sergeant cleared his throat uncomfortably. "Looks like your dog saved your hide, Mr. Michaels."

Po, who had been lying at my feet, wrapped in a police horse blanket, gave a bark of pleasure. She staggered to her feet, trailing the blanket, and walked stiffly over to Jonathan, tail wagging.

I explained our adventure to him, and what a heroine the dog had been. "What about that empty film container I gave you this afternoon, Sergeant?"

Apparently Cinda had brought that with her to her rendez-vous, not knowing how dangerous her customer was. When he realized it was empty, he'd flung it aside and attacked Cinda. "We got a complete confession," McGonnigal said. "He was so rattled by the sight of the dog with the envelope full of negatives in her mouth that he completely lost his nerve. I know he's got good lawyers—one of them's your friend Oldham—but I hope we have enough to convince a judge not to set bail."

Jonathan was on his knees fondling the dog and talking to her. He looked over his shoulder at McGonnigal. "I'm sure Oldham's relieved that you caught the right man—a murderer who can afford to jump a ten million dollar bail is a much better client than one who can hardly keep a retriever in dog food." He turned back to the dog. "But we'll blow our savings on a steak; you get the steak and I'll eat Butcher's Blend tonight, Miss Three-Dot Po of Blackstone, People's Heroine and winner of the Croix de Chien for valor." Po panted happily and licked his face.

# Skeleton Rattle Your Mouldy Leg

## *Bill Pronzini*

*This novelette came into being as a result of two factors.
One is the title. It had been skipping around inside my head for
weeks, ever since I first encountered the phrase in don marquis'
delightful* archy and mehitabel—*a perfect title in search of
a story. The second factor was a mounting desire to make a statement on the plight and treatment of the elderly in this country.
After Bob Randisi called to request a story for this anthology, I
asked myself if it were possible to fit theme and title together
into a case for "Nameless." The answer, obviously, was yes; and
to my surprise the development of the plot required very
little effort. Theme and title, it seems, were made for each other.*

*There's not much else to say about "Skeleton Rattle," except
that it wrote pretty much as I had hoped it would. If you like
it, I'm glad. If you don't like it, my apologies in
advance for inflicting it on you.*

H E was one of the oddest people I had ever met. Sixty years old, under five and a half feet tall, slight, with great bony knobs for elbows and knees, with bat-winged ears and a bent nose and eyes that danced left and right, left and right, and had sparkly little lights in them. He wore baggy clothes—sweaters and jeans, mostly, crusted with patches—and a baseball cap turned around so that the bill poked out from the back of his head. In his back pocket he carried a whisk broom, and if he knew you, or wanted to, he would come up and say, "I know you—you've got a speck on your coat," and he would brush it off with the broom. Then he would talk, or maybe recite or even sing a little: a gnarled old harlequin cast up from another age.

These things were odd enough, but the oddest of all was his obsession with skeletons.

His name was Nick Damiano and he lived in the building adjacent to the one where Eberhardt and I had our new office—lived in a little room in the basement. Worked there, too, as a janitor and general handyman; the place was a small residence hotel for senior citizens, mostly male, called the Medford. So it didn't take long for our paths to cross. A week or so after Eb and I moved in, I was coming up the street one morning and Nick popped out of the alley that separated our two buildings.

He said, "I know you—you've got a speck on your coat," and out came the whisk broom. Industriously he brushed away the imaginary speck. Then he grinned and said, "Skeleton rattle your mouldy leg."

"Huh?"

"That's poetry," he said. "From *archy and mehitabel*. You know archy and mehitabel?"

"No," I said, "I don't."

"They're lower case; they don't have capitals like we do. Archy's a cockroach and mehitabel's a cat and they were both poets in another life. A fellow named don marquis created them a long time ago. He's lower case too."

"Uh . . . I see."

"One time mehitabel went to Paris," he said, "and took up with a tom cat named francy who was once the poet Francois Villon, and they used to go to the catacombs late at night. They'd caper and dance and sing among those old bones."

And he began to recite:

> *prince if you pipe and plead and beg*
> *you may yet be crowned with a grisly kiss*
> *skeleton rattle your mouldy leg*
> *all mens lovers come to this*

That was my first meeting with Nick Damiano; there were others over the next four months, none of which lasted more than five minutes. Skeletons came into all of them, in one way or another. Once he sang half a dozen verses of the old spiritual, "Dry Bones," in a pretty good baritone. Another time he quoted, "'The Knight's bones are dust/And his good sword rust—/ His Soul is with the saints, I trust.'" Later I looked it up and it was a rhyme from an obscure work by Coleridge. On other days he made sly little comments: "Why hello there, I knew it was you coming—I heard your bones chattering and clacking all the way down the street." And "Cleaned out your closet lately? Might be skeletons hiding in there." And "Sure is hot today. Sure would be fine to take off our skins and just sit around in our bones."

I asked one of the Medford's other residents, a guy named Irv Feinberg, why Nick seemed to have such a passion for skeletons. Feinberg didn't know; nobody knew, he said, because Nick wouldn't discuss it. He told me that Nick even owned a genuine skeleton, liberated from some medical facility, and that he kept it wired to the wall of his room and burned candles in its skull.

A screwball, this Nick Damiano—sure. But he did his work and did it well, and he was always cheerful and friendly, and he

never gave anybody any trouble. Harmless old Nick. A happy
whack, marching to the rhythm of dry old bones chattering and
clacking together inside his head. Everybody in the neighborhood
found him amusing, including me: San Francisco has always been
proud of its characters, its kooks. Yeah, everyone liked old Nick.

Except that somebody *didn't* like him, after all.

Somebody took hold of a blunt instrument one raw November
night, in that little basement room with the skeleton leering on from
the wall, and beat Nick Damiano to death.

It was four days after the murder that Irv Feinberg came to see
me. He was a rotund little guy in his sixties, very energetic, a
retired plumber who wore loud sports coats and spent most of his
time doping out the races at Golden Gate Fields and a variety of
other tracks. He had known Nick as well as anyone could, had
called him his friend.

I was alone in the office when Feinberg walked in; Eberhardt
was down at the Hall of Justice, trying to coerce some of his former
cop pals into giving him background information on a missing-
person case he was working. Feinberg said by way of greeting,
"Nice office you got here," which was a lie, and came over and
plopped himself into one of the clients' chairs. "You busy? Or you
got a few minutes we can talk?"

"What can I do for you, Mr. Feinberg?"

"The cops have quit on Nick's murder," he said. "They don't
come around anymore, they don't talk to anybody in the hotel. I
called down to the Hall of Justice, I wanted to know what's
happening, I got the big runaround."

"The police don't quit a homicide investigation—"

"The hell they don't. A guy like Nick Damiano? It's no big
deal to them. They figure it was somebody looking for easy money,
a drug addict from over in the Tenderloin. On account of Dan Cady,
he's the night clerk, found the door to the alley unlocked just after
he found Nick's body."

"That sounds like a reasonable theory," I said.

"Reasonable, hell. The door wasn't tampered with or anything; it was just unlocked. So how'd the drug addict get in? Nick wouldn't have left that door unlocked; he was real careful about things like that. And he wouldn't have let a stranger in, not at that time of night."

"Well, maybe the assailant came in through the front entrance and went out through the alley door . . ."

"No way," Feinberg said. "Front door's on a night security lock from eight o'clock on; you got to buzz the desk from outside and Dan Cady'll come see who you are. If he don't know you, you don't get in."

"All right, maybe the assailant wasn't a stranger. Maybe he's somebody Nick knew."

"Sure, that's what I think. But not somebody outside the hotel. Nick never let people in at night, not anybody, not even somebody lives there; you had to go around to the front door and buzz the desk. Besides, he didn't have any outside friends that came to see him. He didn't go out himself either. He had to tend to the heat, for one thing, do other chores, so he stayed put. I know all that because I spent plenty of evenings with him, shooting craps for pennies . . . Nick liked to shoot craps, he called it 'rolling dem bones.'"

Skeletons, I thought. I said, "What do you think then, Mr. Feinberg? That somebody from the hotel killed Nick?"

"That's what I think," he said. "I don't like it, most of those people are my friends, but that's how it looks to me."

"You have anybody specific in mind?"

"No. Whoever it was, he was in there arguing with Nick before he killed him."

"Oh? How do you know that?"

"George Weaver heard them. He's our newest tenant, George is, moved in three weeks ago. Used to be a bricklayer in Chicago, came out here to be with his daughter when he retired, only she had a heart attack and died last month. His other daughter died young and his wife died of cancer; now he's all alone." Feinberg shook his head. "It's a hell of a thing to be old and alone."

I agreed that it must be.

"Anyhow, George was in the basement getting something out of his storage bin and he heard the argument. Told Charley Slattery a while later that it didn't sound violent or he'd have gone over and banged on Nick's door. As it was, he just went back upstairs."

"Who's Charley Slattery?"

"Charley lives at the Medford and works over at Monahan's Gym on Turk Street. Used to be a small-time fighter; now he just hangs around doing odd jobs. Not too bright, but he's okay."

"Weaver didn't recognize the other voice in the argument?"

"No. Couldn't make out what it was all about either."

"What time was that?"

"Few minutes before eleven, George says."

"Did anyone else overhear the argument?"

"Nobody else around at the time."

"When was the last anybody saw Nick alive?"

"Eight o'clock. Nick came up to the lobby to fix one of the lamps wasn't working. Dan Cady talked to him a while when he was done."

"Cady found Nick's body around two a.m., wasn't it?"

"Two-fifteen."

"How did he happen to find it? That wasn't in the papers."

"Well, the furnace was still on. Nick always shut it off by midnight or it got to be too hot upstairs. So Dan went down to find out why and there was Nick lying on the floor of his room with his head all beat in."

"What kind of guy is Cady?"

"Quiet, keeps to himself, spends most of his free time reading library books. He was a college history teacher once, up in Oregon. But he got in some kind of trouble with a woman—this was back in the forties, teachers had to watch their morals—and the college fired him and he couldn't get another teaching job. He fell into the booze for a lot of years afterward. But he's all right now. Belongs to AA."

I was silent for a time. Then I asked, "The police didn't find anything that made them suspect one of the other residents?"

"No, but that don't mean much." Feinberg made a disgusted noise through his nose. "Cops. They don't even know what it was bashed in Nick's skull, what kind of weapon. Couldn't find it anywhere. They figure the killer took it away through that unlocked alley door and got rid of it. *I* figure the killer unlocked the door to make it look like an outside job, then went upstairs and hid the weapon somewhere til next day."

"Let's suppose you're right. Who might have a motive to've killed Nick?"

"Well . . . nobody, far as I know. But *somebody's* got one, you can bet on that."

"Did Nick get along with everybody at the Medford?"

"Sure," Feinberg said. Then he frowned a little and said, "Except Wesley Thane, I guess. But I can't see Wes beating anybody's head in. He pretends to be tough but he's a wimp. And a goddamn snob."

"Oh?"

"He's an actor. Little theater stuff these days, but once he was a bit player down in Hollywood, made a lot of crappy B movies where he was one of the minor bad guys. Hear him tell it, he was Clark Gable's best friend back in the forties. A windbag who thinks he's better than the rest of us. He treated Nick like a freak."

"Was there ever any trouble between them?"

"Well, he hit Nick once, just after he moved in five years ago and Nick tried to brush off his coat. I was there and I saw it."

"Hit him with what?"

"His hand. A kind of slap. Nick shied away from him after that."

"How about recent trouble?"

"Not that I know about. I didn't even have to noodge him into kicking in twenty bucks to the fund. But hell, everybody in the building kicked in something except old lady Howsam; she's bedridden and can barely make ends meet on her pension, so I didn't even ask her."

I said, "Fund?"

Feinberg reached inside his gaudy sport jacket and produced a bulky envelope. He put the envelope on my desk and pushed it toward me with the tips of his fingers. "There's two hundred bucks in there," he said. "What'll that hire you for? Three-four days?"

I stared at him. "Wait a minute, Mr. Feinberg. Hire me to do what?"

"Find out who killed Nick. What do you think we been talking about here?"

"I thought it was only talk you came for. A private detective can't investigate a homicide in this state, not without police permission . . ."

"So get permission," Feinberg said. "I told you, the cops have quit on it. Why should they try to keep you from investigating?"

"Even if I did get permission, I doubt if there's much I could do that the police haven't already—"

"Listen, don't go modest on me. You're a good detective, I see your name in the papers all the time. I got confidence in you; we all do. Except maybe the guy who killed Nick."

There was no arguing him out of it; his mind was made up, and he'd convinced the others in the Medford to go along with him. So I quit trying finally and said all right, I would call the Hall of Justice and see if I could get clearance to conduct a private investigation. And if I could, then I'd come over later and see him and take a look around and start talking to people. That satisfied him. But when I pushed the envelope back across the desk, he wouldn't take it.

"No," he said, "that's yours, you just go ahead and earn it." And he was on his feet and gone before I could do anything more than make a verbal protest.

I put the money away in the lock-box in my desk and telephoned the Hall. Eberhardt was still hanging around, talking to one of his old cronies in General Works, and I told him about Feinberg and what he wanted. Eb said he'd talk to the homicide inspector in charge of the Nick Damiano case and see what was what; he didn't seem to think there'd be any problem getting clearance. There were problems, he said, only when private eyes tried to horn in on big-money and/or VIP cases, the kind that got heavy media attention.

He used to be a homicide lieutenant so he knew what he was talking about. When he called back a half hour later he said, "You got your clearance. Feinberg had it pegged: the case is already in the Inactive File for lack of leads and evidence. I'll see if I can finagle a copy of the report for you."

Some job, I thought as I hung up. In a way it was ghoulish, like poking around in a fresh grave. And wasn't that an appropriate image; I could almost hear Nick's sly laughter.

Skeleton rattle your mouldy leg.

The basement of the Medford Hotel was dimly lighted and too warm: a big, old-fashioned oil furnace rattled and roared in one corner, giving off shimmers of heat. Much of the floor space was taken up with fifty-gallon trash receptacles, some full and some empty and one each under a pair of garbage chutes from the upper floor. Over against the far wall, and throughout a small connecting room beyond, were rows of narrow storage cubicles made out of wood and heavy wire, with padlocks on each of the doors.

Nick's room was at the rear, opposite the furnace and alongside the room that housed the hot-water heaters. But Feinberg didn't take me there directly; he said something I didn't catch, mopping his face with a big green handkerchief, and detoured over to the furnace and fiddled with the controls and got it shut down.

"Damn thing," he said. "Owner's too cheap to replace it with a modern unit that runs off a thermostat. Now we got some young snot he hired to take Nick's job, don't live here and don't stick around all day and leaves the furnace turned on too long. It's like a goddamn sauna in here."

There had been a police seal on the door to Nick's room, but it had been officially removed. Feinberg had the key; he was a sort of building mayor, by virtue of seniority—he'd lived at the Medford for more than fifteen years—and he had got custody of the key from the owner. He opened the lock, swung the thick metal door open, and clicked on the lights.

The first thing I saw was the skeleton. It hung from several pieces of shiny wire on the wall opposite the door, and it was a grisly damned thing streaked with blobs of red and green and orange candle wax. The top of the skull had been cut off and a fat red candle jutted up from the hollow inside, like some sort of ugly growth. Melted wax rimmed and dribbled from the grinning mouth, giving it a bloody look.

"Cute, ain't it?" Feinberg said. "Nick and his frigging skeletons."

I moved inside. It was just a single room with a bathroom alcove, not more than fifteen feet square. Cluttered, but in a way that suggested everything had been assigned a place. Army cot against one wall, a small table, two chairs, one of those little waist-high refrigerators with a hot plate on top, a standing cupboard full of pots and dishes; stacks of newspapers and magazines, some well-used books—volumes of poetry, an anatomical text, two popular histories about ghouls and grave-robbers, a dozen novels with either "skeleton" or "bones" in the title; a broken wooden wagon, a Victrola without its ear-trumpet amplifier, an ancient Olivetti typewriter, a collection of oddball tools, a scabrous iron-bound steamer trunk, an open box full of assorted pairs of dice, and a lot of other stuff, most of which appeared to be junk.

A thick fiber mat covered the floor. On it, next to the table, was the chalked outline of Nick's body and some dark stains. My stomach kicked a little when I looked at the stains; I had seen corpses of bludgeon victims and I knew what those stains looked like when they were fresh. I went around the table on the other side and took a closer look at the wax-caked skeleton. Feinberg tagged along at my heels.

"Nick used to talk to that thing," he said. "Ask it questions, how it was feeling, could he get it anything to eat or drink. Gave me the willies at first. He even put his arm around it once and kissed it, I swear to God. I can still see him do it."

"He got it from a medical facility?"

"One that was part of some small college he worked at before he came to San Francisco. He mentioned that once."

"Did he say where the college was?"

"No."

"Where did Nick come from? Around here?"

Feinberg shook his head. "Midwest somewhere, that's all I could get out of him."

"How long had he been in San Francisco?"

"Ten years. Worked here the last eight; before that, he helped out at a big apartment house over on Geary."

"Why did he come to the city? Did he have relatives here or what?"

"No, no relatives, he was all alone. Just him and his bones—he said that once."

I poked around among the clutter of things in the room, but if there had been anything here relevant to the murder, the police would have found it and probably removed it and it would be mentioned in their report. So would anything found among Nick's effects that determined his background. Eberhardt would have a copy of the report for me to look at later; when he said he'd try to do something he usually did it.

When I finished with the room we went out and Feinberg locked the door. We took the elevator up to the lobby. It was dim up there, too—and a little depressing. There was a lot of plaster and wood and imitation marble, and some antique furniture and dusty potted plants, and it smelled of dust and faintly of decay. A sense of age permeated the place: you felt it and you smelled it and you saw it in the surroundings, in the half-dozen men and one woman sitting on the sagging chairs, reading or staring out through the windows at O'Farrell Street, people with nothing to do and nobody to do it with, waiting like doomed prisoners for the sentence of death to be carried out. Dry witherings and an aura of hopelessness—that was the impression I would carry away with me and that would linger in my mind.

I thought: I'm fifty-four, another few years and I could be stuck in here too. But that wouldn't happen. I had work I could do pretty much to the end and I had Kerry—Kerry Wade, my lady—and I had some money in the bank and a collection of 6500 pulp magazines that were worth plenty on the collectors' market. No, this kind of place wouldn't happen to me. In a society that ignored and showed little respect for its elderly, I was one of the lucky ones.

Feinberg led me to the desk and introduced me to the day clerk, a sixtyish barrel of a man named Bert Norris. If there was anything he could do to help, Norris said, he'd be glad to oblige; he sounded eager, as if nobody had needed his help in a long time. The fact that Feinberg had primed everyone here about my investigation made things easier in one respect and more difficult in another. If the person who had killed Nick Damiano *was* a resident of the Medford, I was not likely to catch him off guard.

When Norris moved away to answer a switchboard call, Feinberg asked me, "Who're you planning to talk to now?"

"Whoever's available," I said.

"Dan Cady? He lives here—two-eighteen. Goes to the library every morning after he gets off, but he's always back by noon. You can probably catch him before he turns in."

"All right, good."

"You want me to come along?"

"That's not necessary, Mr. Feinberg."

"Yeah, I get it. I used to hate that kind of thing too when I was out on a plumbing job."

"What kind of thing?"

"Somebody hanging over my shoulder, watching me work. Who needs crap like that? You want me, I'll be in my room with the scratch sheets for today's races."

Dan Cady was a thin, sandy-haired man in his mid-sixties, with cheeks and nose roadmapped by ruptured blood vessels—the badge of the alcoholic, practicing or reformed. He wore thick glasses, and behind them his eyes had a strained, tired look, as if from too much reading.

"Well, I'll be glad to talk to you," he said, "but I'm afraid I'm not very clear-headed right now. I was just getting ready for bed."

"I won't take up much of your time, Mr. Cady."

He let me in. His room was small and strewn with library books, most of which appeared to deal with American history; a couple of big maps, an old one of the United States and an even older parchment map of Asia, adorned the walls, and there were plaster busts of historical figures I didn't recognize, a huge globe on a wooden stand. There was only one chair; he let me have that and perched himself on the bed.

I asked him about Sunday night, and his account of how he'd come to find Nick Damiano's body coincided with what Feinberg had told me. "It was a frightening experience," he said. "I'd never seen anyone dead by violence before. His head . . . well, it was awful."

"Were there signs of a struggle in the room?"

"Yes, some things were knocked about. But I'd say it was a brief struggle—there wasn't much damage."

"Is there anything unusual you noticed? Something that should have been there but wasn't, for instance?"

"No. I was too shaken to notice anything like that."

"Was Nick's door open when you got there?"

"Wide open."

"How about the door to the alley?"

"No. Closed."

"How did you happen to check it, then?"

"Well, I'm not sure," Cady said. He seemed faintly embarrassed; his eyes didn't quite meet mine. "I was stunned and frightened; it occurred to me that the murderer might still be around somewhere. I took a quick look around the basement and then opened the alley door and looked out there . . . I wasn't thinking very clearly. It was only when I shut the door again that I realized it had been unlocked."

"Did you see or hear anything inside or out?"

"Nothing. I left the door unlocked and went back to the lobby to call the police."

"When you saw Nick earlier that night, Mr. Cady, how did he seem to you?"

"Seem? Well, he was cheerful; he usually was. He said he'd have come up sooner to fix the lamp but his old bones wouldn't allow it. That was the way he talked . . ."

"Yes, I know. Do you have any idea who he might have argued with that night, who might have killed him?"

"None," Cady said. "He was such a gentle soul . . . I still can't believe a thing like that could happen to him."

Down in the lobby again, I asked Bert Norris if Wesley Thane, George Weaver, and Charley Slattery were on the premises. Thane was, he said, Room 315; Slattery was at Monahan's Gym and would be until six o'clock. He started to tell me that Weaver was out, but then his eyes shifted past me and he said, "No, there he is now. Just coming in."

I turned. A heavy-set, stooped man of about seventy had just entered from the street, walking with the aid of a hickory cane; but he seemed to get along pretty good. He was carrying a grocery sack in his free hand and a folded newspaper under his arm.

I intercepted him halfway to the elevator and told him who I was. He looked me over for about ten seconds, out of alert blue eyes that had gone a little rheumy, before he said, "Irv Feinberg said you'd be around." His voice was surprisingly strong and clear for a man his age. "But I can't help you much. Don't know much."

"Should we talk down here or in your room?"

"Down here's all right with me."

We crossed to a deserted corner of the lobby and took chairs in front of a fireplace that had been boarded up and painted over. Weaver got a stubby little pipe out of his coat pocket and began to load up.

I said, "About Sunday night, Mr. Weaver. I understand you

258

went down to the basement to get something out of your storage locker . . ."

"My old radio," he said. "New one I bought a while back quit playing and I like to listen to the eleven o'clock news before I go to sleep. When I got down there I heard Damiano and some fella arguing."

"Just Nick and one other man?"

"Sounded that way."

"Was the voice at all familiar to you?"

"Didn't sound familiar. But I couldn't hear it too well; I was over by the lockers. Couldn't make out what they were saying either."

"How long were you in the basement?"

"Three or four minutes, is all."

"Did the argument get louder, more violent, while you were there?"

"Didn't seem to. No." He struck a kitchen match and put the flame to the bowl of his pipe. "If it had I guess I'd've gone over and banged on the door, announced myself. I'm as curious as the next man when it comes to that."

"But as it was you went straight back to your room?"

"That's right. Ran into Charley Slattery when I got out of the elevator; his room's just down from mine on the third floor."

"What was his reaction when you told him what you'd heard?"

"Didn't seem to worry him much," Weaver said. "So I figured it was nothing for me to worry about either."

"Slattery didn't happen to go down to the basement himself, did he?"

"Never said anything about it if he did."

I don't know what I expected Wesley Thane to be like—the Raymond Massey or John Carradine type, maybe, something along those shabbily aristocratic and vaguely sinister lines—but the man who opened the door to Room 315 looked about as much like an actor as I do. He was a smallish guy in his late sixties, he was bald, and he had a nondescript face except for mean little eyes under thick black brows that had no doubt contributed to his career as a B-movie villain. He looked somewhat familiar, but even though I like old movies and watch them whenever I can, I couldn't have named a single film he had appeared in.

He said, "Yes? What is it?" in a gravelly, staccato voice. That was familiar, too, but again I couldn't place it in any particular context.

I identified myself and asked if I could talk to him about Nick Damiano. "That cretin," he said, and for a moment I thought he was going to shut the door in my face. But then he said, "Oh, all right, come in. If I don't talk to you, you'll probably think I had something to do with the poor fool's murder."

He turned and moved off into the room, leaving me to shut the door. The room was larger than Dan Cady's and jammed with stage and screen memorabilia: framed photographs, playbills, film posters, blown-up black-and-white stills; and a variety of salvaged props, among them the plumed helmet off a suit of armor and a Napoleonic uniform displayed on a dressmaker's dummy.

Thane stopped near a lumpy-looking couch and did a theatrical about-face. The scowl he wore had a practiced look, and it occurred to me that under it he might be enjoying himself. "Well?" he said.

I said, "You didn't like Nick Damiano, did you, Mr. Thane," making it a statement instead of a question.

"No, I didn't like him. And no, I didn't kill him, if that's your next question."

"Why didn't you like him?"

"He was a cretin. A gibbering moron. All that nonsense about skeletons—he ought to have been locked up long ago."

"You have any idea who did kill him?"

"No. The police seem to think it was a drug addict."

"That's one theory," I said. "Irv Feinberg has another: he thinks the killer is a resident of this hotel."

"I know what Irv Feinberg thinks. He's a damned meddler who doesn't know when to keep his mouth shut."

"You don't agree with him then?"

"I don't care one way or another."

Thane sat down and crossed his legs and adopted a sufferer's pose; now he was playing the martyr. I grinned at him, because it was something he wasn't expecting, and went to look at some of the stuff on the walls. One of the black-and-white stills depicted Thane in Western garb, with a smoking sixgun in his hand. The largest of the photographs was of Clark Gable, with an ink inscription that read, "For my good friend, Wes."

Behind me Thane said impatiently, "I'm waiting."

I let him wait a while longer. Then I moved back near the couch and grinned at him again and said, "Did you see Nick Damiano the night he was murdered?"

"I did not."

"Talk to him at all that day?"

"No."

"When was the last you had trouble with him?"

"Trouble? What do you mean, trouble?"

"Irv Feinberg told me you hit Nick once, when he tried to brush off your coat."

"My God," Thane said, "that was years ago. And it was only a slap. I had no problems with him after that. He avoided me and I ignored him; we spoke only when it was necessary." He paused, and his eyes got bright with something that might have been malice. "If you're looking for someone who had trouble with Damiano recently, talk to Charley Slattery."

"What kind of trouble did Slattery have with Nick?"

"Ask him. It's none of my business."

"Why did you bring it up then?"

He didn't say anything. His eyes were still bright.

"All right, I'll ask Slattery," I said. "Tell me, what did you think when you heard about Nick? Were you pleased?"

"Of course not. I was shocked. I've played many violent roles in my career, but violence in real life always shocks me."

"The shock must have worn off pretty fast. You told me a couple of minutes ago you don't care who killed him."

"Why should I, as long as no one else is harmed?"

"So why did you kick in the twenty dollars?"

"What?"

"Feinberg's fund to hire me. Why did you contribute?"

"If I hadn't it would have made me look suspicious to the others. I have to live with these people; I don't need that sort of stigma." He gave me a smug look. "And if you repeat that to anyone, I'll deny it."

"Must be tough on you," I said.

"I beg your pardon?"

"Having to live in a place like this, with a bunch of broken-down old nobodies who don't have your intelligence or compassion or great professional skill."

That got to him; he winced, and for a moment the actor's mask slipped and I had a glimpse of the real Wesley Thane—a defeated old man with faded dreams of glory, a never-was with a small and mediocre talent, clinging to the tattered fringes of a business that couldn't care less. Then he got the mask in place again and said with genuine anger, "Get out of here. I don't have to take abuse from a cheap gumshoe."

"You're dating yourself, Mr Thane; nobody uses the word 'gumshoe' any more. It's forties B-movie dialogue."

He bounced up off the couch, pinch-faced and glaring. "Get out, I said. "Get out!"

I got out. And I was on my way to the elevator when I realized why Thane hadn't liked Nick Damiano. It was because Nick had taken attention away from him—upstaged him. Thane was an actor, but there wasn't any act he could put on that was more compelling than the real-life performance of Nick and his skeletons.

Monahan's Gym was one of those tough, men-only places that catered to ex-pugs and oldtimers in the fight game, the kind of place you used to see a lot of in the forties and fifties but that have become an anachronism in this day of chic health clubs, fancy spas, and dwindling interest in the art of prizefighting. It smelled of sweat and steam and old leather, and it resonated with the grunts of weightlifters, the smack and thud of gloves against leather bags, the profane talk of men at liberty from a more or less polite society.

I found Charley Slattery in the locker room, working there as an attendant. He was a short, beefy guy, probably a light-heavyweight in his boxing days, gone to fat around the middle in his old age; white-haired, with a face as seamed and time-eroded as a chunk of desert sandstone. One of his eyes had a glassy look; his nose and mouth were lumpy with scar tissue. A game fighter in his day, I thought, but not a very good one. A guy who had never quite learned how to cover up against the big punches, the hammerblows that put you down and out.

"Sure, I been expectin you," he said when I told him who I was. "Irv Feinberg, he said you'd be around. You findin out anythin the cops dint?"

"It's too soon to tell, Mr. Slattery."

"Charley," he said, "I hate that Mr. Slattery crap."

"All right, Charley."

"Well, I wish I could tell you somethin would help you, but I can't think of nothin. I dint even see Nick for two-three days before he was murdered."

"Any idea who might have killed him?"

"Well, some punk off the street, I guess. Guy Nick was arguin with that night—George Weaver, he told you about that, dint he? What he heard?"

"Yes. He also said he met you upstairs just afterward."

Slattery nodded. "I was headin down the lobby for a Coke, they got a machine down there, and George, he come out of the elevator with his cane and this little radio unner his arm. He looked kind of funny and I ast him what's the matter and that's when he told me about the argument."

"What did you do then?"

"What'd I do? Went down to get my Coke."

"You didn't go to the basement?"

"Nah, damn it. George, he said it was just a argument Nick was havin with somebody. I never figured it was nothin, you know, violent. If I had— Yeah, Eddie? You need somethin?"

A muscular black man in his mid-thirties, naked except for a pair of silver-blue boxing trunks, had come up. He said, "Towel and some soap, Charley. No soap in the showers again."

"Goddamn. I catch the guy keeps swipin it," Slattery said, "I'll kick his ass." He went and got a clean towel and a bar of soap, and the black man moved off with them to a back row of lockers. Slattery watched him go; then he said to me, "That's Eddie Jordan. Pretty fair welterweight once, but he never trained right, never had the right manager. He could of been good, that boy, if—" He broke off, frowning. "I shouldn't ought to call him that, I guess. 'Boy.' Blacks, they don't like to be called that nowadays."

"No," I said, "they don't."

"But I don't mean nothin by it. I mean, we always called em 'boy,' it was just somethin we called em. 'Nigger,' too, same thing. It wasn't nothin personal, you know?"

I knew, all right, but it was not something I wanted to or ever could explain to Charley Slattery. Race relations, the whole question of race, was too complex an issue. In his simple world, 'nigger' and 'boy' were just words, meaningless words without a couple of centuries of hatred and malice behind them, and it really wasn't anything personal.

"Let's get back to Nick," I said. "You liked him, didn't you, Charley?"

"Sure I did. He was goofy, him and his skeletons, but he worked hard and he never bothered anybody."

"I had a talk with Wesley Thane a while ago. He told me you had some trouble with Nick not long ago."

Slattery's eroded face arranged itself into a scowl. "That damn actor, he don't know what he's talkin about. Why don't he mind his own damn business? I never had no trouble with Nick."

"Not even a little? A disagreement of some kind, maybe?"

He hesitated. Then he shrugged and said, "Well, yeah, I guess we had that. A kind of disagreement."

"When was this?'

"I dunno. Couple of weeks ago."

"What was it about?"

"Garbage," Slattery said.

"Garbage?"

"Nick, he dint like nobody touchin the cans in the basement. But hell, I was down there one night and the cans unner the chutes was full, so I switched em for empties. Well, Nick come around and yelled at me, and I wasn't feelin too good so I yelled back at him. Next thing, I got sore and kicked over one of the cans and spilled out some garbage. Dan Cady, he heard the noise clear up in the lobby and come down and that son of a bitch Wes Thane was with him. Dan, he got Nick and me calmed down. That's all there was to it."

"How were things between you and Nick after that?"

"Okay. He forgot it and so did I. It dint mean nothin. It was just one of them things."

"Did Nick have problems with any other people in the hotel?" I asked.

"Nah. I don't think so."

"What about Wes Thane? He admitted he and Nick didn't get along very well."

"I never heard about them havin no fight or anythin like that."

"How about trouble Nick might have had with somebody outside the Medford?"

"Nah," Slattery said. "Nick, he got along with everybody, you know? Everybody liked Nick, even if he was goofy."

Yeah, I thought, everybody liked Nick, even if he was goofy. Then why is he dead? *Why?*

I went back to the Medford and talked with three more residents, none of whom could offer any new information or any

possible answers to that question of motive. It was almost five when
I gave it up for the day and went next door to the office.

Eberhardt was there, but I didn't see him at first because he
was on his hands and knees behind his desk. He poked his head up
as I came inside and shut the door.

"Fine thing," I said, "you down on your knees like that. What
if I'd been a prospective client?"

"So? I wouldn't let somebody like you hire me."

"What're you doing down there anyway?"

"I was cleaning my pipe and I dropped the damn bit." He
disappeared again for a few seconds, muttered, "Here it is,"
reappeared, and hoisted himself to his feet.

There were pipe ashes all over the front of his tie and his
white shirt; he'd even managed to get a smear of ash across his
jowly chin. He was something of a slob, Eberhardt was, which gave
us one of several common bonds: I was something of a slob myself.
We had been friends for more then thirty years, and we'd been
through some hard times together—some very hard times in the
recent past. I hadn't been sure at first that taking him in as a
partner after his retirement was a good idea, for a variety of
reasons; but it had worked out so far. Much better than I'd
expected, in fact.

He sat down and began brushing pipe dottle off his desk; he
must have dropped a bowlful on it as well as on himself. He said as
I hung up my coat, "How goes the Nick Damiano investigation?"

"Not too good. Did you manage to get a copy of the police
report?"

"On your desk. But I don't think it'll tell you much."

The report was in an unmarked manila envelope; I read it
standing up. Eberhardt was right that it didn't enlighten me much.
Nick Damiano had been struck on the head at least three times by a
heavy blunt instrument and had died of a brain hemorrhage,
probably within seconds of the first blow. The wounds were
"consistent with" a length of three-quarter-inch steel pipe, but the
weapon hadn't been positively identified because no trace of it had

been found. As for Nick's background, nothing had been found there either. No items of personal history among his effects, no hint of relatives or even of his city of origin. They'd run a check on his fingerprints through the FBI computer, with negative results: he had never been arrested on a felony charge, never been in military service or applied for a civil service job, never been fingerprinted at all.

When I put the report down Eberhardt said, "Anything?"

"Doesn't look like it." I sat in my chair and looked out the window for a time, at heavy rainclouds massing above the Federal Building down the hill. "There's just nothing to go on in this thing, Eb—no real leads or suspects, no apparent motive."

"So maybe it's random. A street-killing, drug-related, like the report speculates."

"Maybe."

"You don't think so?"

"Our client doesn't think so."

"You want to talk over the details?"

"Sure. But let's do it over a couple of beers and some food."

"I thought you were on a diet."

"I am. Whenever Kerry's around. But she's working late tonight—new ad campaign she's writing. A couple of beers won't hurt me. And we'll have something nonfattening to eat."

"Sure we will," Eberhardt said.

We went to an Italian place out on Clement at 25th Avenue and had four beers apiece and plates of fettucine Alfredo and half a loaf of garlic bread. But the talking we did got us nowhere. If one of the residents of the Medford had killed Nick Damiano, what was the damn motive? A broken-down old actor's petulant jealousy? A mindless dispute over garbage cans? Just what *was* the argument all about that George Weaver had overheard?

Eberhardt and I split up early and I drove home to my flat on Pacific Heights. The place had a lonely feel; after spending most of the day in and around the Medford, I needed some laughter and *bonhomie* to cheer me up—I needed Kerry. I thought about calling her at Bates and Carpenter, her ad agency, but she didn't like to be disturbed while she was working. And she'd said she expected to be there most of the evening.

I settled instead for cuddling up to my collection of pulp magazines—browsing here and there, finding something to read. On nights like this the pulps weren't much of a substitute for human companionship in general and Kerry in particular, but at least they kept my mind occupied. I found a 1943 issue of *Dime Detective* that looked interesting, took it into the bathtub, and lingered there reading until I got drowsy. Then I went to bed, went right to sleep for a change—

—and woke up at three A.M. by the luminous dial of the nightstand clock, because the clouds had finally opened up and unleashed a wailing torrent of wind-blown rain: the sound of it on the roof and on the rainspouts outside the window was loud enough to wake up a deaf man. I lay there half groggy, listening to the storm and thinking about how the weather had gone all screwy lately and maybe it was time somebody started making plans for another ark.

And then all of a sudden I was thinking about something else, and I wasn't groggy anymore. I sat up in bed, wide awake. And inside of five minutes, without much effort now that I had been primed, I knew what it was the police had overlooked and I was reasonably sure I knew who had murdered Nick Damiano.

But I still didn't know why; I didn't even have an inkling of why. That was what kept me awake until dawn—that, and the unceasing racket of the storm.

The Medford's front door was still on its night security lock when I got there at a quarter to eight. Dan Cady let me in. I asked him a couple of questions about Nick's janitorial habits, and the answers he gave me pretty much confirmed my suspicions. To make absolutely sure, I went down to the basement and spent ten minutes poking around in its hot and noisy gloom.

Now the hard part, the part I never liked. I took the elevator to the third floor and knocked on the door to Room 304. He was there; not more than five seconds passed before he called out, "Door's not locked." I opened it and stepped inside.

He was sitting in a faded armchair near the window, staring out at the rain and the wet streets below. He turned his head briefly to look at me, then turned it back again to the window. The stubby little pipe was between his teeth and the overheated air smelled of his tobacco, a kind of dry, sweet scent, like withered roses.

"More questions?" he said.

"Not exactly, Mr. Weaver. You mind if I sit down?"

"Bed's all there is."

I sat on the bottom edge of the bed, a few feet away from him. The room was small, neat—not much furniture, not much of anything; old patterned wallpaper and a threadbare carpet, both of which had a patina of gray. Maybe it was my mood and the rain-dull day outside, but the entire room seemed gray, full of that aura of age and hopelessness.

"Hot in here," I said. "Furnace is going full blast down in the basement."

"I don't mind it hot."

"Nick Damiano did a better job of regulating the heat, I understand. He'd turn it on for a few hours in the morning, leave it off most of the day, turn it back on in the evenings, and then shut it down again by midnight. The night he died, though, he didn't have time to shut it down."

Weaver didn't say anything.

"It's pretty noisy in the basement when that furnace is on," I said. "You can hardly hold a normal conversation with somebody standing right next to you. It'd be almost impossible to hear anything, even raised voices, from a distance. So you couldn't have heard an argument inside Nick's room, not from back by the storage lockers. And probably not even if you stood right next to the door, because the door's thick and made of metal."

He still didn't stir, didn't speak.

"You made up the argument because you ran into Charley

269

Slattery, didn't you? He might have told the police he saw you come out of the elevator around the time Nick was killed, and that you seemed upset; so you had to protect yourself. Just like you protected yourself by unlocking the alley door after the murder."

More silence.

"You murdered Nick, all right. Beat him to death with your cane—hickory like that is as thick and hard as three-quarter-inch steel pipe. Charley told me you had it under your arm when you got off the elevator. Why under your arm? Why weren't you walking with it like you usually do? Has to be that you didn't want your fingers around the handle, the part you clubbed Nick with, even if you did wipe off most of the blood and gore."

He was looking at me now, without expression—just a dull steady waiting look.

"How did you clean the cane once you were here in your room? Soap and water? Cleaning fluid of some kind? It doesn't matter, you know. There'll still be minute traces of blood on it that the police lab can match up to Nick's."

He put an end to his silence then; he said in a clear, toneless voice, "All right. I done it," and that made it a little easier on both of us. The truth is always easier, no matter how painful it might be.

I said, "Do you want to tell me about it, Mr. Weaver?"

"Not much to tell," he said. "I went to the basement to get my other radio, like I told you before. He was fixing the door to one of the storage bins near mine. I looked at him up close, and I knew he was the one. I'd had a feeling he was ever since I moved in, but that night, up close like that, I knew it for sure."

He paused to take the pipe out of his mouth and lay it carefully on the table next to his chair. Then he said, "I accused him point blank. He put his hands over his ears like a woman, like he couldn't stand to hear it, and ran to his room. I went after him. Got inside before he could shut the door. He started babbling, crazy things about skeletons, and I saw that skeleton of his grinning across the room, and I . . . I don't know, I don't remember that part too good. He pushed me, I think, and I hit him with my cane . . . I kept hitting him . . ."

His voice trailed off and he sat there stiffly, with his big gnarled hands clenched in his lap.

"*Why*, Mr. Weaver? You said he was the one, that you accused him—accused him of what?"

He didn't seem to hear me. He said, "After I come to my senses, I couldn't breathe. Thought I was having a heart attack. God, it was hot in there . . . hot as hell. I opened the alley door to get some air and I guess I must have left it unlocked. I never did that on purpose. Only the story about the argument."

"Why did you kill Nick Damiano?"

No answer for a few seconds; I thought he still wasn't listening and I was about to ask the question again. But then he said, "My Bible's over on the desk. Look inside the front cover."

The Bible was a well-used Gideon and inside the front cover was a yellowed newspaper clipping. I opened the clipping. It was from the Chicago *Sun-Times*, dated June 23, 1957—a news story, with an accompanying photograph, that bore the headline: FLOW-ER SHOP BOMBER IDENTIFIED.

I took it back to the bed and sat again to read it. It said that the person responsible for a homemade bomb that had exploded in a crowded florist shop the day before, killing seven people, was a handyman named Nicholas Donato. One of the dead was Marjorie Donato, the bomber's estranged wife and an employee of the shop; another victim was the shop's owner, Arthur Cullen, with whom Mrs. Donato had apparently been having an affair. According to friends, Nicholas Donato had been despondent over the estrange-ment and the affair, had taken to drinking heavily, and had threatened "to do something drastic" if his wife didn't move back in with him. He had disappeared the morning of the explosion and had not been apprehended at the time the news story was printed. His evident intention had been to blow up only his wife and her lover; but Mrs. Donato had opened the package containing the bomb immediately after it was brought by messenger, in the presence of several customers, and the result had been mass slaughter.

I studied the photograph of Nicholas Donato. It was a head-and-shoulders shot, of not very good quality, and I had to look at it closely for a time to see the likeness. But it was there: Nicholas Donato and Nick Damiano had been the same man.

Weaver had been watching me read. When I looked up from the clipping he said, "They never caught him. Traced him to Indianapolis, but then he disappeared for good. All these years, twenty-seven years, and I come across him here in San Francisco. Coincidence. Or maybe it was supposed to happen that way. The hand of the Lord guides us all, and we don't always understand the whys and wherefores."

"Mr. Weaver, what did that bombing massacre have to do with you?"

"One of the people he blew up was my youngest daughter. Twenty-two that year. Went to that flower shop to pick out an arrangement for her wedding. I saw her after it happened, I saw what his bomb did to her . . ."

He broke off again; his strong voice trembled a little now. But his eyes were dry. He'd cried once, he'd cried many times, but that had been long ago. There were no tears left any more.

I got slowly to my feet. The heat and the sweetish tobacco scent were making me feel sick to my stomach. And the grayness, the aura of age and hopelessness and tragedy were like an oppressive weight.

I said, "I'll be going now."

"Going?" he said. "Telephone's right out in the hall."

"I won't be calling the police, Mr. Weaver. From here or from anywhere else."

"What's that? But . . . you know I killed him . . ."

"I don't know anything," I said. "I don't even remember coming here today."

I left him quickly, before he could say anything else, and went downstairs and out to O'Farrell Street. Wind-hurled rain buffeted me, icy and stinging, but the feel and smell of it was a relief. I pulled up the collar on my overcoat and hurried next door.

Upstairs in the office I took Irv Feinberg's two hundred dollars out of the lock-box in the desk and slipped the envelope into my coat pocket. He wouldn't like getting it back; he wouldn't like my calling it quits on the investigation, just as the police had done. But that didn't matter. Let the dead lie still, and the dying find what little peace they had left. The judgment was out of human hands anyway.

I tried not to think about Nick Damiano any more, but it was too soon and I couldn't blot him out yet. Harmless old Nick, the happy whack. Jesus Christ. Seven people—he had slaughtered seven people that day in 1957. And for what? For a lost woman; for a lost love. No wonder he'd gone batty and developed an obsession for skeletons. He had lived with them, seven of them, all those years, heard them clattering and clacking all those thousands of nights. And now, pretty soon, he would be one himself.

Skeleton rattle your mouldy leg.

All men's lovers come to this.

# Deathlist

## *Robert J. Randisi*

*Miles Jacoby has appeared in one previous short story,
"The Steinway Collection" (Mystery Monthly, 1/77), although the
character, by the time he arrived in* Eye In The Ring *(Avon,
11/82) had undergone considerable changes. The series, as it now
stands, actually began in that novel, with Jack investigating his
first case as a licensed p.i. What I've tried to do in creating
Jacoby is present his development as a p.i. from day one on,
which means that the* character *has been developing from book
to book—and story to story. The reader gets to watch Jacoby as
he makes mistakes and learns from them. I'm hoping that this
makes Jacoby just a little different from the cliched vision of
the Private Eye as this omnipotent being who never makes mistakes
and is never wrong—a new image which started, I think, with
James Garner and* The Rockford Files.

*To date, Miles Jacoby has appeared in three novels:* Eye In
The Ring *(Avon, 1982),* The Steinway Collection *(Avon, 1983) and*
Full Contact *(St. Martin's, 1984). I hope that this will be the
first of many short story appearances for Miles, as well.*

W HEN the cop on the door stopped me I told him that I was a friend of Detective Hocus' and suggested that he check with Hocus to see if I was to be admitted. He told me to wait, disappeared, and returned in a few moments, saying, "Yeah, go ahead."

I walked into the small apartment, through the living room into the bedroom, where all of the activity was taking place.

Hocus, down on one knee, looked up at me with a frown. "Jacoby? What the hell do you want?"

Hocus wasn't usually that abrupt, so I knew he had a nasty one on his hands.

"I called your office and they told me you were here. What have you got?"

I got the feeling he supressed his first impulse, which was probably to tell me to kiss-off, and instead said, "Take a look," gesturing with his hand and standing up.

There was no one on the bed, so I walked around it and saw what was making him so nasty.

In life the girl had probably been very pretty. Through all the blood I could see the wheat colored hair and the ivory skin, the firm little breasts and the long, lithe legs.

The M.E., an East Indian named Dr. Mahbee, was crouched over her, doing his examination.

"Where's all the blood from?" I asked. I had looked for a throat wound first, but could see none.

Mahbee looked up at me and whether he recognized me or not I couldn't say. He looked over at Hocus, who nodded.

"All over," Mahbee finally answered. "I can't find one wound in particular that would account for this volume of blood, but just off hand—and I won't be able to tell for sure until I clean her up—I'd say she's got a dozen or so wounds here, of various degrees."

"Any one bad enough to have done the job?" Hocus asked.

ROBERT J. RANDISI

"Ah, maybe the one in the abdomen—" he said, then leaned over and moved the body a bit, adding, "—and she's got a pretty deep one in her back."

I looked around the room, seeing splotches of blood here and there, on the floor, the walls, the bathroom door.

"Looks like the killer might have chased her around," I said, "maybe slashing away at her the whole time."

Hocus looked at Mahbee, who nodded and said, "That's the way I see it."

"Okay, thanks, Maybe," Hocus told him. The M.E. frowned and turned his head away from the big detective. He hated having his named bastardized that way, but Hocus knew it and that's why he did it. It was an unconscious thing on his part, now, and he did it even at the worst of times—like this one.

"Let's go outside," Hocus told me, meaning the living room. He told his partner, Detective Wright, where he'd be and he nodded.

In the other room he asked me, "What brings you here?"

"I wanted to ask you about another case," I told him.

"Which one?" he asked, taking out a cigar and lighting it up.

"Another girl, coincidentally. Madeline Dean."

"Redhead," he commented, "about twenty-five, stacked—uh, three days ago, right?"

"That's the one. She was strangled in her apartment. Was that one of yours?"

Jerking his thumb toward the other room he said, "My partner's. Why?"

I shrugged, indicating that there was no offense in what I was about to say.

"Her old man has some dough, says he's not satisfied with the job the police are doing. He wants me to look into it. I told him that it was a police matter and that I wouldn't take the job unless I got the okay from the detective assigned."

"You said that?" he asked.

"I did."

"He's got dough, huh?"

"Loads of it."

"And you said that?"

I shrugged.

"It's only money," I told him.

Shaking his head he said, "I can't believe you just said *that!*"

I just stared at him.

"I'll call Bill out in a minute and you can ask him."

"You going to say something in my behalf?" I asked.

"Jeez," he said, "if I can think of something!"

A few moments later Wright came walking out, carrying something in his hand. It appeared to be a card of some sort, once white but now stained with blood.

"What's that?" Hocus asked.

"Looks like a party invite," his partner answered, handing it to Hocus. "She had it crumpled in her hand."

I felt a chill and asked Hocus, "Can I see that?"

He gave me a baleful stare. "Mind if I look first?"

"Let's look together," I told him, feeling like we'd played this scene before.

With me peering over his shoulder he smoothed out the invitation as best he could and it was the usual you-are-cordially-invited-to kind of thing. The place she was invited to was the home of someone called Leslie Wilford III.

"Jesus," I said, and both Hocus and Wright looked at me.

"What's the matter with you?" Hocus asked.

I directed myself to Wright.

"Did you check the Dean girl's apartment?" I asked him.

"Dean?" he asked, looking at his partner.

"The redhead three days ago," he reminded him.

"Oh, her," he said, remembering. "Yeah, we tossed her place pretty good. Why?"

"Apparently you didn't toss it good enough," I said. I reached into my jacket pocket and came up with a small, stamped envelope addressed to the dead redhead. "I found this in a pile of mail. It hadn't been opened. I took the liberty of opening it."

I opened the envelope then and slid the contents out, held it up to show them.

It was an identical invitation to the same party.

# 2

"So we've got two dead girls—both lookers, by the way—who were killed three days apart, but were invited to the same party," Hocus said, summing things up.

We were back at the 17th precinct with him seated behind his desk, his partner propping a hip on the desk, and me sitting in one of those rock-hard chairs police precincts usually supply for "civilians."

"My client's daughter's body was found on the sixteenth," I said, "the evening after this party." I was tapping the clean invitation, which was sitting on Hocus' desk, next to the other one. "And on top of that, both are made out in different handwriting."

"Yeah," Hocus said, frowning at them. "Now we find this girl's body," he said, tapping the other invitation, "on the nineteenth."

"So the only connection we've got between the two is that they were both invited to the same party," Wright said.

"Yeah, but did they both *go* to the party?" I asked.

"The only way we're going to find out if either one of them went to the party is to ask the man who threw it," Wright said.

"Right," I said, standing up, "let's go."

"Wrong," Hocus said, also standing up. "We'll go," he told me, indicating that his partner and he made up the "we," not me. "You'll go somewhere else, where you won't be in the way."

"Will you let me know what you find out?"

They exchanged glances and Hocus asked Wright, "Should we help the shamus earn his fee?"

"Why not?" Wright said. "He might be generous and buy us a dinner in return."

"You're on," I said.

"Then stick by the phone and I'll call you when we get back," Hocus said.

"Don't forget to get a complete guest list," I said as they walked out.

"Write that down," I heard Hocus tell Wright sarcastically, and then they were out of earshot.

Two people on that guest list were already dead, I thought. I hoped that it wouldn't turn out to be some kind of *death*list.

# 3

I went back to my office and sat behind my desk studying the boxing gloves that hung on my right wall, the ones I'd worn when I was "Kid" Jacoby, boxer and not Miles Jacoby, private investigator. I had nothing else to do while I waited for Hocus' call because I had no clients other than George Dean, the dead girl's old man.

He had come into my office only that morning, offering me an outrageous sum of money to find his daughter's killer and see to it that he was "punished." Of course, the amount wasn't outrageous to him because he *had* money, something no one could ever say about me.

I had fed him the line about checking with the detective in charge, and told him I'd let him know what I decided. He had written a check for two hundred dollars, telling me we would call that a consultation fee, which I could keep whether I took the case or not. He had also given me a business card, and a photo of his daughter, who appeared to be a very young, very healthy, very redheaded, very lovely young lady.

Of course, she was also very dead.

And so was the blonde who had been discovered that morning. Her name, according to Hocus, was Blair Bishop, and she had been 21, three years younger than Madeline Dean.

There was something else I had taken out of Madeline's apartment, and that was a small address and phone book, which had apparently also been overlooked, or deemed unimportant by the police.

I fished that out of my pocket now and began to leaf through it. It was a short trip to the B's, but there it was in red and white: Blair Bishop, 329 W. 23 Street, 253-7096.

I wished I could get a look at Blair Bishop's phone book, as well. I decided I'd ask Hocus about it.

I didn't want to use the phone—Hocus might try to reach me while my line was busy—but I chanced it long enough to call downstairs for a roast beef hero and two containers of black coffee. By the time I had eaten the sandwich and finished one of the coffees, Hocus still hadn't called. I closed my eyes and tried to conjure up a vision of the address on the party invitation, which I had left with Hocus. I was still relatively new at this business, having only recently retired from the ring after a 2½ round debacle against a young fighter named Johnny Ricardi. Not that I was old at 29, but I was old enough to know better and hung up my gloves immediately following that fight. Anyway, Eddie Waters—the other half of WATERS & JACOBY, PRIVATE INVESTIGATORS—who was dead, had always had the knack of automatically remembering little things like that. I didn't, and after a few minutes of fruitless effort, I gave it up.

There was one cold sip of coffee left at the bottom of the second cup when the phone rang.

"Jack, it's Hocus."

"What'd you find out?"

"This Leslie Whosis the third is a guy, not a broad," he told me. "He came on all shocked and dismayed, said he knew both girls well enough to invite them to a party, but not much beyond that. Said he hadn't the 'inclination' to get to know them better, since he was engaged to be married to some rich bimbo—"

"He said that?"

"No, bimbo was my word. Anyway, the guy's getting set to

marry money, so even if he knew these girls better than he says, he wasn't saying."

"Did you get the guest list?"

"Shit, I told Billy to write that down—"

"Hey—"

"We got it, Jacoby. We do know our job, you know."

I fingered Madeline Dean's little phone book and said, "Uh-huh. Can I see it?"

"The guest list?"

"Of course, the guest list."

"Well, lucky for you the Xerox machine is working today. I'm going home, but I'll leave a copy for you here. Just ask anybody for it."

"Okay, Hocus. I appreciate it."

"Just remember that dinner when you collect your fat fee," he told me. "Jeez, you private eye guys have all the luck."

"Yeah, listen, before you hang up."

"Yeah?"

"Did you take Blair Bishop's address book, or phone book, out of her apartment?"

"Why, you gonna look under 'K' for killer, or 'M' for murderer?"

"Funny. Did you?"

"I don't know," he admitted. "We get so many of these goddamn things that we do tend to get sloppy, sometimes. We should have. I told them to bag anything that was pertinent. Hold on . . ." I heard him leafing through some papers. "Shit . . ." he muttered under his breath at one point.

"No, huh?"

"Shit, no—"

"Okay, look, just so you don't think I'm holding anything back, you know? I've got Madeline Dean's phone book—"

"Shit—" he started again, but I kept going.

"I'll bring it in to you, but how about calling the cop on the door at the Bishop apartment, and telling him to let me in. I'll find hers and then I'll bring you both of them. How's that?"

He paused a moment, then said, "It sounds okay, but why do I have this urge to look up your sleeve?"

"Just a Homicide Dick's natural suspicious mind, I guess."

"Yeah, sure, the Private Dick calling the Homicide Dick a dick. Okay, kid, you're on. Have it in my office by morning, pick up your list when you want."

"Okay, thanks, Hocus. Ain't cooperation great?"

"Yeah, try giving more than you receive some time, huh?"

# 4

I had no problems getting into the Bishop girl's apartment, not with Hocus' call paving the way. I had even less trouble finding her phone book, which was right next to her bed on her night table. I slid it into my pocket and left, so that the cop would see that my hands were empty. He didn't ask to search me.

On the subway, riding uptown to the 17th, I opened her book and turned to the D's and was not disappointed. There it was: Madeline Dean, 117 E. 57 Street, 752-5474.

So, not only had both girls been invited to the same party, but they knew each other as well.

I identified myself at the front desk at the precinct, and the sergeant there handed over an envelope with my name on it. I took the IRT back downtown to my apartment on Bleecker Street.

Once I was home I spread out the guest list and the two phone books on my kitchen table. Since Hocus had told me to have the books in his office by tomorrow, I decided to take advantage of the extra time I had with them. I fully expected that Hocus would get around to taking statements from all of the guests at the party, but I didn't want to wait that long. I intended to make my own list of names that appeared in both phone books as well as on the guest list. I hoped that Leslie Wilford III wasn't in the habit of throwing parties where everybody knew everybody.

I lucked out. Apparently Wilford knew a lot of people from different walks of life who were not necessarily acquainted with one another.

I came up with a final list of seven, which included five women and two men. I folded up the list and put it in my wallet, then set the two phone books aside. Since I didn't need them any further, I would be very willing to turn them over to Hocus in the morning. I was not quite so willing, however, to let Hocus in on what I was planning to do. He might not mind, but I didn't want to take the chance of his ordering me to stay away from the people on that guest list.

The following morning I was at the 17th Precinct at 9 a.m. Hocus had already been called out on a case, so I left the phone books for him at the desk in an envelope they kindly supplied.

"Now we're a stationery store," the nice policeman on the desk muttered when I asked for it.

"Thank you very much," I said, and he scowled at me as I left.

There were two names on my list with the same address, and they were both female. As it turned out, they were roommates as well. They both knew Blair and Madeline, but neither girl had been able to attend the Wilford party due to a previous engagement. Neither girl seemed to have any cause for adverse feelings toward the two dead girls, and both seemed genuinely upset about the murders.

The others on my list had all been at the party, but none could tell me anything that would help my investigation. The last man I went to see suggested that I see a girl named Ginny Davis. According to him, she was "Blair's best friend in the whole world." By coincidence, Ginny Davis was the last name on my list, and with that little tidbit of information I rushed to see her.

# 5

Ginny Davis was the prettiest live girl I had seen in some months. She was small, petite even, with ash-blonde hair, green eyes, a small nose and a rosebud mouth. Her hair was parted down the center and she was forever sweeping the two halves away from her face. Behind her, the hair extended all the way down to her cute behind.

When I introduced myself at her door and told her why I was there, she appeared nervous, but invited me in.

"Can I get you a drink?" she asked.

"No thank you."

Her pretty green eyes were somewhat red and swollen. She had obviously been crying.

"I read it in the papers," she told me, pointing to the copy of the *News* that was on her coffee table. "It was such a shock, seeing it that way."

"I can imagine. You also knew Madeline Dean, didn't you?"

"Only through Blair. I can't imagine why Madeline had my name in her phone book. She's never called me once since we met."

"When was that?"

"At a party, a few months ago."

"Was the party at the home of Leslie Wilford?"

"Why no, it was at another friend's house. Why?"

"Just curious. Did you attend Wilford's party four days ago?"

"Why yes. Actually, Blair and I went out there together. Neither one of us had a date. I was hoping to meet someone there, but Blair—"

When she stopped short, I prompted her to finish what she had started to say.

"Well, Blair kind of had her eye on Leslie, you know?"

"I thought he was engaged," I said.

"He is, but that never stopped Blair . . . or Les, for that matter."

"He played around?"

She took a Kleenex from a box on the coffee table, and started twisting it in her hands.

"I shouldn't say—"

"Ginny—may I call you Ginny?" When she nodded I went on. "Ginny, I'm not looking to dig up any dirt on anyone, I'm just trying to find out who killed Madeline Dean. At the same time, I might be able to find out who killed Blair."

"Do you think maybe it's the same person?" she asked.

"I don't really know. What can you tell me about Wilford, Blair and Madeline?"

"Well, Leslie is a notorious playboy, but he acts like he has more money than he actually does. Everybody thinks he's marrying Monica for her money."

"Monica?"

"Monica Quartermain. She's nowhere as pretty as Madeline or Blair . . . were."

"Was Wilford seeing one or both girls?"

"Well, there was some talk that he'd been sleeping with Maddy for some time. He wasn't really seeing Blair, but she was trying."

"Did Madeline go to the party, too?"

"No, she never showed up."

"Is there anything at all that you can tell me that might help me out? Anything at all?"

She thought a moment, but she didn't seem to be able to concentrate.

"I'm sorry," she said finally, "I can't think—"

"You can't think of anything?" I prompted.

"No, I just can't think at all. Not after that," she said, pointing to the newspaper.

"I understand. I'm sorry to put you through this. Maybe in a while, a day or so, you might think of something. Would you give me a call?"

I took out my notebook and pen and wrote my office number, and then as an afterthought, my home number. I ripped out the page and handed it to her.

"Call me anytime," I told her.

Was I telling her for the same reason? She was very pretty, and I found myself trying to think of other questions just so I wouldn't have to leave yet.

Finally I decided to leave the girl alone with her grief, but I promised myself that I would get back to her at a later time, for personal reasons.

"I'll leave you alone now, Miss Davis," I told her, standing up.

She stood up also and said, "I'll call you as soon as I'm able to think."

"I'll be grateful for any help you can give me."

"I want you to find who killed them," she said. "I'll call you."

"Thank you."

# 6

The next day I rented a car and went out to see Leslie Wilford III himself, playboy and host. He had a large home on Long Island, and if he was suddenly having trouble paying for it, that might explain why he was planning to marry, in Hocus' words, 'some rich bimbo'.

As it turned out, the blushing bride-to-be answered the door and, when I ask for Wilford, introduced herself to me as Monica Quartermain.

"My fiancé is in the den," she said. "I'll take you to him."

I followed her to the den and when I saw them together it made even more sense to think that he was marrying the woman for her money.

Wilford was a tall, handsome blonde type, just what you'd expect from a playboy. Monica was a small girl with mousy gray hair and a perpetual squint.

"Mr. Wilford? My name's Jacoby. I'm here about the murders of Blair Bishop and Madeline Dean."

"Really?" he asked, casting a glance at his fiancée. "Why come to me? I barely knew the girls?"

"Really? Why were they invited to your party, then?"

"Invited?" he said, frowning. "I don't know what you're talking about. I didn't invite them. I've already gone through this."

Obviously, he thought I was a cop. Instead of correcting him, I said, "Are you saying they crashed the party?"

He threw another glance Monica Quartermain's way before answering. Was he checking to see if she was buying his story. Was he trying to convince her rather than me?

"Yes, they must have," he said, shrugging, "or else how would they have gotten in?"

I decided not to mention the two invitations to the girls. That was something to hold until later.

"Did you know the girls, Miss Quartermain?"

"No, I didn't know them at all." Her attitude clearly added that she had no desire to, either. She had no desire to know any of the women her fiancé had known before her.

"I see," I said, and turned my attention back to Leslie Wilford. "I suppose, then, that you wouldn't know any reason why someone would want to kill them?"

"Not at all," he said. "As I said, I didn't know either girl all that well."

"I see," I said again.

I decided to back off, then, and think about things. Let Hocus question him as well, and then maybe we'd put our heads together and come up with something. Wilford was lying, that much was clear, but he could have simply been lying to his fiancée, and not to block a murder investigation.

Maybe he'd even tell Hocus the truth, since a policeman would press much harder than I had.

"All right, I guess I'll be leaving then," I said.

"I'll see you to the door," Monica offered.

"Thank you," I said. I turned to Wilford and said, "Good-bye, Mr. Wilford . . . and good luck."

"Thank you."

As we walked to the door I asked Monica, "When is the wedding?"

"Later this morning, at City Hall. Neither of us wants a large wedding."

"I see."

"We'll be leaving on our honeymoon later today. We'll be going upstate for a couple of days."

"Just a couple of days?"

"I have some business," she said, without elaboration.

At the door I said, "Good luck, Miss Quartermain."

"Thank you," she said, shutting the door in my face as if she could read my mind.

I was thinking that she would need it.

# 7

Three days later I was in my office and got a call from Hocus.

"You've been busy, haven't you?"

"What do you mean?"

"We finally got around to taking statements from the guests at that Wilford party," he told me, "and I find that you've been there three days ahead of us."

"I only visited some of them."

"Which ones?" he asked. "How'd you narrow it down?"

"I just compared the list to the two girls' phone books, and visited the names that appeared on all three."

"Good thinking," he said, grudgingly.

"You would have thought of it to, if you had the time."

"That's true."

"Did you talk to Ginny Davis?"

"If her name was on the list, yeah. I can't remember all of them."

"You'll remember this one," I told him, and described her to him.

"Oh, yeah," he said right away, "I remember her. Prettiest thing I've seen in a long time. Kinda skinny, though."

"I'd make all kinds of allowances for the sake of that face."

"I don't blame you. You want to compare notes?"

"You stumped?"

"I'm overloaded with cases, damn it!"

"All right, so don't bite my head off. I didn't tell you to become a cop."

"Sorry," he said, and he meant it. "You want to trade info?"

"Sure, why not? Don't I always cooperate with the minions of the law?"

"Yeah, it's just me in particular you like to screw."

"Bogie's okay?"

"Bogie's is fine. Meet you there in an hour."

As I was about to leave the phone rang, and it was Ginny Davis.

"Mr. Jacoby?"

"Hello, Ginny. How are you?"

"Much better than I was, thanks. I was thinking about what you asked me, and I don't know if this will mean anything."

"What is it?"

"Well, it was at the party. Blair wanted to sneak up to Les' office and leave a note on his desk. You know, as a joke? And as kind of a pass on paper. It had her phone number on it, among other things."

"Yes?"

"Well, she wanted me to be the lookout. I didn't want to do it, but she talked me into it. I stood out in the hall while she went in, opened his desk drawer and put her note inside."

"That's it?"

"It doesn't help much, huh?" she asked.

"Well, I don't know yet, Ginny. Did you tell this to the cops?"

"No, I didn't really think it was important, but then I thought maybe I should tell you."

"I appreciate you calling me, Ginny. I'll let you know if it ends up helping or not."

"All right."

"Ginny?"

"Yes?"

"After this is all over, I wonder if I could, uh, maybe call you for, you know, a drink or . . . something?"

She hesitated a moment, then said, "Sure, I'd like that."

"Okay, then, I'll be talking to you."

"Good luck," she said, and hung up.

When I hung up I was smiling like some kind of a fool.

Bogie's is a small restaurant with a Bogart motif that was owned by Billy Palmer, a friend of mine. Billy had been letting me live in his back office, which was a small apartment, until I could find another place. Mine had burned down, but that's another story.

I was sitting at the bar in Bogie's when Hocus came in, and signalled the bartender to bring over another beer.

"Where's your better half?" I asked Hocus.

"He's back at the precinct."

"I thought it was his case?"

"I took it over because of the similarities between it and the Dean case."

When the beers came we each took a drink, and then he said, "What have you got?"

"Oh, no. This was your idea, you go first."

He told me about his interview with Leslie Wilford III. He said he couldn't remember if either girl had attended his party, and denied having any relationship with either girl.

"That doesn't jibe with what I got," I told him. "There was something going around that he was sleeping with the Dean girl. I also know that the Bishop girl was trying to get something started with him."

"I got that, too," he told me. "Not about the Bishop girl, but about him and Dean."

"You get anything else?"

"Yeah, there was another guest who said that during the party Wilford got an envelope from a messenger service or something. He said that when he opened it up, it looked like bad news. He got all shook up and went straight up to his office."

"The guy didn't get a look at what was delivered?"

"Just that it was a long, white envelope."

"Is that it?"

"No, it's not, but do you notice anything here?"

"What?"

"I'm doing all the talking."

"And doing quite well, too."

He frowned at me. "Okay, one more thing. Apparently the Dean girl was a little kinky."

"Why do you say that?"

"I went back to her apartment and looked around myself. I found a false back in her closet, and inside I found a camera setup aimed at the bed."

"Movie camera?"

He shook his head.

"Stills. If she kept a scrapbook, it wasn't in her apartment."

"What about Blair Bishop?"

"I went over there, but she wasn't set up that way."

"So maybe Madeline was blackmailing a boyfriend, and he killed her."

"That leaves the Bishop girl. Where does she fit in?" he asked. "I guess we could be looking at two different killers."

All of a sudden I didn't agree.

"Let's go and see the Wilfords tomorrow."

"Together?"

I nodded.

"Why?" he asked, squinting at me suspiciously.

"I think I can clear this whole thing up for us."

"How about keeping your side of the deal, here?"

"Tomorrow, when we visit the happy couple."

"What about today?"

"Today?" I repeated. I held my beer aloft and said, "Today I'm buying the drinks."

# 8

The next day Hocus and Wright picked me up in their unmarked car and we drove out to the Wilford house on Long Island. Mr. and Mrs. Wilford—those happy newlyweds—had just arrived home from their honeymoon, but consented to see us.

"We're not even unpacked," Wilford said as we gathered in the living room.

"We just got home," Monica Wilford whined.

"It's all right, dear," her hubby said. "We must cooperate with the police. We don't want the murderer of those young girls to go unpunished, do we?"

"Of course not," she said, but her tone said something else.

In the car Hocus had agreed to let me handle things when we reached the Wilford house, but he seemed to have come to his own conclusion, because I could see him inching his way toward the mousy Monica, ready to pounce when I denounced her.

"I'm glad you feel that way, Mr. Wilford," I said. "I guess that means you're willing to confess."

"Confess?" he said, looking surprised. I could sense Hocus looking at me in surprise, as well. "To what?" He frowned then and asked, "Are you a policeman?"

"No, I'm a private detective, and I'm naming you as the murderer of those two girls."

"You're mad," he said.

"Les, make them go away," Mrs. Wilford said in her whining tone.

Suddenly I was of the opinion that Wilford should thank me for nailing him so that he wouldn't have to spend the rest of his life with her perpetual squint and constant whine.

"What have you got, Jacoby?" Hocus asked, puzzled.

"I've got one and one," I told him, "which, unless my math is wrong, adds up to murder." I held up my left hand with the index finger pointed up and said, "On this hand I've got a girlfriend," and then, holding up my right hand in the same way, "and on this hand I've got a would-be girlfriend."

"I don't have to listen—" Wilford started, but Hocus held his hand up for silence.

"I think we'll listen to what Mr. Jacoby has to say, Mr.

Wilford," he told Wilford, and the look in his eye told me it had better be good.

"Okay," I said, "we've got Madeline Dean, with whom our Mr. Wilford here had been sleeping."

"Les—" the lady of the house started, but he said, "Shut up, Monica," and she lapsed into a shocked silence.

"Now, our Miss Dean has a peculiar hobby, one which Mr. Wilford was not aware of. She liked to take pictures of herself and her boyfriends in bed. My guess is that when Mr. Wilford decided to marry Miss Quartermain, he broke up with Madeline Dean. Miss Dean didn't take kindly to that, nor did she take kindly to being invited to the party here last week, which I assume was in honor of the happy occasion."

"I didn't—" Wilford began, but he cut himself off as I continued to speak.

"Miss Dean was pissed," I went on, "so the day of the party she had an envelope delivered to Mr. Wilford here, the contents of which made him very upset. What was in that envelope?" I asked, looking at Hocus.

"A photograph."

"Right on the button," I complimented him. "A picture of Madeline Dean and Leslie Wilford III in the sack. A pretty damning picture, I'd say, if the future Mrs. Wilford got hold of it. She might even call off the wedding if she found out, and there would go all of that money."

Monica Wilford made a sound halfway between a squeak and a hiccup, then remained silent.

"So what does our Mr. Wilford do?" I asked, facing Hocus again.

"He kills her," he said, playing along.

"Right again. There was no forced entry into her apartment, right?"

"That's right," Hocus replied.

"So in all likelihood she was killed by someone she knew, someone she admitted to her apartment herself."

"Okay, what about the Bishop girl?" Hocus asked.

"He killed her, too."

A sharp intake of breath from the mousy Mrs., but no further sound.

"Why?" Hocus asked.

"Blair Bishop's best friend told me that she had a thing for Wilford, and wanted to try and get something started. The night of the party, she went up to his office to leave him a mash note. She opened the drawer of his desk and left the note inside. Again, my guess is that Wilford left the photo in his desk drawer, to deal with later. When he found Bishop's mash note, he felt sure she had seen the photo, and that made her dangerous. Especially if she tried to use that to make him take up with her. She may or may not have, but whichever it was, Wilford saw his only way out as killing her, too. With both girls out of the way, he was free to marry Miss Quartermain—and her money." I turned to Hocus and said, "Again, no forced entry into the Bishop girl's apartment either. So, she let him in, and he killed her."

We all faced Wilford then, who was standing with his head down, and Hocus said, "What about it, Mr. Wilford? You want to get it off your chest."

He looked up at us through sick eyes and said, "It was horrible. She wouldn't die after I stabbed her the first time. I had to chase her around, stabbing her and stabbing her until . . . until I finally sank the knife into her back." He covered his face with his hands and from behind them repeated, "It was horrible!"

Monica Quartermain Wilford just stood there, staring helplessly at her husband.

"Did you want my money so badly?" she finally asked him.

He dropped his hands from his face and looked at her, then said, "What else would I want from you, Monica? What else could I possibly want from you?"

Wright approached Wilford and touched his arm.

"Let's go, Mr. Wilford," he said.

Wilford looked at me and said, "There's one thing I don't understand."

"What's that?" I asked.

"You said Madeline was angry about being invited to the party. I didn't send her an invitation!"

He was looking at Hocus and me with a puzzled expression on his face.

"Well, if you didn't, who did?" Hocus asked.

After a long moment of silence Monica Wilford said, "I did."

We all turned to face her and Wilford asked, "Why?"

"I'd heard the stories about you and her," she said. "I invited her to see if the stories were true. I wanted to see how you would react when she arrived."

Wilford faced me with a helpless look on his face.

I shrugged and said, "That was the connection between the two killings. That's originally what had us thinking about one killer, instead of two."

So without realizing what she was doing, Monica Wilford had set her husband up to take a well deserved fall for double murder.

When Wright took Wilford out to the car, Mrs. Wilford trotted along behind, ever faithful, ever squinting, ever whining.

"I thought you were zeroing in on her," Hocus said.

"Did you get a look at any of the other invitations?" I asked him.

"No, why?"

After leaving Hocus the night before, I had called Ginny Davis and asked if I could come over to get her invitation. Now I pulled it out of my pocket and showed it to him.

"The handwriting?" he said, handing it back.

"Different," I said, nodding. "She made out the invitation to Madeline Dean, he made out all the rest, including the one to Blair Bishop. He didn't know the Bishop girl would use the party as an opportunity to pull a stunt like the one she pulled."

"That couldn't have told you it was her," he said.

"It didn't," I said, "but I figured that when we came here and faced them, one of them would crack."

"Then you didn't know for sure yesterday?"

"I didn't even know for sure until a few minutes ago," I said. I *had* been leaning toward Wilford himself, but I didn't mention that to Hocus.

"I wonder," he said as we started for the door.

"What?" I said. I was thinking about Ginny Davis. When I picked up the invitation from her, she had agreed to have dinner with me the next night—tonight.

"I wonder how long it would have taken him to decide to kill her, too," he said, referring to Monica Wilford.

Thinking of her mousy gray hair, her perpetual squint and the whine that was like fingernails on a blackboard, I said, "Not long, pal, not long at all."

# Hallam

## *L. J. Washburn*

*This is the first appearance of Hallam, a cowboy who has outlived the days of the old west to become a gun-toting private eye and stuntman in the early days of motion pictures in California.*

HALLAM waited behind the rocks, Colt Cavalry Model .45 gripped firmly in his big right hand. The riders would be here soon and he could go to work. For now, though, he waited. Seemed like that was all he did most of the time since he got into this crazy business.

The clatter of hooves came to his keen ears and he straightened, body taut now with expectation. He was a big man, tall and wide-shouldered, looking right at home in the buckskins and wide-brimmed hat. A full cartridge belt was fastened around his lean hips. Besides the holster for the .45, a sheathed Bowie knife was suspended from it.

The bone handle of the Colt felt good in his calloused palm, rekindled a lot of memories. If he let his mind drift, it seemed almost like he was back in the old days. The days when Lucas

Hallam was a respected—and feared—name in Texas and New Mexico and Arizona . . .

"Get ready, Lucas. They're almost here. Steady now . . . Action!"

Vaguely, Hallam heard the director's commands and obeyed them like the professional he was. But as he swung around the rocks into the open, the rolling thunder of racing hoofbeats filling his ears, he might have been home again.

"Hold it!" he roared, lining the Colt on the group of riders. There was no sound on this picture, of course, but the words came out anyway.

The riders pulled back on the reins and slowed their mounts to a stop. There were five of them, all wearing cowboy clothes and big hats. Bright bandannas were tied around the lower halves of their faces. The men were hard-eyed, glaring at the big man who faced them down without even a hint of fear in his manner.

From his post beside the camera, the director called, "Now, Jerry, go for your gun!"

One of the men on horseback, one who was dressed all in black, sent his hand streaking for the butt of the pistol holstered on his hip. To Hallam's eyes, the draw was pitifully slow, and he had to concentrate in order not to shoot too soon. He let the black-clad actor get his gun all the way out, waited until the muzzle was swinging into line with him.

Then Hallam squeezed the trigger of his own gun, felt the familiar buck against the palm of his hand. Smoke blossomed from the barrel.

The gunman on the horse dropped his pistol and clutched his stomach. His face distorted in mock pain.

"Now ride!" the director shouted.

All of the men urged their horses forward, even the one who was supposed to be wounded. Hallam triggered off a couple of shots, then darted out of the way. The horses galloped past him. He fired after the fleeing men, but they didn't slow down until they were well out of camera range.

"Cut! That was great, fellas, just great!"

Hallam took a deep breath and slid the long-barrelled Colt back in its holster. Playtime was over. With the rolling gait of a man who has spent a lot of his life on the back of a horse, he walked toward the long table where a couple of girls were handing out lemonade to the actors. The California sun was hot this time of day, made a man thirsty.

Before he reached the table, though, the director hurried up to him and stopped him. "Great take, Lucas!" he said. He looked speculatively up at the foot-taller Hallam. "You've got star quality, man. Why do you want to keep on being an extra? You could be as big as Tom Mix if you wanted to. Why, you'd leave Gibson and McCoy and all the rest behind!"

Hallam shook his head. "I'm no actor, Bernie," he said simply. "Just a broke-down old cowboy."

"Yeah, sure. And I'm D. W. Griffith. Listen, Lucas—"

Hallam shook his head with a smile and turned away. The director had made this pitch to him before. Working as an extra got Hallam through the lean times when his agency wasn't attracting any clients, but being a movie star was the last thing he wanted.

Too much hoopla mixed up with that. Wouldn't sit well with a man like him.

There was another interruption before he made it to the lemonade. A long black car pulled up behind the trucks of the movie company. The driver got out, asked a question of a passing script girl. The girl pointed to Hallam.

Hallam saw the exchange and watched the man striding toward him. The newcomer was big, too, but he wore a pin-striped suit and a pulled-down Panama instead of cowboy clothes.

He stopped in front of Hallam, looked him up and down in disbelief, and said, "You're a private dick?"

"I'm Lucas Hallam, if that's who you're lookin' for." Hallam felt an instant dislike for this man, but he kept his voice flat and impassive.

The man jerked a thumb over his beefy shoulder. "Somebody wants to see you, Hallam."

"Question is, do I want to see this somebody?"

The man stiffened. He wasn't used to people asking questions. "You wanna see him if you know what's good for you, Tex," he snapped.

Hallam rubbed his jaw, squinted toward the long black car. He could see a figure sitting in the back seat. "Maybe your boss should do his own askin'," he said slowly.

"Why, you moth-eaten old bastard—" the man hissed. His hand shot out and clamped down on Hallam's shoulder. "You'll come when I tell you to come, you—"

Hallam hit him in the stomach with his left and jerked his shoulder loose. His right swept around as the man gasped and took a step backward. The blow cracked into his jaw and knocked him sprawling. With a growled curse, he reached under his coat and grabbed an automatic out of a shoulder rig.

Just as the gun came clear, the man froze, the point of Hallam's Bowie knife resting easily just under his chin. The blade barely pricked the skin, but it was enough to stop any threat the man wanted to make.

Hallam smiled down at him.

"This ain't a prop, son," Hallam said so softly the man could barely hear him. "You go to movin' too much, it'll slice your head right off. Now take that gun out real slow and put it on the ground."

A crowd was gathering around the two men, but nobody got too close as the man followed Hallam's orders. This wasn't play-acting, and everybody knew it.

A voice cut through the tension. "Very impressive, Mr. Hallam. I'll thank you to let my man up now, though."

Hallam kept the knife where it was. He looked up to see who had spoken, saw a slim man of medium height wearing a lightweight white suit. Everything about him said money, from the carefully cut sandy hair to the Italian shoes on his feet.

Hallam straightened from his crouch and stepped back from the man he had knocked down. The knife went into its sheath. "Need to teach your people better manners, mister," Hallam rumbled.

"You're probably right, Mr. Hallam. I assume that you *are* Lucas Hallam?"

"That's right. Who're you?"

The man extended his hand. "Anthony Rose. I have a job for you, Mr. Hallam, and I'd like to discuss it with you."

Hallam's big hand briefly engulfed Rose's smaller one. "I'll talk to you. Won't say I'll take the job just yet, though."

"Fair enough," Rose replied. "Were you through for the day?"

Hallam looked at the director and got a quick, nervous nod. Bernie knew who Anthony Rose was, just as well as Hallam did.

"Seem to be."

"Good. I'll give you a ride back to town, then."

The big man in the pin-stripes had gotten up by now and was standing nearby, looking murderously at Hallam. He kept his mouth shut, though, and made no move to start more trouble.

"Let's go, Bert," Rose said to him, and the man hurried to the car to open the back door.

The car was big enough that even Hallam, with his long legs, was able to sit comfortably in the back seat next to Rose. The windows were down, and Hallam took off his hat and let the cool breeze ruffle his shaggy gray hair. It felt good after the heat and dust of location shooting.

Rose looked over at Hallam in his buckskins and said, "You don't look like any private detective I ever saw."

"Man's got to eat," Hallam said. "Movie work pays good."

"So do I. Do you know who I am, Mr. Hallam?"

"Course I do." Hallam paused. "You're one of the biggest crooks on the West Coast."

For a moment, Rose seemed on the verge of anger. In the front seat, the pin-striped Bert gaped in amazement that anybody would talk to his boss like that, especially some goofy old cowboy.

Then Rose chuckled and said, "Take us to the *Gilded Lily*, Bert. I'll do my talking there." He turned to his companion in the back seat. "I think you're just the man for this job, Hallam. We're going to get along fine."

"We'll see," Hallam said.

\* \* \*

Rose made small talk during the drive to Los Angeles and the ride in an expensive motor launch out beyond the limit, out to the *Gilded Lily*. Hallam had never been to the gambling ship, but he had heard stories about it. It was only one of Rose's enterprises; a fleet of smaller, quicker ships ran in tons of Mexican booze every year under Rose's direction. The *Gilded Lily* was his pride and joy, though, the place where he could play at being the little tin god he fancied himself.

Hallam had been told all that by friends on the LA force, but now he was seeing it firsthand. The sun was setting by the time they reached the ship, and it was already ablaze with lights. The launch pulled up beside a small platform; a flight of steps led up to the deck from there.

Rose went first, then Hallam, then the still-surly Bert. At the top of the stairs, a man in blue ship's uniform tried to hide his surprise at the sight of Hallam, coming aboard in buckskins.

As the three of them reached the deck, Bert tapped Hallam on the shoulder. "No guns on board, mac," he grated. "Boss's rules."

Hallam turned with a mild look on his face. "Sure," he said. He took the Colt from the holster and handed it over to Bert. "Nothin' in it but blanks, anyway."

Bert tapped him on the arm. "The pigsticker, too, Buffalo Bill."

"Bert . . ." Rose said in a soft, warning tone.

"Don't go nowhere 'thout my Bowie, son," Hallam answered. "And them's *my* rules."

Bert growled and squared his shoulders, but Rose cut in. "Let it go, Bert. You and Mr. Hallam have danced enough already today."

Bert let out a long breath and nodded reluctantly.

"We'll go to my private office, Hallam," Rose went on. "I can explain everything there."

"I'm ready to hear it."

The ship was crowded with drinking, gambling merrymakers

from Los Angeles, and Hallam got several startled looks as he followed Rose through the main rooms to a large, opulently furnished office somewhere in the bowels of the ship. To judge from the thick carpet on the floor and the dark wood panelling, they might as well have been in a high-class office building in the city.

Rose shut the door, leaving Bert outside. Another man was waiting in the office, and he said, "Hi, Tony," as Rose went behind a huge mahogany desk and sat down.

"Art, this is Lucas Hallam, the man I told you about. Hallam, meet Art Burlington, my right-hand man."

Hallam shook hands with Burlington, who was a little taller than Rose, with dark curly hair and a pleasant, open face. "I'm glad to meet you, Mr. Hallam," he said. "I've been learning quite a bit about you."

"How's that?" Hallam asked.

"I had Art do some checking up on you before I ever approached you, Hallam," Rose said. He gestured for Hallam to take the chair in front of the big desk. "I like to know a little about someone before I offer him a job."

"Good policy. What'd you find out?"

Rose glanced at Burlington. "Art?"

"Well . . . your name is Lucas Hallam, and you had quite a reputation as a gunfighter in Texas and New Mexico during the Nineties," Burlington began. "Later, right after the turn of the century, you became a lawman and worked as a Federal marshal, as well as serving as sheriff of several different counties. You were also a Pinkerton agent later, and that led to you opening your own detective agency, a one-man agency, I might add, a few years ago. You also work from time to time as, ah, an actor in Western pictures. Is all that correct, Mr. Hallam?"

"Right enough," Hallam admitted.

"So you're not the simple cowboy you pretend to be," Rose said. "Which is why I want to hire you. I need a sharp operator, Hallam, and you're the guy."

"What's the job?" Some of the twang was gone from Hallam's

voice now. Not all of it, though. He could emphasize the accent at will, but he could never lose it completely.

Rose leaned forward and clasped his hands together on the polished desktop. "I've been cursed," he said, "and I think you can help me put a stop to it."

A smile twitched at Hallam's wide mouth. "Don't see as how I can help you there."

Rose shook his head. "You don't understand. I've had this curse put on me——" He broke off, took a deep breath. "What I really want you to do is find the girl."

"What girl?"

"Her name is Carmen Delgado. She worked for me here on the ship as a hostess, but she was more than that. She and I were . . . well, you understand, Hallam."

He nodded. "Sure. And she took off on you?"

"That's right." A look of pain crossed Rose's smooth face. "So where does the curse come in?"

"From *Mamacita*." Rose's fist banged the desk. "Damn that crazy old lady!" He stood up abruptly, went to a portable bar that was set up in one corner. He poured a drink and downed it, then said shakily, "You tell him the rest of it, Art."

Burlington took up the story. He seemed a bit embarrassed to be relating his boss's personal troubles, but he did as Rose ordered. "Carmen's mother thinks she's a witch. She and Tony don't get along, you see, never did, and when Carmen vanished her mother blamed Tony. So . . . so she put a curse on him."

Rose spun around. "She says I'm going to waste away and die unless she gets her little girl back!" he exclaimed. "Hell, I don't know where Carmen is. I want her back just as much as her mama does."

Hallam looked from Rose to Burlington and back to Rose. "You don't believe this old lady really is a witch, do you?"

"Of course not," Rose said uncertainly. "I don't want the old bat causing more trouble for me, though. She came out here a few nights ago, got one of her fisherman cousins to ferry her out, and raised holy ned. Yelling that I was a demon and that I stole her daughter from her. I thought I was going to have to tell Bert to throw her in the drink before she'd leave!"

"So Tony decided that the best way to placate Mrs. Delgado was to hire someone to find Carmen and bring her home," Burlington put in.

"How'd you decide on me?" Hallam asked.

Rose shrugged. "I've got friends on the force in LA, that's no secret. I asked around. They told me you were smart and honest . . . and stubborn. Will you take the job, Hallam?"

The room was quiet for a long moment as Hallam thought. Then he said, "Happen I do find her and she doesn't want to come back. What then?"

Rose rubbed his eyes wearily. "Then you've got to convince her mama that she's all right. I want Carmen, sure, but what I really want is for that old lady to leave me alone."

Hallam stood up, held out his hand to Rose. "I'll take the job," he said.

Rose shook hands with him, gratitude plain on his face. "I'm glad. You'll find that I'm a generous man to work for, too, Hallam. There's just one more thing. I'd like for Art to go along with you."

Hallam glanced over at Burlington. "I like to work alone."

"Art's my right hand, like I told you, Hallam. We go back a long way, and I want him to be in on this investigation, so he can keep me informed."

Hallam grimaced, thought for a minute, finally nodded his head. "We'll give it a try," he said. He put his hat on. "Come on, Mr. Burlington. I aim to go right to work on this, and I've got to change clothes first."

"Why?" Rose asked. "I think you look great in that outfit! Better than Ken Maynard, even."

Hallam squinted at him. "It may be all right for Hollywood or some floatin' saloon like this here *Gilded Lily*, but I sure as hell ain't wearin' this get-up in the real world!"

\* \* \*

"Might be a good thing you're along," Hallam said to Burlington. "You can tell me where this Delgado gal lives, can't you?"

"Of course." Burlington gave Hallam the address, and Hallam pointed the roadster in the right direction.

They had taken a cab from the dock to the little house in the hills where Hallam lived. He had changed into casual clothes, but somehow he still looked like a cowboy. Night had completely fallen by now, and Hallam's roadster was only a small part of a steady stream of traffic on the gaudy streets.

"You think Carmen's room is the place to start?"

"It's *a* place to start. Might get lucky."

The rooming house where Carmen Delgado lived was on the fringes of Hollywood, in a neighborhood that had sprung up along with the rest of the town a few years before. Hallam found a parking place close to the three-story frame structure. The two men crossed a neat lawn and went up four steps onto a porch that ran the full length of the front of the house.

The door was unlocked. Hallam pushed it open. They stepped into a good-sized entrance hall. Burlington pointed at a flight of stairs on the other side of the hall.

"No landlady?" Hallam asked.

"No need to disturb her just yet," Burlington said, holding up a set of keys. Hallam nodded, headed for the stairs.

Carmen's room was on the third floor. They didn't encounter anyone else while climbing the stairs. Hallam waited until the other man was sliding a key into the lock before asking, "Those Rose's keys?"

"No, they're mine," Burlington said. "Tony has a set, too, of course. I've had to come over here quite a few times and pick up things for Carmen when she was staying overnight on the ship. You know what I mean."

"Yep. I know what you mean."

Burlington stepped back and let Hallam enter the room first. His big hand felt around near the door, found a light switch, flipped it up. A dim bulb in an overhead fixture glowed into life.

Hallam stopped just inside the door. His boots sank into soft carpet. He grunted in surprise. "Room wasn't furnished like this when the gal rented it, I'd say."

"Tony helped her . . . redecorate it."

"Looks like something out of a Dodge City whorehouse."

The carpet was a rich wine-red, and so were the draperies that were hung on the walls. A long white sofa was the main piece of furniture. A huge gilt-frame mirror took up most of one wall. Hallam's assessment of the room was on target, all right.

"The bedroom's right through that door," Burlington indicated.

"Don't know if I'm up to that," Hallam rumbled. "Not after this place."

The bedroom proved to be functional and spartanly furnished, though. Looked like Carmen Delgado did her entertaining in the front room.

Hallam started working, opening the drawers in the dresser, looking in the closet, all the little tasks that made up the main part of his job. Nothing appeared to be disturbed; it looked like all the girl's clothes were there, though Hallam wouldn't have known if anything was missing. Burlington confirmed his suspicion that nothing was untoward.

"The place looks like she just stepped down to the corner for something," Burlington said. "That's what so puzzling. If it had been torn up, we would have suspected foul play."

"The girl's been missing almost a week, right?" Burlington had told Hallam the details during the trip in from the *Gilded Lily*, and now he nodded in confirmation of the big detective's question. "You and Rose been here checkin' on her since then, haven't you?"

"We both came over here to look for her," Burlington replied. "Tony has a place not far from here, so it was easy for us to drop in and see if Carmen had come back."

"You didn't bother anything here, neither of you?"

"We didn't touch a thing. Tony was worried right away, when Carmen didn't show up for work last Saturday night. We came over here then, and he told me to leave everything alone." Burlington sighed sympathetically as he thought of his boss's upset condition. "I think he was scared even then that something might have happened to her. He knew he'd have to call somebody in on the case if she didn't turn up, and he wanted all the evidence left alone."

"You talked to the landlady yet?"

Burlington nodded, then shrugged. "She doesn't know a thing. Claims she hasn't seen Carmen since a couple of days before she disappeared. The rent's paid up through the end of the month, so the old woman doesn't really care, if you ask me."

"Want to talk to her anyway."

"Sure. I'm ready if you are."

They went into the hall, Burlington locking the door behind them. As they started toward the stairs, the door of another room they were passing opened and a young woman stepped out. Her eyes got big as she swung around and saw Hallam.

"You're somebody!" she exclaimed.

"Yes, ma'am," Hallam nodded. "Lucas Hallam."

"No, I know you. You're . . . you're Black Tom Slade! I thought Hoot Gibson knocked you off that cliff!"

"Well, ma'am, I reckon he did." A smile played around Hallam's mouth. "That Hoot's a fine feller. I never should've gone up agin 'im."

"You certainly shouldn't have," the young woman said. "And trying to steal those poor people's range like that! You should be ashamed."

"Yes, ma'am, I am. Powerful ashamed."

Hallam hung his head, and the woman laughed gaily. "Thank you, Mr. Hallam. Lucas Hallam, was it? You knew I was just joking, didn't you?"

"Well . . . I figured as much."

She extended her hand. "I'm an actress, too. Sharron Devlin."

Hallam shook hands with her. "Glad to meet you, Miss Devlin." Out of the corner of his eye, he saw Burlington fidgeting. Burlington had been impatient throughout the whole conversation, in fact.

Sharron Devlin was about twenty years old, with chestnut hair, a quick, bright smile, and a slim figure. That was enough to make any man pause for a moment, even an old cowboy.

And besides, she lived next door to Carmen Delgado.

"Were you and your friend looking for someone, Mr. Hallam?"

"Matter of fact, we were, ma'am. And call me Lucas."

"All right, Lucas. Maybe I can help you."

Hallam pointed to the door down the hall. "Hope so. We were looking for the young lady who lives there next to you."

"Carmen?" Sharron Devlin shook her head. "I haven't seen her in several days. It's been almost a week, in fact."

"Do you remember the last time you did see her?" Hallam prodded.

She frowned prettily. "I think so . . . I believe it was last Saturday night."

Hallam didn't look at Burlington, but he sensed the other man's sudden interest. "Saturday night, you say?"

"Yes. Yes, I'm sure of it now. I was going out, and Carmen was leaving at the same time."

"By herself?"

"Oh, no. Her date was with her." Sharron smiled, revealing dazzling white teeth. "I said hello. You know how it is with actresses, always trying to meet a producer."

"She was with a producer?"

"Well, I don't know for sure that he was a producer. But he looked like the type. You could tell he had plenty of money, anyway. His clothes were a little loud, but he didn't care. That attitude says money to me. And he was pale, real pale, like he spends a lot of time in screening rooms." Sharron shook her head. "Carmen didn't introduce me to him, though, so I guess little

Sharron's unlucky again. Funny, I didn't know Carmen even wanted to be an actress."

For the first time, Burlington joined the conversation. "This man Carmen was with, was he wearing a bow tie?" His voice sounded taut, strained.

"Come to think of it, he was. Do you know him? Is he a producer?"

Burlington shook his head. "No. No, I don't know him."

"Oh." Sharron tried to hide her disappointment. She smiled again. "I've got to run, you know, important things to do. It was very nice meeting you, Mr. Hallam. Maybe we'll work together on a picture someday."

"Would be nice, ma'am. Good evenin'." Hallam would have touched his forefinger to the brim of his hat, if he had been wearing one.

Sharron Devlin hurried down the hall and disappeared around the corner of the landing. Hallam looked at Burlington and said in a low voice, "You recognized that description, didn't you?"

"I know of a guy who's pale and wears loud clothes and a bow tie," Burlington replied with a frown. "But I don't like to think about Carmen being mixed up with him."

"Who?" Hallam demanded.

"His name's Freddy Malone. He's—"

"I know who he is," Hallam cut in. "He's in the same business your boss is. Has a gambling ship, too, if I recollect right."

"You do," Burlington said grimly. "I've got a bad feeling about this, Hallam. Like the only ones with any chance of finding Carmen Delgado are the fishes."

"That's the *Astriel*," Burlington said an hour later. "That's Malone's ship."

They were sitting on a padded bench beside the railing of another motor launch. Bootleg liquor was flowing freely among the other passengers, many of them clad in tuxedos and evening gowns. Money would flow freely tonight, as well, once this group of big spenders and plungers boarded the *Astriel*.

"Will Malone's men recognize you?" Hallam asked in low tones as sea spray misted around them.

"I don't know," Burlington said bluntly. "They might. But there's going to be trouble sooner or later, whether they know me or not." His voice was dangerously soft.

"Like to make it later, if we could. After we've had a chance to ask Malone some questions."

"We'll get our chance. And Malone will tell the truth, if he knows what's good for him."

Hallam watched Burlington's face, saw the tension beneath the masklike impassiveness. There had to be more to Anthony Rose than just another bootlegger and gambler, to inspire the kind of loyalty Hallam was seeing in Burlington.

Both men had donned hats and overcoats, but the broad-brimmed Panama only made Hallam more distinctive. With his size, though, there was no point in trying to disguise him. Malone's men didn't know *him*, at any rate, so there was no worry on that score.

"Wish I'd brought my Colt," he muttered under his breath.

Burlington heard and shook his head. "They search every-body coming on board. Nobody's heeled except Malone and his men. The guy's paranoid."

"Rose does the same thing, don't he?"

"Well, sure, but he has to, the way Malone likes to cause trouble."

Hallam didn't respond to that except to nod slowly. No point in talking about some things.

The *Astriel* was about the same size as Rose's *Gilded Lily* and every bit as flamboyant and brightly lit. Hallam felt his nerves prickling as he and Burlington boarded the ship along with the launch's other passengers, but there was no problem. Evidently, Burlington wasn't as well known as they had feared.

The casino was full and doing a booming business. Smoke and

laughter and the clatter of dice and roulette wheels filled the air, along with the occasional heart-felt curse. Hallam and Burlington moved into the center of things.

"You know where the office is?" Hallam asked, pitching his voice low enough that only Burlington could hear him over the babble.

"No, but I know how to find out." Burlington pressed something into Hallam's hand. "Try to buy into a game with that."

Hallam nodded and turned away from Burlington. He made his way to a poker table, the crowd parting around his big frame. As he stopped beside the table, he dropped the thousand dollar bill that Burlington had given him onto the green baize.

"That get me into this game?"

The dealer, a slim-fingered man with a white tuxedo jacket and sleek black hair, looked at the bill for a long moment and then smiled up at Hallam. "Of course, sir. I'll have your chips brought to you." He reached for the bill.

Hallam's hand came down on the thousand before the dealer could pick it up. "I go where my money goes," Hallam said.

The dealer's professional smile never wavered. "Certainly." He snapped his fingers and a short, broad-shouldered man appeared from the crowd. "This gentleman wants some chips, Max. Kindly escort him."

The man nodded and turned away. Hallam fell in behind him. The man glanced over his shoulder and asked, "How many chips, sir?"

Hallam held up the bill. "This many, son."

"Right this way."

Hallam knew that Burlington was watching and would be close behind. The broad-shouldered man led him across the room to a closed, unobtrusive door. He opened it and stepped back to let Hallam precede him. "Right down this hall, sir. Knock on the far door."

Hallam nodded and entered the hall. He saw the door at the

far end of the corridor. It was simple and unmarked, but he had a feeling that Freddy Malone was on the other side.

His long legs carried him quickly down the hall. He knocked like he had been told, and a voice from inside said, "It's open."

Hallam glanced back down the hall before he opened the door. The first door was still ajar, but Burlington was nowhere to be seen. Hallam took a deep breath, grasped the knob and turned.

Inside, behind a metal desk piled high with paperwork, a man in flashy clothes sat and punched an adding machine. He had crisp brown hair, very pale skin, and a bow tie around his neck. He looked up at Hallam. "You want to buy chips?" he asked.

"Nope." Hallam slowly shook his head. He opened his fingers to let the thousand dollar bill float down to rest on top of the desk. "I want to pass this worthless piece of paper off on you, friend."

Freddy Malone smiled. "You're a cool one, aren't you, fella? Knew all the time my dealer had spotted the queer right off."

"They were sellin' chips outside, lots more than just a thousand. Knew I was goin' to see the boss instead. You *are* the boss, I reckon?"

"You know it, cowboy. I'm Malone. I run this ship. Now, you're leaving, and I'd like for it to be peaceful, okay?"

"Sure." Hallam paused, then said, "Soon as you tell me where Carmen Delgado is."

Malone's palms went down flat and tight against the desktop. "Rose sent you," he snarled, his lips curling. "That bastard! Trying to cover up. . . . If anybody knows where Carmen is, it's him!" He came out of his chair, his whole body shaking with anger. "If he did anything to her, I swear I'll—"

"You'll what, you slimy little snake?" Burlington barked from the door, behind Hallam. Hallam threw him a glance, just enough to see that his clothes were rumpled and that blood was oozing from a scratch on his chin.

"Have any trouble?" Hallam asked shortly.

"Not enough to worry about," Burlington said. "Your goons need to practice more often, Freddy."

Malone shook a finger at him. "I know you! You're Rose's yes-man. Well, you can take a message back to Rose for me. He's through, you understand? Through!" Malone's voice rose shrilly, and his finger came down on a button on the desk.

Hallam sighed. Wouldn't be much time now until things got busy. His hand shot out. The fingers wrapped themselves in the front of Malone's silk shirt, lifted the little man right off his feet.

"Where's Carmen Delgado?" Hallam asked. "You were seen leavin' her place with her last Saturday, and nobody's seen her since. Might just have to take you back and give you to Rose, happen you don't decide to talk."

Malone swatted ineffectually at Hallam's arm. "You're gonna swim ashore!" he howled.

"Hallam . . ." Burlington suddenly said, and his voice carried a warning. Hallam kept his grip on Malone, even when he heard the ominous clicking behind him.

"Shoot the son-of-a-bitch!" Malone ordered.

Hallam looked behind him. Burlington stood with arms raised while three of Malone's men covered the room with pistols. Hallam grinned.

"You can shoot me, boys," he said, "but them popguns won't put me down in time to stop me from twistin' this feller's head right off his shoulders. Fine with me, if you're sure that's what you want."

Nobody said anything for a long moment, then Malone gulped and said, "Back off, you fools! Can't you see the crazy old cowboy means it?"

"Damn straight I do." Hallam stepped away from the desk, and Malone came with him, still dangling from that iron grip. Hallam's arm didn't even tremble as it supported the other man's weight.

"Maybe Malone should go with us as far as the launch," Burlington suggested, lowering his hands now that Hallam was in control . . . at least for the moment.

"Durn good idea," Hallam agreed. "Come on, Malone."

Malone's men fell back. They had no choice. Malone's feet brushed the floor every so often as Hallam carried him out through the casino. The crowd of gamblers was stunned by the sight. The room fell silent for a few seconds as Hallam marched through, Burlington right behind him, then exploded into sound as the little procession reached the deck.

Guns were trained on the three of them all the way down the steps to the platform beside which the launch bobbed, but none of Malone's men dared make a move. When they reached the bottom, Hallam asked, "Can you run this here boat?"

"You bet," Burlington said.

"Fire 'er up. You get on out, sonny," Hallam added to the regular pilot of the launch.

When Burlington had the launch ready to go, Hallam looked at Malone. "I reckon you can swim."

Malone nodded as best he could.

"Good."

Hallam threw him into the ocean.

Guns started to crack even before Malone splashed into the dark water. Hallam threw himself into the launch as Burlington hit the throttle and sent it leaping away from the side of the ship. He heard the familiar flat *whap*! of bullets passing close by his ear, but none of them found their mark in the darkness. Burlington had the launch running flat out, and in less than a minute, they were reaching the outer limits of pistol range.

Hallam got to his feet and joined Burlington at the controls. The smaller man was gulping down lungsful of air in reaction to the tension and danger. "I thought we were dead men," he said.

"Should've knowed better," Hallam told him over the roar of the engine, "I've faced down worse bunches than that in my time."

Burlington glanced at the big man beside him. Hallam's face was calm.

"I'll bet you have," Burlington said. "I'll just bet you have."

"Well, we didn't do much good, did we?" Burlington said as Hallam stopped the roadster in front of an expensive apartment hotel. Rose had rooms there, as well as sumptuous quarters on the *Gilded Lily.* Burlington had told Hallam that the gambler would be waiting for their first report.

"Don't know as I'd say that," Hallam replied. "We found the connection between Malone and the Delgado gal, and we put the fear o' God in Malone. Maybe something'll come of it."

"I hope so," Burlington said as he got out onto the sidewalk. Hallam got out and came around the front of the roadster to join him. They started for the entrance together. The main building of the hotel was set back off the road, behind carefully tended lawns and hedges. A flagstone path led to the glass doors of the entrance. Electric lamps set in wrought iron fixtures atop poles lighted the way at intervals.

The doors of the building opened and a woman came out. She walked quickly down the path, head turned away from Hallam and Burlington. Burlington paused as she passed them, then stopped and looked over his shoulder at her. There was a thoughtful expression on his face.

"That woman sure looked familiar . . ." he murmured, then his eyes abruptly widened in recognition. "Grab her, Hallam!" he snapped. "That's Carmen's mother!"

The woman heard, threw a frightened glance at them, and started to run. Hallam saw a middle-aged woman with olive skin, dark eyes, and fine features, not at all the type who looked like she would be tied up with gamblers and rum-runners. *She* wasn't, of course, but her daughter definitely was.

Hallam broke into a run behind her. "Here now, ma'am!" he called. "Hold up there! We just want to talk to you."

The woman ran faster.

"I'll check on Tony!" Burlington rapped as he started to run toward the entrance. Hallam paid him no mind as he hurried after the fleeing Mrs. Delgado. Chasing down some lady wasn't really his idea of detective work, but if Burlington wanted her caught . . .

His long legs would have closed the gap between them in a hurry if Mrs. Delgado hadn't reached the curb and the car that was parked there. She dove into the vehicle and hit the starter. Hallam heard the growl of the engine catching and bit back a curse.

He stopped as the car pulled away from the curb with a screech of rubber. He'd never been that much of a runner to start with; nobody who'd spent over half his life in a saddle was. Now there was no chance of catching her. He drew a long breath and turned back to the apartment hotel.

There was no sign of Burlington. He had to be inside, in Rose's apartment. Hallam slapped the doors open and strode inside, then paused and looked around the opulent lobby. There was a clerk behind a desk in the corner. His face was wide-eyed and startled.

"Lookin' for Rose," Hallam told him. "Where do I find him?"

The clerk pointed at a broad staircase on the other side of the room. "Second floor," he said nervously. "Mr. Burlington just went tearing up there a few minutes ago. What's going on here?"

"That's what I want to know, friend."

Hallam took the stairs two at a time with ease. When he reached the second floor, he looked down the plushly carpeted hall just in time to see Burlington come out of one of the doors. There was a slight stagger in his step, and his face was pale and stunned.

Hallam took two steps and grabbed his shoulders. "What is it?" he asked urgently.

"Ambulance," Burlington muttered. " . . . need an ambulance . . . and the police!"

Hallam pushed him aside and went to the door of the room where Burlington had emerged. He stopped and looked inside, his face tightening until it looked like a mask of tanned, cured leather.

Anthony Rose was on his back, sprawled on the floor in the unmistakable attitude of death. One hand was flung out to the side; the other was clasped loosely around the hilt of the knife that was buried in his chest, as if he had tried to pull it out before it killed him.

Hallam heard the rasp of Burlington's breathing beside him. "That old lady always hated Tony," Burlington said. "Claimed he

317

was a bad influence on her innocent little daughter. It looks like she gave up on witchcraft and used a more direct method to get rid of him. Damn. Damn it all!"

"Best call the police," Hallam said heavily. "There a telephone here?"

"Downstairs," Burlington answered, still staring distractedly at the body of his friend and employer. "She made sure the curse worked, didn't she? One way or another, she made sure that Tony died."

Hallam nodded. He put a big hand on Burlington's arm and pulled him away. Burlington came along without resistance, numb from his discovery.

Hallam shut the door of the room behind them.


"What the hell! . . . Oh, it's you, Mr. Hallam." The night watchman gulped and passed a hand over his face. "You gave me quite a scare. I mean, I thought I was alone on the lot, and then I saw you . . . Well, no offense, but you're pretty big, and I thought you were a burglar."

"Nope, just an old cowboy," Hallam told him with a smile. "Sorry I threw a scare into you, George."

"That's all right." The watchman's face was puzzled in the pale glow from his flashlight. "Say, what're you doing here, if you don't mind my asking, Mr. Hallam?"

"Just doin' a little ruminatin', George. For some reason, I seem to think a little better in these surroundin's. Hope you don't mind."

"Go right ahead." The watchman's voice dipped. "Between you and me, you're not supposed to be here at night, nobody is, but hell. If you can't trust a man like Lucas Hallam, who can you trust?"

Hallam clapped the little man's uniformed shoulder. "Thanks, George. Them words mean a lot to me."

"Just don't stay too long, okay? I got my job to think of, after all."

"Don't you worry none," Hallam assured him. "I'll just think through a couple of things, then head on out of here."

"Right. Good night, Mr. Hallam."

Hallam watched the man leave the saloon set, then put his back to the bar and rested his elbows on the polished hardwood surface. This was one of his favorite places, all right. Maybe it was all a fake, but it was the closest thing to his past that he had been able to find. Bill Hart had filmed part of *Hell's Hinges* here a few years before; Hallam had played one of the outlaws that Hart ran out of town. The room had been filled with smoke and noise that day as guns crashed and boomed.

He remembered other saloons and other days, when the gunsmoke had been real, when shots exploded and bullets sang and men lived and died by them. Old days . . .

Hallam forced his mind back to the present. Less than twelve hours had passed since Anthony Rose had appeared out on the location to hire him, but a great deal had happened during that time. Hallam went over all of it, replaying it in his mind like a director would replay a picture that he was editing. Certain things stood out. You looked at them one way and they meant something. You looked at them another way, and they meant something entirely different.

Hallam straightened. His hand went under his jacket and came out with several deadly pounds of metal. A stray beam of moonlight filtered into the saloon set and glinted off the long barrel of the Colt. Hallam spun the cylinder, checked the loads.

Then he reholstered the gun, strode to the batwings, and pushed through them, like he had hundreds of times in the past, both make-believe . . . and real.

This wasn't make-believe. This was a showdown. A real live showdown.

He took the regular launch out to the *Gilded Lily*, glad to be able to sit for a while and let the cool sea breeze blow in his face. Despite his determination to see this through to the finish, he was tired. The cops had kept them at Rose's apartment for quite a while, going over every facet of the story that he and Burlington had to tell. The clerk from downstairs had confirmed that Mrs. Delgado had gone up to see Rose just a few minutes before Hallam and Burlington arrived. Other tenants on the floor had revealed that they had heard angry shouting from Rose's apartment.

The police had sent out a bulletin on Mrs. Delgado. As far as they were concerned, the case would be all but closed when she was picked up.

Hallam thought different.

The guards on the *Gilded Lily* remembered him from earlier in the evening, but when he said he wanted to see Burlington, they shook their heads. "The boss said he don't want to be disturbed," one of them told him. "Lots of things to do, you know how it is."

"Yep, I do," Hallam replied. "I still want to see Burlington, though."

The big figure of Bert, Rose's driver, bulked out of the darkness. "Having trouble, guys?" he asked.

The two guards at the top of the stairs from the launch platform shook their heads. "No problem, Bert," one of them said. "Mr. Hallam wanted to see the boss, but I told him he'll have to come back another time."

"'Fraid I've got to go in now," Hallam said flatly. He started to take a step around the guards.

"Bastard!" Bert spat as he charged forward. "You're goin' for a swim!" He swung a looping punch at Hallam's head.

Hallam moved a couple of inches to the side and let the blow whistle by his ear. He stepped in, snapped two quick punches to Bert's belly. Bert started to double over in surprise and pain.

Hallam brought up an arm like a tree branch and slammed it down on the back of Bert's neck. Bert went flat out on the deck, his face crashing into the deck with a soggy thud.

Out of the corner of his eye, Hallam saw the two guards reaching under their coats. Faster than most people could follow, his hand found the butt of the Colt and brought it out, the heavy gun behaving now like an extension of his arm, like an integral part of him. The barrel lined and the hammer clicked back before either man could finish his draw.

"Just be still, boys," Hallam said quietly. "I got no wish to sling lead with you, happen I can get out of it. Toss them guns overboard—slow!"

The guards did as Hallam told them.

He glanced at the activity in the casino, visible through the portholes along the side of the big room. No one seemed to have noticed the short fracas outside, and Hallam had hung back deliberately until all the passengers that had been on the launch with him had entered the casino.

"I figure there's another way to get to the office, besides goin' through the gamblin' rooms. You boys better take me there, right now."

"We can't do that—"

The man broke off and gulped as the black mouth of Hallam's Colt swung his way.

"I'm gettin' on to bein' an old man, son. Don't know how many years I've got left. Reckon it's few enough that I can do a little gamblin' with them. You understand what I'm sayin'?"

The guard nodded. "I understand. We'd better do like he says, Phil."

"Yeah," the second man agreed. "I think we should."

They were agreeing too easily, even in the face of the .45. Hallam motioned for them to get started, and waited for whatever trick they had in mind.

There was another way to the office, through a series of connecting passages that avoided the big gambling room. The three of them didn't encounter anyone else, and then Hallam saw the familiar door to what had been Rose's office.

One of the guards dove toward the door, obviously intending to warn Burlington, while the other spun to jump at Hallam.

Hallam grabbed his assailant's coat with his left hand and threw him to the side, hard into the wall of the corridor. A long step brought him within reach of the other one. His arm lashed out, and the Colt slapped into the back of the man's head. He went down.

Hallam didn't waste any time. He stepped over the fallen man, opened the door of the office, stepped through and kicked it shut behind him.

"Howdy, Burlington," he said as he leveled the Colt at the two people behind the desk. "You'd be Miss Delgado, I reckon. Glad to finally meet you, ma'am."

Burlington came halfway out of his chair in surprise. His hand instinctively started to reach for one of the desk drawers, but he stopped the motion when he saw the coldness in Hallam's eyes.

The woman remained calm. No more than twenty, there was something about her that seemed much older. Her long hair, parted in the middle, was a glossy midnight black. It framed a face of classic beauty, of smooth olive skin and flashing eyes that she had inherited from her mother. Carmen Delgado was lovely. Even Hallam had to admit that . . .

Lovely enough to drive a man to kill for her.

"And you must be Mr. Hallam. Arthur has told me about you," she said. "You seem to be a remarkable man."

"No, ma'am," Hallam said. "But I try to be an honest one." There was an open ledger book on the desk in front of Burlington. Hallam gestured at it with his free hand and said, "Shove that over here."

Burlington hesitated, his gaze intent on Hallam as he tried to gauge the big man. Then, with a shrug, he pushed the ledger across the desk.

Hallam stepped close enough to get a good look at it, but he kept out of grabbing range. Even upside down, he was about to tell what was recorded there.

"That'd be Malone's writin' there, wouldn't it?" he asked.

Carmen smiled. "Perceptive of you, Mr. Hallam. Yes, that book is dear Freddy's private business journal. It's enough to put him out of business, if not in jail, if the authorities should get their hands on it."

"Which same is just what'll happen if he doesn't turn over his operation to you and Burlington here, isn't it? You must be hell on wheels, ma'am, pardon the expression, to get close enough to Malone in a week to weasel that out of him."

"More than a week," Carmen said in reply to Hallam's accusation. "I've been working on him for nearly a month, off and on. Freddy's a hard man to convince, but . . . I have ways."

"I'll just bet you do," Hallam said under his breath. "You even got Burlington to kill his boss for you, so that the two of you could take over the whole shootin' match."

"What the hell are you talking about?" Burlington exclaimed. "You saw Carmen's mother running away from there. You heard what the other tenants said about her and Tony fighting."

"Worked out real convenient for you, didn't it? Got to give you credit for grabbin' your opportunity, Burlington. You had a witness—me—and a ready-made goat, Carmen's mama. But if it hadn't happened that way, you'd've found another time and place."

Burlington's lip curled. "You can't prove any of that. You may call yourself a detective, but you're just a cowboy actor, Hallam! Nobody's going to listen to you."

"Well, now," Hallam said. "You may be right. But if I shoot you right now, Carmen's goin' to be left 'thout anybody to look after her. She can take Malone's records back to him and tell him that you dreamed up the whole scheme and made her take a part. Malone would believe her, you can bet on that. She can lay Rose's murder at your feet, too, and get her mama off the hook for it. Not that she really cares about her mama; hell, anybody can see that."

Carmen was watching him with a mixture of hate and speculation in her dark eyes. "You have no business talking about my mother," she spat, "but the rest of what you say, it makes sense."

"Carmen!" Burlington blurted. "Don't pay any attention to this old coot!"

"This old coot's got the gun," Hallam reminded him. "You can always turn yourself in, Burlington. That, or I start blowin' holes in you."

Hallam didn't know if he would pull the trigger or not. He'd never shot an unarmed man yet, but he didn't like being used. Never had . . .

The explosion slammed into the ship, tilted it crazily, threw Hallam off his feet. He landed hard on the floor.

None of them knew what was happening, but like Hallam had said, Burlington knew how to seize an opportunity. His hand darted to the desk and came up with a little pistol.

Hallam saw the threat and reacted instinctively. The barrel of the Colt tipped up, and he squeezed the trigger without even thinking about it.

Burlington didn't get a shot off.

The big slug caught him in the chest and threw him backward. He was dead before he bounced off the wall behind the desk.

Carmen Delgado screamed. Hallam came to his feet, grabbed her arm, and pulled her into the corridor. The two guards he had knocked out were regaining consciousness now. Hallam paused long enough to tap them with the Colt and send them sprawling again, then headed for the outside.

At least he hoped he was heading for the deck. This maze of corridors inside the ship was more confusing than a prairie dog town.

Men in suits, carrying guns, appeared in front of him. They didn't fire, maybe because Carmen was with him and they recognized her. One of them ran up with a strained look on his face.

"Where the hell have you been, Carmen?" he snapped. "The boss was going crazy worrying about . . . I mean, before what happened tonight. . . . Hell, we ain't got time to worry about that. You and the cowboy better get out of here!"

"What's goin' on?" Hallam demanded. "Maybe I can help."

The man eyed the big gun in Hallam's fist. "Maybe you can, Tex. Malone and his guys are attacking the ship. They damn near blew a hole in the bow with some kind of floating bomb. It's war, looks like." The man hefted the machine gun he was carrying. "Where's Art?" he asked Carmen.

Hallam squeezed her arm and answered for her. "We left him in the office."

The man nodded and waved the others in his party on. "I'll go get him. Why don't you two come with me?"

Hallam nodded. "Sure." He held back long enough for the others to round a corner and get out of sight, then rapped the man on top of the head with the Colt. He folded up, just like the others who had received similar treatment.

Carmen Delgado looked stunned now, stunned by the sudden violence she had witnessed in the last few minutes. Hallam turned to her and asked, "Where do they steer this thing?"

She didn't answer. Hallam put his free hand on her shoulder and shook her.

"I need to know, gal," he said urgently. "Where's the bridge, or whatever they call it?"

"I . . . I'll take you there," she said in so soft a voice that Hallam could barely hear her.

She was true to her word, though. With Hallam right behind her, she found her way up a couple of short staircases and onto the bridge. Two of the ship's officers were there, and they spun around as Hallam and the girl came in.

Guns were cracking all over the ship now, as a full-fledged battle continued between Malone and his men and the crew of the *Gilded Lily*. They weren't Rose's men anymore, Hallam thought, or Burlington's either, though they probably didn't know that yet. The two officers on the bridge each had a pistol on his hip, but the holster flaps were buttoned.

They wouldn't have had a chance anyway.

Hallam's Colt came up. His thumb eared back the hammer. "Where's land?" he barked.

One of the officers pointed a shaking finger off into the night.

"Well, head off that-a-way," Hallam ordered. He swung the muzzle of the Colt from one to the other to reinforce the command.

"It'll take time . . ." one of them said.

"Then you'd best get started."

A few minutes later, the *Gilded Lily* was underway.

"How did you know?" Carmen asked, her voice still showing her surprise and shock. "How could you possibly have known?"

"That you and Burlington were in it together? Hell, gal, I've been around a long time, remember? I saw the same thing happen in Tascosa, then later again in Santa Fe. Any time you've got two fellers goin' up against one another, you've got more folks in the background willin' to take advantage of 'em."

"I did nothing," she declared. "It was all Burlington's idea. He killed Anthony, he bragged to me of it."

"Glad to hear it. And I'm sure these two fellers will testify that they heard you say that. No point in your mama bein' in trouble for something she didn't do."

"No," Carmen murmured. "No point . . ."

The firing was more sporadic now. One side or the other, Hallam had no idea which, was winning. He heard a sudden clatter of footsteps on the stairs leading to the bridge, and he swung around to greet the newcomers.

Freddy Malone, disheveled and dripping blood from a scratch on his face, burst onto the bridge with a gun in his hand. His wild eyes fell on the girl, and he cried, "Carmen!"

She tore out of Hallam's grip and ran to the gambler, throwing herself into his arms. "Freddy! Oh, Freddy, it was awful! *Madre Dios!*"

Malone looked over her shoulder as she buried her face against his thin chest. His face contorted. "The cowboy!" he snarled. "I figured you'd be here. I knew Rose had stolen Carmen, the bastard! Where is he? Where's Rose?"

"Figgered that's why you started this little fracas," Hallam said grimly. "Well, you're a mite late—"

"He killed Rose and Burlington!" Carmen cried as she huddled against Malone. "He's trying to take over, Freddy—"

Then she was turning, a smaller gun appearing in her hand

326

from some hiding place in her clothes. Malone, too, was lining his sights on Hallam.

Hallam triggered off four shots before either Malone or Carmen could fire. The rolling thunder sent Carmen's pistol spinning from her fingers, cylinder shattered. Malone went spinning away as the other three bullets ripped into him.

The silence that fell over the bridge was as awful as the fury that had preceded it.

The first sound was Carmen's sobs as she clutched her nerve-deadened hand. Then Hallam heard the sirens and became aware of the searchlights playing over the ship. He smiled as he realized that his plan had worked. The *Gilded Lily* was inside the limit now, and the Coast Guard, always interested in the gambling ships that sailed up and down off the coast, was converging.

Hallam holstered his Colt. There would be all kinds of questions from the authorities and he might even hear some threats about lifting his license from the District Attorney. Hell, it had been a lot simpler in the old days. Then he could have gotten onto his horse and ridden off into the sunset, like Hoot and Colonel Tim and all the others did now.

That was progress for you.

When it was over, though, he thought he might look up that little actress—Sharron Devlin, that was her name—and chew the fat with her. She had struck him as the type who liked to listen.

There were still some people who liked to hear about the good old days . . .